One L

Hope

A Voyage to Escape Nazi Germany

Formerly *The Voyage*

A Historical Novel set during the Holocaust,

Inspired by True Events

By USA Today Best Selling Author
Roberta Kagan

One Last Hope- The Voyage
Copyright 2012 by Roberta Kagan

This is a work of fiction. Although the *MS St. Louis* did sail, and many of the events depicted are factual, this is in no way meant to be a work of non-fiction. All characters are fictional, and any resemblance to anyone living or dead is purely a coincidence.

Please visit www.RobertaKagan.com for news and upcoming releases.

CONTACT ME

I love hearing from readers, so feel free to drop me an email telling me your thoughts about the book or series.

Email: roberta@robertakagan.com

Please sign up for my mailing list, and you will receive Free short stories including an USA Today award-winning novella as my gift to you!!!!! To sign up...

Check out my website http://www.robertakagan.com.

Come and like my Facebook page!

https://www.facebook.com/roberta.kagan.9

Join my book club

https://www.facebook.com/groups/1494285400798292/?ref=br_rs

Follow me on BookBub to receive automatic emails whenever I am offering a special price, a freebie, a giveaway, or a new release. Just click the link below, then click follow button to the right of my name. Thank you so much for your interest in my work.

https://www.bookbub.com/authors/roberta-kagan.

DISCLAIMER

This book is dedicated to Carli, whose input took the characters off the pages and brought them to life. I would also like to thank my wonderful husband for always being there to support me, and for being my best friend.

So go on and close every door to me. Keep everyone I love from me.
Children of Israel are never alone.
Andrew Lloyd Webber

For all of those who suffered at the hands of the Third Reich, living or dead, and for all of their children. May God grant you peace.

Table of Contents

Introduction

In 1938, President Roosevelt of the United States of America conducted a conference called the Evian Conference. It was a bold attempt on the part of America to express sympathy for Jewish Refugees from Nazi Germany.

Joseph Goebbels, Hitler's Minister of Propaganda, responded to the conference by offering to send the Jews of Germany to any nation that would have them. In fact, he said that he would even transport them on luxury liners in order to rid Germany of their presence, so sure was he that no nation would open their doors and allow them in. Jews, he said, were nothing but vermin, and unwanted anywhere in the world.

When confronted with this proposal by Nazi Germany, NOT ONE country offered refuge to all of the Jews.

In November of the same year, a public display of anti-Semitism took place in Germany that would be a major turning point in the persecution of the Jewish race. It would come to be known as Kristallnacht, the night of the broken glass. Jews were beaten on the streets. Some were arrested and sent to concentration camps, where they were starved and tortured. Synagogues were burned to the ground, destroying sacred Jewish artifacts. The world watched, but no one did a thing to help. This reaction by the rest of the world provided the Nazis with the fuel they needed. They were assured that no matter how terribly they treated the Jewish population, no one would care, and no one at all would come to their aid.

I would like to thank Mr. Herbert Karliner, a survivor of the MS St. Louis, for taking the time to meet with me and tell me his miraculous tale of survival, filled with beautiful mazel. Mr. Karliner is an honorable man, and even with all that he has endured, he still has a heart of gold. He was the person responsible for proposing that Captain Schroder, the captain of the MS St. Louis, be recognized in the Righteous Among Nations, for going above and beyond the call of duty in his treatment of the Jewish passengers aboard the MS St. Louis.

Prologue

FORT LAUDERDALE, FLORIDA

UNITED STATES OF AMERICA

FEBRUARY 4, 2009

Silver tinsel danced softly in the breeze that emanated from the ceiling fan in the large banquet hall. Each table had been adorned with a bud vase containing a blue and white carnation accented with slivers of foil. Beside the arrangements stood sparkling metal stands; each held the name of a country that had once suffered under the occupation of Hitler's Third Reich. Poland, Germany, Italy, France, Romania, and so on. At the perimeter of the room, a group of eager young Jewish students awaited the arrival of the survivors. Soon they would meet the last witnesses still alive who had seen the horrors of the Nazis firsthand.

At precisely eleven o'clock, the busses began to arrive. Florida had plummeted to a chilly thirty degrees that morning in February, a record cold for Ft. Lauderdale. But the celebration of life would go on…the commemoration of the survivors called "Café *Europa*."

In they marched, some with canes, others with walkers, and many still strong. They all entered proudly, slowed with age, but unwilling to miss the event. They knew that as long as they lived, it was their responsibility to make sure the young never forgot what had happened. Each year the attendance grew smaller, and now this was all that was left of the legacy. They came from everywhere: from Europe and from all around the United States, from South Africa and South America.

Finally, the room was full. At the front stood a podium, and beside it an electronic board that continually flashed names. These were the names of the attendees. They hoped by making their presence known they might find lost friends and family who had disappeared so long ago, those who had gone missing during the war, their names and faces nowhere to be found in any register.

A woman who had seen forty come and go walked up to the podium. She wore a dark suit and white blouse. Her graying hair had been cut short in a fashionable style. With a welcoming smile, she tapped the microphone to insure it had been turned on. Then she spoke.

"Good Morning to all of you, and welcome to the annual meeting of the survivors…'Café *Europa*.' We are honored to have all of you here. My name is Rebecca Morgenstern. I am the director for Jewish services here in Florida. Many of you have come from all over the country to be here today, and I was hoping we could offer you better weather, but that, I am afraid, I cannot control." Laughter came from the audience. "However, today we would like to bring a very special guest speaker."

There was an air of excited anticipation; the guest speaker was an important person, someone they all wanted to meet.

The entire crowd rose. Those who could not stand alone held onto the arms of chairs or to the table to steady themselves. They knew who was coming to speak; that was why they were there.

And then such enthusiastic applause rang through the hall that it seemed as if the entire room trembled in response.

Then Mrs. Morgenstern raised her hands in the air to silence the crowd.

The room grew quiet. Everyone was poised to listen, and to finally see the honored guest.

"Ladies and gentlemen," Rebecca Morgenstern cleared her throat, a tear threatening to fall from her eye. "It is a great privilege to present to you..."

Chapter 1

THE PASSENGER LOADING DOCK AT THE HARBOR IN HAMBURG, GERMANY

MAY 13, 1939

The sun on the water sparkled like tiny diamonds in the eyes of twenty-two-year-old Alex Mittelman as he stood in line waiting to board the ship *MS St. Louis*, headed to Havana, Cuba. He could not believe his luck at having made it through the long waiting list of those trying to board this ship out of Germany and escape the tyranny of the Third Reich. The wind picked up a bit of water from the ocean and sprayed the crowd. Alex reached up, attempting to shield his shaved head from the relentless heat of the sun. They'd done that to him in Dachau, taken his hair... If only that had been all they'd done.

A blaring foghorn exploded out of the belly of the massive sea vessel, unnerving Alex as he waited for his turn to board. At any time, the *Gestapo* could appear and force him back to the nightmare he felt he would spend the remainder of his life trying to leave behind. Still, if his former employer had not taken pity on him and paid his way, he would still be suffering in Dachau, and for that he must be grateful.

"Next!" a ship's officer called to Alex. Because of his experience with German authorities, he shuddered. Then, taking a deep breath, he walked forward and made every effort to steady his hand when he offered his official papers.

"Would you like help to find your cabin, sir?"

"No... No, thank you," he stammered, not trusting and not believing any German would call a Jew "sir." Something was wrong.

Quickening his step, he followed the others inside the ship toward the cabins. He took a deep breath and glanced behind him to assure himself he'd not been followed, that this whole escapade had not been another Nazi trick. It took nearly half an hour before Alex found his stateroom. When he walked inside, he saw Manny Silverman, his roommate, sitting on one of the beds.

"Hello... I'm Alex Mittelman."

"Manny Silverman. You have no suitcase?" Manny puffed on a cigarette.

Alex had no possessions, only his life. He shook his head.

"Well, no matter. I have plenty of clothes with me that should fit you, although you are quite tall," Manny assessed. "Still, I don't mind sharing."

"That's very kind of you…very kind."

"Well, it's a *mitzvah*, and let's face it, we Jews had better stick together. Clothes… We can always buy more. People? Life? Well, that's another story."

"God bless you," Alex said, looking away, embarrassed at Manny's generosity, ashamed of his appearance, and suddenly very aware of how dirty he was and how bad he must smell.

"Ech…stop… You can thank me when we get to Cuba. You can take me out for a drink."

"First I'll have to find a job."

"So, I'll take you out. Either way, it doesn't matter. We are the lucky ones, my friend. We are getting out of Germany." Manny smiled.

Manny saw the pain in Alex's eyes as he tried to smile.

Alex sat on his bed, and in disbelief, he gingerly ran his fingers over the smooth, soft pillow. "Do you know how long it has been since I've slept in a real bed?"

"A while, I'm guessing."

"It feels like a lifetime. I was in Dachau."

"Why don't you lie down until dinner is served? I'll wake you."

"I would like that. I would like that very much." Alex considered cleaning up first, but he was far too tired. It had been a grueling night. He'd stood in front of the SS guard at the camp and trembled, waiting with fear and skepticism to be released. The guard had dragged out the paperwork, while Alex had stood sweating, knowing that at any minute, this dream of being free could be thwarted. Then once he'd been released, he'd ridden in the back of a truck filled with other prisoners on their way to the docks. He'd heard of the gassings in the back of trucks, how the Nazis had dropped pellets of Zyklon B through specially-built openings, killing the passengers. The rumors had spread through the camp, and he'd heard them, along with so many other horrific tales. As they rode along, he could not overcome the anxious fear that the Nazis had taken the money that the prisoners had paid for this voyage, and now that they had them trapped in the back of an enclosed truck…it would be just like them to fool these unsuspecting people. The Nazis loved to play with the minds of the prisoners, giving them hope, and then taking it away, or forcing them to make unfathomable choices. All of this played into the absolute cruelty he'd witnessed. Many of the others slept on the ride to the ship, but Alex remained awake the entire night, waiting and watching. And he'd not felt even the slightest peace of mind until now, as he lay upon this bed. However, even now, he knew that anything could happen. He'd seen too much to ever trust the Nazis to keep their word.

Without removing his shoes, Alex lay on top of the bed. Within minutes, he slept, but as he did the muscles in his face twitched like those of a prey animal. Manny watched him. It was apparent even in his tattered clothing, with his shorn head, that Alex had been gifted with enviable good looks. His sturdy, unshaven chin and high, firm cheekbones, and well-built, although lean frame at first glance brought to mind Michelangelo's *David*, while the yielding, sensuous fullness of his lips and insightful warmth in his luminous dark eyes were reminiscent of an artist or a poet. Manny could not help but wonder, although he knew he would be unable to ask, what horrors poor Alex had endured.

Even though Manny tried to be as quiet as possible, he saw Alex's entire body jump every few minutes, awakening him with a start. Then, as they'd been trained to do, Alex's eyes darted around the room, and once he was assured of his safety, he fell asleep again. It was as if he remained in a constant mode of flight.

Manny sat on his bed, his body rocking with the motion of the ship. He leaned his back against the wall. No doubt, he was lucky to be here aboard this ship, to be one of those who would live. Because after *Kristallnacht*, he knew that plenty of Jews would die. He knew it as surely as he knew the sun would rise in the morning. There could be no denying the signs. The anti-Semitic climate in Germany grew every day. Soon it would swallow every Jew that remained there. Of course, there was no need to show his pessimism; why not just put up a positive front? After all, it was his nature to be lucky, and people loved to be around others who were happy and carefree. That was Manny, always the life of the party, at least on the outside. Somehow he'd cheated death, escaped physical pain, and personal Nazi persecution. But not without a paying a price; everything has its price. Manny 's heart was burdened with a deep secret: a secret that nudged his shoulder each time he laughed, or sneaked up behind him and whispered in his ear when he seemed to be most lighthearted. A secret that could only be silenced at night with heavy doses of sleeping pills. A secret that burned him from the inside, and would someday alter his life.

When the dinner bell sounded, Alex jumped and awakened quickly. He bathed and dressed; then he and Manny walked to the dining room.

The mistrust of the Germans ran through Alex's blood, keeping him on constant guard. When he saw the chandeliers twinkling over the white tablecloths and silver flatware, the ship's crew of Aryans serving Jews, it took Manny holding on to his arm to prevent him from bolting and hiding in the cabin they shared. After what he'd seen in the concentration camp, he could not help but be skeptical of the motive behind such a display of friendship and equality.

A large table had been set up with cards that indicated seating arrangements. Once Manny found their names, he escorted his friend to their assigned table. They were seated with two older couples and a middle-aged couple with a ten-year-old son.

"Good evening," Manny said as they sat down. Alex nodded.

"Good evening," the others answered.

A waiter wearing a black and white tuxedo approached.

"We have *sauerbraten* or *wiener schnitzel* tonight… What can I get for you gentlemen?"

Alex stammered, looking around, unsure of what to do. It felt so strange to him to have a German waiter taking his order. He'd spent the last year hearing Nazi guards bark orders at prisoners instead, shooting them dead if they didn't comply fast enough. He'd sat on a long bench, gobbling watery soup, his stomach rumbling with hunger, so in need of food that he often ignored the dead insects at the bottom of the bowl. His bed had been a pile of dirty, disease-ridden hay that had turned green with mold. It felt beyond wonderful to be clean again, it had been a long time since his body had felt the pleasure of soaking in a bath. Now, this white-gloved waiter stood before him as if all were right with the world, wanting to take his dinner order. The clash of his life in the camp and life on this unreal ship was almost too much to bear.

Manny answered for both of them, knowing that Alex would find it hard to speak to the German waiter. "We would like the *schnitzel*, thank you."

"I hope that was all right with you?" Manny asked Alex.

Alex nodded. "Yes, thank you."

Everyone placed their orders and then began talking.

"So, introduce yourself, and where are you from?" said one of the older men with a balding head surrounded by a monk' cap of dark, graying hair. "My name is Samuel Siedlman; my wife is Etta. She and I are from Berlin. I owned orchards in the outskirts."

"Dresden," answered the other older gentleman, his hair full and wavy, and as white as a Christmas snowfall. "My wife is Ruth, and I am George."

"We lived in Munich," the ten-year-old boy said. "And my name is Abraham."

"When adults talk, you keep quiet. Children should be seen and not heard," his father said.

"I apologize. Sometimes he is very brazen."

"Oh, it's all right. He's just a boy," the man with the white hair said. "Besides, Abraham is quite a name. Do you know much about the Bible?"

Before he answered, the boy looked at his father who nodded, giving him permission to speak. "A little," he said.

"We are Michael and Gloria Rifkin," the boy's mother said. "We are also from Berlin. My husband was an accountant."

"Abraham was a very important man in the Bible."

"As important as Moses?"

"Yes, he was the father of our people."

"Do you have family left in Germany?" the woman asked the older man with the white hair.

"No, thank God. My son and his wife left for South Africa last year, and my daughter lives in America."

"I will miss Germany. I will miss our apple orchards and our friends, the lovely smell of apples in the fall, and the crisp taste of the cider. My son and his wife are still there with my granddaughter. I could not convince them to come with us. I am so worried about him. He is a doctor and will not leave his practice behind. I am hoping that we are just panicking for no reason, and that somehow all of this anti-Semitism will just blow over," Etta Siedlman sighed.

"My parents are still there, in Germany, and I can't stand leaving them," Gloria Rifkin said, her eyes glowing with unshed tears. "And all of my friends, everyone I knew… It will be hard to start all over with nothing. And my son, he would have been *bar mitzvahed* at the temple that I belonged to my entire life, and by the same rabbi who performed his *bris*. Our lives are there in Germany… Everything is there."

"Yes, I know. And I agree that it is hard," the white-haired man said. "But we are the fortunate ones. We got out, and at least we will have our lives."

"A life in Cuba? I have no idea what that means. My wife and I enjoy the symphony. I doubt that we will attend another concert. But what is a concert when you are talking about your life?"

"And my son was doing so well in school, but now he will have to begin again, and learn a new language as well."

"We must all learn a new language. But we will prevail… Somehow, we will prevail."

"It just breaks my heart to leave my childhood home, and all of the people I knew and loved behind. " Gloria said again.

There was silence at the table, everyone lost in their own thoughts and memories.

As they waited for their food to be served, Manny noticed a girl sitting alone at a table just a few feet from their own. She had lovely long, golden-brown hair and deep forest-green eyes, and a certain class and refinement that drew his attention. He could not help but stare. When she finally looked back and smiled, he felt self-conscious, but knew he must approach her.

Alex felt himself salivating as the fragrant aromas of rich food filled the dining room. His stomach rumbled. He'd not eaten food like this since before his imprisonment. He held his hands under the table so that the others would not see them shaking with anticipation. As the other diners were served, Alex watched, his hunger almost unbearable, and he could hardly wait for his food.

When the food arrived, Alex was ravenous, and ate with such gusto that Manny feared the food might not stay down. Their plates were prepared to entice the eye as well as the palate. Individual meals were plated and placed in front of each diner. Then steaming trays of crispy potato pancakes with side bowls of chunky sweet apple sauce were placed in the center of the table. Two fresh breads baked to a golden brown, with melting butter, were also served, as well as a platter of hot, buttered asparagus.

The food was delicious, although Alex hardly tasted the chef's magnificent creations. Instead, he gobbled so quickly that he spilled applesauce on the front of his shirt. He turned and apologized to Manny for soiling his garment. Manny just shrugged and smiled. "It's only a shirt. Not to worry."

At the end of the meal, the white-gloved waiters brought out trays of pastries and desserts. There were strudels and cookies; there were cakes filled with fruit; there were puddings. The diners made their choices, and then the coffee and tea service began.

Once everyone had finished eating and the plates had been cleared, a band began to play, and the diners got up to dance. Men in suits and tuxedos led smartly-dressed women across the floor.

"The music is lovely, no?" Manny asked watching the dancers whirl by them.

"I think I will go back to the room." Alex put his napkin down on the table. "Would you like to join me?"

"No, I think I am going to stay and enjoy the music for a bit."

"I'll see you in a while then?" Alex said.

"Yes, I'll be there shortly. Don't wait up for me."

As the band began to play another waltz, Manny approached the young girl who sat pretending she was not aware of his continued interest.

"Hello."

"Hello." When she smiled, he saw that she had dimples and perfect white teeth.

"I'm Manny."

"Anna. Anna Goldman."

"Would you care to dance?"

"Yes…" She stood and followed him to the floor. As they danced neither spoke. Once the song ended, Manny walked Anna to her table.

"Thank you for the dance." He stood, feeling foolish. "Umm...may I join you?"

"Yes, that would be nice."

"I hope your parents won't mind."

"They are not here. I had to leave them in Germany." Her eyes grew moist with tears that she tried hard to hide. Manny looked at her with genuine compassion, which only made her feel more like crying. "I'm sorry. I didn't mean to spoil your evening," she said, and got up to leave. Manny took her hand.

"Stay. You haven't spoiled anything. In fact, you've lit up my entire night."

"Thank you. I'm sorry. It's all just so hard. You know?"

"Yes, I do. I was in hiding. My family left for America several years ago. I was attending university, so I stayed. After *Kristallnacht*, things started to look bad, and so my best friend and his wife took me in. I had a little money saved and I tried to pay them, but they refused. That was how I was able to afford passage and have a little money left over to start a new life in Cuba. So I, too, am alone."

"My parents took their life savings and sold the house, as well, to afford my passage. I didn't want to go without them, but they insisted. We have family in America who will meet me in Cuba and then take me across the ocean to New York, America. All I can think of are my mother and father, and I wish I had stayed in Germany. Whatever would have become of me would have become of all of us, and at least we would have been together."

"Don't talk like that. Your parents wanted you to go…to get out. Once the Nazis are out of power, they will join you, I am sure."

"Do you think the Nazis will ever be out of power?"

"I know they will… Such a radical government cannot last. Once this has all ended, we can return home to Germany, and it will be like waking up from a nightmare." He smiled wryly.

"I hope so. I do."

"Come, let's not be sad. We are here; we are on our way to Cuba. Listen, they are playing a conga. Would you like to dance?"

She nodded.

When the music stopped, Manny turned to Anna. "It's a lovely night. Shall we take a walk on the deck?"

"Yes, that would be nice."

A warm breeze surrounded the couple as they stood looking out over the ocean.

"Do you have anyone left in Germany?" Anna asked.

"No, they are all in the United States. I have a special visa to meet them there. My father moved there on business several years ago, but as I said, I was trying to complete my education before I left."

"Where were you going to school?"

"University of Berlin. I know it may sound silly, but I wanted to study law. Well, the laws certainly have changed. Especially for us... Jews, I mean."

"I know. They've taken away all of our rights, everything. I wish I could understand why they hate us so much."

"I don't know if it is really us they hate, or if they just need *someone* to hate... Do you know what I mean?"

"Sort of, but why?"

"Well, the country is financially devastated, and I guess it is easier to accept if one can put the blame on a race of people. I think Hitler is convincing the population that if the Jews are gone, the problems will be gone."

"But no one could possibly believe that, could they?"

"Well, I don't think that the Third Reich will last very long. I believe it is a passing thing. I know you are worried about your parents, but don't be. It will all be over soon enough and you will be reunited with them."

"If you truly believe that, then why are you leaving?"

"Ach, my father made such a fuss about me going to Harvard... He went as far as using his connections to help me gain admission. It is supposed to be a very good school. So I had to say yes. Besides, the Nazis have made it so difficult for Jews to go to school. They want us out of all learning institutions...at least for now. Actually, before I heard about this voyage I was considering staying with family in Belgium and going to school there. "

"Would you have preferred to stay in Europe?"

"Yes... No... Maybe... I am excited to go to America. I love adventure...new challenges...you know? And Cuba is supposed to be a wonderful tropical paradise. Before we left, I read so much about it, the music...the people... Why, it is filled with island magic. Before I go on to the United States, I want to spend a few days there." He winked at her.

She nodded her head, not convinced.

"And you Anna? Do you have anyone in Cuba?"

"No, all I have are the relatives I told you about in New York, America, my father's very distant cousin. He has agreed to meet me at the dock in Havana and take me back with him to America. I don't even know him. I feel so strange going to live with someone I've never met."

Manny found himself at a loss for words. The silence hung like a heavy fog. What could he say to this girl to lighten her burden? He knew he must speak soon or Anna might break into tears again.

"So, how old are you Anna?"

"I will turn eighteen next month, on the fifth of July. And you?"

"I am twenty-six. I know I have been attending school for longer than I should have, but for much of the time I was just enjoying the ride. I took time off to travel Europe with friends. I suppose I am guilty of enjoying the social life too much," he laughed, and she smiled at him.

"I wanted to go to the university, too." She smiled wistfully. "I wanted to be a teacher. I love young children, I always have. But of course, I was not even allowed to finish high school."

"And so you will. You will do all of it…in America. And then your parents will join you, and after this Nazi nonsense is over, you will all go back home to Germany. Of course, you may choose to stay in New York. I hear America is a wonderful place."

"Do you really believe that it will all be over soon? Even if you don't, it still makes me feel so much better to hear you say it."

"Of course I believe it. Now, don't be silly, and don't be sad. We are off on a journey, an exciting adventure...yes? Look out over the ocean. See how the stars sparkle like silver jewels in the blackness of the night sky? Beautiful, isn't it?"

"Yes, it is." She smiled at him. "Yes, it is."

Chapter 2

"It's a beautiful night," Manny said as he walked Anna upstairs onto the crowded deck.

"Yes, it is." She smiled.

"It looks to me like everyone else thinks so, too."

She nodded. "Manny?"

"Yes…"

"Have you ever looked at the ocean and wondered what was going on deep beneath the surface?"

"Actually, I'd never given it much thought. Do you wonder?"

"I do. I went to the ocean once a few years ago with my parents, and although it was beautiful, like it is now, at night the dark water scared me. It gave a chill," she said, shivering a little in the warm night breeze.

"Well, nothing to fear. We aren't going to sink. This is a nice, safe, large vessel. So you can enjoy the beauty of being at sea without ever being afraid."

"The fear only comes at night. During the day, I don't ever experience it."

"Well, the next time you are afraid, you tell me, and I will chase all of your fears away."

As Manny and Anna sat in lounge chairs, quietly gazing at the water, a group of two couples came out to enjoy the night air. They began talking amongst themselves, loud enough that

Manny and Anna could hear everything they said. They talked about politics, and the conversation quickly turned to the Nazis, to what was taking place in Germany, and all of the speculation about what was going on in the camps.

"I've heard that they are arresting Jews all over Germany and sending them to concentration camps," one of the women wearing a fur wrap and a silver gown said as she slid her matching silver sandal off of her foot.

"Well, yes, I suppose I've heard that too. But of course, I wouldn't believe everything I heard. Besides, as always, that wouldn't include us. We are rich," one of the men said, lighting a cigar.

"Do you really believe that our financial state will keep us safe?" the woman asked.

"It already has. I mean, here we are on this lovely ship. Do you think if I hadn't have been a successful doctor that we would be here?" the man, wearing a black tuxedo with his hair slicked perfectly away from his face, asked his wife, the woman with the silver sandal.

Just then, a man who'd been sitting with his wife on the other side of the deck came over.

"I couldn't help but over hear your conversation. And I must tell you, you and people like you are the reason that the Germans hate us. You," he said, pointing to the woman, "with your fur coat and your attitude. You think that you are different from the other Jews. But, let me tell you, you are not. You are the same as the rest of us. And what I believe is that there are concentration camps, and they are as bad, or worse than the rumors tell us. Things in Germany are bad now, but this is just the beginning. When they escalate, the rich and the poor will suffer alike. The anti-Semitism is growing every day. You are lucky you got out when you did. Soon, money will mean nothing."

"How dare you!" the doctor said. "You are not a part of this conversation. We have family still in Germany. Your senseless words are upsetting my wife. Go on your way. "

"Mark my words, I am not wrong. If you have family still there, get them out now, while there is still time. Use your money instead of hoarding it for yourself."

"Mind your business." The doctor's face had turned as red as a radish.

"Anna," Manny patted Anna's shoulder to divert her attention from what looked like it might become a fistfight. "Would you like to take a walk?"

She nodded, getting up. Manny took her elbow and led her away while the group was still arguing.

They strolled along the deck for several minutes.

"Manny, do you think that what that man said is true? Do you think my parents will end up in camps?""

"I think the only people who are being arrested and sent to these terrible places have in some way broken the law. I don't believe that every Jewish citizen, rich or poor, will be sent to a camp. This is just panic talking."

"You really believe so? I want to agree with you. I want to believe that my parents will be safe until this is all over."

"Of course I believe they will be safe. Don't worry. You are far too young and far too beautiful to be so worried." he said, but he doubted his own words. Manny had heard all of the rumors. He knew several Jews who had been arrested, their only crime being born Jewish. But, it would do Anna no good to think of such things. There was nothing she could do to help her family; it was best to let her believe all was well.

"Alex could tell us more if we asked him."

"Yes, I suppose he could, but he is having a tough enough time adjusting to the ship. He is a nervous wreck. I don't think we should bring it up."

"Do you know anything about what happened to Alex? Why he was in the camp?"

"No, I'm afraid I don't know anything yet. I just figured I will let him tell me when he felt ready."

"That's probably the best idea," she said.

They could still hear the two men arguing on the other side of the deck.

"It's a bad thing when Jews turn against one another. We must try to stick together. The stronger our alliance, the harder it will be for the Germans to wage war on our people. But of course, there are people like the ones we just saw. They differentiate between the rich and the poor. Or between Polish or Danish Jews, for instance, and German Jews. You know the German Jews think they are superior to Jews from other countries. That is so absurd to me. It is just another way that we weaken our own race."

"I've heard that... I mean, about German Jews being superior. In fact, I remember when I was in school, a girl came from Russia with her parents to live on our block. Her family was Jewish, but all the other children treated her as if she were beneath them because she was Russian and not German. You're right. This superior attitude is not a good thing."

"Ach, it's money, country, profession, or something... But sadly, Jews are always trying to outdo one another, when we should be trying to unite," he said.

Anna nodded in agreement.

"I am getting tired. I am not used being at sea, and the night air is making me drowsy. I think I would like to go to my stateroom now," Anna said. "I've had a lovely evening. Thank you, Manny."

"The pleasure was all mine," he said as he walked her to the stairs.

"I can get to my room from here."

"Are you sure you don't want me to walk you?"

"It isn't necessary. Goodnight."

"Goodnight."

Chapter 3

Havana, Cuba

Once the money for the passports had been received and the ship sailed out of German waters, the anti-Semitic Nazi propaganda began. Alex was right; the Nazis did have a vicious trick planned. Goebbels, Hitler's Minister of Propaganda, had no intention of allowing these Jewish refugees to live in peace. To ensure that the Jews would be unwelcome when they arrived in Cuba, the Nazis began campaigns. They terrified the Cuban people by telling them that the Jews were criminals who were coming to take their jobs, to destroy their homeland. In short, Hitler never planned to see the passengers of *MS St. Louis* safely out of the web of Nazi terror. This voyage was merely another deception of the Third Reich. Glimmers of hope, only to be stolen as the devastated passengers were returned to Germany and the horrific concentration camps. And so, this was Hitler's plan...

Chapter 4

A warm breeze floated off the water the following morning as Alex and Manny walked the upper deck on their way to the dining room. A sense of well-being came over Alex that he'd not experienced since Hitler had come to power. It frightened him, and he hated that he could not accept the luxury and kindness on the ship. First, he doubted the authenticity, and that he knew was because of all he'd seen, but more importantly, he thought of the others…those he'd left behind in Dachau. Those who still suffered, starved, and endured the daily torture he'd escaped from. A shiver ran through Alex, and Manny noticed that Alex trembled, but he chose to pretend he didn't see him shudder. Instead, Manny tried to make light of the situation, hoping to pull Alex out of the dark place he'd gone to in his mind.

"I met a young lady last night after dinner."

"Oh?"

"Yes, her name is Anna. She is quite lovely."

It had been so long since Alex had even thought of romance or love. Survival had been his only concern.

"That's very nice. I am happy for you…"

"Maybe you should stay around after dinner tonight. There are many lovely ladies on board."

"I'll see."

Alex found that he could not enjoy the food. It stuck in his throat, which seemed always to be as dry as sandpaper, regardless of how much water he drank to hydrate himself.

While Manny sat talking to Anna, he thought only of his parents and little sister...all had perished...all had been murdered. If only he'd been able to take little Esther with him. If only he could have done something, anything, to save her. Of course, he was not sure they were dead; he'd never seen their bodies, but he'd been told by others whose word he trusted that they were gone. His friend who'd been forced to shove the bodies into a mass grave had assured him as gently as possible that he would not see his family again.

Lost in thought, Alex didn't realize that Manny had left the table. He did not look up from his plate until Manny returned and stood before him speaking.

"Alex, come and join us. This is Anna," Manny said, Anna standing beside him. "We are going to sit up on deck and play cards. Would you like to play?"

Alex looked at Manny, dazed. He could not think about playing cards. His memories would not let him go.

"No, thank you. I think I will go to the ship's library and get a book, if they will allow me to do so."

"Of course they will, that is what the books are for."

"Hello, Alex," Anna said and smiled.

Alex answered with a troubled nod. "Hello, Anna. Nice to meet you."

Her eyes fixed on his troubled face.

"Nice to meet you, too. I would really like you to join us. It's a beautiful day, and we will be sitting up on the deck. You can get a little sun?"

Alex looked at her, so young, hopeful, and innocent. Although he was only twenty-two, he felt as if he were one hundred and twenty-two. He shook his head. "No, thank you..."

"Please, come with us Alex. I hate to think of you sitting all alone in your room." She smiled again, and something in her smile touched him in a remote corner of his soul, a place that he'd vowed to destroy, forcing it to wither and die long ago.

"Very well, if you insist." Alex tried to return her smile. The corners of his mouth turned, but anguish still haunted his eyes.

The sun burned brightly in a turquoise sky as the three walked slowly along the hardwood deck. As Manny and Anna sat at a table with an umbrella, Alex walked to the edge of the rail and gazed out. White-knuckled, he gripped the wooden railing. Looking at the blue of the ocean mingling with the sky, he allowed himself to wonder if perhaps there might be a God after all. But how could God have allowed his family and other innocent people, women and children, to be massacred, slaughtered, without any good reason? His mother's eyes, the color of peat moss, stared back at him from the water. He thought he could hear her voice, but could not make out her words. As he stood up, his feet unable to move, he felt the ship's motion and with it began to think he might become ill. *So many lost; so many dead.* He wished he could cry, longed for the release it might bring. But the tears would not come; instead, vomit rose in his throat, and without a word to his companions, he rushed back to his stateroom.

"Your friend is rather strange." Anna shuffled the deck of cards several times, then laid them on the table and gazed at Manny.

"He was a prisoner in Dachau. He must have seen some terrible things."

"How did he ever get out?"

"I don't know. I almost feel uncomfortable asking him, as if I might be prying into his private world."

"Maybe he needs someone to talk to. He seems so all alone and so lost."

"That he does." Then Manny looked at her lovely face with his dancing eyes. "But we are here and it is a beautiful day, yes? And you, my dear, are far too beautiful to fret over something we have no control over. So...shall we play cards?"

She nodded, but as she looked at the hand Manny dealt, her thoughts were consumed with Alex. The depth of Alex's very essence, and the pain in his soul cried out to her. Who was this man, and why did she want so very much to save him? She, Anna, who had never given thought to saving anyone. She, who had been pampered and adored, an only child, given to a couple gifted with a baby late in life. Anna knew she had been sheltered. And she'd loved her life, loved her parents, and loved her home. Perhaps that was why she wanted to shelter Alex.

They played cards for the better part of the early afternoon, until it was almost time for lunch.

When Manny returned to the stateroom to find Alex curled up on the floor in the corner, he rushed to his friend and knelt beside him.

"Alex, what is it? Are you ill?"

"How can I eat all this fine food and enjoy the weather when so many people are in the camps, so many still suffer?"

Manny put his hand on Alex's shoulder. "Listen to me. You torturing yourself is not the answer to helping thc others. How does your pain make their suffering less?"

"I don't know, but I can't forget them. If I forget them, they will have endured the torture and died in vain. Leave me please?"

Manny nodded and went upstairs on the deck to take a walk.

That night Alex did not go to the dining room. Instead, he remained in the cabin alone. He fell asleep on the floor, too guilty to enjoy the comfort of the soft bed.

Manny and Anna danced after dinner. As they waltzed she looked up at him with genuine concern. "How is your roommate?"

"Could be better, but then how can we know or understand what he has been through? Somehow, you and I were the lucky ones. We were spared. Neither of us was in a camp."

"Yes, and it makes me feel so guilty, as if I must help him. Do you feel that way too?"

"Well, sort of ... Yes, but I cannot. He won't let me."

"So what can we do?"

"Nothing, my dear. There is nothing to be done for him. Let us talk about you. Tell me, so… what were your favorite subjects in school?"

She laughed. "You sound like my Aunt Minnie instead of Manny."

He touched her face, and then he laughed too. "All right then, you can call me Aunt Minnie."

Chapter 5

That night Alex woke startled and covered in sweat. Manny had insisted he sleep in his bed instead of on the hard floor. Quietly, so as not to awaken Manny, he got out of bed and walked up the stairs to sit outside on the open deck. The darkness settled like a blanket filled with silver stars. As he sat alone, Alex gazed up into the sky, and finally the tears he'd held back for so long came like a flood through a broken dam, and he wept. The smell of the musty urine-soaked hay he'd slept on in the camp still lingered in his nose, and regardless of how much he bathed, he could not wash it away. The faces of the friends he left behind, with their jutting cheekbones and emaciated bodies, haunted his every moment. Perhaps it would have been better if he had died, for in truth he could not live, not like this. Alex wrung his hands and looked down at the floor. He was so caught up in thought that he did not hear the footsteps as they approached him.

"Alex?" Anna's soft voice entered his tormented world.

Alex turned his head to look up but he did not answer.

"I couldn't sleep. I needed some fresh air." She smiled, pulling a chair next to his. "May I join you?"

He nodded, hating himself for being unable to communicate, aware of how uncomfortable he made this girl feel. Yet, small talk was not within his power.

"Manny likes you very much."

"Does he? He is a good person."

"Yes, very kind and light hearted."

Alex nodded.

"Alex…" She hesitated until he met her eyes. "You were in Dachau?"

"Yes." He looked out across the water.

"I am sure it must be hard for you to forget."

"I will never forget." His voice sounded angrier than he meant for it to be. When he looked at her face, he suddenly felt ashamed. "I'm sorry. I didn't mean to be so abrupt. It's just that I feel that by keeping the memory of my friends and loved ones in my heart …" His voice cracked with emotion he could not speak.

"I understand. And I agree, you must never forget them. But I also feel that if you stop living, you will have done them a terrible injustice. Your life must have meaning. Somehow, Alex, you have been chosen to live. If you do something wonderful with your life it will be for all of those who were unable to fulfill their dreams."

This was the first time any words had penetrated Alex's grief stricken mind. Perhaps she could be right.

"I was a writer before all of this began, in another time, another lifetime." His voice cracked as the words emerged, barely audible.

"What did you write?"

It felt as if a crab apple had lodged itself in his throat, and he swallowed hard. "Before things got really bad… I guess what I am saying is, before *Kristallnacht*, I wrote fiction, short stories...but then…" Alex looked out over the dark water and wondered how deep the water was. He wondered how it would feel to fall to the bottom of the ocean, his breath sucked from his lungs as he left the world behind.

"Yes, go on, please." Anna's voice brought him back as she took his hand. It startled him to feel the warmth of her touch, and he pulled his hand away. He'd not felt human contact in so long. Then he turned from the ocean to meet her eyes.

"I couldn't help myself. I tried. I suppose I should have tried harder, but, I began to write anti-Nazi essays. They seemed to flow out of me without my control. And worse, I was compelled to allow them to be published…especially in the Jewish communities. Something made me want to shout a warning. To let the others know what I could see coming in the future."

"And so you became an enemy of the Reich?"

"Yes. I was arrested. I expected to be. But what I did not expect was that they would arrest my family." He looked away from her. "They took us to Dachau: my mother, my father, and my sister Esther, my sweet, innocent little sister. If I had known they would take them… If I had known what they would do to them…" Deep sobs broke from within him. The sound filled the silence on ship's deck like the wail of a dying animal.

Helpless, Anna sat beside Alex as he wept.

"Forgive me. I didn't mean to put all of this on you." He stood to leave.

"Don't go, Alex. Please stay." She stood, looking up into his eyes.

"I'm sorry, but I must." With his head bowed, he left the deck, leaving Anna alone.

Chapter 6

Anna walked to the railing and stood gazing up at the sky. Why had the Nazis done this? What had caused such hatred of her people? While Alex had been beside her, she had forgotten her own pain, but now it returned. Could Manny be right? Would her parents ever be able to escape? Would she see them again? As a child, she could never have imagined a life without her family. The future seemed so simple then. She would grow up, marry, have children, and live within the same community she'd grown up in. She would shop at the same markets and have her parents over at her house for Sabbath dinners. Her Mama and Papa would never be far away. She would have children and bring them to visit their grandparents. That had been the plan. Now, everything had changed. She traveled to an unknown place, to meet distant relatives she'd never seen, who would take her to a country she'd only heard about. She knew she would think about the safety of her parents constantly, and her life would always feel incomplete. Anna felt tears sting the back of her eyes. Alex's loss broke her heart, but she, too, had been forced to give up so much.

The clicking of high heel shoes against the hard wood floor of the deck startled her, and she turned to see a young glamorous blonde.

"So, another one with insomnia?" the blonde laughed. "I couldn't get to sleep."

Anna returned the smile, impressed by the well-dressed stranger in the dark burgundy cotton dress with the black belt and matching shoes.

"Hello, my name is Elke, and you are?"

"Anna."

"Nice to meet you."

"Likewise."

"So, this is an exciting trip, no?"

"Not really, not for me," Anna said." I would much rather be at home."

"Oh, come now, we're going to Cuba… It's beautiful, I hear."

"I had to leave my family behind."

"Yes, I had to leave my mother, but I can tell you this. I won't miss her."

Anna turned to look at her companion.

Elke laughed. "I'm sorry to laugh, but you look so shocked. My mother and I have been at odds for years. She was kind enough to use me to get special favors from the Germans. I have the blonde hair and blue eyes that they like so much. And when I turned thirteen I developed into a woman… I guess I was the perfect bait."

"Use you? How?"

Elke avoided the question. "You are young and naïve, my friend. Well, no matter. It all served me well in the end. Her *Gestapo* friend took pity on me and sent me here to this ship. I guess in their way they liked me. So, I am off to a new and exciting place." She laughed again. "You look so stunned."

"I don't understand."

"Well, perhaps as we become better friends I will explain it to you." Elke winked at Anna.

The two girls sat in silence for a few moments. Then Anna asked, almost in a whisper. "What do you think Cuba will be like?"

"A sultry haven, far away from Germany and my mother."

It was nearly dawn before Anna went to her stateroom. As she dressed for breakfast, an overwhelming sadness came upon her like an outbreak of influenza. Her head and body ached. Even though she'd tried to convince herself that somehow, some way, she would see her family again, in her heart she felt she would not. Never before had she been so fatalistic, and here, blessed with an opportunity to leave Nazi Germany, a dream that most Jews would have given anything to be a part of, she could not shake her depression. *You should be ashamed of yourself, Anna. Stop this self-pity. You must believe that your parents will find a way out. There will be another ship…something will happen to save them. They will meet you in America. You must believe.*

When Alex left Anna on the deck, he returned to his cabin where he sat on the floor, awake, thinking. He was damaged, and he felt that he would never recover. If he had been less outspoken, perhaps his family would be alive. This guilt haunted his every moment. As he sat watching the sun rise, Alex felt the ship come to a stop. The easy swaying motion ceased, and he knew that they had docked somewhere. His first instinct was that they had returned to Germany. It had been a trick all along. The Nazis had given them two days of peace only to return them to hell. Sweat beaded on his brow. His hands shook so badly that he could not steady them. Alex knew he must rise and awaken Manny. He stood up, his knees wobbling beneath him, and walked over to where Manny slept, unaware of what had happened.

"Manny, get up," Alex said, shaking Manny's shoulder. "Get up, the ship has stopped moving."

Manny rolled over on to his back and looked at Alex, confused, still hazy with sleep.

"What are you talking about?"

"Sit up. Do you feel it? We've stopped moving. I am afraid they have returned us to Germany. I think perhaps this has all been a trick, and now we are all going to concentration camps."

Manny sat up in bed. It took a few minutes for him to acclimate himself, but once he did, he realized that Alex was right. The ship had docked...somewhere.

"What are we going to do?" Alex said, more to himself than to Manny. "There is no place to hide on this ship. They have us. We are their prisoners." He got up and began to pace the small room. "I would rather jump into the sea and drown than ever see another concentration camp. I can't take the torture, not again..."

"Alex, you are getting ahead of yourself. Now please, nobody is jumping in the water. Let me get some clothes on and I will go up and see why the ship has stopped. Perhaps we are having some trouble with the engine or something. All right? Don't panic, give me a chance to see what is happening."

Alex sat on the floor while Manny dressed.

Manny looked over at Alex. Could he be right? Could he have been right all along? Maybe they were back in Germany, and it had all been a cruel Nazi trick to bring those who were in hiding out into the open, where they could be caught and sent to camps. *Oy*, this was not good. But before he would allow himself to believe the worst, he would try to stay optimistic. That was always his way. Manny could find the good in the most terrible situations. And he would not abandon hope, not yet.

"I'll be right back. You stay here, and don't do anything crazy. Give me a few minutes, and I'll find out what is what."

Alex nodded as Manny left the cabin, closing the door.

Manny walked up onto the deck. There were people everywhere…boarding the ship. He walked over to a crewmember who stood assisting the new passengers, with their luggage and room assignment.

"Excuse me," Manny said. "May I ask why we have stopped and who all of these people are?"

"We are in Cherbourg, sir. We've come to pick up additional passengers. It should only be a few hours before we are on our way to Cuba. I am sorry for the delay."

"Thank you," Manny said, breathing a sigh of relief as he heard a couple speaking in Yiddish with a French accent.

As quickly, as he could Manny raced back to the cabin, to tell Alex. Alex was still sitting on the floor when Manny opened the door.

"We're all right. We're still in France. We've picked up some more people. I saw them. They are boarding. One of the men from the crew told me that we should be leaving here soon."

"Do you believe him?"

"I saw the passengers boarding. I do believe him. We are all right, Alex. Everything is fine." Manny bent to pat Alex's shoulder. "Come on, get up from the floor. Let's go upstairs and watch the others come aboard."

Chapter 7

Manny had arranged for both himself and Alex to change their table and sit with Anna. But because she was so tired from staying up through the night, the conversation lagged.

"I am going to my stateroom to take a nap. I'm sorry; I couldn't sleep last night," Anna told the men after breakfast.

"Perhaps later this afternoon we could all go for a swim after lunch? That should give you time to get some rest." Manny smiled as he buttered a fresh hard roll.

"All right, three o'clock?" Anna glanced over at Alex, who sat staring at his plate. She realized he'd hardly eaten. "I'm afraid I may miss lunch, so if I oversleep, I will meet you both on deck at three. Good?" Anna nodded as she stood to leave.

"Yes." Manny smiled. "Have pleasant dreams."

"Alex," she spoke softly. "Will you be there...please?"

He looked into her eyes and nodded.

Chapter 8

Manny was convinced that Anna's pity for Alex compelled her to assure him that they wanted his company. Although he liked his roommate, Manny would have enjoyed a few hours alone with Anna. She had begun to captivate his attentions. Women had come and gone in the past and he hadn't cared much. But something about this small, troubled girl played upon his mind. If he were honest with himself, he would have to admit that Anna, lovely as a spring blossom, was still not the most beautiful girl on the ship. Regardless, she held his interest like no other, and since they'd met he'd begun to feel she might be his *bashert* (all Jews believe that there is one special someone that God has created for them alone, their *bashert*). *Maybe I am just thinking absurd thoughts because of the situation we are in.* But he continued to wonder…

Chapter 9

The sun illuminated the deck of the ship, dazzling the water of the pool invitingly. Anna and Manny both wore bathing suits, while Alex had refused Manny's offer to loan him one. Alex sat at a wrought-iron table under a colorful umbrella. He'd brought a book with him, but instead of opening it, he sat drumming his fingers on the leather cover. Manny and Anna, both good swimmers, swam laps in a mock race. After a few minutes, both out of breath, they stood in the shallow end catching their breath and laughing.

Elke had just come outside and when she saw Anna, she waved. Anna waved back. Elke put her towel on a chair and jumped into the pool. Then she swam over to Anna and Manny.

"Elke, this is my friend Manny. Manny, this is Elke."

"Hello." He couldn't help but notice her voluptuous, full breasts, the gentle curve of her hips, and her long, shapely legs.

"Very nice to meet you," She smiled.

One of the German officers was acting as a lifeguard. He was a handsome young man with a muscular build. His blond hair caught the rays of the sun as he watched Elke. She was beyond beautiful.

To an outsider it would seem as if all were right with the world, that this was just a group of young people swimming and enjoying a summer's day. But a closer look would reveal a depth of pain in each of their youthful faces. And if one looked even closer, one must take note of the flag with the swastika flying high at the bow of the ship.

A blond waiter wearing white gloves approached Alex. He carried a silver tray.

"Can I get you something to drink, sir?"

Alex jumped at the approach. He had not expected the crewmember to speak to him. Unable to lift his head and look into the man's eyes, Alex stared out at the sea.

He shook his head. Regardless of the kindness the Germans showed the Jews on this voyage, Alex still did not trust them. He'd seen too much. There had been so many times while in the camp that he'd witnessed horrific murders with his own eyes. The Nazis had killed without reason. Once, he'd seen an old man shot standing in line at role call. His crime? He'd become ill and coughed. This alone had been reason enough for the young Nazi to pull a gun and shoot the old man in the face. Alex's body trembled. Then, his voice cracked. "Thank you, no…nothing." Alex arose quickly, grabbed his book, and retreated out of the sun and into the dark safety of his cabin.

Manny, engaged in conversation with both women, did not realize that Alex had left. But Anna saw him go, and her heart ached as she longed to follow him.

"Shall we get some sun?" Manny asked the girls. "Come, I'll set some towels on the chairs for us. After the harsh winter in Germany, it will feel good to enjoy the warm sunshine."

As they lay on the lounge chairs, the young German officer watched Elke. Could she really be a Jew? She looked so Aryan. He must approach her. He must learn her name.

"Hello." The officer walked over to where Elke was enjoying the afternoon. "My name is Viktor. You are?"

"Elke." She looked up, his face was blocked by the bright rays of the sun.

"May I join you?"

Manny and Anna both watched the Nazi officer, worry on both of their faces.

"Of course. I believe there is another deck chair on the other side." Elke was not afraid; she'd had plenty of experience with Nazi officers. This was just another one.

"Well, let me go and get one, and I will sit beside you." He smiled.

As the officer went off to get the chair, Manny sat up and turned to Elke. "Do you think it is wise to be so friendly with one of them?"

"I don't think it could hurt anything."

"Aren't you afraid?" Anna asked.

"Not at all," Elke said. "I can handle him." She smiled.

Viktor Hahn was carrying a heavy lounge chair in one hand when the cries of a child came from the pool.

A woman in an old-fashioned black bathing suit began to scream, "She's drowning! My daughter is drowning!"

Viktor dropped the chair and jumped into the pool. Manny not believing his eyes, sat up straight to watch as the German officer swam out and grasped the child, pulling her out of the water, then giving her mouth-to-mouth resuscitation. A Nazi treating a Jew in this manner was unthinkable. Anna and Manny exchanged glances. Perhaps things had changed for the Jews on this ship. Perhaps they really were leaving all of the persecution behind.

Elke rose from her chair and ran to where Viktor worked diligently on the little girl. She gazed at him, wondering what it was that made him act this way. She'd known Nazis better than most Jews had ever known them. But even the ones who were kind to her were never like this. They were kind because they were getting something from her. She was fulfilling a fantasy. But for Viktor this child meant nothing, and still he seemed to care enough to want to save her life. It was hard for Elke to believe that he did this out of kindness. The only thing she could figure was that his actions were to gain her admiration. But why would he need her admiration? After all, she was only a Jew. He was the one with the power.

When the child vomited water and began to cough, everyone cheered. With ease, Viktor lifted the little girl and placed her on a chair beside her mother. Then he picked up the lounger he had been carrying, smiled at Elke, and began heading back to the spot on the other side of the deck, where Manny and Anna watched with their mouths gaping open.

For a long time the four sat in silence as the sun put the color back into Manny's, Elke's and Anna's skin. Finally, Elke turned to Viktor. He was lying on his back. By the golden hue of his skin, Elke knew he'd spent a plenty of time in the sun.

"Viktor, may I call you Viktor?"

"Of course, I would have it no other way." He half sat up, turning to her with a white-toothed smile.

"Why did you do that? I mean, why did you help that little girl? I know it's not my business."

"I don't' mind answering. It was the right thing to do. And besides, at 22 I am one hell of a specimen of a man, I am gallant, generous, attractive, and everything a woman would want in a man…" he said, laughing. "Just joking. Really, I did it to impress you."

"You did?"

"Partially, yes. However, how could I let a child drown? Every day one or more of them gets into trouble in the pool. I help when I can."

"Even though they are Jews?"

"Yes, even though. You know our captain said that we are to treat our passengers the same as we would treat every other passenger, regardless of the fact that they are Jews. Besides, I don't have anything personally against Jews. I think all of this nonsense is rubbish."

She studied him. If she were to take a lover, Manny was surely the better choice. This man, although, far more attractive, was still a Nazi, and in the end he would always be a Nazi.

"You're looking at me with such surprise. You know not all of us Germans believe in this propaganda about the Jews. I grew up with plenty of Jewish friends."

She nodded.

"Have you met our captain? I have great respect for the man. I've sailed with him many times before. His name, in case you don't know it, is Captain Gustav Schroder. He isn't a typical Nazi either. In fact, we've had a bit of trouble with a crew member who has been showing disrespect to our Jewish passengers. The captain has severely reprimanded him."

"You must know that for me, a Jewish woman, this is an unusual way of talking for a German officer. I want to believe you, but history..."

"Let my actions prove my words, fair enough?"

She smiled at him.

"You will, of course, sit beside me at the captain's table for dinner tonight?" Viktor had made special arrangements to sit at Captain Schroder's table. It was considered an honor, and he'd begged to be allowed to do it just this one night. He hoped it would impress Elke, and make her see him as a man of importance, and not just another crewman on a ship.

"If you insist." She would rather have been with Manny, Alex, and Anna. This familiarity could either go in her favor, or be the reason for her demise.

"I do. I absolutely do. I would love to present you as my date."

"Very well, then."

"Shall we take a swim?"

"If you'd like," Elke said, her eyes darting to Anna, who bore a look of concern. She smiled with a reassurance she did not feel. Then Elke followed Viktor to the pool.

For the rest of the day, Viktor was attentive to Elke's every need. The more he tried to cater to her, the less she trusted him. She wondered if she should take him to her bed. If she did, she was sure he would lose interest, and then she would be free of him. But what if for some reason she needed his help? Best to keep him at bay, at least for now.

By the time Manny arrived back at the stateroom, he had only a half hour until dinner. He opened the door to find Alex sitting in the chair at the small desk. In front of him lay a pile of papers.

"You've been writing?" Manny thought about telling Alex what had happened at the pool with Nazi officer, but he decided against it. Alex was unstable enough; this would only unnerve him more.

"Yes." He nodded.

"May I?" Manny asked as he reached for Alex's writing.

Again, Alex nodded.

Manny picked up the pile of documents that had been strewed wildly across the top of the desk. Written in black charcoal pencil, the words had smeared into the white paper as if they'd burned onto the parchment from Alex's core.

Sitting down on the bed, Manny began to read account after terrifying account of the cruelty Alex had witnessed at Dachau, each episode written down in explicit detail.

"Why? Why do you do this to yourself, Alex? It can do you no good to hold on to this."

"Because the world must know, Manny. We must never forget our people. Each person killed or tortured was a living human being, a mother, a father, a son, a daughter, a brother, a sister." He hung his head. "They all mattered... Every one of them was a part of someone's life."

"Yes, they mattered, but so do you. They are dead. You can do them no good by carrying this burden in your heart. You are killing yourself over the past."

"And you, what are you doing? Enjoying life? Of course you are. I am sure that is all you have ever done."

"That's not fair."

"Isn't it? Have you any moral purpose Manny? Or is your only purpose to serve yourself?"

"I won't listen to you. I can't see any point in going over this again and again. It won't bring back the dead. I am going to clean up for dinner. Come to the dining room if you like. I don't care what you do."

Alex never came to dinner. Instead, he continued his quest to use the gift God had given him to write. He could not stop the atrocities, but he would remember and write them as clearly as he could. As he purged his pain onto the paper, it left him for a moment feeling a small bit of peace.

In the dining room, Elke sat beside Viktor at the captain's table. The music played. Anna and Manny danced. It was like a luxury cruise, with an underlying agenda.

Viktor even danced with Anna after dinner. Although she was terribly nervous and skeptical, she waltzed with the eloquent German officer.

But Viktor's moment with Anna was only to be polite; he was in fact taken with the beautiful Elke. He could not stop looking at her. She would turn to catch him staring, and he would turn away, embarrassed.

When Manny returned carrying a sandwich, Alex realized how rude he'd been. Manny had shown him nothing but kindness and he'd answered with criticism and judgment. After all, who was he to pass judgment? Perhaps Manny was right. They were still alive; their suffering could not save those already dead. If only he could be more like Manny. If only he could let it all go and live in the moment.

"I'm sorry for how I behaved earlier this evening."

"It's all right. I understand. This is all very hard for you."

"Yes, it is…and I don't know what to do except write. It helps me to get my feelings out and put them on paper. In many ways, it has been my only salvation. But I never meant to hurt you. You are a good friend and a fine person. You have gone out of your way for me. You have done all you could to make my life here on this ship a little easier. I had no right to say that you just lived for the moment. You do live a life of purpose…"

"Come…eat…and forget about what happened. I am not angry. I have forgotten already." Manny put the food in front of Alex.

"I am very hungry."

"Of course you are. Eat, relax… Put this stuff away for a little while."

While Alex gobbled the sandwich, Manny gathered the papers in to a neat pile and put them in the top drawer of the desk, away where Alex could not see them, if only for the moment.

Chapter 10

The following morning the crew announced that a movie would be shown in the ship's theater after dinner that night. It had been some time since Jews were allowed into the cinema, so this came as a rare treat. An air of excitement surrounded the evening's events. The women talked about what they would wear, and everyone wondered what film would be shown. As the ship continued to sail, while the passenger's ate fine food and enjoyed the sunshine, little by little they began to leave the horror of Nazi Germany behind them.

Before the *MS St. Louis* sailed, the captain had gathered his crew. He had made it clear that anyone who showed disrespect to the Jewish passengers would be severely punished. This angered many of the workers, as they were pure Aryan's and the *MS St. Louis* flew under the Nazi flag. However, the captain refused to bend on this rule and enforced it with the utmost authority.

"I am the captain of this ship," he'd said. "While I am in charge, there will be no contempt toward our Jewish guests. They will be made to feel comfortable in every way."

"You are not a member of the Nazi party?" A tall, well-built, blond crewmember asked.

"I am not, and this is my ship. As long as I am alive, I am in command here. If you cannot follow my rules, I suggest you leave the ship before we sail. Any defiance of my wishes will be considered mutiny."

Chapter 11

"It might do you good to watch a film. Take your mind off things for a few hours. So Alex, what do you think?" Manny asked him.

"Yes, perhaps you're right. It has been a very long time since I did something so frivolous."

"Well, it might be good for you."

Manny loaned Alex another pair of black pants and a white cotton shirt. Next to the shirt, he placed a thin gray-and-black tie.

After taking a long, hot bath, Alex dressed for dinner. When he had finished, Manny marveled once again at his roommate's good looks. Then, shaking his head and smiling, Manny watched Alex scrutinize the necktie. After rejecting it, Alex popped open the top button of his shirt, choosing comfort over formality with little consideration of his appearance.

"You are a handsome devil," Manny said.

Alex smiled and shook his head.

Elke joined the three after dinner, and they proceeded to the auditorium. Viktor was already there, waiting. He'd saved seats for all three of them. When Elke saw him smiling, she could not help but return his smile.

"I didn't see you in the dining room."

"You were looking for me?" Viktor asked.

"I was, I must admit."

"That makes me so happy." Viktor smiled. "I was upstairs arranging some things in the engine room and I couldn't get away. You have my true apologies."

Alex looked through the corner of his eye at Viktor. What was a Nazi officer doing with his friends? This was dangerous. He wished he'd stayed in his room, but to leave now would only draw attention to him.

The soft hum of conversation petered out as the lights dimmed and the curtains opened. An instrumental of a German love song played, filling the theater with lovely sound. The movie was to be a lighthearted romantic comedy. But before the feature film, a short came blaring onto the screen. There right in front of them all, larger than life, was the face of Adolph Hitler ranting about his hatred of Jews. Red faced, with hands flaying about in anger, he raved. As the movie clip continued, one by one the audience left the theater in horror.

Viktor stood up his voice rose "What the hell is going on here? Who is responsible for this outrage?"

No one answered. The film continued.

Manny turned to look at Alex who sat glued to the screen. Anna watched Alex as well. His face contorted with fury. With a firm grip on Alex's upper arm, Manny tried to break the spell.

"Come let's go from here. We'll go up on the deck and get some air."

Viktor turned to the others. "I am terribly sorry about this. I am going to the projection area to find out who is behind all of it." Viktor left.

The girls stood ready to leave. The lights in the theater had been turned on and someone had silenced the film but had not turned it off. Hitler's face remained frozen on the screen as Alex remained frozen in his chair.

"Alex." Manny shook his arm "Alex... Alex..."

Alex shook Manny's hand off him. Tears began to slide down Alex's face. Then Anna walked over to the chair on the other side of Alex and sat down. She gently placed her hand upon his. For several moments she did not speak. But once he noticed her presence by the heat of her palm in his, he looked at her face.

"Alex, it's all right." With her other hand, Anna wiped the tears from his cheek. "We should leave here. Please...come with us." She smoothed the skin under his eye with her thumb. "Let's go up on deck? Yes? Come please?" she urged as she squeezed his hand.

From the distance, they could hear Viktor shouting in German and the voice of another man apologizing as the screen went white.

Alex nodded. He rose and the group left the auditorium.

That night, although he did not speak much, Alex stayed with the other three and watched carefully. Tonight's incident had only served to increase his distrust. He sat on deck with Anna and Manny as Manny smoked Cuban cigars and told stories of his escapades traveling around Europe. "Better times," Manny called them. "Before the New Germany."

Elke walked over to where they were sitting. Her platinum blonde hair took on a silver hue in the moonlight, and it did not go unnoticed by Manny. He found her to be ravishing. With her curvaceous figure, high heels and blue eyes, he knew he would have enjoyed a night sharing her bed. But so unlike his usual self, Manny decided against the seduction because of his feelings for Anna. In the past, he would have already been pursuing this magnificent creature, and because he wasn't, once again he wondered if he had fallen in love.

It was over an hour before Viktor came up on deck.

"I thought I might find you here," he said to Elke. "Again, please, all of you, accept my apologies for tonight."

Manny and Anna nodded. Elke did not meet Viktor's gaze. Instead she looked out across the ocean.

"Elke, will you take a walk with me?" Viktor asked.

She nodded.

They got up and walked as the moon began to rise in the sky.

"That should never have happened. The man responsible will be punished."

She nodded.

"Elke, what are you thinking?'

"The truth?"

"Of course."

"I'm wondering what it is that you want from me Viktor. And…I am afraid of you, of your power to cause me trouble."

"I would never ca

use you trouble."

"Even if I told you to go away and let me be with my friends, and to stop trying to act as if we were living in normal times? I am a Jew and you are a Gentile, a Nazi too. This could turn out very badly."

"Do you really want me to leave you alone? I will if you tell me to."

"And then what will happen to me? To my friends?"

"Nothing. The only thing that will happen is my heart will be broken."

"I am sorry for your feelings, but yes, Viktor, please leave me alone. This is not a good thing for either of us. Why begin something that can only cause us pain and suffering? You are going back to Germany. I am going to America. I can never return to Germany. We have only a few days left together before the ship docks in Havana. It's best if we don't even start a romance."

"Fine, I wouldn't want you to feel pushed into anything." He turned and walked away without looking back.

That night, as Elke lay in her bed trying to sleep, she remembered everything that she'd been forced to do with the men from the *Gestapo*. She was just a child when it began, only twelve. They were so taken with her Aryan appearance that they'd avoided arresting her or her mother in order to continue the "evening dates" with Elke. That was how they referred to the nights they would bring sausages and bread, or sugar and flour. There were four of them, all friends, all in agreement as to how much they enjoyed their time with her. Often they came one at a time, but once in a while they all came together. Sometimes they would bring dinner, but she could never eat. Because she knew what was to come next, and she dreaded the physical union. When the men were ready, they would take her to the small bedroom where she still kept her dolls and stuffed bear on the shelf over her bed. It had only been a few years since she'd stopped playing with them. And then it began. The first few times the pain had been terrible, lasting well into the following day. But as time went by, the pain ceased, and she learned that she could use her beauty to manipulate men. And so she did. That was how she'd gotten on to this ship. She'd promised them all something very special in exchange for her freedom. She'd delivered, and surprisingly they'd kept their promise. Once she'd set sail, she assumed that her mother had probably been arrested. It saddened her, but in some ways, the resentment she felt for her mother's having allowed these men to have the evening dates with her still lingered. Perhaps someday she would find it in her heart to forgive her mother, but for now, she couldn't.

Viktor… What a puzzle he presented. She thought about him. He was a man, and men wanted only one thing, and he was a Nazi, to boot. If she were placing a bet, she would bet that Viktor was no different from the other Nazis she'd known. Best to be done with him now.

Now, Manny, he was a different story. Manny, had grown up with money and class; he reeked of it. When he'd told the stories of his travel through Europe, she knew that he'd never wanted for anything. The hotels where he'd stayed were the most luxurious. He didn't even realize that he sounded as if he was bragging. To Manny, this was his way of life, plain and simple. He knew no other. Well, this was the life Elke yearned for, a life of opulence, of plenty. His family waited for his arrival in America. They were rich, no doubt. If she could win Manny's affection, her life would be mapped out for her, once she left the ship in Cuba. She would go off to America at his side, marry him, and forget her past. Yes, Manny was the one she wanted.

Chapter 12

In the morning, while all the passengers were in the dining room having breakfast, the captain's voice rang clear over the loudspeaker, offering an apology for the behavior of his crewmember in the theater the previous night. He assured the passengers he'd had no knowledge of the film that aired causing such distress among the passengers.

"It is my promise to you that the perpetrator of this offense will be punished. And while I have your attention, I would like to extend the offer of *Shabbat* services on Friday nights, if anyone would like to attend. We have a rabbi on board who is willing to officiate. The services will take place before dinner in the main ballroom. Once again, I apologize for last night. I remain your captain, officially in charge of the *MS St. Louis*."

"*Shabbat* services? He seems like a decent fellow." Manny smiled at the girls.

From the side of her eye Anna glanced at Alex who remained silent, but looked at Manny as if he were a fool.

"Would you believe I have never attended a Jewish service? My mother tried to raise me like a Christian. She said that with my coloring I would pass for a German. I even wore a cross," Elke said as she ran her hand over the white tablecloth.

"Even when you were little, before the Nazis?" Anna asked.

"Yes, she wanted to be a part of "their society," always. Before it was Hitler's henchmen, it was Hindenburg's crowd. My mother had high aspirations for me...but mostly for herself. However, once the Nazi's took power, they knew instantly from our background that we were Jewish. So, my mother's pretense had no effect on them at all. Cross or no cross, to the Nazis we were nothing but Jews."

"If you would like to see a *Shabbat* service, I would love to go with you." Anna smiled. "It is very beautiful."

"You know, until *Kristallnacht*, my mother never made much reference to the fact that we were Jewish. I knew I was, but not really… I mean all of my friends and our family friends were Gentiles. In fact it wasn't until we had a visit from the *Gestapo* that I realized what I was." Elke looked down avoiding Alex's accusing eyes.

"Well, don't worry too much about all that. You were just a child. You had no idea." Manny smiled at her.

"I hope you realize now what it means to be a Jew. No matter how hard you might have tried to hide your identity…Hitler has decided that you are a Jew. And you will suffer the same fate as the other Jews." Alex glared at her.

"Alex, don't be cruel. It isn't her fault. She was just a little girl." Manny took a sip of water.

"We should be proud of our Jewish heritage. If more of us had been proud and stood up for what we believed in, before they had the chance to put us into camps, all of this might never have happened." Alex glared at Manny.

Anna's eyes filled with admiration as she listened to Alex speak.

"I too, am guilty of not standing up." Manny looked over at Alex. "Not because I was ashamed, but I just never thought it would turn out to be this bad. I had Jewish and Gentile friends alike, and my religion never seemed to be of importance. We weren't religious…my family, I mean."

"Neither was mine, but we were Jews...and when the Nazis started their miserable propaganda against us...well...I stood up. I wrote... I wrote to the papers..." Alex hung his head. "Ahhh, Manny, maybe you're right. All my writing...so what did it do? Where did it get me? It got my family killed; that's what it did. And it got me a first-class place in a filthy, disease-ridden bunk in Dachau. Things are not good for Jews in Germany now, but somehow, I feel this situation is going to get a lot worse. We haven't begun to see the Nazis in full force..."

"I hope not, but at least we won't be in Germany to witness it."

"Yes, Manny we won't be there...but what about all the Jews that will not be so lucky?"

Manny shrugged his shoulders. He had nothing to say.

For a long time everyone was silent. Thoughts of Anna's parents weighed heavily upon her mind. If things got worse in Germany, it would greatly affect their lives. Silently, she said a prayer for their safety, but even so, the little voice of terror inside of her could not be quieted.

Chapter 13

Unbeknownst to the passengers aboard the doomed, *MS St. Louis*, as the vessel sailed out of the port of Hamburg, all of their visas were already invalid. It was due to a change in the Cuban Government. This new leadership ruled that only 28 of the passengers had valid passports. They would be the only ones allowed to leave the ship and enter the country.

To make matters worse, Goebbels had been successful in creating a strong anti-Semitic climate in Cuba. Word spread like a plague to the Cuban people that a group of Jewish criminals was on its way to their harbor. Five days before the ship was scheduled to dock, 40,000 Cubans participated in a demonstration that strongly opposed the entrance of the Jewish immigrants to Havana. This had a marked effect on the government's future decision to refuse entrance to all but 28 passengers.

Chapter 14

THE DAYS SLIPPED BY WITH EASE AS THE SHIP SAILED TOWARD HER DESTINATION. ABOARD THE MS ST. LOUIS, ONE COULD FORGET THAT HITLER LURKED IN THE SHADOWS. GOOD FOOD, CLEAN WATER, MUSIC, SUNSHINE, AND DANCING HELPED THE PASSENGERS TO LEAVE THE PAST BEHIND AND TO ONCE AGAIN ALLOW THEMSELVES TO HAVE HOPE FOR THE FUTURE.

At close to midnight one evening, the ship's bell clanged loudly, awakening the passengers. It was an alarm so astoundingly loud that within moments everyone had come on deck to see what had caused the ruckus. Alex felt his body tremble uncontrollably, even though he stood in the warm tropical breeze of the Atlantic Ocean. Manny, Anna, and Elke stood beside him. Manny tried to give his friends strength by appearing confident that nothing serious had taken place. Anna's eyes were still half closed with sleep, and Elke looked surprisingly young and vulnerable without all of the makeup she wore during the day.

Together, the four friends stood awaiting an announcement as to why the bell had summoned them. As he glanced around him, Alex saw people crying. Some of the men had begun praying, swaying as the Hebrew words of prayer were whispered into the night.

It felt like hours, but within a few minutes, the captain appeared at the front of the deck. Perfectly dressed in his uniform, he stood before the crowd. His crew stood behind him in their white uniforms. From where Elke stood, she could see Viktor. His eyes met hers, and then he quickly turned away.

"As your captain, it is my responsibility to inform you of any goings on upon this vessel. So it is with great regret that I must tell you that someone has fallen from the ship. We believe it to be a crewmember; however, that has not yet been confirmed. There is no evidence as to how this happened. Perhaps it was a suicide, or maybe an accident. We don't know at this point. We may never know. I have dispatched a rescue crew. I will keep all of you up-to-date as to the outcome of this tragic event. Please return to your rooms and try to get some sleep."

After the captain left, the crowd began to disperse. Then a woman of middle age, her salt-and-pepper hair wild with the night wind and her face ragged with premature wrinkles, began to scream.

"I think it's a murder. I think they plan to kill us all… They're Nazis. Look…" She pointed with a quivering finger to the Nazi flag that flew at the front of the ship. "How can we trust them…How?" She wobbled on the brink of hysteria as a man who appeared to be her husband put his arm around her shoulder leading her away.

Now, as Alex glanced over at Anna, he saw that she was crying. It amazed him that after all the tragedy he'd witnessed in the camp, he could still feel such compassion for this small, fragile girl. He loathed sentiment; he hated to allow himself to feel. It was dangerous. In Dachau, he'd learned that to care was to hurt deeply, to die inside. To love meant loss. It left you weak and vulnerable, even more open to cruelty. Alex could bear his own pain, even his own death, but not the death of a loved one, not again. And yet, he couldn't help himself. Whatever had come over him was well beyond his control. For the first time in as long as he could remember, he reached out with trembling fingers and touched another person. His hand rested tenderly on Anna's upper arm. This gesture, although it was small, was monumental to Alex. The warmth of connecting to another human being sent tingles of electricity through his entire body as he stood paralyzed by the realization that he was still alive. He could still feel he could still care. The Nazis had taken so much, but God had given him his humanity and no one could take that away. She turned to him, surprised at the gesture. But she, too, felt the shock waves that ran through her with a startling emotional bond. Then, through her tears, she gazed up into his eyes. There she saw great empathy and knew the true essence of Alex. Neither of them spoke.

For a long while, the noise all around them muffled in their ears and they could no longer hear the outside world. In this strange and magical moment, something significant had occurred.

Chapter 15

The following morning at breakfast, Anna moved from Manny's side to sit between Manny and Alex. For the first time since he'd boarded the ship, Alex had a smile on his face and his skin seemed to have lost its chalky pallor. In fact, he appeared almost radiant. But his eyes still reflected the depth of a dark world few had ever known. Still, because of Anna, Alex had joined the living. And he'd begun to allow himself a small sliver of joy.

After they finished eating, the group went up to the deck to enjoy the morning. There was a great deal of excitement on board because they were coming close to Havana. The ship had been at sea for ten days. It would only be four more days before they would enter Cuban waters. Then their new lives would begin in earnest. As the group of friends looked out over the ocean where it met with the blue cloudy sky, they were each lost in their own thoughts. Soon this friendship they had built together and come to lean on like surrogate family during the voyage would be done, and they would go their separate ways. There could be no telling if they would ever see each other again.

Manny watched as Alex and Anna seemed to speak to each other without words. The tenderness they felt for one another reflected in their eyes. His own feelings bubbled up in a quiet rage of jealousy. He'd wanted Anna. They had been together first. Then Alex came along with his neediness and something had stirred within her. Manny could not bear to watch them together. Instead, he suggested that they all go for a swim.

"I am going to have to decline. I'd like to spend a few hours in the library." Alex got up and stretched.

"Would it be all right if I went with you?" Anna asked.

Manny was livid.

"Of course, if you'd like," Alex said.

"Well, only if you would like me to…"

"Yes…I would," he replied.

"That's fine, then…it's settled. "Manny tried to smile. "Elke, would you take a swim with me?" Manny asked, as he looked away in an effort to hide his resentment. After all he'd done for Alex; Alex had rewarded him by stealing his girl.

"Sure…let me get my suit." Elke smiled.

Chapter 16

When Elke walked over to the pool, everyone turned around to look at the tall magnificent blonde. She shook her long hair out of a ponytail and smiled at Manny, who returned the smile in kind.

Viktor, who had been swimming, looked up as Elke walked out on to the deck. His eyes betrayed his longing for her. She was everything he'd searched for his entire life, and she would not even look at him. Most women fell at his feet, but she refused his advances. Why? What could he do to change her mind? He watched the sunlight catch her hair and his heart ached with yearning. He must find a way.

Manny saw the undeniable beauty in Elke and his sexual desires were fueled by his anger toward Alex. With all of the previous experience, Elke had with men she knew instantly by the look in his eyes what Manny wanted. She considered his desires and her own. After all, there was no guarantee of the future. This entire trip could have all been another trick of the Third Reich. She might leave the ship and be shot, or sent back to Germany to a camp. Or even worse, be used as a sexual toy, forced to endure the cruel whims of her Nazi persecutors. She'd been through that before, and she'd suffered. There was no telling what the next few weeks held. Elke considered all the possibilities. Then she measured the joys of a tender sexual encounter with Manny. After all, this might be the last one she would ever have, the final time a man would hold her gently in his arms, stroke her body and whisper kind words in her ear. She wanted that; she needed that memory to survive whatever was about to happen. And

just suppose that by some miracle things went as planned…
What if they landed in Cuba and all was well? What if Manny
fell in love with her and she married him? Oh, what a dream,
to live a life of privilege, to be respected, to be a part of
society, to be the wife of a prominent man, instead of the
mistress of many.

After a quick dip in the pool, the two dried off in the sun.
Elke turned to Manny, "Would you like to come to my
room?" Her eyes and wet skin glistened in the morning light.
Of course, she already knew his answer before he spoke.

Momentarily, the pain of losing Anna was gone and
Manny felt only the pure desire of long-repressed sexual
need. "Yes," he said. "I would like that very much." Manny
smiled at Elke.

She stood up and wrapped her towel around her waist.
Then Manny followed her to her room, while Viktor sat
watching.

Chapter 17

Anna and Alex sat in the library. He'd taken the manuscript he'd written along with him and presented it to Anna. She read his memoirs. She was clearly disturbed, but she remained silent as she continued reading, asking no questions, and wanting no answers. Three hours passed, then four. The document was long, over two hundred pages. She was not nearly finished when, finally, he turned to her.

"So?" he asked, barely above a whisper. "What do you think?"

"My God, is all of this true?" She indicated the manuscript that Alex had written. "Is this really what is going on in the camps? I had no idea. I don't think most people know."

"Yes, this and more. They are murdering people by the thousands. I fear it is going to escalate from here."

Tears formed in her eyes. Alex did not try to stop her crying. Instead, he allowed a tear of his own to fall.

"How can people treat other people this way? How do they find it in their hearts? Aren't they human beings, just like us? Don't they go home and play with their children, hug their wives, share an evening meal with their families? How can they do this, and then go on as if things were normal? I don't understand it at all. Do you?"

"I never did understand. I couldn't hurt anything. But I saw the evil firsthand. I saw such unbelievable cruelty that I will never forget the terrible things that happened in that place."

She lay her head on his shoulder.

"Thank God you survived," she said. "And thank God you are on your way to a new life, far from Germany and Dachau."

"Yes, I am grateful to God. But I am guilty too. Why was I chosen to survive, and my little sister, who never said a bad word about anyone or anything, was murdered?"

"I have no answers," she said. "Maybe it is selfish of me, but I am glad you are here and alive."

He put his arms around her. It was not his intention to make her so sad. Why was it that such misery followed him? Why was it that everyone who loved him suffered?

Tears flowed from his eyes as he looked at Anna and remembered his family. She saw his tears, and she could not hold her own back any longer.

Together they wept for everyone they'd loved and lost, and for all of the souls still in Germany, especially those still in camps, frightened, and alone. Those who could not get out, who were still held as prisoners in the hell Hitler had created, waiting for the Nazis to inflict their cruelty upon them.

Chapter 18

Manny proved to be a caring and experienced lover. He worshiped the beauty that lay naked before him. His admiration of her beauty filled Elke with the warmth she longed for. But she knew the difference between passion and love. When they lay spent, she turned to him, wise beyond her youth and said, "It's no use. You're in love with Anna."

"You can tell?"

"Of course, anyone who can see would know what you are feeling. It is as plain as the sky."

"It is that obvious, huh? Do you think she knows?"

"No... I am sorry, but I think she's in love with Alex and cannot see beyond that."

"I know." He folded his arms across his chest in disgust.

"Don't be angry, Manny. She can't help how she feels. I am sure she did not intend to hurt you."

"I know that too. That's what makes it all so hard. And Alex..."

"Yes, and Alex... For him, this is an unexpected chance at living again. When I first saw him, I felt sure that Alex was just a breath away from suicide."

"That's true. I knew that too."

"Now, he's found love."

Manny nodded his head.

"Manny, you will love again and again. You are just that type of man. I wish I were the girl, but sadly, I am not. However, Alex... Well...this is a onetime thing for him. Either he will be with Anna or he will be alone. I don't believe he will ever find anyone else."

"Oh, Elke, this leaves me with so many questions...and no answers. I thought she might be my *bashert*...but if she was, wouldn't she love me as much as I love her?"

Elke shrugged, she couldn't answer his question. She didn't know, so she just looked into his eyes and smoothed the hair off his forehead. "I have faith in you, Manny. You'll know the right thing to do."

Chapter 19

When the MS *St. Louis* pulled into Havana Harbor, guards awaited the ship. The vessel was not permitted to dock, and the passengers were not to be allowed to disembark.

The warning bell rang, calling the passengers to come to the deck where the captain awaited them. He would be forced to tell them the news.

In his white uniform, the captain stood before them, his eyes bloodshot with worry and lack of sleep.

"Ladies and gentlemen…I am your captain. At the present time, Cuba is refusing our ship entry. We are anchored outside of the docks awaiting further instructions. As difficult as this is for me, I must inform you of the situation. It seems that your visas are invalid and at present, you are not able to enter Havana. However, negotiations have begun for your safe release here on the island. All we can do at this point is wait and hope that this is resolved favorably. I am truly sorry from the bottom of my heart to bring this information to you. But please note that I am the captain of this ship and the well-being of each and every one of you is my utmost concern. I will do all that I can to insure your safety. For now I leave you… I will summon you again when I have an update."

The stifling heat hung down, smothering the passengers. Now that the ship had stopped moving, the breeze no longer cooled the atmosphere. An odor of human sweat, mingling with fear, wafted through the stagnating air. Howls like those of wounded animals came from the crowd. Some fell to their knees as the ship tipped and teetered nauseatingly in the ocean's waves. Several of the people vomited over the side of the deck. The sound of splashing vomit hitting the water added to the hideous atmosphere of despair.

All four friends stood together, but no one spoke. Each had secretly entertained the possibility of something like this occurring at some point during the voyage, yet none had ever acknowledged their fear aloud, none but Alex. Now together they faced the realization that they might never leave the MS St. Louis to a safe haven.

Anna turned to Alex and took his hand in hers. She gazed up into his eyes. "Whatever happens to us…at least we had this short time together."

He squeezed her hand. If they were to be sent back to Germany, to the camps, he would prefer to die rather than to see her suffer. Alex had seen the concentration camp first-hand. He knew torture, and he'd witnessed suffering. Little Anna…tender, small Anna, like a sparrow… What would they do to her? He could not bear to think of it. In that moment, the coward within him wanted to leap from the deck into the water and drown. But he could not; he would never leave her there alone. Once he knew for sure that they were returning to Germany, he planned to suggest a double suicide to Anna. As much as he cherished life, he saw no other way to save her from suffering.

Manny's wrath grew as he watched Anna and Alex. What did she see in Alex that she could not find in him? Instead of losing his desire for her, the more he saw them together, the more he wanted her for his own. Even Elke had known his feelings; how was it that Anna and Alex did not? They'd betrayed him, especially Alex. Alex knew he cared for Anna. How could Alex, being his friend, have allowed himself to have feelings for her? Manny, always the optimist, refused to believe that the negotiations with Cuba might be unsuccessful. Instead, he pulled a blanket of denial over his head, assuring himself that it was simply a misunderstanding that would soon be resolved. When they worked all of this out, Manny, Elke, Anna, and Alex would be on their way. But he and Elke would be alone... Alex and Anna would be together.

Elke knew the Nazi mentality firsthand; she'd endured their strange habits since childhood. This turn of events came as no surprise. It would be just like them, she thought, to dangle a carrot of freedom and life in front of all these desperate people, only to thwart it at the very last second. Oh, yes, it is most painful when a dream is taken just as it is about to be realized. That was how the Nazis operated, with the utmost cruelty...pure evil. How often had an SS officer treated her with kindness, bringing her and her mother food? Then, out of nowhere, that same man could turn when he was aroused, and slap her face until her lips and nose bled, or worse. Nazis loved the element of surprise and cruelty, but mostly they worshiped power. And often the supremacy they held so dear became the only method that enabled them to derive sexual pleasure. She'd come to know that. Somehow, she did not believe she would be murdered or sent to a camp. No, not with her blonde hair, blue eyes, and Aryan good looks... She would be tortured in other ways. Her heart pounded with fear as she looked at her three friends. For them she already mourned; they would be tormented in one way, but at least they would be together. For herself, she knew she would be alone, and she lived in terror of what the future held.

Chapter 20

The person who had fallen from the deck of the *MS St. Louis* into the Atlantic Ocean was never recovered. The body could not be located. But it came to be known that only an hour prior to the accident another death had occurred on the ship. An elderly man, already in grave condition when he boarded, had passed away by natural causes. After his quiet burial, at sea the strange incident of the "man overboard" had taken place.

A nervous energy spread through the ship like an influx of lice. Everyone walked around the ship on edge. The elaborate dinner parties that had been taking place in the evenings stopped abruptly, and no one wore formal wear to the dining room anymore. Several relatives of the passengers on board who waited on shore in Cuba charted small vessels and came out to the ship to see their families and to promise to do all they could to ensure entrance to Havana. The captain tried to foster an atmosphere of well-being by demanding that the band continue playing, but now no one got up to dance. People waited in the nail-biting stillness for answers. They prayed; they bargained with God. They hoped against hope for an amicable outcome as the negotiations with Cuba continued. For the passengers on the *MS St. Louis* knew that the only alternative was death.

Chapter 21

An atmosphere of unspoken contempt grew quickly in the stateroom that Manny and Alex shared. Alex attributed his roommate's foul mood to the insecure nature of the future of the voyage. Alex was sure that Manny now realized they might all be transported back to Germany, and he was convinced that the reality had hit Manny in the stomach like a punch from a prizefighter. Very little conversation was exchanged between the two. And often Manny took meals alone. The change in his friend concerned Alex, but since he had no answers, he felt that all he could do was allow Manny his freedom to be alone to think things through.

Manny was so caught up in his anger at what he perceived as his friend's betrayal with Anna that he hardly considered the tragic state of the *MS St. Louis*. Instead, he walked the deck, consumed with anger, frustration, and longing for the woman he'd fallen in love with.

Chapter 22

On the fifth day of waiting outside the docks of Havana, the captain came to the passengers again.

"As your captain, I have come to give you an update on our situation. From what I understand, the Cuban government is requesting an additional five hundred dollars per passenger in order to allow entrance. Presently the American Jewish Joint Distribution Committee is in negotiations with the Cuban President. However, some of you already have valid passports. Those of you with valid passports will be permitted to leave the ship. The others whose passports have been declared invalid will be forced to wait for the results of the negotiations. If you are one of those who will be going ashore, you will be notified. Otherwise, we wait together for answers. I remain your captain. And please be assured, that, as always I will do everything in my power to see you to a safe harbor. Thank you."

After the captain left, a blood-curdling scream came from the throat of a woman standing at the deck. The passenger beside her had slit his wrist. Blood poured like someone had put a hole in a garden hose. It spilled across the deck in a dark red river, and as the victim moved his body, it splattered on to the clothing of surrounding passengers. Now more screaming ensued. The man who'd cut himself jumped from the deck into the water. When a crewmember saw the incident, he set off the alarm, and a rescue team was sent out immediately. The man was pulled safely onto a rowboat as the rest of the passengers watched in horror, sweating profusely in the hot Cuban sun. Then the bleeding man was taken ashore. No one saw him again.

Alex put his arm around Anna, who shivered in spite of the blistering heat. She turned her face away from the scene, burying her head in his chest. "Come on, let's go into the library… It's quiet there," Alex said, smoothing Anna's hair gently.

She nodded and continued to lay her head against his chest as they walked slowly to the library. Anna sobbed so quietly that only Alex heard her. The pain in his heart grew as each whimper sliced into him as if it were his own pain.

"Anna, Anna… Shhh… It's all right." Alex whispered the words softly…gently…lying to her…hoping to comfort her… He knew that things didn't look good. Five hundred dollars per passenger was a steep price… There were almost a thousand passengers… No one could pay such an amount, even if they wanted to. He was sure that the American Jewish Joint Distribution Committee could never collect enough donations to rescue every living soul on board.

Alex and Anna found a private cubicle in the study corner of the library. There, with their hands gripped together, Anna laid her head against Alex. Neither of them spoke.

Then through her tears, Anna tried to smile "Well, if we do go back to Germany, at least…perhaps I'll see my parents again."

Alex nodded. "Yes, perhaps." There was no telling where the passengers would be sent. Alex knew that the chance of Anna seeing her parents were slim, but he couldn't tell her that…couldn't bear to see her suffer more than she already did.

"Alex," she whispered, her voice hardly audible, "I'm a virgin."

He didn't answer…didn't know what to say.

"I don't want to die a virgin."

Again, he remained silent.

"Will you come to my room? Will you make love to me, Alex?"

He could no longer hold back, and a single tear ran down his face as he gazed into her lovely eyes. If the Nazis had never come into power this beautiful young girl would be standing beside him under a *chuppah* (marriage canopy). It should not be like this, it shouldn't, but it is, he thought.

"Yes, let's go to your room," he replied.

Before they stood, Alex took the hand that he held in his and brought it gently to his lips. "My beautiful, precious Anna…" he whispered.

They walked to her room in silence, hand-in-hand. Anna was nervous; she had never thought that she would make love to a man who was not her husband. She had waited for marriage, done what her parents told her was right. But in the last few hours, when it seemed that she would never leave the ship safely, that she would most likely be sent to a concentration camp, everything had changed. Her dreams of the future were shattered. She would never stand beneath a *chuppah*, never say I do, never have a husband or children of her own. These precious hours that she was about to share with Alex would be all she would ever have to cherish in life.

They arrived at her room. She had a private room, so there was no roommate to disturb them.

For the first time their lips touched timidly as both of their hearts beat in unison. Alex's hand caressed the maple-colored hair that fell freely about her innocent face. He cherished every small piece of her as if he were Adam, and had been alone on the earth until God bestowed Eve, the greatest of all gifts, upon him. And he relished that gift… His soul sang out in gratitude for the wonder that was Anna. The sharing of their young love, flesh upon warm flesh, and the life giving force of passion took over as the lovers lay in each other's arms. Hours passed as they tenderly stroked each other's skin, offering comfort and tenderness, a safe haven in an uncertain world gone mad. But mostly, they knew that they were creating memories… Memories, they both felt sure, would soon enough be all they had left.

Chapter 23

When Alex returned to his stateroom, Manny awaited him. Somehow, although he could not be sure, instinct told Manny that Alex had been in bed with Anna.

"You stole my girl." Manny's face was crimson with anger.

Alex stood looking at Manny, stunned, his arms hanging helplessly at his sides.

"You knew how I felt about Anna… You knew."

"I knew you liked her, but I hadn't realized your feelings had become serious."

"Well, you knew I wanted to be with her."

"Yes, but I thought it was just a casual thing with you, Manny… For me, this is not a passing fancy. I love Anna."

Manny could not answer. He could not speak.

"She loves me, too. Soon, we might all be dead. For this moment…for this one moment, Manny, we wanted to be happy… I'm sorry… I'm sorry… The last thing I would ever want to do is to hurt you."

Alex reached up, as if petitioning the heavens for understanding. And Manny walked out of the room, slamming the door behind him.

Chapter 24

Manny had enough money to leave the ship. He had enough to leave and then an additional five hundred dollars to start his life. He walked the deck all night rather than going back to the room where Alex waited. In the morning, he would go to the captain and try to buy his freedom. Then he would depart this ship and leave all of this pain behind. Who was this girl anyway? He'd had so many girls before. What was it about her that made him want her so much? Maybe it was because she didn't want him, he thought…a stupid reason…

Manny felt sure his friends would perish when the ship returned to Germany. All night he reflected on their future. Poor Elke, she would probably end up a slave to some Nazi officer. And Alex, he would surely find himself back in a concentration camp. His body was strong; he might survive the ordeal, but Anna…never. Anna was too tiny…too petite. Her return to Germany would mean certain death for her. Perhaps if he offered to take her with him, she would go. He had just enough money for two visas. That would leave him with nothing to begin his life, but he would manage. Somehow, he'd find work until he could contact his family. They would send him the funds to come to New York. The plan sounded good… he would go to the captain…but first he would talk to Anna.

The following morning at breakfast, the four sat together, as always. Manny watched as the lovers held hands and looked at each other with such affection that it hurt his heart. Manny wanted to make his offer known to Anna. After breakfast, he would ask if he could speak to her.

Once they finished eating, the group walked upstairs to the deck. Havana harbor stood like an unattainable prize hanging just over their heads, only a few miles in the distance.

"Anna... I would like to speak with you alone." Manny would not meet Alex's eyes.

Anna squeezed Alex's hand, and Alex nodded at her that it was all right with him.

"Come this way, please." Manny escorted Anna to the other side of the deck. Once they were, alone he turned to look into her eyes. "Anna... I care for you very much." He cleared his throat. "I have enough money for two visas into Cuba. Will you come with me?"

"Manny, I hardly expected this."

"I understand. I realize you were unaware of my feelings for you."

"I had no idea."

"Well...let me say that I will try as best as I can to give you a good life."

She turned away from him and looked out over the water. A heavy silence hung over them for several minutes before she answered.

"Manny... I'm sorry. I'm so sorry. I can't go with you. I am in love with Alex. I must stay with him and whatever his fate is to be...well...it will be my fate also."

"You will be sent back to Germany...back to the camps...you will be killed... Most assuredly...you will die." He grasped her shoulders trying to make her understand that the decision she made was a fatal one.

"I know. I know, Manny...but this is my choice. I love Alex. I can't leave him alone to face what is to come. I must be there beside him. You are a dear friend to offer, and I will always be grateful for your generosity, but I must say no. Again, I'm sorry."

There was nothing left to say. Manny nodded. Then he turned and walked away, toward the captain's quarters.

Chapter 25

"Captain, sir, I know you are busy but I've come to ask if there has been any progress with the negotiations." Manny stood looking at the captain, who appeared disheveled, as if he carried a personal burden.

The captain sat at his desk, running his hand over his thinning white hair. "Sit down, please."

Manny sat across from him and waited.

"It doesn't look good. The Cuban government wants too much money."

Manny nodded. He was sorry to hear it but it was the answer he'd been expecting.

"I have money… I want to purchase two visas." Manny pulled a wad of Reichsmarks that had been secured with a band from his pocket.

The captain counted it out. It came to the equivalent of a thousand American dollars. Then he put the money into an envelope sealed it and asked, "What are the names that you would like printed on the visas?"

"Anna Goldman and Alex Mittelman," Manny answered.

Chapter 26

"I cannot accept this from you." Alex shook his head as Manny handed him the visas.

"Don't do it for me...do it for Anna. If you don't go with her, she won't leave the ship. We both love her. Save her life. Alex. You have the opportunity. You are the only one who can do it... You must."

Alex looked at the official papers. He touched them and his stomach flopped with nausea. If he left the ship with Anna, they would both have a chance at life, but Elke and Manny... What would become of them?

"You must," Manny repeated.

Trembling, Alex took the visas. "I owe you my life."

Manny looked at him and nodded. "Then go... Go and get Anna, and get out of here... Get off the ship... Do something wonderful with your life... Live a life with a purpose... And don't forget, Alex...tell the story. It is what you were meant to do. Tell what happened. Never let it be forgotten, never. I know you will you do this for me, for all of us. Go now... Hurry and leave the ship."

Alex walked over to Manny and embraced him. Manny returned the embrace.

Then Alex went to find Anna.

Chapter 27

Alex and Anna left the ship and entered Havana through a fortress on the bay called *El Morro* Castle, an ancient structure of white stone that had once served as a political prison. Anna looked out one last time at the ship. "Alex, the sky is turquoise. Look at how it meets the water. And the water is so clean and blue. It's incredible."

"I've never seen the sky that color or the ocean so clear."

"No, neither have I," he replied.

She squeezed his arm. "Alex, I'm so glad we are here, and we are together. I have so many emotions right now. I'm a little scared, a little excited, and…"

"And in love?"

"Yes," she smiled, "in love."

"And a little guilty?" he asked, his voice barely a whisper.

"Yes, that too."

They walked through the old city, with its narrow streets and sidewalks, its open-air cafés and beauty salons, and the lure of Latin music coming from the markets and night clubs filling the warm tropical air.

"How different this is from Germany," Anna said.

"That's for certain."

"I wish my parents were here with us."

"I know, Anna."

"But it is beautiful, isn't it?"

"It is, and so are you." Alex put his free arm around Anna's shoulder.

They passed grassy parks sprinkled with vibrant colored flowers and palm trees swaying in the breeze. They found themselves surrounded by a bustle of humanity, tourists from every country speaking in their native tongues, bargaining with the Cuban merchants. It was easy to see why Cuba was known as the Pearl of the Caribbean.

"We should find a cheap hotel where we can stay until I can contact my uncle about securing visas for us into the U.S.," Anna said, as she looked into the open doors of a nightclub to see women dancing in vivid costumes.

"Why should he take me in? Anna, he is only counting on one person. I don't want to ruin your chances. I will stay here. You go to New York." Alex carried Anna's suitcase, the only luggage they had between them.

"Are you crazy? I would never leave you. Maybe I was wrong in assuming…"

"Assuming?" He looked at her puzzled.

"Never mind," she said, folding her arms across her chest as she looked down the street away from him to where a woman sat in a manicurist's salon covered only by a small orange-and-yellow striped awing, in case of rain. The women held her hands out in front of her, smiling and admiring her nails, which were the color of the inside of a ripe cantaloupe.

Oh… It suddenly dawned on him, and he knew what she was talking about. "Anna, of course I want to marry you, more than anything in this world. But I have nothing to offer you. What kind of a life can I give you?"

"I don't expect you to have anything to give me, Alex, just your love…" she said.

"You have my heart. You know that," Alex said, as they passed a group of men playing dominos at benches in a small park, their hands wrapped around cups of what Alex and Anna would later learn was strong Cuban coffee.

"And together we will build a life in America. You know they say that the streets are paved with gold," she laughed.

"Yes, I've heard." He smiled, and she glanced over at him to see that his eyes were once again clouded, and she knew his depression was never far from the surface.

"I'm feeling terribly guilty about Manny. I am glad to be here, to have the opportunity to live again, to be far away from Hitler…from Germany… But, Manny…" Alex said, shaking his head.

"Oh, Alex, Manny is a survivor. He will be fine. Don't worry. His family will send him more money. He'll get out and probably contact us when he gets to the United States."

"Do you really think so?"

"Of course. You know how Manny is. He's the type of person who will always land on his feet," she said. "Don't get me wrong; it was good of him to give us this money. He saved our lives; we are forever indebted to him. But, he will be all right. I know how Manny is. He has important friends and his family has connections. Don't be troubled about him."

"I want to believe you."

"Then believe me," she said, squeezing his arm.

They found a cheap room in an apartment building where the service people from the nightclubs lived. It was a small kitchenette, already furnished with a double bed and a wooden table and two chairs. When the landlady showed them the room, Anna saw a large black insect that looked like a giant cockroach crawl quickly across the wall. She screamed. The landlady laughed and explained that they weren't roaches that came from dirt; they were just tropical bugs, and they were everywhere. Anna shook, and scratched her head. To her it felt as if the bugs had built a nest in her hair, and she wanted to cry.

"I'm sorry," Alex said. "It hurts me that I cannot do more for you, and that I can't pay for a better place for us to stay."

"I know. It will be all right." She smiled at him, trying not shiver when she thought about the insects.

"Do you know where I can go to send a wire?" Anna asked the landlady.

"Down the street past the pharmacy," the woman answered in broken German, trying her best to communicate with the foreign guests.

"We should buy some books and try to learn Spanish," Anna said to Alex. "I am not sure how long we will be here, and it would help if we spoke the language."

"I think we are better off trying to learn as much English as possible, if we are going to America. It will be too difficult trying to master two languages at once. While we are here in Cuba, we'll pick up as much Spanish as we need to survive. I speak some English. Do you?"

"A little, yes," she said, and slipped her pocketbook under her arm. "I am going to send a wire to my uncle Max. I'll be right back."

"No, I'll go with you. We don't know anything about this country. I don't want to risk having something happen to you," Alex said.

"What could possibly happen to me, Alex? I'm not a child."

Chapter 28

Anna gave Alex a look that told him that he'd better not follow her. Then she left the apartment and headed toward the little store that sent telegrams. The language was unfamiliar, and as she walked down the street, she saw men leaning against buildings in alleyways. They beckoned to her.

"Hey, lady," one said in broken English. "You American? What you looking for? I have whatever you want!"

Anna walked faster...

"Lady, come here..." one of the men called after her.

Why was she so headstrong? Her feet could not carry her fast enough. He was gaining on her. She felt her heart beating in her ears to the sounds of the Latin music on the street. She broke into a run.

"Lady, slow down!" he cried, his greasy hair slicked onto his forehead.

He was close enough now that she could smell his body odor. She could not out run him; he was faster.

"God please help me to get away."

The man caught up with her; he grabbed her arm with his grimy hand.

"Why you run? You scared of me?" the man purred as he stroked her arm with his free hand.

She felt the tears forming in her eyes.

Chapter 29

Sometimes Anna really got on his nerves. She had her own mind and could be so stubborn, Alex thought, as he walked around the apartment thinking that he should have gone with her. If I go after her, she will be angry... He sat down in the chair by the window to wait until Anna returned.

Chapter 30

"You such a pretty lady." The man had Anna's arm. He reached down and pinched her buttocks.

"Let me go!" she yelled with a confidence she did not feel.

"Where you want to go? Huh? You tell me, yeah?" The man began trying to pull her into the lobby of a nightclub. Anna fought him as hard as she could; then she started screaming. But nobody paid her any attention.

"Why you so difficult? I am only wanting to take you inside, have maybe a drink, and visit with some of my friends. You would have a good time."

"Let go of me. I don't want to go anywhere with you." Anna began screaming again "Help me! Someone help me!"

"They think you my wife, or maybe I'm your pimp and we having a fight, don't no one want to get involved. Stop carrying on so much. Let's have us a little fun."

She was hysterical, crying and screaming as he tugged at her arm. He was strong and he almost had her inside the building.

Chapter 31

Alex could not sit still. They had no food in the apartment. He decided he would go out and buy a few things. That would also give him the opportunity to check on Anna without her knowing. He walked up the street toward the store where Anna had gone to send the wire and heard her screams. Alex ran toward the sound to find Anna being molested by a stranger. Alex came from behind, and although Alex was not a fighter, he whipped the man around and punched him as hard as he could in the face. The man was stunned. He fell backwards.

"Get away from my wife," Alex said.

"Hey, I meant no harm. Don't be so touchy," the man said, and he walked away.

Anna was shaking. "I'm glad you came."

Alex took Anna into his arms and kissed her all over her face, hugging her tightly. "Anna, my Anna…"

She sighed.

"Are you all right? I was afraid you'd be angry…that I came…" Alex was out of breath. He hated violence.

"Thank God you came," she said, and laid her head on his shoulder. What do you think he would have done to me? Do you think he'd have drugged me and forced me into prostitution?"

"I don't know, Anna. I don't know what he wanted. We are in a different culture, and we are not at home. Everything is different. You and I don't know how things work here, so we have to be careful, you understand?"

She nodded.

"Now, let's go send that wire…" he said, and he kissed the top of her head.

Chapter 32

The following day Alex went out to look for work. He spoke very limited Spanish, so he walked the streets in search of anyone who would hire a foreigner. The nightclubs and restaurants required that he speak and write in Spanish, enabling him to take the customers' orders. He offered his services as a dishwasher, but all of the jobs were taken. Distraught, he walked the streets until he saw two men sitting on stools with a long table between them. There was a huge barrel of tobacco and a pile of thin brown papers. Alex watched, fascinated, as the men rolled cigars and cut them with a silver guillotine-type instrument. I could learn this, he thought.

"Hello, my name is Alex Mittelman. I am looking for work." His Spanish was weak but understandable.

"You know how to roll cigars?"

"No, I am sorry. But I am a fast learner."

"I don't need no help that I have to teach."

"Thank you," Alex said, and he turned to go. Then he thought of Anna. He would not live off her small savings. He wanted to provide for her, not the other way around. Alex turned around and looked at the old Cuban, with his copper skin lined with age and wisdom, his dark, knowing eyes studying Alex.

"Please," Alex said. "I am begging you… Please, just give me a chance. I am new to this country. I have a wife and no way to support her. I will work hard…"

"Hmmm," the old man said. He'd known poverty, and he'd known hunger too. He saw the look of pain and suffering in Alex's eyes. He cleared his throat, got up, and extended his hand to shake Alex's hand. "My name is Raul Perez. This is my shop. All right, I will teach you to roll cigars. I make the finest cigars in the world." Raul Perez picked up a fat sausage-like cigar. "Don't make me sorry for agreeing to hire you."

"You won't be sorry. I will learn this, and I will do it well. I appreciate everything. You cannot know just how much," Alex said.

Raul nodded his head. He had some idea of just how desperate Alex was.

Alex began working the following day. He hated leaving Anna alone in a strange city, and begged her not to leave the apartment without him. He was determined to keep this job, even though the pay was low, and he found that his shoulders ached after a few hours of rolling. Raul noticed how hard Alex was working and wondered if he would return the following day. He did. It was difficult for Alex to learn to roll these cigars, but he couldn't afford to lose this job. So he worked through his lunch, sweating in the tropical heat. The cigar business was harder than he would ever have believed. Raul showed him again and again how to roll properly, but when Alex began to work the paper in his hand, his fingers seemed to be clumsy and unable to achieve the desired results. Who would have ever thought that something that looked this simple was really an art? Raul watched him with a frown, and Alex was afraid his boss regretted hiring him, and he feared his days of employment might be numbered.

Chapter 33

The first time that Alex began screaming in the middle of the night, Anna awoke terrified. She opened her eyes to see him sitting up in bed, only half-awake, crying out, his hands whipping about wildly, his words unintelligible.

She quickly sat up and put her arms around him, shaking him, trying to wake him from the nightmare that had his body rocking frantically. In the light of the moon that filtered through the window, she could see that his face contorted and was covered with tears.

"Alex... shhhh… It's all right. You were dreaming. You are here with me…safe." Anna repeated this until Alex slowly became conscious of his surroundings.

As soon as he realized where he was, Alex hugged Anna tightly, gripping on to her, his breathing ragged.

"Shhh…Alex."

She said again, feeling his body, cold against her own, trembling and bathed in sweat.

"Come, let me turn the light on and make you a cup of tea."

"No...no… Don't move. Stay here. Let me hold you."

So he lay down, pulling her down beside him.

And he held her through the night. But she could not close her eyes. Once he relaxed and began to doze off, she breathed a sigh of relief. However, still even as he slept, she could hear him sometimes gently sobbing.

Anna looked at her handsome, damaged husband, his newly sprouting dark wavy hair still wet with sweat, and wanted to join him and cry too. But she knew she must not. He needed her, and she must be his strength.

There would be many, many, nights like this, when Alex could not shake the memories, even to sleep.

Chapter 34

Anna found the days long and lonely. She cleaned the apartment from top to bottom, scrubbed the wood floors until they turned white. In the cabinets, she found a few unmatched dishes, a couple of rusty pots, and three forks, knives and spoons that she washed in boiling water. Anna became friendly with the landlady, Rosita, an older woman who always wore a brightly colored scarf on her head and had a warm, toothless smile. Rosita had five grown children and seven grandchildren living in the building. They came and went and Anna learned their names. Rosita taught Anna to prepare rice covered with black beans, and fried plantains, which were sweet island bananas.

Each day when Alex returned from work, the two went to check and see if any word had come from Uncle Max. It was two weeks before they received a telegram stating that Max would help them to apply for their visas. When Anna had sent the telegram, she'd told her uncle that she and Alex were married. He responded with surprise, and a warm welcome to the newlyweds.

The following Monday, with permission from his boss, Alex left work. He and Anna went to the city hall, a beautiful old Spanish building with tall white columns, where they were married in a civil ceremony. Before they said their vows, Alex whispered in Anna's ear, "Someday we will do this again, under a canopy. You'll wear a real gown and I will buy you the most beautiful gold band. I am sure that when you were a little girl this was not the wedding that you dreamed of. I am sorry for that. But I love you, and someday, I swear I will find a way to make this right."

She squeezed his hand. "This is exactly the wedding I dreamed of, because I am madly in love with my future husband, and he loves me too. What else is important?"

Alex swallowed hard to keep the tears from coming. If someone had told him when he was dying in Dachau, that such a blessing would befall him, he would never have believed them. Then he remembered something his mother had once told him when he was just a little boy. She'd said that when God worked a miracle, everything fell into place. A man could plan for something for years and it would not go the way he hoped. But when God decided that something should be so, it would be so. He wished that his mother could be there to see his new wife, and that his sister could have also called Anna sister. His father would have been proud that Alex had taken a wife. He missed them; he would never stop missing them. But he was alive, and life must go on. Again, Alex glanced at Anna and whispered his thanks to God. Then he kissed her hand and looked into her eyes. "Anna, my Anna, you are my wife."

She nodded, her eyes glistening.

Their evenings were lovely; the two shared their meager meals, with looks of passion that only those young and in love can share. They played cards, and Alex learned to play dominos from Raul. He taught the game to Anna, and they spent many hours stacking the black wooden squares.

But Anna was still bored during the days when Alex was gone. She decided not to ask him, because he was such a worrier; instead she asked the landlady if she would accompany her to see if she could find work. She agreed. As Anna expected, Rosita explained that she knew which streets were safe to walk, and where it was not safe. She would take Anna down the main thoroughfare, where the businesses that might be hiring would be located. They walked up and down the avenues, which were a surprisingly pleasing temperature, in spite of the heat. The landlady explained that the streets and sidewalks were built very narrow so that the buildings could block the glaring sun from melting everyone in the city. As she walked past the *Plaza Vieja*, Anna remembered the beauty salon where she'd seen the woman sitting at the manicurist's table. From what she remembered, there were no men inside this shop, making it a very safe place to apply for work. Most of the salon was outside, except for the shampoo bowls, which were half inside the building. An awning covered the hairstylists' chairs and the manicure tables in case of rain.

"When I first came to Cuba I saw a beauty shop. I think I would like to apply there. It is right down the street."

"Yes, I know the one. It is a very safe walk from the apartment to this area. Come, I'll accompany you. We'll see if you can get hired."

"May I help you?" A young pretty girl with golden skin and auburn hair said as Anna walked up to the desk.

"Yes, I am looking for a job."

"Can you shampoo?" the girl asked.

"Yes, I think so."

"Mama!" the girl yelled, and an older woman with her hair dark hair piled high on her head and black eyeliner came walking out of the back room. She wore a tight skirt and white ruffled blouse. "Mama, this lady needs a job, she says she can shampoo."

The woman looked Anna up and down then tilted her head. "Why not? You try; we see how you do." She smiled, and Anna returned the smile.

Alex was not pleased that Anna had gone out without him and found a job. Consequently, they had their first fight. But when she began to cry, his heart broke and he apologized.

Alex was a true romantic. Sometimes when he was unable to sleep, he wrote beautiful poetry and left it on the table for Anna, declaring his undying love for her. Even though money was tight, he often brought her a single flower or a box of candy. He made love to her as though she were the most cherished goddess of all time, and he just a mortal put on earth to worship her. Careful, gentle, almost afraid she would break.

Anna learned that her boss's name was Claudia, and her daughter was Lucia. They owned the popular beauty shop where most of the performers at the nightclubs got their intricate hairstyles done. A large clientele of tourists also frequented the salon, which not only offered all kinds of hair and nail services, but also cosmetic applications for the showgirls. The shop was a hotbed of female gossip, from who was dating whom, to the latest on the American movie stars. Anna enjoyed the hustle and bustle of the high-fashioned women who came and went daily. She listened to their stories and sympathized with their problems. It was here at the shop that she learned just how effective Goebbels anti-Semitic propaganda was on the Cuban people. While the MS *St. Louis* had sat in the harbor waiting, the people were demonstrating in the streets against allowing the Jewish passengers entrance. The visas into Cuba were nullified by a decree, called the 937. This was the first Anna learned of such a decree. She was shampooing the wife a government official when she overheard the story as the woman explained it to another customer. Well, no matter, Anna knew that all of the names and numbers of the decree were just that, names and numbers. The truth was that Hitler had organized a hate campaign so powerful that it destroyed the poor Jewish passengers, even when they arrived at a country so foreign and far away from Germany that it should have been impossible. Each week Alex bought a German newspaper. Finally, he discovered that the passengers had been allowed to enter the Netherlands, England, Belgium, and France. They had been divided between these countries. He told Anna, and they both sighed with relief. Anna was right; soon Manny would contact them and perhaps Elke too. Then they would have a wonderful reunion.

Uncle Max flew to Cuba in the beginning of August. He helped Anna, his brother's only daughter, and her husband to fill out the forms to apply for their visas to America. But it was common knowledge in the United States that the Americans had become leery of foreigners, especially Jews. Anti–Semitism was rearing its ugly head into the city of New York. Max had seen political demonstrations and parks with signs that read: "Jews Keep Out" and "NO JEWS ALLOWED." Would Hitler come to America? Max wondered. The country was desperately trying to pull itself out of the depths of a deep depression. For the most part, Roosevelt was beloved amongst the American people. He was working hard, there was no doubt, but creating jobs was a difficult proposition, and the streets were still filled with unemployed people, hungry and begging for spare change. The lines at the soup kitchens could be seen twice a day: men, women, and children, desperate for a meal. Contrary to the European concept, America was not prospering. This was the state Germany was in when Hitler acquired his popularity; would the same thing happen in America? Max could not help but worry, but he decided not to share his concerns with the young, hopeful couple whom he had just met. When he looked at Anna, he saw his brother. Although she was a very feminine girl, he could catch small glimpses of her father in the way she raised an eyebrow, or how she sometimes winked just before she giggled. Yes, Max had a little money put away and no children of his own left alive. He and his wife Edith had endured a stillborn, and then once they had a little boy, he had died in an epidemic of tuberculosis. So, for Max, this young couple was all the family he had left. There would be payoffs to get them to America, under-the-table money to officials, and even then, no guarantees, but he would do what he could. For now, Alex and Anna were on the waiting list for visas and there were no guarantees that they would ever receive them.

Max Goldman left at the end of the week. He had to go home, had to get back to the butcher shop where he worked. Both Alex and Anna hugged him tightly; they would miss him. He vowed to himself that the next time he came he would bring a care package of food and clothing. It was the least he could do until they were in New York.

Chapter 35

If Alex lost this job, they would be on the street in no time at all. He had to learn this business. It was imperative. He began taking the tobacco home with him, and spent many a night rolling the cigars, until he was able to do it correctly. One morning he brought a pile of rolled cigars into the shop with him. Raul was sitting on his bench. He looked up at Alex and frowned. Alex knew Raul wanted to let him go. With hope that he'd done well, Alex laid the box of cigars in front of his boss.

Carefully Raul picked each one up and turned it over in his fingers.

"Not bad, not bad at all," Raul said a bright smile coming over his face.

Alex heard the relief in his voice. He knew Raul was glad not to have to fire him.

"I think you are going to make it as a cigar roller," Raul said, smiling so widely that his oversized yellow horse teeth jutted out of his mouth "Looks to me like you have a job here."

Alex said a silent prayer. He'd mastered the art of rolling Cuban cigars, and for now he and his wife would be all right.

Chapter 36

It was almost *Rosh Hashanah*, the Jewish New Year, followed by *Yom Kippur*, the highest holy day in the Jewish calendar. Anna searched for a synagogue where they could attend High Holiday services. She found a small Jewish temple off the main street, and went in to talk with the rabbi. Anna explained that she and Alex could not afford to buy tickets, but they longed for the camaraderie of other Jews, and to hear the *shofar* blown to welcome the New Year.

"Of course you are welcome in our temple," the rabbi said. "You and your husband will come to my house for *Yom Kippur* and break the fast there. My wife will be very pleased to meet you."

"Oh, Rabbi, you don't have to do that…"

"Ahh, my child, I want to. Besides, the book will be open, and it is a wonderful *mitzvah* that you give me the honor of performing. Both my wife and I would love to spend the High Holidays with such lovely young Jewish newlyweds."

"Are you from Europe?"

"Yes, I am from Germany," the rabbi said.

"I thought I recognized your accent," Anna smiled.

"You speak Yiddish?" the rabbi asked.

"A *bissel*," Anna smiled.

"Good, for you know that Yiddish is the language of God."

She smiled at him again. "Thank you, Rabbi, for all of your kindness."

In the Jewish religion, it is believed that God has a book where he determines the fate of all of his people. On *the first day of Rosh Hashanah*, which is the Jewish New Year, God opens the book. He looks at the behavior of every living thing over the previous year. It is at this time that God will decide who will live to see the New Year the following year and who will not. Over the week between *Rosh Hashanah* and *Yom Kippur*, the assessments are made. From sundown the night before until sundown on the night of *Yom Kippur*, Jews will fast for their sins. Once the sun sets, the book is closed, all decisions have been determined, and the Jewish people celebrate with food, music, and the joy of life.

When Alex arrived home, Anna was excited to tell him about the invitation from the rabbi, but when she looked at Alex, he seemed nervous, anxious. She waited. Something was wrong.

Chapter 37

Alex did not speak, he didn't kiss her the way he always did when he entered the house; instead he went to the sink and began to wash up. Anna watched as Alex continually splashed cold water on his face. He bent over the sink and took deep breaths, holding his temples.

Alex's behavior frightened Anna. It was true that Alex could be overly sensitive, even moody, but she had never seen him like this.

Finally, she could no longer bear his silence. The sun began to set on a golden September day, a warm breeze drifted off the ocean. Everything should have been perfect. She had been waiting for him to come home so that she could tell him about the services for the high holidays, and now... Did she do something to offend him?

"Alex?"

"Yes..." he answered, distracted.

She saw his hands trembling, white, pale, and colorless.

"Alex, look at me please," she said.

He turned around to face her. "What?"

"Alex, did something happen at work?" she asked. He may have lost his job. The crevice cut between his brows as deep as a river.

"No, for now I have a job. Thank God," he said.

"What's wrong? Have I done something? Did something happen?"

He realized that he'd upset her. How foolish of him, how inconsiderate. He'd come home in a foul mood, and he'd put it all upon her. Alex took a deep breath. He realized that often he was lost in his own emotions and forgot to consider the feelings of others. Before he'd married it had not mattered, he could go inside of himself and think, but now he must watch this behavior more carefully.

"I'm sorry, sweetheart. I didn't mean to upset you. Yes. Something happened. I'd rather not discuss it."

"How can you say that to me? You don't want to discuss it? Alex please if it is distressing you, I need to know."

"I will be all right. Just give me a few minutes."

Alex went outside on the patio. Anna did not follow him. She just stood there, watching. What was troubling him? What could it be?

Chapter 38

Alex didn't touch her that night as they lay in bed. This was the first night since they had been married that he had not made love to her. He lay beside her without speaking. His breathing pattern told her that he hadn't fallen asleep. Anna did not know what to ask him, what to say, so she curled up, held her pillow, awake, and filled with worry. At close to four that morning Anna drifted off to sleep, only to awaken three hours later to the sound of the alarm. Alex was not in bed beside her.

Her head ached from lack of sleep and she felt dizzy, but she must find her husband. So Anna ran outside and searched for Alex, but he was not to be found. She didn't want to go to work; she was too upset. She wanted to go and find Alex; he must be at his job, to yell at him, to shake him, to demand to know what was bothering him.

But she didn't. She went to work.

Chapter 39

Anna couldn't concentrate. She had no idea what had sent Alex into this strange silence and caused him to distance himself from her. The clients chattered at her, telling her about their lives, their husbands, the families, complaining, bragging, joking, but Anna could not hear them. Instead she just continued to nod with a frozen smile on her face.

It seemed as if the day would never end, but it did. Anna decided that she would stop and pick something up to make for dinner, something special that Alex would really like. Perhaps if she put together a romantic candlelight dinner he would open up to her. She went to the butcher and bought a roast. Then, she went to one of the street vendors and bought some potatoes. He would love this meal. Anna splurged and bought a bottle of wine and two white candles. She went home and unlocked the door. When she entered, she stood at the door stunned; the entire apartment had been ransacked. They had been robbed. Anna dropped the bags and ran through the rooms to see what the thieves took. The little bit of money that she and Alex had saved was gone, and so were the few pieces of jewelry that Anna had been given by her mother. She picked up the bag of groceries and put it down on the table. Then she sat down and wept.

After a few minutes, she shook her head. What good would it do to sit and cry? What was done was done; no use in dwelling on it. She got up, steeled herself, and began to clean up the mess the burglars had left. Then she put the roast in the oven and the potatoes too. She set the table, and lit the candles. Then she waited for Alex.

He didn't come directly home from work. Anna opened the wine and poured herself a glass, then another. She waited until well past dark before she put the food away and went to bed, wondering if Alex would ever return.

Chapter 40

As tired, as she was she still could not sleep. Every time she closed her eyes, she felt strong anxiety grip her entire being. Where had Alex gone, and why? She sat up in bed and watched the sunrise. Alex still had not returned.

In the morning, she dressed for work, her heart heavy and her head aching. She took her handbag, and then she went to the landlady's apartment. The locks would have to be changed. Someone had broken in. She told Rosita.

The landlady agreed to take care of the problem that day.

As Anna was walking down the boulevard toward her job, Alex passed her walking toward home.

"Where have you been?"

"Walking, worrying…"

"Alex…" She shook him. "Talk to me. Tell me what happened."

"I didn't want to tell you I wanted to protect you, but I suppose you should know. I saw the news in the German newspaper. Hitler has invaded Poland."

Her hand went to cover her mouth in shock and horror.

Alex took Anna in his arms and held her tight. They stood like that for a long time. Then Anna asked, "Are you hungry? I have food from last night in the ice box."

"No, I can't eat."

"Neither can I," she answered.

"Alex…"

"Yes."

She was going to tell him that they had been robbed, but he was far too upset. Anna knew how delicate Alex could be; best to keep bad news from him right now.

"Never mind," she said reaching up and touching his face. "I will see you tonight when I get home?"

"Yes. I'll be here. Anna…I'm sorry, I only wanted to protect you."

Thank God he'd come home safely, she whispered to herself as she smiled at him and squeezed his hand. "It will be all right, Alex. It will be all right."

Two days later, on the third of September, France and Great Britain, in honor of their pact with Poland, declared war on Germany. Alex was obsessed with the German newspapers. Every morning on his way to work, and on his way home in the evening, he checked the headlines. When he arrived at home, his shoulders slumped and he sat quietly staring out the window. Anna sat beside him and took his hand.

"Do you have family in Poland?" she asked, carefully.

"Friends, people I used to know. God, how my heart goes out to them." he said. "But that's not even the point. "First the Studenland, now Poland? We were hoping they would fade away, but from what I can see, the Nazis are becoming even more powerful. And that is dangerous for Jews everywhere, all over the world. Who knows? Maybe here, maybe even in America."

"I don't understand why he invaded Poland. I thought I remembered my father saying that Hitler gave Poland a promise that he would never invade them."

"Yes, well, a man's word is as good as his character. And Hitler's character is one that leaves a lot to be desired," Alex said.

"What do you think he will do next?"

"There's no telling. But I feel we would be the safest in the United States. And even in America, we are never completely safe. Still, I think it's the best place. I don't know how to get our visas, but we must get there as quickly as possible." His eyes were wide with fear. "You can't imagine what the Nazis can do, how cruel they can be…"

Anna had always known that whatever had happened to Alex in Dachau had made him unstable. Bad things had a more intense effect on him than they did on the average person. And once he got an idea in his head, there was no changing his mind. Right now, he was certain that they must find a way to go to America, and she knew that he was determined to do this.

Because she loved him, and longed to banish all of his demons, Anna would find a way. Whatever it took, she would get them to America.

`

Chapter 41

Even as a child, Anna's parents' friends had called her refined. She knew when to speak, and what to say. She also knew when not speak, and this won her many friends at her job at the salon.

One of the manicurists was a young woman striving to become a dancer at a posh nightclub on the Calle 23 in the *Veado* district. When she was hired as a chorus girl, she left the salon without notice. There was no one to cover her appointments and Claudia was distraught. She sent her daughter, a hairdresser, to the manicurist's apartment to see why she had not come to work. When Lucia returned, she explained what had happened.

"What are we going to do? All of her customers will go to our competitor. There are a hundred other salons right here in this area; they don't need to come here." Claudia ran her fingers through her hair nervously. She shook her head and bit a nail.

"Mama, do you think Anna could do it? She is very neat and precise," Lucia asked.

"Anna? But then who will do the shampoos? I have a full book of clients today, too," Claudia said.

"We will all have to shampoo our own customers."

Claudia considered the idea.

"I could teach her, quickly," Lucia said.

"You think you could teach her before your own customers start coming in?"

"I think so. But maybe we should ask her."

"Anna…" Claudia called.

And it was that day in early September when Anna became the most popular manicurist in the salon.

From her customers, she learned English and Spanish. She polished the fingers and toes of showgirls and wives of political officials, of Americans and Europeans, as well as natives of the island. They loved her. Anna was a good listener; she never repeated what was told to her, and for that she became their confidant.

That December, the couple who had grown up in Germany with cold winters sat outside, lighting the inexpensive *menorah* that Alex had bought. It was 70 degrees outside, on their first *Hanukah* together.

They clasped hands as Alex said the prayers.

"Blessed are you, Lord our God, Ruler of the Universe, who has sanctified us with Your commandments, and has commanded us to kindle the lights of *Hanukkah*…"

She looked over at her handsome husband wearing the *yarmulke* she'd made for him.

Anna squeezed Alex's hand and he looked at her, his eyes shining with gratitude for all he'd been given.

After the candles had been, lit Anna served a dinner of potato *latkes*. It had been such a long time since they'd eaten Jewish food.

"You even got apple sauce," Alex said.

"I made it from apples and sugar."

"It's delicious."

"I'm glad you like it. I've been serving you so much rice and beans that I almost forgot how to prepare our food."

"Well, you remembered quite well…and by the way…"

"Yes?" She ate a forkful of applesauce and potato pancake.

"Wait here."

Alex got up and went to the other room. He took a small box out of his pants pocket, "Happy *Hanukkah*, my sweetheart."

"Alex, we agreed we were not going to buy gifts. We agreed that we were going to save our money." She held the box.

"This is from my lunch money. I saved it to buy this for you."

She felt the tears. "Oh Alex. I wish I had gotten you something too."

"You give me something every day. You give me a reason to live," he said.

She looked at him and shook her head, smiling through her tears. "Alex…"

"Open it…come on. I've been waiting for two weeks to give this to you. It was hard to keep the surprise. I was so excited that I wanted to give it to you as soon as I got it."

She pulled the lid off the small white box. Inside was a thin gold band, encased in black velvet.

"I had it engraved," he said. "Look inside."

She felt the tears running down her cheeks as she read the script "For Anna, my love, my life, my salvation."

"Alex…"

"Here give it me. Let me put it on you."

She handed him the band. "Are you sure we can afford this?" she asked.

He didn't answer.

"With this ring, I thee wed," he said, his hand trembling as he slipped the ring on her small finger, "For richer or poorer."

"In sickness and in health," she said, the words catching in her throat with emotion.

"Forever and for always…till death do us part." Alex kissed her hand and held it to his cheek. "Happy *Hanukah*, Anna, my Anna…"

"Happy *Hanukah*." She kissed him.

Chapter 42

Over the next eight months, Alex and Anna learned to speak Spanish almost fluently through daily conversations with the natives, and English fairly well from books Alex purchased. They set aside the waltz, which they'd brought with them from Germany, to learn the *bolero-sun*, a hot rhythmic dance, much like the *rumba*. Even though Raul was much older than he was, Alex made friends with the man, and he and his wife occasionally went dancing with Alex and Anna. However, Alex and Anna tried to save every penny that they could. With an uncertain future such as theirs, money could be a safety net. If they had enough, and could make the right connections, they might be able to buy the visas to America. Still, they both knew that they might never leave Cuba, that for reasons beyond their control they might never see the United States. They had discussed this. It upset Alex more than Anna. He felt that, in America, Jews would be safe. However, both of them had become acclimated to their lives in the tropical paradise. There was no doubt that they were surrounded by beauty, not only in the old city, but also just a few miles away in the new city. Alex missed his career; he missed his love affair with words. He'd become fast and efficient at rolling cigars, but he longed to go back to journalism. And Anna secretly yearned to finish her education. But for now these were dreams, and with all that the Jews faced in Europe, they considered themselves fortunate to be earning enough money to live and even put a little away with hopes for a future.

Every month a letter arrived from Uncle Max, and sometimes another from Aunt Edith. They were doing what they could to obtain the Visas, but so far they were being shuffled around without any concrete answers.

Alex began going to the library. He wanted to learn to read and write in English. He read books written in English, and began writing his own critiques on them. Words had always been his strongest allies, and he planned to use them to convince the Americans to approve their visas. And if not, he would try to find a job in the new city working as a writer for one of the tourist papers.

On most Sundays, Alex and Anna packed a picnic basket and walked through the park or along the ocean. They splurged and bought second-hand bathing suits so that they could feel the warm salt water upon their skin. Alex had lost the pale, chalky-white pallor he'd had when he first arrived, replacing it with a healthy bronze glow. Anna, too, had been kissed by the sun. The sunshine and good food helped Alex to regain his health. He gained weight and his body filled out. To look at him, no one would ever know he'd been starved and tortured in Dachau.

For Alex and Anna, every day their love only grew stronger, and spending every night wrapped in each other's arms was the true highlight of their lives. The landlady gave Anna a box fan, and at night they listened to the hum and the chirping of the crickets. Anna lay with her head on Alex's chest, gazing out at the full moon.

"Sometimes I wish that we could have a child," she said. They had taken great care not to conceive.

"I know you do, and so do I, but I don't think we should until we know what is going to happen with our visas. If we have a baby they might not let us in to America."

"Do you care so much about leaving here and going to America?"

"Yes and no," he said. "I love it here. It's beyond beautiful, but I am afraid that if we stay in Cuba, we will always be poor. And this country is small, not nearly as safe; its government isn't as reliable as the United States. We are Jews, Anna. We must never forget that if there is trouble, Jews are the first ones that they go after. Besides, there is so much opportunity in America. There, I can work hard and give you the life you deserve."

"If that is what you really want, I am going to start asking my customers if they can do anything to help us get our visas," Anna said.

"You mean to tell me that you have not asked them?"

"No…" she said, "I'm sorry."

'You don't want to leave?"

"It's not that. It's just that I am comfortable. I feel secure. Our lives are what they are, but at least we know what to expect. After the ship and everything we went through to get here…"

"I know. I know," he said, kissing the top of her head.

"In America, we will be starting all over again, not knowing where to go or what to expect…" she said.

He nodded. "It's beautiful here, and I am comfortable too. But after what happened in Germany, I've learned never to become too comfortable. America, in my mind, is still the safest place for us. The government is stable, Anna…"

"I sent a letter to my parents several months ago. They still have not answered."

"Why didn't you tell me?"

"Because I didn't want to upset you. I kept waiting, thinking that the letter would come the following day…" Her voice cracking with concern, "It didn't…"

"But you are upset? If you are upset, you should always turn to me. You know that I'm here for you. Even if there is nothing I can do to help, I will always listen. Oh, Anna, my Anna…" Alex picked up her hand and kissed her palm.

"Do you think they are all right?" she asked.

"Yes, of course they are," he said, but he knew that he didn't sound convincing.

"I am afraid for them. Before I left they begged me to write, and promised that they would write too. But they haven't, Alex."

"Do you think it might have been the mail? Maybe they never received it. Why don't you write again?" he said.

"I will try. I'll write tomorrow."

"That's a good idea." He said a silent prayer that her parents were safe, but after what he'd been through in Dachau, he doubted it.

Chapter 43

Alex followed the news coming out of Germany every day and Anna could see how worried he was. Cuba had its own problems with anti-Semitism, and she knew that Alex was afraid that the Nazis would infiltrate the government there. It was well known that many of Hitler's SS came to Cuba on holiday. They were accepted, and even welcomed. She decided that it was probably a good idea to start asking some of the officials' wives if they could help her and Alex get their visas.

Every time Anna had the opportunity, she asked her customers. Most said that they did not interfere in their husband's business affairs, and brushed off her request to discuss their latest party or the newest fashion.

One afternoon an old woman came into the shop, perhaps seventy-five, maybe eighty, but she kept her hair coiffed in a teased-up do that stood high on her head like a crown. Her hands were parchment-white, with raised, thick, purple veins, and she wore long crimson nails that curved under her slender fingers. Her name was Benita Garcia, and everyone at the salon both feared and disliked her. She was a strong woman who demanded immediate service, and expected excellence at every turn. Benita's reputation for cruelty included being the cause for several of the hairdressers leaving and going to work for a competitor, just to get away from her. However, even though she'd been asked to leave and not return by Claudia, Benita continued to patronize the shop. When Anna had done her shampoos, she demanded a long massage, and then after Anna had taken the knots out of her long, thin hair, she expected her neck and shoulders rubbed. Some of the girls complained, and even refused to comply because she was known to forget to tip, even though everyone knew she was very rich. But nobody could say where her money came from. Several of the girls speculated she'd been born an heiress, but no one knew for sure. Anna never refused any of Benita's requests. She'd always shown Benita the respect the older woman demanded, never arguing with her or expecting a tip for her services. Then, when Anna was promoted to the manicure table, she spent extra time massaging Benita's old arthritic hands, and allowed Benita to take as much time as she needed to select the perfect nail polish. Because of all of this, Benita had always liked Anna, and even occasionally remembered to give her a small tip.

Anna dared not ask Benita for help with her visas. She knew the older woman could be caustic, and expected a refusal followed, by a reprimand, and heaven knew what else. If Anna said the wrong thing, or asked the wrong question, Benita could see to it that it cost Anna her job, or worse.

On a busy Friday morning, Benita came into the shop without an appointment. Claudia simply did not have room to fit her into the schedule with any of the hairdressers or manicurists. Benita responded by throwing a tantrum.

"I have been a customer of this salon for years. You mean to tell me that you cannot take me today? I have a very important dinner tonight with my husband's colleagues, and their wives. I need to have my hair and nails looking perfect," Benita said, banging her fist on the reception table.

"I'm sorry. I cannot help you." Claudia hoped that Benita would leave the salon permanently and go to another one; she'd had enough of this old woman's antics.

Again Benita hammered the reception desk. "Do you hear me? I need to have this done…today!"

"There is nothing we can do for you here," Claudia said. All the other customers grew quiet, watching the old woman's outburst.

Anna, seated at the manicurists table just a few feet away, had just finished polishing a customer's nails. Gingerly, she got up and went to the reception desk.

"May I offer to help?" Anna said.

Claudia looked at her, relieved, wondering what Anna could possibly do.

"I have been watching the girls do Benita's hair since I started working here. I can forgo my lunch hour today and do her hair and nails. Of course, that is if it's all right with you," Anna said.

"Do you think you could do it right? My hair I mean?" Benita asked.

"I believe I can," Anna said.

"If you want her to try, I would agree to it," Claudia said.

"It's not like I have much choice, but if I don't like it…well… I am not going to pay for something I don't like."

Anna worked on pure commission, so Claudia waited for her to decide.

"It's up to you, Anna," Claudia said

"I will try for you, Mrs. Garcia."

"All right, I suppose. What else can I do? Well, don't just stand there; let's get started."

Anna felt the sweat bead under her arms. Benita Garcia demanded perfection. But Anna did her best, and by the time she'd finished, Benita sat looking in the mirror. She glanced at Anna, and a smile came over her wrinkled face.

"You know, Anna, you never cease to amaze me. You have more patience than anyone I have ever met. In fact, I hate to admit this, but sometimes I push people just to see how they will respond. I suppose it is just age that makes me ornery. However, you have done a wonderful job today."

"Thank you, ma'am. I appreciate your loyalty as a customer to the shop."

"You're about the only one who does. They think I don't know that they talk badly about me and that they wish I would leave this shop forever. Of course I know. Nothing gets by me." She laughed. "But they don't have the guts to throw me out permanently. They've asked me to leave, but always welcome me back when I show up. Ahh, well, at least they all know who I am; I'm not just some person who comes to get their hair done and remains anonymous. I'd rather have everyone talk badly about me than just not talk about me at all."

Anna was not sure how to respond, so she just smiled. "I am glad you like your hair and nails."

"Anna, there is something I would like to discuss with you, but not here. It's a bit of a secret. Can you meet me after work, for a cup of coffee, perhaps? I won't have much time to spend with you, because I have that dinner to attend, but a few minutes are all I will need."

Anna tilted her head and looked at the old woman, bewildered. What could Benita Garcia want with her?

Benita smiled, then winked, "So, you'll be there?"

"Of course I will meet with you. We close at 6:00 tonight. I hope that is all right. I will come immediately after we close," Anna said. Alex would be a little upset at her being late to celebrate the Sabbath, but Mrs. Garcia's proposal intrigued her; she wanted to know more.

"There is a little cafeteria right around the corner, the one right by the park where the men play dominoes? Are you familiar with that place?"

"Yes, of course, they are famous for having the best coffee in Havana."

"Meet me there. Don't be late. I will be waiting."

At the workday's end, Anna hurried through clean up. She wanted to get to the coffee shop as quickly as possible so that she could get home before dark. All day she contemplated what the old woman might have on her mind. She decided that Mrs. Garcia probably planned to offer her a job doing her hair and nails privately. Claudia usually frowned upon taking customers from the shop and doing their services at home, but Anna knew that Claudia would be glad to be rid of this particular customer. And for Anna it meant full payment for her work, not just commission, making it a nice sum of extra money. She and Alex could use the cash. Every penny they saved was a penny closer to getting to America. And Alex still did not know that all of their previous savings had been stolen. Because Anna knew how delicate Alex could be, she had continued to put off telling him. However, before Anna mentioned anything to Claudia about taking this customer privately, she would first meet with Benita Garcia to be sure that is what Mrs. Garcia had in mind.

When Anna arrived, Benita was sitting outside under an umbrella, drinking a cup of thick black Cuban coffee. She had another mug filled for Anna sitting on the table waiting. Anna sat down and glanced at the contents of the cup; it looked like wet mud.

"That was rather brave of you today, Anna, to agree to take care of me, even though you have very little experience doing hair, and I can be such a pain in the ass, and then to sacrifice your lunch hour too."

"I wanted to see to it that you to had everything done for tonight. You said you had an important dinner."

"You have always been kind to me," Mrs. Garcia said. "You are good girl, not like the others. They are such trash. Hmmm, I know trash when I see it. I know class too. I can tell you were raised properly." Benita sipped her coffee, blowing on it first to cool it down. "Your parents should be proud. I would tell them myself, if you would like. Are they here or still in Europe?"

"I suppose you know that I am from Europe by my accent?"

"Of course, dear, you speak broken Spanish with a German accent. It is rather obvious." Benita raised her eyebrows; then she smiled.

"I suppose it is," Anna said, looking down into her coffee cup.

"What is it Anna? Something is wrong…tell me. I am not a patient woman, but you may just find that contrary to popular consensus, I can be a very good friend, to someone who deserves that friendship."

Anna had never discussed everything that happened on the *MS St. Louis* and all that had taken place before she'd boarded. She doubted that Mrs. Garcia even knew she was Jewish. But something told her to tell the woman the entire story. How her parents had sacrificed everything to get her out of Germany, even that Alex had been in Dachau, and his entire family had been murdered. Anna looked into Benita's dark eyes, and suddenly she realized that the mean old woman was merely an act. This woman was kind and compassionate, and maybe too kind, so she hid what she thought was a weakness by being hard and uncompromising.

"I know you are in a hurry, but I will be as brief as possible. I am going to tell you something I have never told anyone," Anna said.

Mrs. Garcia nodded. "Go on Anna… I'm listening."

A breeze rustled the trees; Anna ran her index finger along the top of the coffee cup. She bit her lower lip, swallowed, and began to speak.

Then Anna told her the entire story, from the time she left her beloved parents in Germany, until Manny had paid for her and Alex to leave the MS St. Louis.

Mrs. Garcia sat, silent, looking directly into Anna's eyes. She did not speak until Anna had finished.

Then Mrs. Garcia nodded, blew on her hot coffee, took a sip and spoke.

"So you and your husband are trying to get visas into the United States and you are having a difficult time?" Benita Garcia asked.

"Yes." Anna nodded. "We are trying. My uncle is in America and he is doing what he can to assist."

"I see," Benita Garcia said, wrapping her red-nailed fingers around the warm coffee mug. "I think I might be able to help. I don't know if you will need some money. But if so, can you get any?"

"I will contact my uncle and see what can be done. My husband and I have a little bit saved. We have both been working hard and saving everything we could. But recently our apartment was broken into and the thief took everything. My husband doesn't know. He is an emotional man. It stems from his time in the concentration camp, and I just haven't had the heart to tell him. " Suddenly Anna was crying.

Benita Garcia nodded again.

"I understand," she said, "Don't tell him. After his being tortured in a camp, I can see why he is an emotional wreck. Let this just be our secret for now, and let me see what I can do. Give me a week or two. I'll come into the shop and ask for you when I have some information."

"Mrs. Garcia…"

"Yes?"

"Thank you."

"I haven't done anything yet." Benita Garcia had turned back into the hard old woman hiding her feelings. She got up slowly and for the first time, Anna noticed how arthritic she was. Then Benita Garcia bent over and stretched her back, patted Anna's shoulder, and left.

Chapter 44

Every two weeks Anna sent a letter home to her parents in Germany. Finally, she received an answer. When she recognized her mother's handwriting on the envelope, she felt her heart begin to beat faster and let out a small cry of excitement. Then she tore the envelope and read.

My Dearest Anna,

Your father and I were so happy to hear from you. It warms my heart to know that you are all right, but I must admit that Papa and I were very surprised to hear that you had gotten married. We pray that he is a good person and that he treats you well, loves you, and gives you a decent life. Oh, how I wish we could have been there with you to see you take your vows. Your papa would have been so proud to see you under the chuppah. *But times are not so good, and we must be thankful that at least you have married a nice Jewish boy, and you are happy. You see, before I received your letter, news of what happened on the* St. Louis *had reached us, and we were worried. At least now we know that you are safe and not alone in Cuba. This is a comfort to Papa and me.*

We are all right here. So far, we have not had any problems. Please do not worry about us. Soon this Nazi problem will all be over and done with. The German people are too smart to allow this to continue. After all, this is the country that gave the world Mozart and Beethoven; it is far too civilized to put up with Hitler much longer. And once this monster is gone and we can get out, your papa and I will join you in America or maybe you and your husband will choose to come home to Germany. For now, may you be healthy and safe, and may God watch over you and guide you, my dear and precious child. I send all of our love to you.

Mama

Anna held the letter to her breast. Her mother had touched this very same paper. She held it to her nose, hoping to get a whiff of her mother's perfume.

"Mama," she whispered, kissing the letter.

Then she sat down at the small kitchen table, got a piece of paper and a pen.

She wrote:

Mama,

I was so glad to get your letter. It means everything to me to hear from you. I think of you and Papa every day, and I pray you are both healthy and all is well. Alex, that's my husband, knows how much I miss you, because I must tell him a hundred times every week. When we are all together again, it will be the happiest day of my life. Our reunion is never far from my thoughts. I look at Alex and I know that you will be pleased with your son-in-law. He is a good, kind man, and he will be good to you and treat you as if you were his own parents. I love you and Papa more than you will ever know. In fact, I never realized how much I loved you until I was forced to leave you. It was the hardest thing I have ever done. When the war is over, and we can only pray that Hitler will be defeated, God willing, I will come back to Germany to find you. But no matter what happens with the war and everything, I want you to know that I swear on my life that I will never forget you and Papa. Your grandchildren, when they are born, will know everything about you. I will tell them how wonderful it was to grow up with parents like you. And I will pray that I can do even half as good a job of parenting my children as you did for me. You will always be with me in my heart and in my spirit, and someday, with God's help, we will be reunited again.

Always and forever,
Your Anna

Chapter 45

True to both her word and to her nature, Benita Garcia came into the salon two weeks later, demanding that Anna take care of her hair and nails immediately. Claudia bit her nail, anticipating the tantrum that would ensue. She explained that Anna had a full book of clients that day and would not be able to accommodate another customer, even Mrs. Garcia.

"I'm sorry Mrs. Garcia. I am looking at the book right now, and she has someone every half hour. It would be impossible for her to fit you in."

"I don't want to hear what you have to say. Go and ask her," Mrs. Garcia said.

"I'm sorry, but it is impossible. She is not even scheduled to take a meal break today."

"I said ask her." Mrs. Garcia raised her voice and pounded her fist on the reception desk, daring anyone to defy her.

"Wait here. She's in the back doing a shampoo for one of the girls. I'll ask her, but I doubt she'll be able to help you."

Claudia found Anna wrapping the client's newly-washed hair in a towel and sending her off to wait for her hairdresser.

"Anna, I know how busy you are today. Your manicure just got here waiting. She's waiting in the front. But Mrs. Garcia is here and she is raising hell, as usual. Do you want to come up to the front and tell her that she needs to make an appointment for tomorrow? You are not available today."

Anna straightened her shirt; it was covered with water and soap from the shampoo she'd just finished. Her face was wet with sweat, as it was an extremely hot day and the fans were not working. "I'll take her, right now. My other client will have to wait. Or she can make another appointment," Anna said.

"But Anna, that's not right."

"I know, but I want to take Mrs. Garcia first. I can do her hair and nails quickly. Then I will work on the other one."

"Are you sure? It's a lot of pressure on you," Claudia asked.

"Absolutely," Anna said. She could barely contain her excitement. Had Mrs. Garcia come with news about the visas? Anna said a silent prayer that it would be good news. Then she raced up to the reception desk, where she found Benita Garcia tapping her foot.

"What took you so long?" She asked Anna.

"I'm sorry, Mrs. Garcia. I will do your hair and nails immediately."

"Now, that's more like it. Let's get started shall we? I've been waiting for almost an hour."

As they walked toward the back of the salon to wash Mrs. Garcia's hair, Anna saw Claudia silently say shaking her head. "She's only been waiting five minutes."

Anna nodded and smiled to let Claudia know that it was all right. She could see by the look on Claudia's face that her boss was amazed at her patience.

After the shampoo, Anna escorted Mrs. Garcia to an open hairdressing station and began to set pink rollers into her hair. Mrs. Garcia did not speak and Anna could hardly keep her hands steady. She was afraid to ask, so she waited. Benita's hair was nearly all rolled up before she said anything.

"I can't help you. It is impossible to obtain visas into the United States," Benita said.

Anna could not control the tears that were swelling in her eyes. She was so disappointed that she could not speak. Instead, she just nodded and began to help Mrs. Garcia to a seat in the sun, where her hair would dry more quickly.

"Thank you for trying, anyway," Anna finally managed. She was glad she had not told Alex about the conversation with Mrs. Garcia. She'd wanted to surprise him. Now at least she would not have to thwart his dreams.

Benita Garcia laughed loudly. "Anna, my dear, I was just joking. I have the visas."

"Mrs. Garcia...." Anna took the old woman into her arms. "Tell me what you need. I will give you all the money that we have."

"Well, I had to grease a palm or two, but it's done. And you needn't pay me. I have plenty of money…"

"God bless you, God bless you." Anna was crying, and everyone in the salon had stopped working to watch the interaction between the most difficult client and the quiet girl who was always kind to everyone.

"Enough, you're ruining my reputation. We wouldn't want them to think I did anything nice, now, would we?" Benita Garcia laughed again. Then she continued, "You and your husband report to the immigration office first thing tomorrow morning. Ask for Jorge Garcia; he is expecting you. You said that you have an uncle in the United States?"

"Yes, my uncle Max."

"He will need to sponsor you and your husband by signing an affidavit that he will promise to support the two of you financially. America will only accept immigrants that they are sure will not become a burden on the already strained economy."

"I understand. I am sure my uncle will sign whatever is necessary. He has been trying to help us for a long time."

"Yes, well, usually it takes at least two to three years for your number to come up, even with help, but I've made these other arrangements, and that will speed the process. Do as I say and go tomorrow, ask for Jorge Garcia. He will direct you from there."

"I will do what you tell me to do." Anna smiled through her tears.

"Now hurry up and get my nails polished. You know how I hate to wait," Benita said. Her voice was caustic and demanding, but her smile was warm and loving.

Chapter 46

After a year and a half in the tropics, Alex and Anna boarded a ship headed for New York. They held hands as their hearts beat with excitement. Soon, they would be in America, the land of opportunity.

The ship they were able to afford passage on was nothing like the *MS St. Louis*. There were no bands or fancy food. In fact, they shared a bunk bed deep within the belly of the vessel, surrounded on all sides by other hopeful immigrants. Neither Anna nor Alex had experienced seasickness on the *St. Louis*, however here they were both nauseated for most of the voyage. Because a large group of people had been stuffed into a small, enclosed room, sometimes violent fights broke out, not to mention all of the illness that spread through the germ-infested air.

But in spite of its cargo, the ship sailed up the coast of the Atlantic Ocean, passing the beautiful beaches of Miami and continuing toward the port of the city of New York, and the gateway to the land of plenty, Ellis Island.

As the ship came into port, the passengers rushed up to the lower deck where they were able to see the Statue of Liberty, holding her torch high and welcoming them into the new world. Although there were over a hundred people, no one spoke. They were all in awe of the beauty of the copper statue, the symbol that meant they had arrived. Alex leaned over and kissed the top of Anna's head.

"I can't believe we are actually here," he said.

"I know. We are in America... It's like a dream," she said, and looked up at him, her eyes glowing with excitement.

When they left the ship, they were directed into a line which had formed on the bridge into the port. Alex carried the cardboard suitcase with all of their possessions as they went to the end of the line. It took hours to reach the front, where they were examined by doctors and dentists. They saw others walking around with markings on their bodies, such as H, or E. They had no idea what this meant, only that these people were to be detained and held in quarantine.

"Look healthy, pinch your cheeks," Alex heard a man say to his young daughter. The girl was pale and had been coughing for most of the trip.

Alex squeezed Anna's hand, and gave her a wink and a worried smile as they were separated to see the doctor individually.

The exam was extensive. Not only were they checked for physical defects, but mental defects, as well.

Several hours later, Alex waited outside the building until Anna finally joined him. They had passed the test. Then they boarded the ferry that took them to Manhattan. They were now in the United States of America.

Uncle Max had wired them directions to the apartment he shared with Aunt Edith, and although Alex had done a fair job of learning to read English, the bus numbers and street names were still difficult for him to navigate. But they asked directions and made their way to the Jewish section of Manhattan. When they arrived, they climbed three flights of stairs in a red brick building to find the apartment. Anna knocked on the door. A plump woman with a bright smile and graying brown hair opened the door.

"You made it…" she said. "I'm your aunt Edith." The woman opened her flabby arms to take them both into a big bear hug. "Come in, come in… Don't stand in the hallway."

Anna walked in first; then Alex followed her. She looked around at the small apartment, clean and modestly furnished.

"Sit, sit, you must be tired, yes? You must be hungry, too. Well don't you worry, I'm gonna make you something right away. In fact, I have a little chicken soup left from last night. I'll make you both a bowl with a piece of *Challah*. How does that sound? *Oy*, Max was right; you are a pretty little thing. Am I rambling? I ramble sometimes. I'm sorry. It's just that Max works for such long hours, and I am all alone, with no one to talk to. It will be good to have you here. There I go again; I am rambling. I'm sorry. Let me get that food. I'll be right back."

When Aunt Edith went into the kitchen, Anna smiled at Alex.

"She's excited," he said.

"She's funny," Anna said.

Anna sat down on the sofa and Alex sat beside her. Neither of them spoke, but their eyes caught, and they could see in each other's expression that they were comfortable here at Anna's uncle's house, at least for now.

The food was delicious, good, old-fashioned Jewish cooking, the way that it had been so long ago when they were just children in Germany. Anna's attempts at preparing their old favorites had been good, but this was truly authentic.

"It reminds me of my mother's chicken soup," Anna said.

"Yes, it's strange, but I felt the same thing. My mother used to make it just like this, too," Alex said, sipping a spoonful of hot broth.

Aunt Edith refilled their bowls twice, and they both finished every drop, and then thanked Aunt Edith a thousand times.

"You two look tired. Let me show you the room where you will be staying."

It was a pleasant room with a red and yellow flowered bedspread and matching curtains, the dresser was light blond wood, and there was a small closet to hang things. Both Anna and Alex were too tired to unpack. They took turns going to the bathroom to clean up, and then went directly to bed, where they slept all the way through until the following morning. Even though they arose early, Uncle Max had already left for work. He was a butcher, Edith explained. The customers began to come early. He kept terrible hours.

"We don't have a lot, but Max does all right. People will always have need for a kosher butcher, thanks be to God," Aunt Edith said. "And we always seem to have enough to eat...so for that I am thankful, too."

"Yes, wherever our people settle, be it here or anywhere else, they will always need a kosher butcher, so it is a very good profession to be in." Alex smiled.

"Max says that he will take you to work with him, Alex. He says he is going to teach you, apprentice you; I think that's what he called it. Then you will have a trade. You will be a butcher, too."

Alex smiled at her, but inside he was cringing. He could do almost anything, almost anything but this. The killing of animals sickened him; he couldn't bear to see the blood. This was going to be a challenge, but he couldn't let Anna down. He had to try.

"I want to get a job, too," Anna said. "I have experience working in a beauty shop. Do you think they would hire me here?"

155

"I don't know. You can try if you want to…"

"Yes, I will do that today."

"Why don't I go along with you to make sure that you are safe? Again, Anna, we are in a new place, we don't know much about the neighborhoods," Alex said.

"All right. Come with me, then."

None of the beauty salons were interested, they already had their staff, and besides, Anna's English was still limited.

"I don't know what I am going to do," Anna said.

"Well, perhaps I will do well enough as a butcher to support us, and you can go to school instead of working."

"I want to do both. I plan to go to school. But I want to bring some money into the house; I cannot just live with my aunt and uncle and not contribute."

"But my contribution will be for both of us."

"No, I feel that I need to do something as well. I need to be productive."

"Sweetheart, let me do this for you. If we find that it is necessary, you can get a job, but for now, can we just try it my way? You stay at home and learn how to make that special chicken soup, so that you can make it for our children when they are born, all right?"

She nodded, but since they had landed in Cuba, Anna had grown from a child into a woman. She had earned her own money, and learned her own self-worth.

Chapter 47

Aunt Edith meant well, but she watched over Anna as if Anna were a child. She would not allow her any freedom. Anna, having lived in Cuba, alone with Alex, was not used to anyone hovering over her constantly, and she began to feel annoyed.

"I would like to go to school and work on my English, so that I can get my citizenship and maybe a job," Anna said as they were rolling out bread dough one morning.

"You don't need to go to school. Women don't need an education. The only education you need is how to cook, clean and take care of babies."

"Yes, but I want to. I would like to maybe become a teacher."

"This is nonsense. That's a job for an old maid. You have a husband to take care of you. What do you need to do all of this for?"

Anna shrugged. "I had a job in Havana. I had friends too. I feel a little bit lost here."

"You have me. And you have all the young girls from the neighborhood who come to sit outside on the steps with us in the evening."

Anna nodded. She did have Aunt Edith, and every night the family sat outside on the steps and the sidewalks with all of the other families in the neighborhood. The children ran through the streets playing kickball, while the adults talked. Because of these nightly gatherings, Anna had become friendly with several of the other young woman who lived in the building. News traveled through the neighborhoods at these informal groupings. In fact, as the sun set one night, Anna and Alex sat on the stairs with Uncle Max and Aunt Edith when they overheard a conversation between two men who lived in the adjacent building.

"Hitler has taken France and Belgium, they are now under Nazi rule, and he is bombing the hell out of England," one of the men said.

"Are you sure?" Alex interrupted the conversation.

"Absolutely. It's all over the newspapers."

Alex looked at Anna to see if she had heard what the man said, and by the expression of horror on her face, he knew that she had. Neither of them spoke the words aloud, but they both knew that Manny and Elke could be in any of those countries. Those were three of the countries that had accepted the passengers from the *St. Louis*.

Anna and Alex also learned that America was not immune to anti-Semitism. Outside on the sidewalk they heard about the street demonstrations against Jews, and the American Nazi Party. Their Jewish neighbors tried to brush it off as nothing but insignificant rabble-rousers. But when Alex heard that America had a growing Nazi Party, he'd spoken up, and because Alex was usually so quiet and mild mannered, when he raised his voice, heatedly explaining that the Jews must pay careful attention, and they must do everything possible to ensure that the Nazis never came to power, the others listened. He told them that he had been in Dachau; then he explained how it all began, how the Nazis took over in Germany. "Open your eyes! You are in danger! Act now, while you still can! Once they are in control, you will have no rights at all! And they HATE you! They hate ALL Jews! They will do things to you and your families that you never dreamed human beings could be capable of doing to another human being!" Alex said, and he made them afraid.

It was also on one of those evening that Anna had overheard one of the girls talking about job openings in the factories in the garment district. Anna wasn't sure how far this was from her home, or which streetcar she would need to take to get there, but the idea of having a place to go and money in her pocket, money that she had earned, excited her. She planned to find out more information.

But she hardly had the chance to look into working, because try as they might to prevent it, Anna had become pregnant. Although they had hoped to delay the beginning of their family until they were sure they could afford it, both Anna and Alex were excited. Max and Edith assured them both that they, too, would welcome a child.

But secretly, Alex was not well. He'd become deeply troubled. He could not bear being a butcher, could not force himself to participate in the killing of animals. The slitting of their throats, the draining of the blood and the carving of their bodies haunted him. He could not sleep and gagged when he tried to eat meat of any kind. At night, he had dreams where he saw the slain animals turn into his family members. His mind twisted and turned as he slept, his body bathed in sweat. In his dream, Alex saw himself dressed in a perfectly pressed black SS uniform. He woke shivering, his mouth dry, his throat parched, his heart racing. Before the Nazi's had taken power in Germany, Alex had been a man of words, a man of learning, a gentle man who could never see himself capable of killing anything. But he knew he had to continue to try, to try not to fail for Anna's sake, especially now with the baby coming. He went to work every morning with Uncle Max. Alex stood beside Max, shuddering as he butchered the creatures, then secretly went behind the building and vomited. Alex saw the eyes of the young lambs and thought of his sister. Even after he left the butcher shop, he still heard the sounds of the animals. His hands began to shake, and as the weeks went by and he ate less and less. He grew thin and pale.

Anna knew something was wrong with Alex, but he refused to tell her what bothered him. She thought he must be concerned about earning enough money to care for a child. He'd only just begun his apprenticeship; he had a lot to learn before he could expect full pay as a butcher. If only she could find a way to reassure him. As her belly grew bigger, Alex got worse. He withdrew into himself and hardly spoke to her or the others. When the family went outside of the tenement at night to gather with the neighbors, he did not join them.

In spite of Aunt Edith's disapproval, Anna decided that she would get a job. One afternoon when Edith lay down for a nap, Anna dressed and left the apartment. She waited for the streetcar on the corner, and then asked directions to the garment district. Because of her broken English, she was ignored by most people walking by. She boarded the streetcar, hoping that she would find someone to help her. Anna took the streetcar until she saw what looked like factory buildings. She got off and walked around looking for any help-wanted signs, but did not see any. Instead, she saw lines of people in ragged clothes outside of Christian missions waiting for food. The streets were filled with people of all sorts, boys selling newspapers, men scurrying off to work, even prostitutes in tight skirts and low-cut blouses, selling their wares. Anna heard loud noises above her and she looked up to see workers laboring on dangerously tall buildings. They looked as if they might fall to the ground any minute. Anna trembled and looked away. She began to feel as if Edith might have been right. Perhaps she should have just stayed at home. New York City loomed over her like a living, breathing giant, one she knew very little about. Anna turned to the left, then the right; nothing looked familiar, and now she couldn't remember where she had gotten off the streetcar or even what number streetcar she'd taken. Automobiles honked their horns as the drivers hollered at each other. Anna felt her heart begin to pound. She tried to find a landmark, but all of the streets looked the same. A car right in front of her honked its horn. She jumped at the loud noise, just as a man came from around the corner. He rushed at her so quickly that she hardly knew what happened. With his left hand he punched her in the face, while with his right hand he grabbed her purse. Anna tried to run, but she tripped over the curb and fell hard against the concrete, her nose was gushing blood. She let out a scream, but the thief had disappeared into the crowd. Several people gathered around her. A tall, slender woman wearing high-heeled shoes and a stylish hat bent down to help her to sit up.

Anna sat on the curb, the blood from her face flowing like a river onto her blouse.

"Are you all right?" the woman asked.

"I don't know," Anna said. "My stomach hurts. I have a lot of cramping."

The woman looked down; then she smiled a frozen smile back up at Anna, trying to hide her shock. Anna was bleeding from between her legs.

"Officer, officer…this woman needs help. She needs an ambulance…"

Anna passed out. The officer helped to load her in the back of an ambulance that screamed all the way to the nearest hospital.

Chapter 48

"You wouldn't listen to me. Now, *oy vey*, I can't believe this happened." Aunt Edith pulled her hair.

Anna opened her eyes to find Alex holding her hand.

"Anna, my Anna…" He kissed her hand. "I've been so worried," Alex said, and she saw that his eyes were red and he'd been crying. "I was so afraid I would lose you…"

"I'm all right…" she said, but she wasn't. The doctor set her nose with bandages, blood filled the whites of her eyes and the skin surrounding them had begun to turn black and purple. Her hand gripped her belly where she felt terrible cramping. "The baby?" Anna squeezed Alex's hand hard. "Is the baby..?"

"I'm sorry… Dear God, I'm sorry," he said.

"I lost the baby?"

He nodded.

She sighed and her shoulders slumped.

"I told you it was dangerous to go out by yourself. Now just look at you. Your pretty face will be ruined." Edith shook her head. "Such a stubborn girl you are…"

"Is my nose broken?" Anna asked.

"Yes," Alex answered.

She just nodded. She'd lost the baby. It was all her fault. Edith was right; she should never have ventured out alone.

"Can Alex and I be alone please?" Anna asked.

Uncle Max took his wife's arm "Come on Edith, let's get a cup of coffee…"

"*Oy vey*, I should never have taken that nap. She would never have gotten out of my sight…."

"Come…" Max's voice was firm as he pulled Edith a little harder.

After Max and Edith left the room, Anna began to cry. "I am so sorry, Alex. It's all my fault. I could see that you were troubled. I thought that maybe you were worried about earning enough money to have a child. I wanted to help… And now…look what I've done."

"Anna, it's all right…"

"I'm sorry."

"I don't blame you. You wanted to help me."

"Yes, I wanted to contribute. To make things easier for you, so you wouldn't feel that you had to carry the burden of supporting us all on your own," Anna said.

Her face was drained of color. She'd lost a lot of blood, and she was tired, but she wanted to talk to him, to ease his mind. Lately he'd been so tense. So even though she fought to stay awake, she felt she had to at least try to make all of this right.

"Anna, you don't have to do these things… I am a man. I should be taking care of you. For some reason I seem to be too weak to help the people I love."

"You are not weak, Alex. You are doing your best. I just wish I knew why you have been so tense ever since we came to America. Is it living with my uncle? Is it me? Please, Alex, I need to know. "

"Maybe then this is a good time to tell you."

"Tell me, yes. Please tell me." She was afraid of what he might say. Could he possibly have met someone else? Perhaps he'd fallen out of love with her. She felt a cramp in her lower belly, but she bit her lip so that she did not make a sound. She wanted him to speak, so she waited in silence to hear what he had to say.

Alex sighed. He hated to burden her with all of this, but perhaps if she knew what it was, then she wouldn't feel that it was something she had done.

"I can't keep working at the butcher shop, Anna. It's horrifying to me. I am afraid I am going to have a nervous breakdown." He began to weep, his shoulders trembling. "I'm sorry, Anna. I've failed you. The truth is that this is all my fault and now here you are in this hospital. I wasn't there to protect you when you needed me, and worse, I can't even keep this job. It's a good opportunity, one most fellows would be happy to have. I owe you at least this... Why, why can't I just do it?"

"Shhh, is that what has been bothering you? Is this why you don't eat or sleep well? Why I find you awake in the middle of the night, sitting in the living room looking out the window?"

"Yes, I am so sorry. I tried, Anna. I've tried."

She nodded. "It's àll right...shhh... It's all right."

"Yes. I can't bear it. I can't stand to see the animals die, and the blood, Anna, the blood. I can't eat meat any more. "

"It's all right," she said. "Listen to me." She took his hand, and with all the strength that she had she squeezed it to let him know that she understood. "We will work together. We will find a way. First, you'll look for another job, and then you'll have to help me to find work in a safe place. Next, we must move out of my uncle's house so that you don't feel obligated to work with him. He means well, but you are a gentle man, an artist, a poet. It is not meant for you to be a butcher."

"Can you forgive me?"

"Of course, I can, and I do. There is nothing to forgive. I love you. I knew who you were when I married you, and I have never regretted my decision. We will have more children. But first let's find a way to live on our own again. We were doing just fine together when we were in Cuba."

He nodded.

"Don't mention anything to my aunt and uncle just yet. Let me get my strength back; then we will explain together."

He nodded again. Then he bent to kiss her and watched as she drifted off to sleep.

When Max and Edith returned, Alex was still sitting on the edge of the bed holding Anna's hand as she slept.

"I think we are going to go home for a while. Are you going to join us Alex?" Max said.

"No, I am going to stay here with Anna."

"All right, Edith and I will come back to the hospital when I get home from work tomorrow," Max said.

Alex nodded.

After they left, Alex watched Anna. How could he be so blessed to have the love of such a strong and wonderful woman? He bent to gently kiss her forehead. She stirred. He did not want to wake her. She needed to rest.

Chapter 49

Three days passed without any sign of Edith or Max.

"I wonder why they haven't returned," Anna said. "It's not like Uncle Max, or Aunt Edith not to come back to the hospital."

"I'm sure Max is working. They'll probably come on Sunday when Max is off. It will be easiest for them. I mean, after all, when Max gets home it's late and he's tired. It's hard to start traveling all over the city on streetcars at that time of day."

"You're right. They will probably wait until Sunday."

But Sunday came and went. Alex had not been home even to change his clothes in over a week. He'd grabbed food in the hospital cafeteria and stayed at his wife's side. Finally, at her insistence, Alex agreed to go home, bathe, change, and return. It would also give him the opportunity to check on Max and Edith while he was there. Perhaps one of them had fallen ill. Hospitals were known to be hotbeds of germs; they might have caught something while they were there with Anna.

Uncle Max had taken up smoking cigars ever since his first visit to Cuba. He loved the way the rich smoke filled his lungs, relaxing him. In the evening after work, he'd allowed himself the indulgence of a cigar and a glass of brandy. These were his only vices, and he enjoyed them to the fullest.

After they returned from the hospital, Edith had prepared a light dinner and gone off to bed. She was emotionally drained from the whole incident, she told him. No matter, Max was glad for the time alone. It was peaceful to enjoy his nightly

166

smoke and drink without her constant nagging. Max loved Edith. He'd spent his entire life with her. In fact, he could not even remember life before her, but she could be annoying there was certainly no doubt about that. Perhaps she would have been better if they'd had children. It would have given her something else to focus on rather than just him. But although they tried, she'd never conceived, and so he'd been the center of her universe for as long as he'd known her. When Alex and Anna arrived, she'd taken to mothering Anna so strongly that he could see how Anna found it unbearable. Edith was full of love, but in many ways her love was as vast as the ocean, and once you were a part of her world she could easily drown you.

Max inhaled another puff of his cigar. It was one of the thick brown hand rolled cigars that Alex had brought with him for Max from Cuba. There was certainly no doubt that Cuban cigars were superior. Everyone said it and it was true. Max stretched his back in the easy chair in front of the window and put his feet up. He was tired, but enjoying this time alone far too much to go to bed. It was a starless night and the moon was barely a sliver. He thought about Anna. What had happened horrified him. It was bad enough that she lost the baby, but could have been killed. It took a while for immigrants to know the ropes in the city. He'd seen plenty of them fall victim to their ignorance, by going to the wrong neighborhood, or trusting the wrong people. Well, at least this time Anna would be all right. Before Max had left the hospital, he'd spoken with the doctor who'd treated Anna. He said that Anna had come through all of this quite well, and that she would be all right. And most important she would be able to have more children. Max could not go home and relax until he heard these words. The night was so dark and peaceful. He decided that since Edith was asleep he would have another glass of brandy. It was such a luxury and he enjoyed it so much. His back hurt when he got up to pour the

167

second cup. Lifting half cows was hard work, and although he'd not told anyone because he didn't want to complain, Alex wasn't much help. His stomach was too weak to handle the butchering, and his muscles weren't strong enough to carry the butchered carcasses. Max wondered if Alex would be able to make a living as a butcher. His efforts so far did not look promising. Max smacked his lips as he took another sip of brandy and felt the warm drink caress his insides. This brandy is so good, he thought. Then he leaned his head back on the cushion in the chair. Exhaustion took over and his eyes closed slowly.

Neither Max nor Edith ever awakened. The cigar, still lit, fell to the ground and rolled over to the drapes that hung over the picture window, igniting the carpet on the way. The fire began slowly, then, as it grew, the scorching orange fingers of the blaze consumed the drapes and the furniture, filling the entire apartment with smoke. Next, the raging flames spread quickly through the wooden tenement structure, devouring everything in its wake. The flames rose like an erupting volcano into the night sky, and the fire department battled until the sun rose in an effort to contain the destructive force before it consumed the neighboring buildings. Most of the dwellers in these shoddy tenements did not awaken until it was too late to get out, and the massive clouds of grey and black smoke filled their lungs, smothering them and forever silencing their dreams of a Golden America filled with opportunity. A few escaped. But none of those who'd gotten out of the building alive knew Alex or Anna well enough to know about Anna's hospital stay. When they didn't see Alex or Anna, they just assumed that they had fallen victim to the fire like so many others. However, unbeknownst to Alex or Anna, several of the neighbors who'd been severely burned were brought to the hospital and put in room's right down the hall from where Alex sat beside his wife. Later that morning the nurse arrived to check Anna's vital signs.

"Good morning, Mrs. Mittelman, how are you feeling today?"

"Better, thank you."

"Let me take your pulse."

Anna gave the nurse her hand.

When she'd finished, the nurse popped a thermometer in Anna's mouth.

"I'm sorry if I'm dragging a bit today," the nurse said. "There was a terrible fire last night, and we got several burn victims on this ward, so I've been here all night."

"You must be exhausted," Alex said.

"Oh I am. I'm leaving right after I am done in here. And I'll be glad to get home and get some sleep." She took the thermometer out of Anna's mouth and held it up to the light. "Perfectly normal," she said and smiled. Then she left the room.

Anna and Alex had no idea that the building that had burned was the one where they'd been living.

When Alex arrived at the apartment, he saw the burned-out building. His mouth fell open and he let out a gasp. He remembered that there had been talk of a fire amongst the nurses in the hospital. They said that many of the victims had been brought there. Alex had never even considered the possibility that this had happened in his own home, in his own building. Perhaps Edith and Max were in the hospital, and that was why they had not come. He could not bear to think that they might have died. But he knew there was a very good possibility. One of the ladies who lived across saw Alex standing in front of the ashes and burnt wood beams. She was one of the older women who gathered on the steps outside each evening.

"Alex!" she called out, squinting as she looked across the street. "Is that you?"

Alex turned around quickly to see the old woman calling him.

He was surprised she'd remembered his name. He didn't remember hers.

"You are looking for your in-laws, yes?"

"Yes. My wife is in the hospital. This is the first time I have been home in a week. What happened here?"

"There was a fire. Nobody knows what caused it. But there was a lot of damage."

"I can see that. Do you know where Max and Edith are?"

"Yes," she said, and then touching his arm. "I am sorry. I saw their bodies, when the fire department pulled them out. They are both dead."

Alex suddenly felt as if he might vomit. He had wanted to leave Max and Edith, but not in this way. It was as if his wish were granted by some macabre force. The bile rose in his throat, and he ran away and vomited on the street. Had his wish really caused this? That was crazy thinking, but he couldn't help but consider the possibility. He had not meant for such a terrible thing to happen. How would he ever tell Anna? She would be distraught, and in her present condition..."

His mind was racing. Edith and Max dead? Dear God, how would he tell Anna? He kept walking, just walking, unsure of where to go or what to do. Then he realized that all of their money, everything that he and Anna had in the world was in that building. They had nothing: no place to go, no money, no food...nothing. When Anna was discharged from the hospital, they would be homeless, destitute.

Alex walked the streets. Like most people, he'd heard of the tent city in Battery Park. If he were alone, he would not have cared, but Anna? How could he do this to Anna? Alex could not bring his beautiful young wife to live in a tent city, with its criminal elements. She would be in danger. A dull, pounding pain began above his right eyebrow. He should never have taken the money from Manny. If he'd been any kind of a man, he would have tried to convince Anna to go with Manny. Manny had money, and connections, he could have taken care of her, at least done a better job than Alex had. Alex had no marketable skills; he was nothing but a writer, a man of words, a poet, a romantic, and a goddamned fool. Who needed another journalist in New York? They needed strong construction workers to erect tall buildings. They needed factory workers to manufacture the planes, bombs, and equipment that America was sending to England to help her fight against Hitler. But they certainly did not need a writer or a poet, a weak man with a nervous condition. And he was nothing but a plague to Anna. She deserved so much better. If it weren't for Anna, he would have taken his own worthless life… However, if he did, Anna would be alone, and penniless. And the least he could do was to be there for her.

It took Alex almost an hour to get to Battery Park on foot. When he looked around, he saw that it was worse than he'd anticipated. Mostly all men, but a few ragged women too, and even a few waif-like, dirty children, lying on the ground, or on benches, in old tattered clothes. Trash was scattered about and burned-out garbage cans lay on their sides, abandoned for now, from the fires that the bums had made in them the previous winter. What would become of these poor souls in a few months when once again the freezing winter set in? What would become of him and Anna? Especially Anna.

As Alex walked along the bridge by the water, he noticed a group of hard looking young men in their early twenties eyeing him. They were leaning against a bench just a few feet away. One of the boys licked his lips, and smiled a crooked smile. Alex felt his heart begin to beat faster, his palms begin to sweat. He assessed the situation. If there is a fight, he thought, I will surely lose. After all, there must be at least ten of them.

So this was life in America. Alex tried not to let them see him watching them.

"Hey, Jew boy!" one of them yelled.

Alex took off running.

Chapter 50

Anna shared her hospital room with an Italian girl who had broken her leg when she'd slipped on oil while she was at work in a factory that made sewing machines. Her name was Gabriella.

"But everyone calls me Gabby," she said.

"I'm Anna."

"Nice to meet you."

"Nice to meet you too."

"So, why are you here?"

"I'm kind of embarrassed to say. But I was out looking for a job and I'm not so familiar with this city…"

"I can hear your accent. Where are you from?"

"Germany."

"Oh, so everybody thinks you are best friends with Hitler, the same way they think I am with Mussolini. If I was so crazy for Mussolini, I'd be in Italy. But just try and explain that to the Americans. They hate us for where we came from," Gabby said, shrugging her shoulders.

"Well, I'm no friend of Hitler's. That's for sure. I'm a Jew. He's torturing Jews in Germany. I am not sure how badly now, because I've been gone for a year. But before I left, Jews couldn't go to school anymore or own businesses. The Nazis were beating us up on the streets."

"A Jew? You have it worse than I do," Gabby laughed. "Everyone has problems with Jews."

Anna grew quiet. She was offended.

"Listen, hey, I didn't mean to hurt your feelings. In fact, I know a few Jews; they live down the street from me, nice people. I'm just saying that you folks have as many problems as we do, maybe more."

"Well, you did sort of hurt my feelings."

"Will you accept an apology?"

"Yes, sure. Why not?" Anna said, "It's hard being an immigrant. We are all from different places, all learning about each other. I can't hold that against you."

"Then we'll be friends?"

"Yes, of course."

Anna and Gabby were close in age. They talked about leaving their homelands. Gabby was not yet married, but a marriage had been arranged for her.

"His name is Mario. I met him for the first time last month. I don't know if I like him so much. He is not handsome, and he doesn't really have much to say. Shy, I suppose. But we are to be married in the spring. My papa had decided, so I must do as he says."

"It must be hard for him too. Meeting you for the first time, he was probably trying to make a good impression. That could be why he was so quiet. Perhaps he didn't want to say the wrong thing." Anna offered.

"Yes, very possible." Gabby nodded. But Anna could tell that she was not happy about the upcoming wedding.

"You are married, yes? That man who was here with you all last week, he is your husband?"

"Yes…"

"He is very handsome."

"Yes, he is."

"Your parents arranged this?"

"No, I met him on a ship."

"On the ship you took from Europe to America?"

"It's more complicated than that…"

"I have time; you have time. Explain?"

"Sure, why not..?" Anna said. And she told Gabby how she met Alex, and the story of the *MS St. Louis*. It took the better part of the afternoon, and by the time they'd finished lunch the girls were laughing together like old friends.

Anna wondered why Alex had not yet returned. It didn't take him that long to wash and change his clothes. She assumed that Uncle Max must have needed his help at the butcher shop. Nothing to worry about, he would return that night.

Chapter 51

That evening Gabby's family had come and gone, bringing her cookies, which she generously shared with Anna. They were a nice, friendly group of people, warm and outgoing. But Anna was distracted. Something was not right. Visiting hours ended at eight thirty, and still Alex had not returned. Had something happened to him? Anna tried to rationalize the situation, but she could not help but worry.

When the nurse came in to take their nighttime vitals, Anna asked her if there had been any calls for her. If anyone, her uncle, her aunt, her husband…had left her a message.

"No, honey, I'm sorry. Nobody called for you. But let me double check. I've been so busy. We've really had our hands full with all the burn victims from the fire the other night."

"A fire? Where? "Gabby asked.

"I'm not really sure," the nurse said.

"When?" Anna asked. Her heart sunk. Could there have been a fire? Could Alex have been involved somehow? Was she thinking crazy? Didn't the nurse mention something about a fire the night that Alex was here? She hadn't really been listening. Well, Alex had disappeared before, when there was something that was bothering him. He was probably distressed over what had happened to her and needed time to collect himself. She hated that quality in him, his inability to cope. She remembered how he'd had the same reaction to Hitler's invasion of Poland. Would he disappear every time something became difficult? Oh, Alex, she thought. I don't know if you are lying dead somewhere, God forbid, or if you are sick, or if you have been burned in a fire, or if you are just emotionally distraught again.

"A few nights ago," the nurse said.

"Do you happen to remember if it was on a night when my husband was here at the hospital?" Anna was pretty sure she remembered the nurse mentioning something about a fire.

"I don't remember if he was here or not. I'm sorry. I'll ask the other girls at the desk for you, to see if anyone called. And I'll let you know if there are any messages."

The nurse returned a few minutes later to say that there had not been any messages; however, one of the nurses recalled seeing Alex the morning after the fire.

"Was she sure?"

"Yes, quite," the young nurse laughed. "Please don't take this wrong, but all the girls can't help but notice your husband. He is such a handsome man. But I'll bet you've heard that before."

Anna nodded. "Handsome, yes… Stable, no."

The following morning Gabby's brother Valente came to see his sister. Anna had seen him the first day she was in the hospital but she had not really spoken with him.

"This is my brother, Valente. This is Anna."

"Hello Anna," Valente said. He wore a cap and loose-fitting pants with a dark tight tee shirt that displayed the well-formed muscles in his arms.

"My brother is a construction worker. He works on high-rise buildings."

"That must be challenging," Anna said

"It's good money. You get used to the height. I don't mind doing it."

"My mother hates that he does this kind of work. It is so dangerous. Men are always falling from those buildings."

"Ah, yes, my sweet sister, but I am like a cat, very graceful." He made his hands like cat paws and moved then toward Gabby; then he laughed.

"If I could move my body, I would hit you," Gabby said, laughing.

"My sister and my mother, they worry about me. But I do just fine." He smiled at Anna. His dark eyes danced with mischief.

He was attractive, not as handsome as Alex, who had movie-star good looks that made females of all ages turn to look at him wherever they went. Alex with his dark, mysterious, and brooding eyes, made women want to delve into his life, to rescue him from his demons, to be his salvation. Valente on the other hand, had even features, a warm smile, and a contagious, carefree disposition.

"So, when are you leaving here?" Valente asked Anna.

"I don't know. I feel fine, but the doctor will tell me when I can go," Anna said. She did feel fine, except for the depression that lingered from losing the baby and the anger she felt at Alex for disappearing again when she needed him.

"My mama says you and Gabby have become good friends. Maybe you're going to come to our house one Sunday for Sunday dinner. My mother, she makes delicious gravy."

"Thank you. That would be very nice."

"She's a pretty one," Valente said to his sister, but pointing to Anna.

"She's married, Valente."

"I shouldn't be surprised; all the pretty ones are taken." He smiled at Anna, but she saw by the look on his face that he was not discouraged.

Chapter 52

A week went by and Alex did not return to the hospital, neither did Uncle Max or Aunt Edith. However, the doctor had come and gone, giving Anna a clean bill of health and telling her that she would be discharged the following morning. Gabby's family had been at the hospital every day. They had come to like Anna, even brought her cookies and candy when they brought things for Gabby. She knew they wondered what had happened to Alex, but no one said a thing.

Anna vacillated between anger, fear, and despair. She could not figure out why she had not heard from Alex at all. Even in Cuba, when he'd done something like this before, he'd returned the following day. This had been over a week. What if he were dead? Anything could happen in New York. Hadn't the attack she'd just suffered proved that? What if they were all dead: Alex, Aunt Edith, Uncle Max? They could have been killed by a robber. So many possibilities, but if they were all right, then would they not at least have called? Something terrible had happened. She felt it.

She would be leaving the hospital the following morning. Soon she would have some idea of what had happened. At least she hoped she would.

Chapter 53

Alex could not take his wife home from the hospital to sleep on a bench in Battery Park. He had to find a way to get some money. For hours he'd wandered the streets; he had no money to buy anything to eat or drink. He was hungry, but more than that, he was distraught. As he passed a Red Cross building, he read the sign in the window. "Blood Donors: Get Paid for Your Blood."

He read the sign again.

Then he went inside. The nurse wrapped his arm until his vein stood up at attention, and then she pierced it with a needle. He sat watching as his blood filled a vial. When he was done, she gave him a glass of orange juice and a dollar.

"You must not give blood again for a month, all right? You see, it takes a month for your body to recoup the blood you have lost today," she said.

"I understand," Alex said, stuffing the dollar in his pocket. He would need ten dollars to rent an apartment for a month.

"Are there other blood donation centers in the city?"

"Yes, they are all over the city. Would you like a list?" The nurse asked.

"Yes, I would," Alex said.

"Now, remember, you must not give blood again for at least a month."

"I remember," Alex said.

He left and began walking toward the next blood donation center. If he could donate ten times, he would be able to take Anna home to a safe apartment somewhere.

By the third donation, Alex began to feel weak, nauseated. He'd had no food and he'd donated three pints of blood. He was dizzy, but he would go on to the next Red Cross center as soon as he could. First, he had to take a moment to sit down and rest.

Alex sat on the side of the street, his hand in his pocket gripping the three precious dollars. Only seven more… He wanted to lie down and sleep, just for a little while.

As he lay his head on the sidewalk, although his vision was foggy, he could see the faces on the passersby as they looked at him with disgust. His mind began to drift off as he remembered how he'd felt when he'd first come to New York and he saw the hobos on the streets. It was a mixture of pity and fear. Secretly he'd always feared that he would end up as one of them, and now he had.

Alex heard a loud voice from across the road, a voice he remembered. With difficulty he forced his eyes to focus, and then he saw him.

"Jew boy?" Alex heard the voice but he couldn't move. "Is that you?"

Alex tried to force himself to get up. He wanted to run, but try as he might, he could not will his muscles to move against the exhaustion. If that boy got a hold of him, he would steal his precious money. Alex's fingers, too weak to maintain their grip, released the dollar bills in his pocket. God help me, Alex thought. Then he passed out.

Chapter 54

When Anna was discharged from the hospital, she had no money for carfare home because her purse had been stolen. Embarrassed, but desperate, she asked Gabby to loan her the money to take the streetcar home. She explained what had happened, how she'd been robbed.

Gabby understood, but she had no cash with her in the hospital.

"Can you wait for an hour or so? My brother is coming. He will give you the money. I am sure of it."

"Yes, of course I can wait, and I don't want him to give it to me, just to lend it. Oh, Gabby, I am so ashamed to have to put you in this position," Anna said.

"Don't even think about it. What happened to you was not your fault. It could happen to anyone, especially here in New York. "

"I will pay you back. I promise," Anna said.

"It's Valente who has the money, not me. He is the one in my family who is earning much money."

"Then I will pay him back every cent."

Chapter 55

Alex opened his eyes to see the same group of boys he'd seen earlier that day in Battery Park. Although his mind was dim and clouded, and a nauseating ache pulsed at his temple so strongly he thought he might be having a stroke, a spasm of terror shot through the haze and he sat up straight. His hand immediately went to his pocket to check for the money. It was still there. Who were these young men? What did they want with him? And why had they not taken his money? He wished he had the strength to get up and run.

Chapter 56

"I'm going to see to it that you get home. I wouldn't think of letting you take the streetcars alone, coming right out of the hospital." Valente said.

"You don't have to do that. I'll just borrow the carfare and you can give me an address where I can send the money back to you as soon as I can get it. It might be a few weeks. I don't know. But I'll send it as soon as I can."

"I'm not worried about it. You needn't pay me back. Let's just say it is my way of thanking you for being such a good friend to my sister."

"I want to pay you back."

"For now, let's just get you home safely. We don't need to discuss the money just now. All right?" He smiled and took her arm.

"You take care of my friend, Valente, and please be a gentleman. Don't embarrass me. Remember, she's a married woman," Gabby said.

"Yes, yes, I remember. But thank you for reminding me again, Gabby." He bowed to his sister. "She is the queen of our family. We have to bow to her."

"Shut up, Valente," Gabby said, laughing. "He's always teasing me."

"Now, that is because you are so easy to tease," Valente said.

"When we were kids he used to torture me with insects."

"Did you?" Anna found herself getting lost in the banter that was so familiar to these siblings.

"Yep, I did," Valente said to Anna. Then, turning back to Gabby, "Ahhh, but when anyone else teased you, Gabby, who was there to protect you?"

"You were, of course," Gabby said, smiling at Valente.

"See, I'm not such a bad fellow…." Valente said to Anna.

"Will you be back later tonight?" Gabby asked, "I'm going to be lonely in here with Anna gone."

"Of course. Would I leave my baby sister alone in the hospital without anyone for company?"

Gabby just shook her head at him. "See you later, Valente." Then she turned to Anna. "I'll miss you. Will you keep in touch?"

"Of course. You know I will," Anna said.

"I'll see to it," Valente said. "You have our address, yes?" He asked Anna.

"Yes, Gabby gave it to me last night."

As they walked down the hall and out the doors into the street, Valente turned to Anna. "Why don't we stop and have a nice breakfast before you go home? It's on me."

"Oh, I don't know…"

"Come on, I'm hungry. I can't travel so far without eating. You have to stop and get something for my sake," he teased.

"Don't you have to go back to work?"

"Are you forgetting? It's Sunday… In fact maybe, just maybe you are going to come to our house for dinner tonight."

She looked at him skeptically.

"You'll bring your husband, of course," he said.

Anna wondered if Valente had noticed that Alex had not been at the hospital the entire week. She thought he might have, and she felt her face grow hot with shame.

Valente was a gentleman. He opened the door to the restaurant, ordered for her, and in many ways made her feel protected and cared for. Sitting across the table from this smiling, attractive Italian, with his carefree attitude and his willingness to spend a little bit of his cash, made her wish Alex could be a stronger man. With Alex, Anna had to be the backbone of the relationship. It had been that way from the start, and in the beginning, she'd liked it. It made her feel in charge. But as time went on, and she saw how easily Alex could fall apart, it became a burden.

"So, tell me all about you," Valente said.

"There is really nothing to tell."

"Such a pretty lady has nothing to tell?"

"Not really, just that I am looking for work and finding it very difficult here in America."

"Yes, it can be difficult. Our family came from Tuscany, beautiful country. My father was a farmer there; I too would have been a farmer. But we were the lucky ones, no?" He said, and smiled a wry smile. "Now I am living here in the land of opportunity, in a small, crowded apartment, stuffed to the brim with my parents, my sister and her husband, their three young children, Gabby, and myself. Usually we don't have hot water. And the toilet almost never works right, so with all these people crammed in this dump, the place always stinks. I only stay because they need the money I make to help them survive." He shrugged his shoulders. "And almost every day, in this wonderful city of New York, a man falls to his death doing the same job I am doing. One of these days maybe it's gonna be me." He sighed. "What can I do? The family needs me. I have to keep the job."

He'd been so lighthearted in Gabby's presence, but now Anna saw another side of Valente."

"Sometimes I resent them all. I wish I could just go off on my own and not have to worry about them. But Papa is so old, he can't do much anymore."

"Are you married?"

"No, not yet, although he would like me to be. I don't want my Papa to bring a girl over from Italy. I want to choose the woman I spend my life with." His dark eyes locked with hers, black as a starless sky. She was taken aback by his serious expression, but as soon as he saw that he'd made her uncomfortable, he changed his expression. His eyes twinkled again and he smiled warmly.

"It is very nice of you to help me."

"Can I be so bold as to say something? I hope I am not going to be offending you."

"Yes, go ahead."

"I just wanted to say that if I were your husband, I would have never left you alone in the hospital. I would have been with you every moment that I could."

She looked away and gazed out the window as she felt the tears building behind her eyes. Oh Alex… she thought. Where are you?

"I'm sorry. I didn't mean to upset you."

The food arrived, but Anna could not eat. She felt a lump in the back of her throat.

"Eat, please?" he said.

She nodded and picked up her napkin.

"Come on…" He smiled. "I've eaten here before. The food is very good. Well, maybe not so good as my mama's, but it isn't bad."

She smiled back at him and picked up her fork.

"Don't be so sad, Anna. Such a beautiful lady should not be sad," Valente said, and he reached over and touched her hand.

She looked up from her plate. Their eyes met.

Chapter 57

"Don't be so damn sensitive. So I called you Jew boy. So fucking what?" The boy had a thick New York accent. He wiped his crooked nose with the sleeve of his shirt, then handed Alex a hot dog he'd bought from the nearby vendor. "Eat this. You look like you're dying."

"Thank you," Alex said.

"Hey, you probably never guessed, but I'm a Jew too. My name is Abe Kohan. You are?" Abe asked.

"Alex Mittelman." Alex took a bite. He felt the salvia increase in his mouth as he began to gobble the food.

"Now you probably want to know why I been following you, right?"

Alex nodded.

"Ya see, I'm a business man. I got a whole group of fellas who sell newspaper subscriptions for me. They stand out on the corners. Every time they make a sale, I make a few cents. Got it?"

"So you want me to sell papers?"

"Well, ya see, that's just it. I don't want you to sell papers. I got enough men doing that. I'm trying to recruit a few boys to sell sandwiches outside of the World's Fair. From what I hear, the food inside the fair is real expensive. Mothers with lots of kids will be looking to feed them cheap. That's where you come in. Every morning you're gonna make sandwiches. Wrap 'em up and stand outside the gates of the fair. The loaf'll cost you about five cents, the jam another five. You sell the sandwiches for five cents apiece. And for every one that you sell, you're gonna pay me two cents. You got it? Now, if you turn out to be an ass and you try to do this without me, I'll send my boys over and they'll make you sorry. You understand?"

Alex nodded. He needed a job. This proposition felt like a godsend.

"So what do you say? You wanna do it?"

"Yes, of course I do." Alex squeezed the three dollars in his pocket.

"What's a matter?" Abe said.

"Nothing," Alex answered, still afraid that one of these street hoodlums might steal his money if they found out that he had some.

"Come on, what's your beef? I can see you got a problem. You might as well tell me."

"It's not with you I have a problem. You see, my wife is in the hospital. When she gets out, we have no place to live. Our apartment building was burned down. I have a few dollars but not enough to rent a place."

"Hmmm…" Abe said. "So you want me to cuff you the dough to get an apartment?"

"I don't know what you mean."

"I mean you want me to make you a loan?"

"Oh no, I couldn't expect that."

"Well, I got an idea. Finish your food and follow me," Abe said.

Alex stuffed the rest of the hot dog into his mouth, got up, and followed Abe.

"You speak good English for a greenhorn." Abe looked over at Alex and saw the look on his face, and then Abe laughed. "Hey, what's the sense in you taking offense? My folks were greenhorns. Nothing to be ashamed of."

"What's a greenhorn?" Alex asked.

"An immigrant, coming from Europe, that's all." Abe patted Alex's back. "Come on, I think I know a fella who can help you."

They walked for two miles, until they reached an area very similar to the one where Alex and Anna had lived with her aunt and uncle.

"Wait here," Abe said as he started walking toward the door of a rundown tenement. "Hey watch it." Abe said to a child who accidently hit him with a ball he was throwing.

Just as Abe walked up the sidewalk, a short stockman limped out of the building. In fact, before Alex saw his face he thought he was a child with a deformity. Now Alex knew that the man was a dwarf.

"Gimpy!" Abe said. "How you doing?"

"All right, Abe. You?" They shook hands.

"Can't complain. Listen, you still got that garden apartment for rent?"

"Yeah, nobody wants it. It floods when it rains and it still stinks from the last flood. Fulla mold, too."

"I got a business proposal for you."

"Yeah, so what else is new? I wouldn't expect anything less from you Abe. Go ahead, spring it on me."

"I got this guy who needs to rent a place. He don't have too much dough, but then again that place ain't worth too much, right?"

"I ain't saying nothing. I'm just listening."

"He'll give you two dollars and fifty cents for the first month. Then from then on he'll pay you three dollars. What do you say?"

"That ain't enough. Come on Abe? It's still an apartment."

"Gimpy, right now you ain't getting' nothing.' the place is vacant. It stinks; don't nobody want to live in it. And let's face it, two bucks-fifty is more than you had before I got here, right?"

Gimpy rubbed his head with his short, fat fingers. Alex watched and listened, saying nothing. He was holding his breath, praying that the little man would accept the offer.

"Yeah, I guess so…better than nothing. What the hell, I'll take it."

"Good. Good. Now, you gotta pay me a little finder's fee. I mean, shit Gimpy, we all gotta survive."

"I expected that too. I know you better than to do something for nothing, Abe. So, I'll give you a dollar for finding me a tenant; that oughta do it. Then, I'll get it back from the owner of this dump. He'll be glad I rented that place. It's been vacant forever."

"Good enough," Abe said, shaking his hand. "Come on over here Alex, I want to introduce you to your new building manager."

Chapter 58

The apartment needed a lot of work, but at least they would have a roof over their heads and a place where Anna would be safe. As soon as he earned enough money, Alex would move them out. But for now, it seemed as if God had intervened with a blessing.

"I left you with a little dough to buy the loaf, the jam and pick up a little food for yourself. You're also gonna need money for the subway to the fairgrounds. It's in Queens. Have you ever been out that way?"

"No," Alex said.

"I'll give you directions. When can you start?"

"Tomorrow?"

"Yeah, that's good. Here, let me spot you a little extra cash in case of an emergency. You'll owe it to me from your first day's pay. Now don't be a rum-dumb and try to run out on me. I know where you live," Abe said.

"I wouldn't do that. I appreciate your help, so much," Alex said, and there were tears in his eyes.

"Hey, hey… Don't start bawling like a little girl. Go on and get your wife. I'll drop by your apartment tomorrow night to collect my share."

Alex bit his lip. The emptiness that always plagued him like a wound deep in his chest seemed more pronounced and aching right now. His hand went to his throat, which was as dry as the sand on a scorching afternoon in the desert.

"Thank you," Alex said as Abe walked away without ever hearing him, because his voice never rose above a whisper. Cruelty made Alex nervous and angry, but kindness made him cry.

Chapter 59

"What do you mean she was discharged and she is not here?" Alex asked the nurse in Anna's room when he found another girl in the bed she'd occupied.

"She went home this morning. My brother took her," Gabby said. She was a little disgusted by the fact that it had taken Alex so long to show up.

"When?"

"A few hours ago."

"Oh my God!"

"What?" Gabby asked.

"Anna doesn't know..." Alex said.

"Doesn't know what?"

But Alex was already running down the hospital corridor.

Chapter 60

"I'm sorry," Valente said. "I didn't mean to offend you."

Anna nodded. She wanted to be offended, the way a married woman should feel when another man flirted with her. But in truth, it scared her just how much she was enjoying Valente's company.

"Can you forgive me?"

"Yes. It's all right," she said.

"It's just that, I feel that there is something very special about you..."

"Valente, don't. I am married, very married. I am not in the market for a boyfriend on the side, if you understand what I mean."

"Again, I am sorry. It's just that..."

"Perhaps we should go. I need to get home," Anna said.

He called for the waitress and requested the check.

"I feel so funny, you paying for my food. I will pay you back everything you have given me. I will pay you for this food and for the carfare."

"It is my pleasure. I would not accept any money from you, ever. You insult me by offering."

"Well, thank you."

"You are very welcome," he said, and his smile made her tingle in a way that made her feel very guilty.

As they walked down the street, Anna noticed how Valente walked on the outside toward the curb. His manners impressed her.

"It is a beautiful day. Soon it will be cold. Why don't we take advantage of the nice weather and walk through Central Park?" Valente suggested.

"I don't think I should."

"Please, do it for me?" he asked.

Anna was angry with Alex, tired of his emotional breakdowns. She had endured enough of the constant threat that he would collapse at any moment. There was no telling where he had disappeared to this past week. All she knew was that he was not going to continue working with her uncle, and he would have to find work elsewhere. When she'd first met Alex she'd been so taken in by his broken spirit. Anna had longed to hold him, to mother him, to save him from the demons that haunted his tortured soul. Instead she'd found that now her spirit was sinking and she had begun to feel trapped by his needy, depressive, self-indulgent behavior.

She was still young. She longed to be young, to enjoy life...

"Valente?" She said, turning to look at him.

"Yes..."

"Why don't we take that walk through the park?"

"I'd love to, Anna..."

There was an old man on the corner selling single roses. Valente ran ahead of Anna to the vendor. After flipping a coin out of his pocket and handing it to the old man, he selected a red rose. Walking back, he handed it to Anna. Then he took her hand and kissed it.

She smiled, she felt good, like dancing on the clouds, even though she still felt terribly guilty.

Chapter 61

Alex's heart beat in his throat as he ran all the way back to the charred remains of the tenement where they had lived.

Even though it had been days since the fire, the area smelled of smoke for at least a block on either side of the building.

Chapter 62

"Oh my God!" Anna said as she approached the burnt out ruins. She ran forward, her hand covering her lips.

Valente followed close behind her.

Two women who lived next door stood on the stoop outside while their children played. A pile of orange peels lay on the step as they divided the slices between them. Anna recognized them both. She ran over to the women.

"What happened here?" Anna asked, pointing to the burned-out ruins.

"You don't know?"

"No, I've been sick. I was in the hospital."

"What was wrong with you?" One of the women with a long grey wool dress asked.

"Nothing, it was nothing. What happened here, please tell me?"

The other woman, known to be one of the neighborhood gossips said, "There was a fire." She got up from where she was seated, and put a hand on Anna's shoulder "I'm sorry. You're aunt and uncle didn't make it."

"What? Uncle Max? Aunt Edith?" Anna asked. She could hardly catch her breath. "Are you sure?" she asked, but she didn't wait for an answer. She knew that the women spoke the truth. That was why her aunt and uncle had not returned to the hospital. Anna's face was hot. She could not catch a deep breath, and she was afraid she might pass out. But she had to ask, she had to know, "My husband? Was my husband in the fire too?" Anna suddenly felt the love she had always felt toward Alex come creeping up and filling her with fear. God help me if anything has happened to him. I will never forgive myself.

"No, I saw him here the day after it happened. He's fine."

If he was unharmed then where was he? Anna felt her head spinning. She leaned against the iron rail that led to the apartment building. Damn you, Alex, she thought. You've run away again, disappeared when I really needed you, leaving me to face the loss of the baby, and now this, all alone. Once she knew he was all right, she was angry with him again. It was time to face facts. Alex could not be depended upon. He would never be a man she could count on through bad times. She would miss him, miss everything they'd shared together, but perhaps it was best that he was gone.

Valente touched her shoulder from behind. "Anna."

She whirled around, remembering that he was there.

"Anna, I'm sorry. Come, you can stay at my house. My mother will understand," Valente said.

But Anna just stood there; her feet were glued to the pavement.

"Come." His voice was tender and his arm felt strong as he enveloped her shoulder.

She was trembling, leaning against him.

"Come…" He whispered again.

Chapter 63

There was no use just standing there in front of the ruins of her life. Anna clumsily thanked the two women and then turned back to Valente.

"Are you sure your mother won't mind? I will only stay until I can get a place of my own."

"I am sure." Valente smiled. "Very sure. Everything will be fine. I'll take care of you. Come away from here. Let's go."

It felt good to just drop the burden for a few minutes and let Valente lead her away. She rested her head on his shoulder and he gently squeezed her arm.

Anna's thoughts weighted heavily on her mind as she began to walk away. She had so many questions, and none of them could be answered. Valente pushed their way through a group of children playing with jacks and a ball, gently leading Anna, then another group of little girls playing hopscotch.

Where was Alex? Would she ever see him again? Anna wondered. He was such a troubled man. Even she could not help him. Alex.

Valente and Anna were halfway down the street, almost ready to turn the corner, when Anna heard Alex cry out.

"Anna..! Anna! Please…"

She turned around to see him standing there, his hands limp at his sides. He looked so small and helpless that she felt as if her heart was breaking. His hands went up in a gesture of desperation.

"Anna…" he cried again.

Tears fell from her eyes. What was she going to do with him?

"Please…" Alex ran toward her.

She glared at him. She had so many questions, but all she could do was shake her head.

Alex glanced at Valente, and Anna saw the hurt in his eyes. She wanted to turn and walk away with Valente, to leave Alex's constant need to feed off her strength behind. It was becoming exhausting to watch his every move and wonder if he was going to have an emotional episode and disappear for an undetermined amount of time, or leave a perfectly good job in a terrible economy because of something that troubled him from his past. Anything could set him off, anything at all, and he needed constant reassurance from her that no matter what happened, she would be there, she would understand, and she would love and nurture him. That afternoon with Valente, she'd allowed herself to imagine a life where for once she could be the weak one, where she could have the indulgence of leaning on someone else, and he would be there and be strong enough to lift *her* up.

"Anna..." Alex said. "Anna, my Anna?" His hands went up in a gesture of helplessness. His handsome face contorted with pain.

She shook her head, and tried to turn away, but not before she saw that there were tears in his eyes.

"I love you, Anna."

Again, she shook her head.

"I can't, Alex…"

He fell to knees, and she heard the crack as his knee caps hit the pavement. "Please, Anna, don't leave me. You are my whole life, my everything… The reason I get up in the morning, the reason I am still alive… Anna, please."

She was angry. He'd evoked feelings of guilt in her and she resented them.

"Then where in hell were you, Alex? I was in the hospital for a week. I had no idea what happened here…to Uncle Max and Aunt Edith. I was coping with the loss of our child. But you? No Alex, you had to go off alone. Yes, our lives always have to revolve around what Alex needs. I can't do it anymore. I just can't."

"Anna, please listen to me. I had to find us a place to live. I couldn't bring you home from the hospital without a place. I wouldn't let you live in the park like a bum and subject you to constant danger. So, I sold my blood in order to get enough money to rent an apartment. As soon as I found somewhere to take you, I came for you. I was never going to leave you…"

"Oh God, Alex."

"Please Anna. I have a job, too. It's not much, but it's a start. Please, don't leave me. Give me another chance. I promise I will never do this again. If I feel that I must be on my own for some reason, I will talk to you about it. I won't run away. We will work it out together."

She loved him.

As she watched her incredibly handsome husband begging her on his knees in the middle of Delancey Street, her heart began to melt. Dear Lord, Alex was truly handsome. There was no doubt about that.

"Do you promise never to disappear again?"

"Yes. I promise. Please, Anna. I love you…"

She turned to Valente, and carefully removed his arm from her shoulder; then she gently took her small bag from his hand. "I'm sorry," she said. "Thank you for everything today. I will pay you back all of the money that you spent, but I must go with my husband now."

Valente nodded. "If you ever need me. You have my address…"

"Yes. Thank you. I will mail the money to you."

Anna watched Valente straighten his back and walk away. Then she reached down and took Alex's hand. "Let's go home to that apartment you were talking about."

"It's not as nice as I would like it to be, but as soon as I can I will get us a better place to live."

Chapter 64

The first day at the World's Fair, Alex sold his entire loaf of sandwiches before ten o'clock. From where he stood, just outside, he could see many of the exhibits. Right inside the gates there was a Bavarian village that was so reminiscent of Germany it made him long for home, and a Hall of Nations that gave him a glimpse into countries he had never seen. There were automobile exhibits, futuristic refrigeration, and a big poster of a black and white cow that said, "It sure makes you proud to be an American." But of all the exhibits, the one that he most longed to enter was the Jewish Palestine Pavilion. Ever since he was a little boy, he'd heard talk of a Jewish state, a place somewhere far across the seas, in a land called Palestine. For the Jews, this land represented hope, dreams...a future where Jews would live in safety.

On the second day, Alex invested his entire share of the money that he'd made the previous day and bought several loaves of bread. Anna helped him to prepare the sandwiches.

Abe was right. Many of the mothers bought his sandwiches for the children because they were far less expensive and much less rich than the food at the fair.

By the end of the week, Anna was baking cookies to sell and she and Alex were making up several loaves of bread each day.

Abe was pleased with his share, and even offered Alex another opportunity to earn some cash.

"Listen Jew boy, I have a couple of ideas," Abe said when Alex paid him for the week. "Why don't you and your wife make up lots of sandwiches and cookies for all the other fellows too? They can pay you a percentage, and that will give you some extra dough. Of course you'll have to give me a little for a finder's fee."

"Yes, Abe, we can certainly do that," Alex said. He knew Anna would help him. Together they would do all right, and they would manage.

At night after work, Alex studied his English. He'd become fluent in writing and reading, as well as speaking the language.

When Alex was at work, Anna cleaned the apartment. She opened the windows and tried to air the musty smell from the flood out of the tiny rooms. However, she knew that the first hard rain would bring another flood. So, as soon as possible, she and Alex hoped to move. The water when it worked ran ice cold. In order to bathe, Anna boiled water on the stove and added it to the tub until it was lukewarm. The neighbors Anna spoke to warned her that in the winter the entire population of the building frozen from lack of heat. They kept the ovens on in their apartments all day, in order to stay warm.

Every day, Anna thought of Max and Edith. They had been kind to her and Alex, and she missed them. She missed her parents too, but they never answered her letters.

One night after they finished their evening meal, Anna was tired and went off to bed early. Alex couldn't sleep. It had been years since he'd felt the urge to write, but tonight it came back to him. He wanted to put down in words all of the things he'd seen at the fair. And so he began to pen articles.

Alex missed having a typewriter, but even working manually with pencil and paper he felt as if he'd come home. He was a writer. Before he'd been arrested in Germany, he'd been a journalist. It was in his blood, and now that he was writing again, he began to feel the depression he constantly battled begin to lift a little.

One morning as she was sipping coffee and wrapping sandwiches, Anna happened to read one of the articles Alex left on the table. It was about the Jewish Palestine Pavilion at the fair.

"This is very good," she said as he Alex walked into the room. "Did you write this last night?"

"Yes, I've been writing little articles about the different exhibits. I want them as reminders of what I have seen. Besides that, it makes me feel good."

"Alex…"

"Yes, love?"

"Why don't you submit this to the newspaper?" Anna said.

"Oh, I couldn't. It isn't that good."

"But it is…"

"No, I don't think so. This is America. My English is not good enough. And, besides, who wants to read about Jews here? People are demonstrating their hated for us in the park. It's just a little article about Palestine, for my own enjoyment," he said, kissing her cheek, then gathering the sandwiches and putting them into a basket.

"Here," she handed him the bag for the other sellers. "And here are some extra cookies too."

He took them and left.

It had rained lightly the night before, and a quarter of an inch of dirty water and sediment had seeped in to the apartment through the foundation. There was always the smell of mold and sewage to contend with in this filthy place. Anna looked around her on all sides. It would take another day's worth of heavy cleaning to make this hole in the ground even moderately livable.

She looked out the window and sighed as she saw Alex walking quickly toward the subway. He was doing his best. She couldn't fault him for that. But perhaps he needed a little help.

As soon as Alex was out of sight, Anna got dressed and went to the corner, where she bought a newspaper. Although she was not as advanced in English as Alex, she could read and write enough to understand. The address of the newspaper office was right on the inside front cover of the paper.

She did her best to construct a letter of introduction. Then she went through Alex's papers and chose the best articles she could find. They were all about the World's Fair. And right now, the World's Fair was the most exciting thing going on in New York, and everyone wanted to know more about it.

After folding the articles neatly, she carefully addressed the envelope, walked downstairs and purchased a stamp at the post office, then sent them off to the newspaper.

Alex never missed the articles. He never realized that they were gone until he received an answer from the paper three weeks later. They wanted him to come in for an interview.

Chapter 65

"You sent these articles to the newspaper?" Alex asked.

"Are you angry?" Anna looked into his eyes.

"No, I just didn't expect this."

"Well, you are an excellent journalist. This is what comes naturally to you."

He nodded. "What would I ever do without my Anna?" he asked and smiled at her. Then walking over, he kissed her lips lightly. "Anna, my Anna…" He smiled.

"So you'll go for the interview?"

"Of course I will go."

The paper bought Alex's articles and asked for more. He wrote freelance for the next six months while Anna continued to prepare the cookies and sandwiches for the other sellers.

A blast of heavy snow fell upon New York City that November of 1941. As the neighbors had promised, the heat hardly worked. Alex and Anna wore coats even when they were inside, and Anna felt as if she would never be warm again. Then, like a blessing and a curse, the weather warmed up for a few days, giving them a break from the bone-chilling cold. But it was just enough time for the snow to melt, leaving Alex and Anna with two inches of dirty water on the floor of their apartment.

"Let's move. We can afford it now," Alex said. He was doing fairly well with the paper, earning almost fifty dollars a month, and even though the fair had ended and that source of income had dried up, they had saved enough to move to a decent flat.

The new apartment was furnished, overlooking the street, on the second floor of a well-maintained building just a few miles from the newspaper offices. The hallways and vestibule smelled a little like boiled cabbage, but other than that, it was a fine new home. The neighborhood was better and the apartment much cleaner.

Every night Alex and Anna studied until they passed the test and became citizens of the United States of America.

Alex began writing news articles and the editor of the paper loved them. He offered Alex a salaried position with the paper, which paid him well enough to keep him and Anna comfortable.

"Can I go back to school now that things are better for us?" Anna asked.

She had always wanted to further her education. Alex knew this, and he put great value on learning, so he was pleased at her request.

Before she could attend college, Anna had to finish high school. She didn't mind. She loved every minute that she spent in the classroom. It was then that she decided that someday she would like to be a teacher.

Chapter 66

On a very cold morning a few weeks before the Christmas holiday, Alex dressed for work. He wore heavy gray wool pants, and a white shirt with a black jacket and black tie. After wrapping a heavy wool scarf around his neck, he kissed Anna goodbye and left.

Most of his colleagues at the paper were Christians and they were looking forward to the coming holiday. The offices would be closed for Christmas Eve and Christmas Day so they could enjoy time with their families. In celebration, the newspaper had put together a small office party, a luncheon spiced with a little alcoholic holiday cheer that would take place that afternoon at a nearby restaurant.

At eleven forty-five, the office closed for the day so that everyone could attend the gathering. They walked in groups of two or three for half a block, sliding on the slippery pavement to the restaurant. Icicles hung from the awnings of buildings and the branches of trees. It had snowed the night before, dusting the city with a thin white powder that had turned to black slush where the cars had driven through the streets.

The waiters brought out steaming and delicious platters of roast turkey, stuffing, cranberry sauce, and mashed potatoes. A piano player crooned old-fashioned holiday songs while everyone joined in.

Alex was talking with a man who he'd met a few times at the office. They sat across the table from each other, discussing cigars, as the man puffed like a locomotive on a thick Cuban cigar. He said his name was Mike and told Alex how surprised he was that Alex knew so much about Cuban tobacco.

"You're not from Cuba. Your accent doesn't sound Spanish to me," Mike said, prying a little, wanting to know more.

"No. I'm not." Alex tried not to tell anyone that he came from Germany. It saved the aggravation of explaining.

"You immigrants never cease to amaze me," Mike said.

Once lunch was over the party began to break up. The boss came around the tables and handed out envelopes containing Christmas bonus checks.

"Merry Christmas," he said as he handed Alex the envelope. "I wish it could be more, but the economy has been so bad…"

"Thank you, sir." Alex had never received a gift from his employer, and he appreciated whatever he might find in that envelope.

Just as everyone was saying their goodbyes and wrapping themselves back into their winter coats, scarves and boots to head for the subway, the owner of the restaurant came in to the room. His face was as white as a funeral lily.

"We've been attacked," he said. "The United States has been attacked. The Japanese just bombed Pearl Harbor, in Hawaii."

It was December 7, 1941. Japan and Germany were allies.

Alex imagined Nazi flags hanging from the buildings in New York, pictures of Hitler inside his office, all of his friends turning on him when they discovered his Jewish heritage. He felt his entire body grow hot and clammy. The room turned dark. He felt dizzy and lightheaded.

Alex fainted.

When he awoke, Anna knelt there beside him. Next to her stood his boss and all of his fellow employees.

"You gave us quite a scare, Alex," his boss said. "I telephoned your wife and she took a taxi right over. Come on, let me help you up."

Alex stood on wobbly legs and leaned on Anna as they walked outside to flag a cab. The cold wind sobered him, and he remembered what had happened.

"Have you heard the news?" Alex asked Anna.

"Yes. I know. We have been attacked. Come on, Alex. You must try not to upset yourself. We'll discuss this further when we get home."

All the way to their apartment in the taxi, Anna heard Alex's labored breathing. She was worried that he might pass out again. When they arrived, she helped him up the stairs to their flat. Then she laid him on the sofa and put up a pot of water to boil for tea.

Alex sat up and turned on the radio. He'd purchased a secondhand radio just a few months prior. As he listened, he could hear the shock in the voices of the announcers. No one had expected this.

Hitler, Alex thought. Did Hitler have something to do with all of this?

Anna sat beside Alex and gave him a cup of tea. Neither of them slept. They barely spoke as they listened through the night, anxiously awaiting news.

At 12:30 the following day, President Roosevelt came over the radio and declared the United States officially at war.

"This is a day that will live in infamy," the President said.

Alex looked at Anna, his eyes glaring, his face white as the snow that fell the night before.

"Don't disappear on me, Alex," she said, shaking his arm when she saw the look in his eyes. "I can't cope with that again. You promised. Please, Alex. I don't need the extra worry."

He nodded. Then he took her hand in his and put it to his cheek. "I won't disappear. I am here. We'll see this through together."

She brought his hand to her heart. "Alex. Oh, Alex… Don't worry. We will be all right," Anna said. She had a secret that she had planned to tell him on *Hanukah*, but now she didn't know if she should tell him at all. He was so delicate, so unstable, and she couldn't be sure how the news might affect him.

Chapter 67

Anna couldn't say exactly when Alex started drinking heavily. All she knew was that he seemed to bury all of the demons that followed him in the bottom of a whiskey bottle. She worried about him constantly. However, as much as he drank, he never allowed it to interfere with his work. And for that at least, Anna was thankful.

Once she conquered the English language, school became fun. Anna enjoyed the challenge of learning new things, and although she was much older than the other students were, she made friends.

When he was not at work, Alex listened to the radio obsessively. Each night when he arrived at home, he didn't even take the time to change his clothes; instead, he immediately flipped on the radio and sat down with a grave expression on his face. When President Roosevelt gave his fireside chats, Anna dared not interrupt. She knew not to say a word.

"I feel terribly guilty every day," Alex said, "I am here, living well, eating good food, and sleeping in a warm bed. I am safe, while other American boys are fighting overseas, and Jews are being persecuted in Europe. These American soldiers are dying for me… I should be there. I should be with them. They are keeping Hitler from coming, sending his troops to the United States."

Anna had been preparing dinner, but she stopped to sit down beside him.

"Do you ever feel guilty?" Alex asked

"Of course I do. I feel guilty because I left my parents, and my friends. But what can we do Alex?"

"I think of Manny all the time. I see his eyes in my dreams and wonder if he is suffering somewhere."

"I know. He did a lot for us. If not for Manny we would be in Europe, probably under Nazi rule."

"Yes, and we might be dead. He gave us our lives. And me? I have done nothing, nothing for anyone except for being the cause of the death of my whole family," Alex said. His hands were balled up in fists on his lap as he leaned forward, shoulders slumped and head down.

"You have to stop thinking about that. There is nothing you can do to change the past, Alex, nothing."

"I know. I know, and that is why it bothers me so much."

"Perhaps Manny and Elke got married. Maybe they went to England," Anna said.

"The Germans are bombing the hell out of London. If they are in England, they are in constant danger."

When Alex fell into one of his depressive states like this, Anna had learned that there was nothing she could say or do to pull him out of it. It just had to run its course.

He filled the shot glass with golden brown whiskey, which he poured down his throat in a single swallow.

"You have been drinking quite a bit lately."

"It's the only thing that makes me feel better."

Anna glared at him. She gritted her teeth. All of their married life, he had been so damned much work. Then she poured herself a shot and forced it down quickly. The bitter taste burned her throat, but the effect was good. It calmed her nerves and quelled her anger, at least for a moment.

The following day, Alex did not return from work on time. Anna began to worry. He had been very depressed the previous day, and she always feared that he might disappear again. The sun set, and it was almost bedtime before Anna heard Alex's key turn in the door. She sighed with relief.

"Anna, I am sorry I'm late. But there is something I must discuss with you."

Chapter 68

It was a good thing that Anna had not told Alex about her surprise. All day long she had been having terrible stomach cramps. She'd missed school, and then Alex had been very late coming home, so she hadn't had a chance to tell him. Perhaps the constant worry over Alex had gotten to her. Perhaps she just could not carry a child full term.

"Anna…" Alex called again. "I'm home I need to talk to you."

"I'm in the bathroom. I'll be right out," Anna said.

There was blood on her underwear and blood in the water of the toilet. Anna felt like crying, or screaming, or beating her fists against the wall, but she knew it wouldn't help. She was less than a month pregnant, and now she'd lost the baby.

"Anna, are you here?"

Damn him, she thought. Can't I have a single moment that is not about taking care of his needs? I am upset, my heart is breaking. Can't I just be left alone?

"Anna…"

"I'll be right there," she said.

"I'm sorry I'm late." Alex said.

"I said I'll be right there."

Anna washed away the blood that had stained her inner thighs, and then she put the rags she used for her menstrual period in place. She had been so hopeful that this child would fulfill her need to love something pure and undamaged.

Leaning her head against the cool cement of the bathroom wall, she sighed; then the tears came, and she lost control and wept.

"Anna, are you all right? I said I need to discuss something with you."

"Yes, I'm fine." She frowned, annoyed, as she splashed cold water on her face. Then she dried off and walked out into the living room to see what Alex had in store for her now.

Chapter 69

"I've enlisted in the army," he said, placing his enlistment papers on the table next to his uniform.

"My God, Alex," Anna sunk down into a chair. "You should have talked this over with me first."

"I know, but now at least I will be doing something to help. I won't be so useless. I will be fighting against the Germans."

"Alex. Come on, you're not a fighter. My God, you could be killed."

"Yes, I realize that, but this is something that I must do. I will be an American soldier." He smiled at her, a strange, sad smile.

She could feel the deep furrow between her eyes, but she just nodded. It was no use to argue with him.

"I will be paid fifty dollars a month. I'll send you money to live on until I return."

Anna was tired, physically, emotionally, and mentally. She was too weak from the loss of blood and the loss of the baby to cope with the bomb Alex had just dropped on her.

"Your dinner is on the stove. I am going to bed," Anna said.

Chapter 70

When Alex left for boot camp, Anna felt lost and so alone. Except for when Alex had been gone for a week during her hospital stay, and when she'd boarded the *St. Louis* by herself, Anna had never lived alone.

She continued to go to school, but classes only lasted a few hours a day, and then she would return to the dark, lonely apartment and wait for a letter from Alex. As she had expected, he corresponded regularly, and she promptly answered. From what his letters told her, Alex was stationed at Camp Benning in Georgia. "Besides learning to fight, I am learning to repair vehicles, tanks, planes, and automobiles." His letters explained how rigorous his basic training was; each morning he was awakened before sunrise and put through an intensive exercise regimen. Alex wrote of his difficult, demanding drill sergeant, and of how he had almost no time to himself. But at least, he said, he did not have very much opportunity to dwell on his depression. At night when he lay down, he was so exhausted that he fell asleep immediately.

Anna was lonely. She had no real friends. Her school friends were all much younger, and although she asked them to come to dinner, none of them ever came. With no one to cook for but herself, she hardly ate, so her already slender figure grew sickly thin. Staring out the window, reading, or listening to the radio all night was maddening. The days faded into one another. She began falling asleep as she read, sitting in her chair. To Anna it felt as if she'd become an old woman with no place to go and no one to talk to. Hers was not a fulfilling life. Realizing this, Anna decided to go to work.

The following morning she walked to the corner and bought a newspaper. Then she returned home, put on a pot of coffee, and began to search the want ads. With all of the men going off to war, the jobs had grown more plentiful. There was an opening in a meat packing plant for a secretary. Anna could type, but not very fast, and she had never learned shorthand. She continued to scan the list of jobs that met her limited qualifications. Housekeeper for a family on Long Island, a waitress in a family diner, a line server in a hospital cafeteria, an elevator operator... She took a pen and put a check beside each one. Then, as her eyes moved down the page, she saw an opening for a sales person to work in the women's dress department at Gimbels department store. Anna loved fashion. This was a job she would enjoy.

Anna got dressed, and with paper in hand, she headed to the subway. She wore a straight black skirt that came to her mid-calf, and a starched white blouse with a peter pan collar, and a simple, but stylish black wool coat. Her shoulder-length hair was parted on the side and combed neatly into a pageboy.

Why not start by applying for the job she would most prefer? Anna took the subway to 34th Street, got off, and began walking. Although it was already April, it was still cold outside. Now the snow had begun to melt and turn to gray slush, making way for spring. Anna pulled the collar of her coat tighter around her neck. She knew right where Gimbels was located. Occasionally, she'd come downtown shopping, and as she'd passed the window she couldn't help but stop and stare at the beautiful window displays.

"Excuse me," she said to a young girl straightening a gorgeous pair of black velvet opera-length gloves in the millinery department. "Can you direct me to personnel, please?"

The woman laid the gloves on a glass table next to a wide-brimmed black hat sporting a red feather plume. "Sure, right down that hall and then to your left, there's a big sign that says 'Personnel.' You can't miss it."

Anna loved the click her low-heeled pumps made as she walked along the white marble floor, clutching her small leather handbag. The overhead lighting cast a glow over everything in the store. When she happened to catch a glimpse of herself in a mirror in passing, she decided that the lighting made her look prettier than she actually was. A good selling tool, she thought. If people looked good in the product, they would buy without hesitation, especially women. Even though the war effort had taken all of the silk and nylon, the stockings of cotton and rayon that were presented were stylish and well made. Each department displayed gorgeous items in the latest fashion, and she couldn't help but turn look at each one. As she passed the perfume counter, a whiff of a light floral fragrance rose up to greet her. This was where she wanted to spend her afternoons. This store was where she wanted to work.

Anna entered under the sign that said Personnel Office.

"May I help you?" A pretty young girl with clear skin as pale as fresh cream sat behind a mahogany desk.

"I would like to fill out an application for the position that you have advertised in the paper," Anna said.

With a smile, the girl handed Anna a clipboard with the application and a pencil. "Just let me know when you are finished, and I will tell Mrs. Parker."

"Thank you," Anna said, and she sat down.

When Anna finished writing her answers with careful penmanship, the girl took her application and asked Anna to have a seat and wait.

A few minutes later, a woman entered. Her dark hair was cropped in the latest style; she wore a knee-length dress that fit her slender frame perfectly. She picked up the clipboard at the reception desk, and then extended her manicured hand to Anna.

"I'm Grace Parker," she said, "I will be interviewing you for the position."

Anna smiled and extended her hand.

"Nice to meet you, Mrs. Parker."

"Come into my office."

Fifteen minutes later Anna had a job. She could not believe that it had been that easy. Grace Parker said that she liked Anna's style. She also appreciated Anna's willingness to work long hours. For now, Anna would put her education on hold. She thought it best to save as much money as she could, and when Alex returned, perhaps they could move out of the city and put a down payment on a house.

She wanted to get home to put her clothes together to decide what she would wear tomorrow, because tomorrow would be her first day of work.

As soon as she got her first paycheck, she would send Valente the money she owed him.

Anna stopped at the store to pick up a few grocery items, and then she went home. When she arrived, she checked her mailbox. There was a letter from Camp Pendleton, but the address was not written in Alex's hand. "Oh my dear God," she thought as she unlocked the door to her apartment. "What now?"

Chapter 71

Although she was a nervous wreck and she wanted to rip the envelope open, Anna forced herself to go to the kitchen to get a knife to open the letter. She had manicured her nails that morning and wanted to keep them looking groomed for work the following day. Grace had made a point of telling her that since she was working in ladies dresses, it was important that her nails be manicured and her hair styled at all times.

Anna could hardly hold the letter straight to cut the envelope open, her hands were trembling so badly.

As she carefully put the knife into the top of the envelope, there was a knock on the door. Since Anna almost never had visitors, she jumped. Was it the army, with bad news? She looked at the front of the envelope again. It was definitely not Alex's handwriting; if not his, then whose? And why had someone else needed to write to her? Was Alex dead?

Breathe, she thought. Just breathe.

The knock came again. Anna stood up. She straightened her skirt. Then she opened the door, calmly.

"Anna Mittelman, right?" It was a woman. She looked to be close to Anna's age, but unlike Anna's, her clothing was old fashioned and her hair styled in a bun, like a grandmother. She was heavyset and had thick skin and a ruddy completion.

"Yes, I am Anna Mittelman."

The woman pushed herself inside. "We are neighbors. I was wondering if perhaps you had some onions I could borrow."

"No, I'm sorry; I don't have any right now," Anna said, looking at the strange woman with annoyance.

"I was cooking and I ran out."

"Sorry I couldn't help." Anna still stood at the door holding it open, expecting this odd creature to leave.

Instead the heavy set woman sat down. "Do you have a cup of coffee?"

"Not prepared but I can brew a pot, if you would like." Anna found the woman irksome and wished she would leave.

"Yes. I would love that. By the way, my name is Wera Krubinsky. My husband was just shipped overseas, to somewhere in the Pacific. I got a letter today, but he said he couldn't give me the exact location. I'm really sorry to bother you, but I just needed someone to talk to. That's why I came over. I don't have no family here. My family is Europe, Poland. And now with my husband gone..."

Anna nodded feeling sorry for the woman. "My family is in Europe as well."

The coffee began to percolate and the smell filled the apartment. Anna looked over at the envelope. She wished this Wera woman would go and leave her alone so that she could see what the letter contained.

"I'm so worried. My Joey, he was shipped off yesterday. I'm beginning to wish we had never become citizens of this America. Maybe then he would not have felt like he had to go. What if he gets killed? What am I going to do without him? I can't go back to Poland, not with Hitler there."

The more Wera Krubinsky talked about her husband, the more Anna's anxiety increased. Please, Wera Krubinsky, go home already, Anna thought. Any other time she would have welcomed the company. But now all she wanted was to be alone so she could open that letter.

"I'm sorry, Wera. I must get ready for school," Anna said after a half hour had passed.

"Why don't you come across the hall for coffee tomorrow?"

"I am starting a new job. I won't be home until seven tomorrow night."

"Then, I will make supper for the two of us. You'll come?" Wera smiled. She seemed so happy to have a friend.

It would be good to share some time and a meal with a friend. Anna smiled and nodded. "Yes, I will come. Thank you for dropping by."

"I'll see you tomorrow then?"

"Yes, tomorrow."

"Don't worry; just come over whenever you get home, even if you are late or early. I will be waiting."

Anna nodded again. "I will." She smiled and closed the door.

God bless that poor woman, Anna thought. She is lonely. She needs a friend. So do I.

Then Anna sat down and picked up the envelope; then with a deep sigh she opened the letter.

My dearest Anna,

I am dictating this to a fellow soldier because I am unable to hold a pen. I was bitten on the index finger of my right hand by a rattlesnake while out on a training mission. I must admit it hurt like hell, but the medic who was in the desert with us had a syringe with an anti-venom serum. So, I am fortunate to be alive, and for the most part, I am all right.

We train in the hot desert sun all day. It is exhausting. I have seen scorpions, tarantulas, and all varieties of snakes, including the one that bit me.

I think of you constantly, and I keep your picture in the breast pocket of my uniform, close to my heart. You are my one true love, Anna, my Anna. From the day I first saw you, I knew that we were meant to be together. I think of those days on the ship, and I think of Manny. He loved you too. He was the reason I held back in the beginning. But of course, you know all of this. I only repeat it because now that I am here without you, the past becomes clearer, the memories more tender and distinct, and I miss you so very much.

Know always that you have my love,

Your husband, Alex

A snakebite. She ran her hands through her hair. Well, at least he was not going to be going into combat for a while.

Chapter 72

From the first day, Anna loved her job. It was not easy, especially physically. She had to stand on her feet for ten hours wearing high heels. And for the most part, the wealthy customers could be snooty and demanding. However, the first week of her employment, Anna sold the most dresses on the floor. Women simply wanted to look like Anna, to share her sense of style, and to emulate the elegant way that clothing draped across her slender frame.

There was no doubt that the other saleswomen in her department resented Anna, the new girl who had no problems making a sale. In fact, she made it all look too easy.

So when the girls in her own department shunned her, Anna made friends with two girls from other departments in the store. There was Alice, who worked in men's clothing, and Bette, from perfumes. The three took lunch together every day. Alice was dating a customer, although it was strictly forbidden. And she told the others all about him. He was a handsome man born in Texas, she said, and although he never said how he came by it, he had plenty of money to spend. Bette, like Anna, was married to an enlisted man. His name was Paul, and according to Bette, he was terrible at writing letters. The last time she'd heard from him he was on a small island somewhere in the Pacific. He was not at liberty to tell her the name. The three women shared their love of fashion and brought magazines to thumb through on their breaks.

Although, Anna saved a little of what she earned, and all of what Alex sent her, she still managed to buy a few new dresses, a pair of black high heels, and a tube of creamy crimson lipstick.

Often Wera and Anna had dinner together. Wera did not have a job, so she insisted upon cooking, and Anna insisted upon paying for most of the food. Although they rarely discussed it, they shared a common bond, a fear of what might be happening to their husbands far away from their homes.

In July, Gimbels had its annual summer picnic. The company had barbeque grills up in Central Park, while the employees and management challenged each other to friendly games of softball and participated in a three-legged race. The employees voted, and prizes were awarded for outstanding behaviors. One of the men who sold shoes won a trophy and five dollars for being the best at telling jokes. Another woman who worked in cosmetics won for creating the prettiest displays. Anna received the prize for best dressed. She giggled like a schoolgirl as she was awarded a small trophy and a ten-dollar gift certificate to the store.

Even though all seemed well at Gimbels, it wasn't. Employees had begun to complain of long hours and insufficient pay, which enticed the unions to come pounding at the door. They began by infiltrating the staff, meeting the employees at off hours, and promising a forty-hour workweek and two dollars additional pay.

Alice was a staunch supporter of the union and she constantly tried to sway Bette and Anna.

"I work too hard to give my money up for union dues," Bette said. "I need every penny. I just can't spare anything right now."

"Yes, you're right we will have to pay union dues, but the extra money the union will get us when they bargain with the management will pay the dues, and then some. We will be much better off than we are now."

"What if they fire all of us?" Anna asked.

"They won't. They can't. That's why we have to make sure that everyone joins. If everyone joins, then they can't fire any of us or we will all threaten to strike. Then they won't have anybody to work. If we stand together, we have power. What you don't realize is that they need us more than we need them. We do the work, we keep this place going."

"They could hire outside people," Bette said.

"And if they do, and those people cross our picket lines, we will make then sorry. The union calls people like that scabs."

"It all sounds good, but I'd hate to lose my job," Bette said.

Anna nodded in agreement.

"We won't lose our jobs. I promise you that. Now, if it comes to the point where we are going to take a vote, you two have to vote yes for the union. Come on, promise me…"

Anna and Bette both nodded reluctantly.

At the end of the day, Anna walked to the subway. Her high heels hurt her feet after standing for ten hours with only a half-hour break for lunch. Perhaps, Alice was right. Maybe the employees did need to stand up for themselves.

Even though the sun had gone down, it was still hot and sticky outside. Anna took some hair pins out of her handbag and quickly twisted her hair up into a bun. A nagging thought kept creeping into the back of her mind. She tried to push it away, but it came rushing back. It had been two weeks since she'd received a letter from Alex.

Chapter 73

"There's a union meeting tonight," Alice said the following morning. "You two have to attend. I'll be there. It's at eight o'clock. Here is the address." Alice handed them both a small square of paper.

"I don't know." Anna shook her head. "The company really frowns on this…"

"Of course they do, look at the way they treat us. If we had a union, they couldn't work us so damn hard. How many times have you been forced to work right through your lunch? And all day without a break? Ten hours…no break…no lunch…"

Bette nodded. "I have."

"Come on, Anna, you know you have too."

"Yes, of course I have. But I don't want to end up unemployed. That would be worse."

"Well, who does? I need this job too. In fact, I probably need it more than you two gals. Your husbands send you money. I'm not married. I'm on my own, but why should we be treated like animals just because we need the work? We do a good job and we are human beings. We deserve respect," Alice said.

Anna shot a glance at Bette. Bette shrugged.

"All right, I'll be there," Anna said.

"Me too," Bette answered.

The meeting was in the apartment of one of the employees whom none of the three girls had met. He worked loading merchandise at the dock, and his name was Fred. He welcomed everyone at the door, and even set out a plate of cookies, and coffee.

Anna's eyes darted around the small room; perhaps one of these people had come as a spy for Gimbels. They could be taking down the names of the employees who showed union support."

"Okay, order, everyone… Come on, take your seats," Fred said as he stood in front of the crowd. He was a big man, with thick red eyebrows, and a bush of matching hair. A sprinkling of brown freckles covered his face. "Come on, these fellas can't stand around here all night."

Card chairs had been set up in rows, and everyone took their seats. Anna sat beside Bette, with Alice on Bette's other side.

"I'd like to thank you all for taking the time to come tonight. I know how busy everyone is, and I sure am glad we have such a good turnout," Fred said. "I'm not going to stand up here and talk. I'll get right to the point." He smiled. "I'd like you all to meet a friend of ours, a friend of the working man. He is a real important fellow, the National President of the Retail Wholesale and Department Store Unions. For those of you who don't know him yet, his name is Samuel Wolchok. Let's give him a real warm welcome."

Fred began clapping, and the others joined in. Mr. Wolchok walked up and raised his hands to silence the crowd.

"Thank you," he said. "I'm here to help you form a union. But first let me answer a question everyone has been asking me tonight. What is a union? What is a union, you ask…? It's when the labor force all bands together and becomes one powerful force. Because every single worker is part of this whole, the owners of these big companies can't treat their employees any way they to want to anymore. When the workers unite, they have power. They can demand fair wages, reasonable hours, and humane treatment. You are the workers. It is the sweat of your labor that makes the owners of these big stores rich. Why shouldn't you be treated better? You bring in lots of revenue, but how many of you can afford to shop in Gimbels? I'll bet you can't. I'll bet you shop at Kleins or Ohrbahs. Not that there is anything wrong with those stores, but you spend your ten hour days catering to the rich clients who demand that you kiss their asses so that Gimbel can live in his big, fancy house. Do you have a big fancy house?" The crowd grunted. "Hmm… I thought not. Well, if you decide to form a union of the workers here at Gimbels you'll become powerful. Your bosses will be forced to pay you better, because if they don't they won't be able to keep their store open. Why, you ask? Because if the entire labor force goes on strike, there will be nobody here, and they sure as hell don't know how to do our work, couldn't do it if they tried, right?"

"Yeah!" the employees cried out in unison.

"Then they are going to have to listen to us," Wolchok said.

The crowd of workers cheered and stood up, clapping.

"So, let's get going. I got some of my best boys here to help you get started signing up for that union."

"What about dues?" one of the men from the back of the room asked, "Union dues?"

"The dues are a very small percentage of your pay, and with the raise the union will get you, you won't even notice the dues."

A few others asked questions, but Anna could see that the group was all fired up, and no matter what the questions or answers, Gimbels would have a union very soon.

Lines formed in front of the three organizers who had come to sign the workers up as new union members.

Alice took Bette's and Anna's arms and led them into one of the lines.

When they got to the front, the union organizer at the table handed each of them a form. He looked up and his royal-blue eyes caught Anna's glance. He nodded to her and smiled as his long, raven-black hair fell over his forehead.

Anna thought he looked a great deal like Clark Gable.

"Hello… I'm Benny," the man said directly to Anna. The fire in his eyes and the passion he exuded for the workers cause gave Anna a tingle up her spine.

"I'm Anna."

"Come on…let's go. I can't stand in this line all day." a short, chubby man with slender little hands standing behind Anna said.

"People are waiting," Anna said.

"I don't care." Benny smiled.

"Come on," the little fat man said again.

"All right, all right," Benny said. "Can we talk after I get done here?"

Anna shook her head. "Sorry, I'm married," she said.

"I didn't ask you about your marital status. I just wanted to talk to you," Benny said.

Anna was suddenly embarrassed. Perhaps she was attracted to Benny and he just wanted to plug the union.

"I don't know what made me say that. Of course we can talk." Anna's face felt hot and she knew she was turning bright red.

"Jeez, come on…" the little fat man stomped his foot.

Anna took the union form and pencil, and walked back to her seat.

Everyone walked around for the rest of the meeting, talking, and sharing cookies and coffee. The organizers made their way through the small crowds, trying to spend time with each group. Benny did not approach Anna. And the more he seemed to be ignoring her, the more she wanted him to come over and chat with her and her friends. She stood on the side of the room with Bette and Alice, trying not to glance over at Benny as he spoke to the others, his smile friendly, but his voice strong, echoing through the room, filled with conviction.

At ten-thirty, people began leaving. They all had to be up in the morning to be at work by seven. Everyone said their goodbyes and headed out into the night.

Outside the building, Anna, Bette, and Alice separated, each headed in a different direction. Anna tried to avoid the subway at night, so she decided to spend the extra cash and flag a taxi. As she stood at the side of the road waiting for a cab, Benny walked over to her.

"Sorry, it seemed like everyone wanted to ask questions tonight. I meant to get back over to you, but I just didn't get the chance."

"Oh, that's fine. I was talking with my friends," Anna said, keeping her eyes on the street as if finding an open cab were the most important thing in the world to her.

"Have you eaten?"

She hadn't. In fact, she realized that she was hungry. "No, actually I forgot to eat."

"Why don't we go and grab something and I can tell you a little more about the union."

"I don't think so," Anna said, "Thank you anyway."

"Please, I hate to eat alone. You aren't going to make me eat alone are you?"

She looked at him. He gave her a silly expression, and she couldn't help laughing.

"Oh, why not? Yes, let's go and get something to eat," she said.

"Do you like Chinese food?" Benny asked.

"I've never had it."

"Well, my dear girl, you are in for quite a treat," Benny said. "Come with me. No need to fear the subway at night when you have a Knight of the Shining Union with you."

She laughed.

They took the train to Chinatown.

"I know the best place for Chinese food."

"I'll just have to trust you…"

The restaurant was small, only five tables, but it was late so they got a booth in the corner immediately.

"Shall I order for you?"

"I guess you're going to have to. I have no idea what to have."

"Then leave it to me," he said.

"I should tell you that I don't eat pork or shell fish."

"Me either. I am a Jew," he said.

"Really?" Anna looked at him, surprised. "I thought with that black hair and your blue eyes that you might be Irish."

"Nope, I'm a full blooded Hebe."

"Hebe?"

"It's slang for a Jew." He smiled. "Would you like a drink? They have a wine called plum wine that's delicious."

"No thanks."

"I'm still in shock that you're Jewish. I can usually tell other Jews," she said.

"I can tell you're Jewish. I knew it when I first saw you."

"Really, how? Do you think I'm stereotypical?"

"Nothing about you is stereotypical. You, Miss Anna, are one of a kind. Maybe it's just that I have a sixth sense."

"Is your name really Benny, or is that just a name you use for the union. I've heard that some of the organizers didn't use their real names."

"Where did you hear that? Not true, not true at all. My real is name is Benjamin. But I like Benny 'cause it's sort like Benny Goodman, you know?"

"Sure I know Benny Goodman. I love his music."

"Do you dance?" Benny asked.

It had been a long time since Alex had taken Anna dancing. In fact, they had not gone since they left Cuba. She hadn't given it much thought until now that Benny brought it to her attention.

"I do dance. In fact, I love to dance." She'd forgotten how much she loved it.

"So your husband must take you dancing all the time?"

"No, he's in the service."

"Overseas?"

"I don't know, I haven't heard from him in a couple of weeks. The last I heard he was in Georgia."

"Georiga is beautiful, one of my favorite places."

"You've been there?"

"Yeah, I've been all over the place."

"I'd love to travel." Anna said as she watched the cars outside the window.

"You should join the union organizers."

"Oh, I don't think so. From what I have heard, it is dangerous."

"Yeah, I suppose it is. We get ourselves into some serious trouble sometimes. We make a lot of friends and we help a lot of people, but in turn we make some serious enemies, too."

"How long are you staying in New York?"

"That depends…" A sexy smile broke over his face.

"On what?" she asked. She couldn't help being drawn to his magnetic eyes and alluring smile.

"On you…" Benny said.

She looked away from him. Twice in one night he had made her blush. Alex, think of Alex, she told herself.

After dinner, Benny escorted Anna back to her apartment.

"Thanks for having dinner with me."

"Thanks for all the information about the union," she said.

"See you soon, I hope…"

"Thanks again, for dinner and everything," she answered, and walked up the stairs to her apartment.

Chapter 74

The following day Anna received three letters, each postmarked a few day apart. Alex had written consistently. His letters had been held up in the mail.

For the most part the letters told her about what he was learning. He was still stationed in Georgia, and would not be re-stationed for at least another six months; then there was a good chance that he would be transferred somewhere out in the Pacific. But if he had his choice, he would put in for a transfer to Europe. Alex wanted to fight the Germans, not the Japanese. He had no issues with the Japanese, he said. He wanted to pay the Nazis back for the deaths of his family, for their hatred of the Jews, for his time in the camp, and for their deception on the *St. Louis*. He explained to Anna how during gun training he imagined the targets to have the faces of the Nazis he'd remembered from Dachau. When he turned the machine gun on them full blast, he said he felt elated. And because of this he'd become an excellent marksman.

"The strange thing here is that the other soldiers think I am German just because I have an accent and I was born in Germany. This automatically makes them leery of me. They think I am some kind of a spy for the Nazis. Can you imagine? If they only understood that Hitler does not see me as a German, only as a Jew. If they would only accept the fact that I am on the side of America even more than the Americans are because the survival of my entire race hangs on the outcome of this war. I try to explain this to them, but their heads are too thick and they are unwilling to believe me.

"I do not fear my own death. I only fear that I will somehow lose you, that something terrible will happen to you. Sometimes at night, I can't sleep because of this fear. As you know, I have lost everyone I have ever loved. If I should be killed, my only concern is that it would cause you pain, and I hate to think of myself as the cause of any unhappiness for you. I am not worth it," he wrote. "Anna, if I should die you must go on; you must forgive me and not grieve. This war is something that I must be a part of, it is something I must do in order to make things right in my own mind. When Hitler killed my family, he declared war on me personally, and I want to be sure that I give him just what he deserves. I only hope that I have the opportunity to kill plenty of Nazis."

She read his letters and was afraid that he was spiraling down into madness. Anna knew that Alex was angry, and rightfully so, but he seemed to be obsessed with murder and revenge. If only he'd not gone so far away… She could not protect him from himself now. And he needed protection; his mind had been unsound before he left. "Now, without me to lean on, God only knows what will become of him…." she whispered aloud.

Chapter 75

A vote was taken. The union won, hands down. Gimbels employees were now a part of the RWDSU.

Anna came into work on a Monday morning to find a letter waiting for her behind the counter where she worked.

"This is for you." Her supervisor, Joan said. It came with the mail this morning.

"Oh, no…" Anna said. "I hope it isn't about my husband."

"Go in the back and sit down and read it. I'll watch the counter." Joan said. Anna was a good, reliable employee, who stayed out of trouble. Joan liked her.

"Thank you," Anna said, taking the envelope and walking to the break room.

Three women whom she knew from different departments were pouring coffee. She didn't want to stop and talk, so she took the letter into the bathroom, locked herself in a stall, and tore the envelope open.

It read:

"Just wondering if you've had a craving for egg rolls lately, no pork, of course? Or maybe you've had a hankering to go out dancing? I'll be at the diner next-door at seven when you get off work tonight. Come on over and say hi to your friendly union rep, Benny, at your service."

She tore the paper into small pieces and flushed it down the toilet. Damn him, she thought. I have enough to worry about without him bothering me.

Anna ignored Benny's request, and three days later a dozen red roses arrived at Gimbels for Anna. All the salesgirls who saw the delivery boy carrying the box wrapped in silver paper came rushing over to see who the flowers were for.

"It must be from your husband overseas," one of the girls said as Anna thanked the delivery boy.

"How beautiful... May I get Anna a vase from the housewares department?" another one of the girls asked Anna's boss.

"That won't be necessary. I believe we have something in the back that Anna can use." Joan smiled at Anna. "Come with me and bring your flowers. We'll put them in water."

"Aren't you going to open the card?" another salesgirl asked.

"Perhaps Anna would prefer to open that in private. Come along, Anna." Joan put her arm around Anna's shoulder and led her away.

Anna tucked the card into the pocket of her skirt. She had a feeling that the flowers were not from Alex. How could he send flowers all the way from Georgia? They had to be from Benny, and she would prefer that the others not know about his interest in her.

Joan filled a vase with water and put the flowers in one-by-one. "They are lovely."

"Yes, they are."

Joan never asked who the flowers were from. She put them on the table in the break room and left.

Once she was alone, Anna opened the card.

"This act of sending flowers is not really my style, but you are a rare find. So, how about that dinner? You know how I hate to eat alone. Benny."

He was really beginning to get on her nerves.

Chapter 76

Anna never responded to the flowers, and she did not hear from Benny again. But three weeks later, at the beginning of August, labor and management negotiations began. Mr. Broido, the vice-president in charge of the employees, seemed to be on fairly good terms with Mr. Wolchock, and because of this the employees were hopeful that they would be granted what they asked for. The demands were not outrageous. The employees were asking for a forty-hour, five-day workweek and two dollars a day additional pay.

Within a few days, the employees had a resolution. The company agreed to a dollar fifty raise per day and a forty-two hour workweek. The employees were not satisfied. They wanted the forty-hour week, wanted it badly enough to strike.

Anna was worried about a strike. If the union said everyone must walk out, she would be forced to join them, and that meant no pay until the strike ended. She had some money saved, but she was hoping to have a down payment for a house when Alex returned. This could be a setback, depending upon how long the strike lasted.

On August 18th, William Michelson, the leader of Gimbels local two ordered a strike.

That night Anna had dinner with Wera in her apartment.

"I cannot believe that I am going to sit on a picket line instead of working. It seems like such a waste of time."

"Yes, maybe, but maybe it is good for the company to put these rules in place. In the long run it's gonna be better for you and everybody else who works there."

"I suppose you're right. "

"Listen, I made you a present," Wera said.

"A present, for me? Why?"

"I have nothing to do all day, so I made you a pair of pants. I saw a poster of Katherine Hepburn wearing them. Maybe you will want to wear them on the picket line."

Wera got up and pulled a pair of gray trousers out of the drawer of her sewing dresser. "Come on, try them on so that I can fit them to you."

Anna held the trousers up and looked at them. She'd never considered wearing pants before, but the idea was sort of attractive. Why not? She put them on. They were too big. Wera pinned the sides until they hung just right.

"I'll have them all ready for you tomorrow," Wera said.

"Can I at least pay you for the fabric?"

"No need. I had this fabric left over from a customer I made a dress for. You are so small and thin that it was enough fabric." Wera occasionally did sewing work for private clients.

"Oh, Wera, thank you so much for thinking of me."

"You are my friend, my only friend," Wera laughed. "And after all, you are like a movie star, always the first one to wear the latest fashion. I wanted you to be a style-setter like Katherine Hepburn and Marlene Detrich."

"I think these pants would look wonderful with my white cotton blouse."

"Yes, so do I, but I had a little time and a little black silk left over from another customer, so I made you a blouse, too."

"Wera?" She smiled. "Thank you."

"No need to thank me. You help by paying for the food."

"And you hardly even let me pay for that," Anna said.

"You do plenty." Wera smiled. "Now, come in the morning and I'll have these clothes all ready for you."

"Are you sure? There is no hurry. You can take a few days."

"Of course I'm sure. I'll even have a couple of sweet rolls and a pot of coffee for us. We'll have a little breakfast before you go."

Anna leaned over and kissed Wera's cheek.

When Anna arrived on the picket line wearing her new outfit, all of the women came rushing over to her.

"You look marvelous. I love the way the trousers make you look, so stylish."

They raved, and Anna felt good. She wasn't earning a salary, but the picket line wasn't so bad. It was fun to socialize with the other girls. They never had time to sit and chat for very long while they were working. Anna was given a sign to carry that said: "Don't shop at Gimbels. They treat their employees terribly."

Everything went fine for the first few days, until one of the well-known, affluent customers came to Gimbels and tried to break through the picket line.

Anna had never seen her fellow employees get so angry and volatile. The female customer was testy, spoiled and demanding, not uncommon for the typical prosperous Gimbels customer. For years the employees had been forced to cater to the whims of the well-to-do customers, whom they had come to hate. Now, they refused to back down. They called out obscenities at the woman, and frightened her away.

As the strikers grew in number, the workers grew bolder. They hurled strong insults at Gimbels' wealthy clients who tried to cross the picket line. Then things went too far when Helen, one of the sales girls, threw a bottle of red ink at a woman. Anna had seen Helen around the store. She always appeared quiet, and reserved; there had been no evidence of this fire brewing within her. Anna watched as the police came rushing over. They handcuffed Helen, and she was arrested for assault.

As the time went on, the strikers became more daring in their approach until finally someone released a swarm of bees into the store.

Anna was not violent by nature, and she didn't like the screaming of obscenities in the streets. But she understood how the employees felt.

A few days later, several workers from Quills TWU came to join the strikers, as the picket line grew larger and more aggressive.

Bette and Alice invited Anna to join them as they sat on the curb eating sandwiches. Anna sat down. She was wearing another pair of brown trousers that Wera had made for her, and a cream-colored blouse.

"I have an extra sandwich, Anna. You want one?"

"No, thanks."

"Look over there..." Bette said. "Remember that handsome union organizer, Benny? He's coming this way and he really looks good in that fedora."

"Jeez, he's handsome," Alice said.

"You know what I heard?" Bette said.

"What?" Alice asked.

"I heard that Benny gives lots of his own money to help picketers, you know, like guys with families who have to be out of work because of a strike."

"Where did you hear that?" Anna asked.

But before Bette could answer, Anna looked up to see Benny sauntering over to them. Several of the other strikers tried to stop him and engage him in conversation, but he was heading straight for Anna.

Chapter 77

Alex was on a plane on his way to England. He was to work on bombers and tanks. This was the first time he'd ever flown and the altitude bothered his ears. A sharp pain shot from the back of his ear down his neck. As he sat in the dark cabin of the plane, he thought of Anna. Poor Anna, she'd put up with so much from him, Now he'd left her alone to fend for herself in New York City, and if he died, then what? He hated himself. It had not been fair of him to marry her. When they met, Alex already knew that he was damaged. He should have stayed away from her. She was so young and innocent. She could have married so much better. She should have married Manny. But she'd been so kind to him and cared so much about him, that he'd fallen in love with her so deeply that even now the depth of his feelings left him breathless.

Perhaps enlisting had been a mistake; perhaps he owed Anna more than this. Dear God, if only he could be more decisive. Everything he did always seemed wrong after the fact. But he could not go on living the way he had been, constantly feeling as if he should be doing something, anything, to fight against the Nazis.

His time in boot camp taught him many things, but the one that had been the most difficult was discovering that anti-Semitism stretched its ugly head into the U.S. armed forces. Once the other soldiers learned that he was Jewish, some of them refused to sit next to him in the mess hall, and one even refused to bunk on the bottom of his bunk. They acted like he had a contagious disease.

The plane hit some turbulence, rocking and shaking like it might fall out of the sky.

Alex shivered. Anna...

It felt strange to be going back to Europe. He'd worked so hard to get to America. Well, at least once he got to England he could begin searching for Manny. A day never passed that Alex didn't remember that both he and Anna owed everything to Manny, and he would not rest until he found him.

Although the cabin of the aircraft was dimly lit, Alex took a pencil and paper out of the breast pocket of his uniform and began to write a letter.

"Anna, my Anna..."

Chapter 78

"Anna, banana..." Benny said as he approached. "So, how have you been?"

"I'm fine." She hadn't meant to sound so curt.

"Well, that's sure good to hear." He smiled "How are you two girls doing?" he asked Bette and Alice.

Alice nodded, and then Bette nodded too.

"This is sure some strike. I think they're gonna cave pretty soon. Old man Broido is starting to realize that he better take this labor union seriously."

"Well, that's good. I hope he agrees to the five-day, forty-hour week," Alice said.

"He's gonna have to. We just won't let up until he does."

"Yes, but a lot of these men are the sole supporters of their families, Benny. Who is going to feed their children, you?" Anna asked.

"Anna, why do you dislike me so much?"

"I don't. But I think that sometimes you are far too idealistic."

"That could be true. But if we don't stand together as one force, the management will always be able to do whatever they want to the workers. Is that better? Should people work so hard that they end up in an early grave?"

Anna folded her arms across her chest. She understood, and even agreed with what Benny was saying, but she didn't want to let him know that he was right.

"Come on, don't be like that. We are all in this together," he said, flashing his white-toothed smile.

"And I suppose you are taking a cut in salary, too, while all of this is taking place?" Anna said.

"Actually, yes, I am. And I would gladly do so for the principle of the thing," Benny said.

"Hmm…" Anna crossed her arms over her chest.

"Can we stop arguing? You look far too pretty today to fight," Benny said.

Alice gave Anna a questioning look.

Anna shrugged.

"Have you had lunch?"

"No, she hasn't. We tried to feed her, but she won't eat. Pretty soon she's gonna get so skinny that if she stands sideways you won't be able to see her," Bette said.

"Come on, let's walk over and get a hot dog. You know how much I hate to eat alone," Benny said.

Anna glared at Bette, who shrugged her shoulders.

"Oh all right." Anna handed her sign to Alice and picked up her pocket book. "I'll be right back."

"Take your time." Bette smiled. "We aren't going anywhere for a while."

Anna and Benny turned the corner away from the picket line. A hot summer sun glared down at them from a royal-blue cloudless sky. Anna felt her blouse sticking to her. She pulled her hair into a knot at the nape of her neck and secured it with a few hair pins from her handbag.

"Now, how is it that you looked beautiful before, and now that you've pulled your hair up, you look even more stunning?"

"Have I told you lately that I find you infuriating?" Anna said.

"No, you haven't told me. But I am kind of beginning to get the picture."

"What is it you want from me? You know I am a married woman."

"I want a torrid love affair."

"That's vulgar. I am leaving."

"Hey, hey, I was just kidding. Can't you take a joke? Why are you so serious all the time?"

She shrugged her shoulders. "I don't know. I guess because I have been through a lot of bad things in my life," she said.

"Well, then, just let loose for a few minutes and let's just enjoy a hot dog. I'm not asking you to forgo your morals or anything. Will you just do that?"

She nodded.

Benny bought two hot dogs from a vendor, and he and Anna walked as they ate.

"How about the turnout for this strike?"

"It's bigger than I thought it would be. I thought it would be just Gimbels," she said.

"When I see a group of workers coming out and picketing for the laborers' rights, it reminds me that all the work I've been doing has been worthwhile."

"Do you really think they'll give us what we are asking for?"

"Eventually they are going to have to. You see that's the beauty of a union. Anna, the world is changing. The labor force is becoming strong, powerful. We have a voice. Not just in this industry, but in every industry. The rich company owners can't take advantage of us anymore. And believe me, it took a hell of a lot to get to this point. Heck, when I first started I faced such resistance from the workers. I was a young kid fresh out of college. Nobody trusted me."

"You don't look that old now. How old are you?"

"Now you know a man never tells his age..." He winked. "I'm going to be thirty-five in April."

"You don't look your age. You went to college?"

"Yep, I'm an attorney. Benjamin Lewis Berman, attorney at law. But I decided to give up practicing law in order to do something important with my life. My father was a transit worker. He posed as an Irishman. They didn't hire Jews, but like me, he had the black hair and blue eyes, so he passed for Irish. That's where he met Michael Quill. Quill was an Irish immigrant. Smartest man I ever met. Fair too."

"You mean Quill from Quill TWU? That's the union that's out on the picket line helping us."

"Yep, that's right. Michael Quill is the founder. He is one hell of a nice guy, with a heart as big as New York. In fact I met him when I was just a kid; my father brought him home a couple of times. He had a hell of an effect on me. Between watching my father face terrible abuse at the hands of the subway bosses, and the influence of Mike Quill, I became a union man."

"How does your wife cope with the danger of your job?"

"It is dangerous, but it's important. The same as the guys out fighting for America in our armed forces, I'm fighting a war right here on our home front, a war between the rich and the poor, between the owners and the workers. I believe in what I am doing. I know it is the right thing and in the years to come long after I'm dead, the work I've done will continue to make a difference in the world."

She nodded…

"Oh yeah, I forgot… You asked another question." He winked.

Anna felt her face turning red; she looked away so he wouldn't see. Why had she asked about his wife? Why did she care?

"I'm not married. A man like me can't be married. I'm traveling too much for that. It wouldn't be fair."

"It's none of my business, but don't you ever get lonely, and want a family of your own?"

"Sure, all the time, but I know that if I don't continue this work, I'll never forgive myself."

"This really means a lot to you."

"Yeah, I could earn at least three times the amount that I am making with the union if I were to work as a lawyer. But at the end of the day, I wouldn't feel as if I'd accomplished anything important."

"You're a real idealist, Benny. When you've lived through what I have lived through, ideals go out the window. For me it's always been about survival."

"I know this is going to sound crazy, but I believe that we are all put here on earth with a purpose, something that we are supposed to do. Once we find that purpose, we must go forward until our job is complete. Does this make any sense to you?"

"Yes. I understand. But, I have no idea what my purpose might be. I'm not even sure I have one."

"I'm sure you do. For some people it takes longer to find their purpose. Others never find it."

"I would like to find mine. I mean, I'd like to know why I am here on earth. And just why I had to leave my family behind in Germany. I guess I am saying I'd like to know God's plan. "

"Are you religious?" he asked.

"No. I believe in God, and as you know, I am Jewish, but I wouldn't say I'm religious."

"I'm not either. I'm a Jew, but for me it's more of a tradition than a religion. I don't believe in religion. It's just another reason for war."

"You are a strange man Benny. I don't think I have ever met anyone like you."

"Does that mean that you'll have dinner with me tonight?"

"Oh, Benny, I don't think it's a good idea."

"You said you had to leave your family behind. What happened?"

"It's a long story, a very long story."

"Well, that's all the more reason for you to have dinner with me. I'd like to hear your story."

"You are insistent."

"Yes, I can be. I like you Anna. I don't expect you to be anything but a friend to me. But I could be a good friend if you give me a chance. Come on out for dinner tonight. Tell me what's in your heart, what's bothering you. I'll listen. I'm a good listener. Come on…say yes."

"Yes." She couldn't believe that she agreed. But there was something about him. Maybe it was his warmth, or his desire to do the right thing and help those less fortunate. Or perhaps it was the sparkle in his eyes, the way he made her feel full of life, full of dreams, full of possibilities…but what about Alex?

"Would you like to go to little Italy? I know an Italian restaurant that I think you'll love."

She nodded. "Yes, I've never been to an Italian restaurant." Anna was realizing all of the things she'd missed over the years, and suddenly she wanted to experience every one of them. She wanted to be young, to go out dancing, to try different foods, maybe even to go to a movie theater. Benny brought the joy of living back to her.

Chapter 79

"You're going to eat with a man? Anna, are you crazy?"

"I don't know, Wera. I might be." Anna said as she carefully drew the red lipstick over her lips.

"Anna, you're married. What are you doing?"

"Wera, I suppose I am being selfish. I want to go out and have fun. When Alex was here, I had to be so careful not to upset him, not to throw him into one of his depression fits. When we were in Cuba, at least he would go out dancing once in a while, but once we got to America he always seemed to be brooding, and I was always afraid of what he might do. Then he just up and left to go overseas. He never even discussed it with me."

"But you're still married, Anna."

"I know."

"If something should happen to Alex, you're never gonna forgive yourself."

"Don't say that…" Anna snapped. "It's bad luck."

"I'm sorry." Wera sounded sad. "I'll go back to my apartment. I'll see you tomorrow."

"Wait," Anna said. She went over and hugged Wera. "I'm sorry. I know you mean well, and you want what's best for me. And God knows, you are probably right… This is probably a mistake. But, Wera, I've had far too little laughter in my life. I just want to grab a little bit of sweetness while I can."

"Believe it or not, I do understand. I too have had far too little pleasure in my life. Go, Anna, enjoy yourself. But please be careful. Don't get involved with this man. It will only make a mess of your life."

"I know. You're right."

Chapter 80

Anna and Benny had agreed upon eight o'clock, and at five minutes to eight, Benny was ringing the downstairs bell. Anna grabbed her handbag off the sofa and ran down the stairs. Benny stood in the vestibule, looking handsome in his black pants and white cotton shirt.

"Hello there…"

"Hello," Anna said.

"You look incredibly beautiful. But then again, you always do," he said.

He took her arm and led her to the taxi he had waiting.

"From the first time I saw you, I said, 'That girl is different, she's elegant, like a First Lady.' I don't know what it is, I guess it's something in the way that you carry yourself. But, Anna you should know it, you are special."

Benny opened the car door and Anna slid into the back seat. Then Benny got in beside her.

"We're going to Little Italy. A place called Alfonzo's." Benny told the driver.

Then he squeezed Anna's hand. "And if you want to, tonight, you can tell me all about Germany and what happened."

She wanted to tell him, to cry on his strong shoulder, to release her burden.

Anna looked over at Benny he was gazing at her. Their eyes met and locked. She felt a rush of desire, fear, and excitement all at once.

Chapter 81

The warning sound of the air raids blared so often that they became commonplace as the bombs fell over London. Germany bombed England, and England bombed Germany. But Hitler's insatiable desire for power could not be stifled. He already occupied most of Europe, but his fatal error was greed, and he would not rest until he took England and Russia. Stalin proved a formidable enemy, and Hitler would soon learn that he'd made a mistake. Before America joined the war, Churchill had struggled to keep the Nazis at bay, and even with the planes and supplies from the United States, he had been in peril of losing Great Britain. However, now, with America and Canada allied with England on the west, and Russia allied with England on the east, defeating the Nazis began to look more promising.

Alex found himself running for shelter just a few feet from a blast. He'd not seen hand-to-hand combat, but the bombing had sobered him into the realization that war caused death and destruction, and had little to do with glory. Although he still wanted to kill Nazis and somehow right all of the wrongs that burned in his soul, he'd now come to know the terrifying sights and sounds of war. His memories of Dachau still lingered, and they were beyond terrible. But the deafening blast of a building bursting into rubble, and the splatter of blood or the flying body parts unnerved him.

For Alex, who was not outgoing by nature, the army was a lonely place. He had difficulty making friends, and spent most of the time he was not working reading books. Alex knew that his sergeant didn't like him. Perhaps it was because

Alex was too withdrawn, but he always seemed to be selected for the harder jobs.

He wrote to Anna and told her all that he saw, and all that he felt. The letters kept him from feeling as if he was all alone in the world, and he waited daily for the mail, hoping she'd written back.

Chapter 82

The union strike was settled. Management realized that the labor force had the power to hurt their business and because of this, they gave in.

The union gave a big party to celebrate the victory. Benny and Anna, along with Alice and Bette, attended. They had buffet tables of food, and a small local band.

"I told you we would win. I told you that the union would get us what we need," Alice said.

"I can't believe we got a forty-hour, five-day workweek," Bette said. "It's wonderful. Now I can have time to do some of the things I've always wanted to do."

"Yeah, like what?" Alice asked.

"I dunno, but I'll have time."

"The world is changing, girls. I've seen it in every industry. They can't walk all over us anymore. Once we organize, labor becomes a force stronger than the owners and the managers of any company. They don't do the work, they don't even know how. We do; they're dependent on us, and because of that they know that they had better pay attention when we make demands," Benny said.

"Well, they sure did pay attention," Alice said, and she smiled.

Bette nodded.

"I am going to go and get some punch," Anna said.

"Let me get it for you," Benny offered.

"Sure," Anna said.

Benny went to get the punch.

"He's crazy about you," Bette said.

"No, we're just friends," Anna answered.

"Maybe that's all you're feeling, but he's falling for you. I can see it; it's all over his face. Shoot, I wish he were falling for me. I'm single after all," Alice said.

Anna felt guilty. She'd been selfish, wanted just a little sweetness in her life, and now she was about to hurt two men, one who meant a great deal to her.

It all began so simply. Benny was a friend who occupied the lonely hours for Anna. But somehow, it grew. He was funny, charming, and more than willing to take her anywhere. They went dancing and took long walks together along the river. One night Benny introduced her to Woody Guthrie and his pro-union music. They went to a coffee club in the city to hear him play. Woody did not play with a band. He was a one-man troubadour with an acoustic guitar and a gritty honest voice. The simple words and music of his songs expressed the very heart of the working man. Until Benny had brought her to see Woody play, Anna had only listened to orchestras and big bands. She'd never heard music like this. One couldn't dance to it; instead it touched the listeners deeply, forcing them to think.

"Do you like Guthrie?" Benny asked.

"I don't know. Sometimes some of the things he says in his songs are like a slap in the face. By that I mean it's like they are saying, 'Wake up and look around you. See what is happening.' Does that make any sense?"

"Yes, because that is exactly what the music is saying. Woody began his union work with the migrants in California."

"Migrants?"

"Yeah, the folks who work picking fruit, and vegetables, that kind of thing. It was terrible for them. They were working for a dollar a day and that was when they could find work. And it wasn't enough to feed their families, so they had to borrow from the company stores, which were owned by the same people who employed them. So the migrants were always working off their debt; they could never get ahead. You see there were a lot of them. After the dust storms hit Texas, Oklahoma, and all the states out that way, the farmers who lived there lost everything. So they had to leave their homes to find work."

"Dust storms?" Anna tilted her head to the side.

"Yep, there were some big old dust storms. Clouds, big and black, stretched as far as the eyes could see. The dust covered all their crops and they couldn't plant anything."

"So they went to California?"

"They had to. The storms kept coming and they were causing these farmers all kinds of lung problems, not to mention starvation because the storms killed all their crops. Then, because the farmers were leaving their little towns, the people who ran the stores where they shopped had to close too. And the towns became like ghost towns."'

"But why California?" Anna asked.

"Well, California needed pickers, so they sent out flyers telling the farmers that there was work out West. When the farmers saw the flyers, they headed out that way. But when they got to California, there weren't enough jobs for all the people that showed up. So they set up all these tent cities where people lived, hoping to get work. Now, the owners of the farms saw just how many desperate folks had showed up and they took advantage of the situation. They lowered the pay and worked the poor pickers real hard."

As they sat at a table in the back of the small coffee house, Anna listened to Benny, intently her chin on her fist.

"So what happened?"

"That's when the unions came in. Little by little, the unions are making their mark on the world."

"And this is what you want to do?"

"Yep. I want to make a difference."

"If I hadn't seen the results with my own eyes, I'd call you crazy."

"You can call me anything you want, but till there is some kind of equality in this world, I'll keep going out on a limb."

"Anna," Benny said, "We've been seeing each other for a while now, and you have come to mean so much to me."

"I like you a lot. You have made everything brighter for me in this lonely city, but I am married. I told you that when we first met. All we can ever be is friends."

"I'll take your friendship rather than lose you. But I have to be honest, I want so much more."

"I know you do, and maybe it's best that we stop seeing each other this way. It is too tempting for both of us. And my Alex is out somewhere fighting. I can't do this to him."

"So you want to stop seeing me?"

"I think it's probably best. Don't you?"

"No, but if it's what you want, I would never force you."

Woody Guthrie took off his cap picked up his guitar and sat down in a chair on the stage to do his next set.

"How you all doin' tonight?" he said. "I want to play this here song for you. I wrote it while I was ridin' the rails from California to New York. It's in honor of a friend of mine, a hobo who I met while travelin.' A fine man and a talented artist, his name is Leadbelly…"

"I think we should go," Anna said.

"So you probably had enough of my talkin,' you all came here to hear the music, so let me get this going."

Woody began to strum his guitar.

"If you want to leave, I'll take you home," Benny said.

Anna got up and Benny followed her. He flagged a cab. They were silent the entire ride.

"Goodnight. And thank you," she said at the door to her building.

"I guess this is goodbye?" he asked.

"I'll see you at work."

He nodded. She thought she saw the trace of a tear in his eye, but he turned away too quickly for her to be sure.

Then he got into the cab. It rolled down the street, turned the corner, and he was gone.

Anna lay in her bed that night thinking about Alex and Benny, and work and unions and everything. She would miss Benny, but if this so-called friendship continued, she was afraid she might break her marriage vows.

It was for the best.

But as she closed her eyes and fell asleep, she dreamed of Benny's lips on hers. The passion and life force that radiated off him surrounded her, giving her purpose.

"Benny…" She fell into his arms. But she was only dreaming.

Chapter 83

Each night a selected crew went out carrying searchlights looking for German bombers. When Alex's turn came, he waited until sunset and then joined his troop. Only a sliver of a moon shone on that starless night. As he walked in the darkness, Alex tripped over a rock. Pain shot through his leg as he tried to get up. It was difficult to walk, but he made it back to camp. In the morning, his ankle had swollen and he could hardly stand on it.

His sergeant frowned as Alex was taken on a stretcher to the medic's tent. That boy's not cut out for the service. He's a lazy, uncoordinated Kike, and a German to boot. I am not sure we can trust him, Sergeant Gregory Sife, thought. I wish he were in someone else's platoon.

It embarrassed Alex to be lying on a stretcher with a broken ankle, next to men who'd been really injured during a bombing. The guys all talked amongst themselves, but Alex was all in knots he withdrew deep inside of himself, and never joined in their conversations. Instead, he turned his face to the wall, and let his mind carry him away.

"Hello." A young British nurse came over to examine Alex one morning. "My name is Nelly." She said in a cheerful voice. Her blonde curls framed her face, as she looked at him with emerald eyes.

"Nelly, it's nice to meet you. I'm Alex."

"You have an accent. Where are you from?"

"Germany."

"Germany?"

"Yes, I'm an American citizen. But I am also a German Jew."

"Oh my gosh. Well, I'll bet the others give you a real hard time. They are against anything German, and hardly understand that German Jews are hated by the Nazis as much or maybe even more than the Americans."

"How do you know all of this?" Alex sat up on his elbow, suddenly fascinated. This Nelly girl was the first person he'd met in the service that understood what it meant to be a German Jew.

"Because I know that the Nazis hate Jews, and to them you are even less German than I am, and I'm not German at all."

Nelly began to examine Alex's ankle. Her touch was light and gentle.

"You're English, right?"

"Yep, born right outside of London."

"So how is it you know so much about the Nazis anti-Semitism?"

"I guess you could say I read a lot. I like to stay informed."

"I used to be a writer, a journalist."

"That's interesting. I'd love to hear more about it. Did you write for magazines or newspapers?"

"Both when I lived in Germany, then for a paper in New York."

"Did you always want to be a writer, even as a little boy?"

"For me, writing was always a way to free my soul. I've never fit in, not even as a youngster. And sometimes if feels as if I am all bound up inside of myself. Do you know what I mean?"

"Sort of. Not really."

"I feel as if I can't find the words to speak to tell anyone what is causing me to hurt inside, so I just shut down and then I write. And writing eases my pain. I not only write for work, lately I've been finding that I want to write some short stories."

"What kind of short stories?"

"Oh you don't want to know. They are just tales from my past. I feel that maybe they would free me."

"From your past?"

"Yes, you see, I spent some time in a concentration camp."

"Oh my God!"

Alex saw the shock on her face and wished he'd kept quiet.

"It was long ago, nothing to be concerned about." She was looking at him like he was a victim. Sometimes Anna looked at him that way, and it always made him feel terrible, weak, disturbed. He despised that look of pity. "Before I left New York, I had a good job. In fact I wrote articles for a newspaper, all about the World's Fair. Now that was something to see." He tried to sound cheery.

"I'm impressed. You're famous."

"I'm hardly famous. I am just a simple writer, not really very gifted at all, and certainly not well known, but lucky enough to find work doing what I love. And then, I've had plenty of other jobs too."

"Nelly..." the other nurse who was making rounds with Nelly called to her from the other side of the infirmary. "I need you over here."

"I'll be right there. I'm just finishing up," Nelly answered across the room to the other nurse, and then she turned back to Alex.

"I'd love to hear about what it's like to work for a newspaper, but I can't stay and listen right now. I have rounds to make. I'll be back to see you tomorrow. By the way, your ankle is sprained, not broken."

"Well, that's good news."

"It is! The doc will have to come by and confirm it, but I've been a nurse for a while, and I'm pretty sure I'm right." She smiled.

"So you will be back tomorrow?" Alex asked.

Nelly wound the last bandage around Alex's ankle. She could not help being drawn by this deep, dark, mysterious man with his soft, sensitive voice that made her long to protect him. As far as she knew, Alex was the first Jew she'd ever met.

Not only did Nelly's visits break the monotony of lying in a hospital bed, but also Alex had finally found a friend. Since his arrival in the armed forces, he'd felt alienated and alone. Nelly enjoyed the stories of his life, and the more she encouraged him, the more he talked. First he talked about the newspapers and magazines he'd written for, which led to an explanation of the article that had gotten him arrested in Germany. From there he told her about the camp and the *St. Louis*, and all about America and Anna. After several days, when he'd finished, Nelly told him her story, which was a sad one as well.

"I had a baby by my teenage sweetheart. I am ashamed to tell you this, but we were not married. As soon as he found out I was pregnant, he left town. My mother called his parents. She was livid, not only with him but even more so with me. She wanted him to marry me, but he was already gone and nobody knew where to find him. If they did, they weren't talking. So, mom insisted that I find a career. Once you have a child, she told me, you're going to have a very hard time finding a man who is willing to take you seriously, and chances are you won't be getting married. After the baby came, I dated a little and found out that what she said turned out to be true. Men thought because I had a child, I'd be easy, just a girl to have fun with. At that point, I realized that I had nobody to depend upon but myself. My mother has been wonderful, helping me with the baby, and financially too, but she's getting older and I want to take care of her now. So to earn decent money I had to learn a trade. That's when I decided to attend nursing school. But school was expensive and we couldn't afford to pay for it. That's why I joined the army. They sent me to school. My mother watches my son, John Michael, and I am here serving the troops. I miss my little boy terribly, but I couldn't see any other way. I suppose we are all doing what we feel we must in these hard times."

"Yes, it's true, we are."

"Do you have any children?"

"No." Alex shook his head. "Not yet."

Nelly didn't ask why, and Alex was glad because he didn't want to talk about what happened that week that Anna spent in the hospital.

Nelly came every day and Alex looked forward to her visits. After two weeks, she helped him to begin walking again. He leaned on her shoulder. The feel of being so close to her brought an undercurrent of sexual need to the forefront of his mind. He could smell her perfume and feel her hair brush against his face as he leaned toward her. He fought the feelings, but his body responded with the physical response of a man's desire, overwhelming him with guilt.

The friendship between Alex and Nelly continued even after Alex left the hospital. As she got to know him better, Nelly saw Alex's loneliness and detachment from the other men, and she began to try and break him out of his shell. She introduced him to friends of hers, other soldiers, and they all joined in nightly card games. There was something about this boy that made him different than anyone Nelly had ever met. Maybe his being Jewish, forbidden and alien to her, had something to do with her desire. She knew he had a wife, and even knew how much he loved his wife. He'd told her more than once. But this was war, any day any one of them could be blown to bits. Nelly wanted him, and even if it were only for a short time, just to fill the loneliness, she would have him.

Chapter 84

The next time Anna saw Benny, he stood by the coffee pot, hovering very close to Alice in the break room. Alice leaned forward pressing against him blushing and giggling like a schoolgirl. Anna wanted to leave the room, and she would have if Bette had not come in right after her.

"Anna, are you taking lunch now?"

"Yes, I was."

"Come sit with me." Bette said then she glanced over and saw Benny and Alice. She gave Anna a look that told her she didn't understand what was happening between Benny and Alice.

Anna shrugged, trying to appear as if she were indifferent to Alice and Benny, when in fact she felt terrible. Why the hell did he have to become interested in one of her friends? Couldn't he just go away where she didn't have to see him all the time?

"Can we join you?" Benny asked, stealing a side-glance at Anna.

"Sure," Bette said.

Anna took the sandwich she'd brought from home out of the brown paper bag and laid it on a napkin. Then she put a single sugar in her black coffee.

Benny pulled the chair out for Alice and she sat down.

"How have you been, Benny? I haven't seen you around in quite a while," Bette asked.

"I've been doing just fine. Spent a few months out West, but I had to come back to New York for Christmas. I love the hustle and bustle of the city during the holiday season."

"Yeah, there's no place like New York during Christmas, with the store windows and all," Bette said, nodding. "The big department stores really do it up right."

Anna took a bite of her sandwich. Her throat was so dry she felt like she couldn't swallow.

"How have you been, Bette, Anna?" Benny asked.

"Fine," Bette said. "Not much news here."

"Anna?"

"Fine."

When Benny had stopped coming around, Anna had been adamant in telling both of her girlfriends that she and Benny had never been anything more than just friends. Bette and Alice accepted this, even if they found it hard to believe. Neither of the girls would have allowed themselves to be interested in Benny if they thought Anna were interested in him. But Anna made it clear that she would never break her marriage vows. Now, it seemed as if it all had backfired on her, and Alice and Benny were romantically attracted to each other.

"I'm having a Christmas party," Bette said to Anna and Alice. "Both of you have to come. Of course, Benny is coming."

Alice smiled at Benny and touched his chin with her thumb.

"When is it?" Alice asked.

"Next Friday night."

"I'll be there. What can I bring?"

"Yourself," Bette said. "Can you come, Anna?"

Anna had fixed her eyes on the table. She didn't want to meet Benny's gaze. She was afraid he would see how she felt.

"I think Wera and I have some plans already," Anna said.

"Bring her with you. It would be good for her to get out," Bette said. Then she turned to Alice and Benny. "Wera is Anna's neighbor. She never leaves the house."

"I don't know if she'll want to, but I'll ask her," Anna said. "I have some shopping to do before I go back to work, so I'll see you later." Anna got up and threw the rest of her food in the trash. Then she rushed out of the break room.

Anna still had twenty minutes left of her lunch break. Perhaps she'd take a walk outside. The cold air would do her good. Anna grabbed her coat and scarf, and walked through the store and out the front door. Only a week and a half remained until Christmas. Crowds of shoppers made their way through the slushy streets, as the window decorations flickered and holiday music filled the air. Why did she feel so sad? Alice and Benny were both single, they should be dating. She had Alex, and for better or worse, she'd vowed to stand by him. Hadn't she? There could be no doubt that he'd been a difficult husband, and many times she'd considered divorce, but she didn't think he could bear the loss, and there was no telling what he might do to himself. He needed her, he leaned on her, and she had to be there. She'd promised she would be there. A tear rolled down Anna's cheek. She'd married so young. She'd married a man she thought she could save, and now she found herself drowning, falling deeper and deeper into the bottomless sea of his depression. Why had he enlisted? Why? Finally, after all they'd been through, just struggling to have a place to live and food on the table, he'd finally gotten a decent job, one he enjoyed. Everything had begun to look brighter. They'd made friends with the people he worked with at the paper, and it seemed as if they might

281

be settling into a comfortable middle-class existence. Then the bombing of Pearl Harbor had set Alex rolling into one of his states of deep despondency. When he descended into one of his dark periods, nothing she said or did could reach him. And sadly, these episodes always ended with a radical act of desperation on his part. When she'd first met him, she believed that she could be the candle that lit the darkness inside of him, and she'd strived to be, but it never worked. When he should have turned to her for support, he always turned away.

Anna pulled her coat closer to her body. She felt frozen inside. If only she could go home, and curl up in her bed and sleep. But she couldn't. She was expected back at her counter, and so she headed back to the store.

All afternoon Anna felt miserable and tired. She wasn't herself. At the end of the day, Bette and Alice asked her if she wanted to stop and have a cup of coffee, but she declined. Instead she took the subway home.

When Anna got home, she quietly unlocked her door. She wanted a few minutes alone before Wera came over. Anna laid her head back on the top of the sofa. Right now, she hated Alice. *Alice has always been loose. Easy would be a good word to describe her. In fact, as soon as Benny showed her the tiniest bit of interest, she fell at his feet. I wouldn't be surprised if she's already been to bed with him.* The more she thought about Alice, the more furious she became. *Well, if he's willing to settle for trash like her, then I am glad that he's out of my life, even if we were only friends.*

Wera knocked on the door. "Anna, are you home?"

Anna sighed and got up from the sofa. She would have preferred to spend the night by herself. The way she was feeling, she knew she wouldn't be good company. But she opened the door.

Wera tilted her head "Are you feeling all right? You look pale."

"Yes, I'm just tired."

"Come, I have a nice dinner ready. You'll eat and then get some sleep."

Anna nodded. "Let me change first. I've been wearing this dress and high heels all day."

"I have an idea. Come over in your warm pajamas. It's just across the hall and you'll be much more comfortable."

"I like that idea tonight, Wera."

"I thought you would."

Anna hardly spoke during dinner, as she pushed the food around her plate.

"It's that man you've been seeing isn't it?" Wera asked.

Anna shrugged. "We don't see each other anymore."

"You're better off."

Anna shrugged again.

"Anna, you like him, don't you?"

Anna looked away.

"You can talk to me. Believe it or not, you can. I understand. I know how lonely it is to wait for your husband and not know where he is or if he is all right. It's easy to become caught up with a man who is here in the flesh and gives you the attention you are craving."

"I can't get involved with Benny. I have to think of Alex."

"Yes, that's true. But something tells me you are already involved. What happened?"

'I broke up our so-called friendship, because he was developing feelings for me. Now he is dating a girl I work with who I used to think was my friend."

"Does she know how you feel?"

"No, I don't even know how I feel. I feel so many things. I want to be with Benny, but I am sick with guilt over Alex. Oh, Wera, I am a mess."

"I don't think so. You're just a woman. We are complicated creatures."

"Have you ever had feelings for a man other than your husband?"

"Sure, I think every woman has an attraction now and then. It's just deciding how far to let the attraction take you."

"I like Benny. He's a gentleman, and he has shown me so many new and exciting things. Besides all of that, he is strong, so strong and unafraid. I can tell him anything, and he understands. He is so different from Alex."

"Oh, I think you are wrong there. I think Benny and Alex are both very much alike."

"Do you? I can't see how you think that."

"Benny may be a little stronger. He might have his mind a little more settled. But both men are passionate and driven by something they believe in."

"Yes, that's true. I never realized it. But Alex is so much needier than Benny."

"Exactly, Benny is the way Alex would have been if he'd never gone through what you told me he went through in Germany."

"Perhaps you're right, Wera."

'I think so."

"So what do I do now?" Anna said.

"What do you want?"

"I want both. That's terribly selfish, I know. But I do."

Wera nodded her head. "If you let this thing with Benny go any further, you might fall in love with him."

Anna shook her head and felt the tears sting the back of her eyes "If I am not already."

"Would you divorce Alex?"

"I don't know. I am so afraid of what would happen to Alex if I left him."

Wera nodded. "So what will you do?"

Anna shrugged her shoulders and took Wera's hand.

Chapter 85

Anna planned to forgo the party on Friday. She would have a quiet dinner with Wera and play a game of cards. But when she told Bette that she wasn't coming, Bette insisted.

"Come on, Anna, don't be so selfish. It would be good for your friend to get out of the house. The two of you burrowed into that building like two moles is not at all good for either one of you."

"Bette, it's cold and snowy, and we'd have to take the subway. I don't think Wera would want to do all of that."

"Why don't you give her the option?"

"Bette…"

"Come on, it's Christmas, and it won't be the same without you." Bette smiled.

"You win. I'll be there. I don't know about Wera. I'll have to ask her."

"Fair enough. I'll see you tonight then?"

"Yes. Eight o'clock, right?"

"Yep," Bette smiled.

Wera surprised Anna. She wanted to go to the party. Wera insisted upon baking cookies for the two of them to bring.

"I made my famous *kolachkes*. Taste one."

"You didn't have to go to all that trouble." Anna took a bite. "Oh my, these are delicious."

Wera winked. "Come on, get your coat. We'll be late for the party."

Chapter 86

When they got to Bette's apartment, the women outnumbered the men at a ratio of three-to-one. This is war. Anna thought. The men all gone off to fight, the women alone and worried, but surviving. Still, even with Alex away and the constant concern about his welfare, she was glad that America had entered the war. Without the help of the Lady of Liberty, Hitler might just be unstoppable.

Wera got a glass of punch for herself and one for Anna. Although her old-fashioned dress looked out of place, Wera did not seem at all intimidated by the other more fashion-forward young women. When Benny walked in with Alice, Wera looked directly at him. Even though she'd never seen him before she knew he was the one that had turned Anna's head. Incredibly handsome, well-spoken and self-confident, Benny made his way around the room, saying hello to all of the employees who knew him from the union strike. Now that she saw him in the flesh, Wera could see what had attracted Anna. From what Anna, had told her of Alex, Wera still felt that Benny was a great deal like Alex. But Alex lacked Benny's self-confidence and his immediate likeability, which brought him lots of friends. Benny cast a ray of sunshine as he made his way through the crowd toward Anna. Here he comes, Wera thought.

"Anna Banana, I just wanted to wish you a happy *Hanukah* and a happy New Year."

"Thanks, Benny. The same to you."

"Isn't tonight the last night of *Hanukah*?"

"Yes, it's the 22nd." Anna noticed that Benny had a black eye.

"And the oil burned for eight days. Right? Isn't that the premise? You know I'm not religious, but I actually have a little bit of knowledge of the Jewish holidays."

"Yes, Benny, that's the premise. There is more to it, but you have the basic idea."

"Wanna tell me the rest of the story?" Benny smiled.

"Not now." The words caught in her throat. "What happened to your eye?" Anna asked.

"Hey there, Benny! I've been looking all over the place for you. You go off to get a girl a cup of punch, and you don't come back for a half-hour. I guess that's what I have to cope with, dating Mr. Popular, the union rep." Alice smiled. "Hi, Anna, this must be your friend Wera?"

Anna nodded. "Yes. Wera, this is Alice. Alice …Wera."

"Nice to finally meet you. Anna says such nice things about you at work," Alice said.

"A pleasure," Wera said.

"Just look at our poor brave Benny. He was attacked by union-busters the other day," Alice said, and she gently touched the bruise beneath Benny's eye. "Without this fellow we would never have won our contract." Alice said to Wera. "Isn't that right, Anna?"

"Benny works very hard for the union," Anna said.

"Well, nice to meet you, Wera. Good to see you, Anna," Alice said, wrapping her arm into Benny's. "Let's go get something to eat. I'm famished."

As they walked away, Benny quickly glanced back over his shoulder. Anna saw the longing in his eyes and turned away.

"You might as well accept it. You really like him," Wera said.

"Yes, I know. But I am trying to fight it, and the harder I try, the stronger the feelings are."

"It can be that way sometimes."

"Hi, Anna. I'm so glad you came." Bette gave Anna a warm hug. "This must be Wera?"

"Yes."

"I'm so glad you could come to my party."

Even as Bette was talking to Anna, she was stealing glances at Benny, who had his arm around Alice. Alice was laughing. Then Alice walked over to a table decoration and picked out a piece of mistletoe. She stretched to hold it above Benny's head. Then she kissed him. Anna quickly turned away. But something forced her to look back and she saw that although Benny was kissing Alice, his eyes were open and he was staring at Anna.

"How are you holding up?" Wera asked Anna after Bette left to welcome another guest.

"I don't know. It hurts to see him with her, but I have no right to him. I'm a married woman."

"Sometimes our emotions don't know right from wrong."

"I know how he feels about me. I can see it in his eyes."

"I wish I could give you some advice. I don't have any. All I can say is that I am your friend and I will be here for you no matter what you do."

"Oh, Wera, thank God for you. What would I ever do without you?"

"You're a strong woman, Anna. You would manage."

Throughout the night, Anna stole glances at Benny, only to find that he had stopped paying attention to her and was focused on Alice. Anna wanted to leave; she felt sick, but she didn't want to ruin the party for Wera, who had made friends as people came up to compliment her on her cookies.

It seemed as if the night might never end, but as the clock ticked toward one o'clock, the party began to break up. Anna and Wera thanked Bette for having them, and then they both wrapped themselves in their winter clothes and began their walk to the subway. Anna had never taken the train this late at night. A bitter cold wind brushed across their faces as they walked the empty street.

"Got any spare change?" A bum in ragged clothes hardly enough to protect him from the cold asked.

"Come on, Anna." Wera grabbed Anna's arm. They tried to walk faster, but the sidewalk was slippery with ice.

"Can't you find it in your cold heart to help a guy who's down on his luck?" The bum came chasing after them.

Anna felt her heart pounding. She thought about the time she was robbed when she'd ended up in the hospital.

"Leave us alone," Anna said, trying to sound firm and unafraid.

"Heartless bitch." The bum was so close that Anna could smell the alcohol on his breath.

"Hey, what the hell is going on here?" Benny said as he came walking up with Alice.

"Nothing. We're fine," Anna said.

"Come on, leave the girls alone. You're scaring them," Benny said to the bum. He took a quarter out of his pocket and handed it to the man. "Now get outta here."

"Thank you," Anna said.

"He's just a drunk, looking for money for liquor. Probably pretty harmless. Why don't I take you ladies home in a taxi? It would ease my mind to know that you got home safely," Benny said.

Anna looked at Wera. She saw the relief on her face and felt the same gush of relief. "That would be wonderful," Anna said. "Thank you."

Benny flagged a cab and opened the door. The three women piled in and Benny got into the front. He strategically gave the driver Alice's address first.

"Benny, didn't you want to come over tonight?" Alice said. "Why don't we drop them off first?"

"I'm kinda tired, Alice. Maybe another time. Besides you live the closest. It would be easiest to drop you off first."

Alice didn't say another word, but the tension grew thicker ever minute as the cab made its way to Alice's flat.

"Goodnight, "Anna and Wera said as Alice got out of the taxi. Benny got out and opened her door, then walked her up the walkway. Then he turned and got back into the cab. Anna saw Alice huff, then go inside as the cab eased away from the curb and back onto the street.

"Don't wait for me," Benny said to the driver as the three got out in front of Wera and Anna's building.

"It's not necessary for you to walk us inside," Wera said. "We are fine from here."

Anna's heart was on fire. She was confused, angry, but fatally attracted to Benny.

"I insist," he said. "It will ease my mind to know you are safe."

Even with that black eye, he was handsome, rugged, and unafraid. Anna wanted to run away, and at the same time, she yearned to fall into his arms, to collapse and feel his kisses all over her. *What am I thinking?*

Benny paid the driver and walked the two women up to the door of their building.

"Goodnight," Anna said as she fumbled with the keys. "Thank you for taking us home."

"Anna…" Benny's deep voice cracked with emotion.

"Yes?"

"Please?"

She cocked her head.

"Can I speak to you alone for just a minute?"

"Oh yes, of course, "Wera said, and she turned to Anna. "I'll go upstairs. I'll see you in the morning."

Anna nodded. She watched Wera disappear into the building.

"I know what you said. I know that you want me to go away, to leave you alone. And I tried. I really tried. Hell, I even went so far as to start seeing Alice, but Anna…I'm crazy about you. I think I might even be in love with you. I can't think of anything else."

She felt the same way, but she couldn't tell him. She had to think of Alex.

His eyes were so naked, that she knew he had told her the truth.

"Please, Anna. Don't send me away again. I know that you feel the same way about me…"

"I don't. I love my husband."

Anna turned to open the door. Benny stopped her. He turned her around to look at him. His desire for her was like a magnet, pulling at her body and her heart. He took her into his arms. She struggled but only for a second. Anna felt wonderfully weak in his arms. Here was a man she could lean on. The warm strength of his touch, filled her with yearning and she grew limp in his arms. It felt like dream, a fantasy, as he leaned down and their lips met for the first time.

Chapter 87

Three Christmases and three summers passed as the war continued to escalate and the death toll continued to rise.

The friendship between Alex and Nelly grew stronger, and because of Nelly, Alex found some acceptance from the other men in his platoon. There were still those who called him the dirty Jew, but there were others who had begun to look past his ethnic background and befriended him as a fellow soldier.

Sometimes Alex would lie in bed at night and find it hard to remember Anna's face. He would picture her, but as time went by the picture began to fade. He still wrote, but less frequently. And she still answered, but less frequently.

As Alex and Nelly came to know each other better, he learned more about her son. The boy was born with a clubfoot, which caused him to walk with a severe limp. With just Nelly and her mother to support the child, there had been limited funds for medical treatment. Nelly had never told anyone except Alex how guilty this made her feel.

"Perhaps a really good doctor could have done something to make it easier for him to walk. The other children laugh at him and it just breaks my heart," Nelly told Alex.

"I don't know if anything would help. But then again, who knows what a good doctor could do? What I do believe is that you've tried to do everything in your power to give the boy a good life; haven't you?"

"Yes, I've tried."

"Well then, you've done your best. Just give the boy your love, Nelly. That's the finest gift anyone can ever receive."

At Nelly's request, Alex wrote children's stories for her son, which she tucked inside the care packages that she packed for him. Her mother read the stories aloud to the boy at night, and wrote to tell Nelly how much the child enjoyed them.

"You're a talented writer," Nelly told Alex.

"I don't know. I've often wondered if I really have talent or if I just think I do. I suppose for me, writing is my voice. Do you know what I mean?"

"Not exactly."

"I've always had difficulty relating to other people. I've always felt like an outsider, except with you and Anna. You two are the only people I've ever been able to truly be myself with."

"I'm glad that I can be here for you."

"I'm glad too." Alex smiled at her. It was getting dark. Nelly usually left the men's barracks earlier, but on this night, she'd stayed late.

"Will you walk me home?"

"Of course," Alex smiled at her. "I'd be happy to."

It was a cold night in late January of 1944. Nelly had forgotten her gloves. As they walked, she tucked her hand into Alex's pocket and folded her fingers into his waiting hand. As soon as he felt her presence, a shot of electrical energy ran through him.

"Do you think I'm pretty?" Nelly asked.

"Beautiful," Alex answered. "Why would you ask such a question?"

"I've always wanted to know. I've always been afraid that I wasn't attractive enough, and that's why my son's father ran away from me."

"My guess is he was probably afraid of taking on the responsibilities of a family. It can be scary for a man. You must realize that the man is the one who must earn enough money to take care of his wife and children. It's a big responsibility."

"But you married Anna. Would you have married her if she were pregnant?"

"Yes, I would have."

"I wish I had a man who loved me, really loved me, a man like you," Nelly said and she squeezed his hand.

"Look, there's a shooting star…" Alex said.

"I see; it's beautiful. Make a wish."

They had arrived at her room.

"Goodnight," she said, squeezing his hand but not letting it go.

Alex looked down at her blonde hair glowing in the starlight. She looked up at him.

"Well, goodnight," he said.

"Alex?"

"Yes…"

"Would you like to come in and stay the night? My roommate is on leave. She won't be back until tomorrow. I have the room all to myself..." Nelly said.

Alex looked into her eyes. They shined like candle flames in the moonlight. It had been a long time since he held a woman in his arms, a long time since he'd felt the wonder of release…

"Alex..." Nelly said, cocking her head and smiling just a little. Then she opened the door and beckoned to him...

Chapter 88

Benny took Anna on a trip up to Boston. She loved the cozy restaurants and friendly neighborhood bars. They walked hand-in-hand through Harvard square, and then toured the hallowed halls of the famous university. For three glorious days, they explored the history of America. Anna marveled to see so many of the landmarks she'd learned about when she had studied for her citizenship. Then Benny rented a car and they drove up to Maine, where they ate lobsters and spent entire days lying in bed and making love. Benny didn't earn as good a salary as he might have as a lawyer, but his generosity toward Anna made her feel like a goddess. In turn, she sacrificed time with her friends, even Wera, and spent every free moment with him. Neither Benny nor Anna ever mentioned Alex, but for Anna he was always there, a presence in the room reminding her of her commitment. She worried about him, prayed that he hadn't been killed, or worse, captured. Strangely as happy as she was with Benny, her heart still belonged to Alex.

But Anna had never before felt so carefree, so adored, and she couldn't resist being swept up in the wonder of it all. She had no doubt that whatever cards the future dealt to her, Benny would be there standing behind her, holding her up if need be. And because his fervor was so contagious, she came to believe in his causes and to admire the way he cared and worked to protect the less fortunate.

The other salesgirls at Gimbels began to gossip. They saw Anna leave work with Benny every night, and they noticed that whenever Anna took time off work, Benny disappeared as well. She discussed the situation with Benny and asked him to try and be more discreet. He agreed to make the effort, for her sake. Personally, he said, he didn't care what people said about him. He loved Anna and he wasn't ashamed of his feelings. But because it mattered to her, when Benny held a union meeting, he treated Anna as if they were only working colleagues, but anyone could see the electrical current that ran between them. The way that they glanced at each other, the secret smiles they shared...

Even though Benny made every effort to be careful and he used precautions, Anna became pregnant. She was distraught. It had been three years since she last time she had been with Alex. If she gave birth to a child, there would be no doubt that Alex was not the father.

"I think we should see if we can find a doctor who is willing to help, or even a medical student," Anna said as they sat on the sofa in her apartment.

"That is far too dangerous. I refuse to put you at risk like that, Anna."

"But I can't have the baby. What would people say? What about Alex? I can't do it."

"You can if you divorce Alex and marry me..."

"I thought you weren't the type of man to ever get married."

"That was before I met you..." Benny said and he squeezed her hand.

Chapter 89

Spring came slowly to England, melting winter's last attempt at blanketing the earth in snow. Alex had become fairly good at his job. It took some effort to learn mechanics, but he'd done well.

After he finished working one evening he was on his way to the mess hall to meet Nelly when Sergeant Sife came walking up to him. Alex greeted his superior as was expected.

"You know Mittelman, I don't much care for you. And I don't take it too kindly that you been seeing that girl, Nelly. You're a Jew and she ain't one. You ought to stick to your own kind."

Alex said nothing. He just stood listening.

"You hear me, Private?"

Alex nodded.

"I can't hear you. I said do you hear me?"

"Yes, Sergeant."

"And are you gonna quit seeing that girl?"

"No, sir, I'm not."

"Like I said, Mittelman, I don't like you. And me not liking you won't do you no good; in fact it could just turn out to be your biggest mistake. You see I got it in for you. I can't make you leave that girl alone, but I sure can make your life a living hell. You understand me, Private?"

"Yes sir."

"And you still gonna go on seeing that Nelly?"

"Yes, sir, I am."

"Stupid bastard," Sergeant Sife said, shaking his head as he walked away.

The repercussions of that conversation were not immediate. In fact, Alex had almost come to believe that the sergeant was only bluffing. But almost a week later, he discovered what the sergeant had planned. Alex lay on his bunk when he received a message that he had new orders. Alex would be sent to join a platoon going into combat. They would be leaving for France in a few days. Alex did not have the exact location where they planned to land; none of the soldiers did, in case there were spies amongst the troops. However, he heard that the Allies had begun bombing northern France, giving Hitler the impression that they would land somewhere in the North. This led Alex to believe that the attack would take place in the South. However, he was not sure of anything. He could find himself landing in Poland for all he knew. But what he knew for sure was that he was about to see combat and he had a good chance of being killed.

That night Alex took Nelly for a walk after dinner. There was a full moon and the night sky was almost blue in color.

"I've received new orders. I am going into battle."

"On land?" Nelly asked.

"Yes, I think so."

"Oh my God, Alex, You are a mechanic, you're trained to fix planes. You should complain. Tell them that you would be of more use working on equipment."

"Who should I tell this to?"

"Your sergeant?"

"He's the one who requested my transfer."

"Why? Why would he do that to you? You're good at your job. You never answer him back. Why would he want to send you into such a terrible, dangerous situation? And you haven't even been properly trained for it."

Alex shrugged. "I'll be all right."

Nelly started crying.

"Shhh, don't cry. I wanted to fight Nazis. I joined the service for that very reason."

"Alex you could be killed."

"I know. But I have to do this. If I do, maybe the demons that haunt me will finally go away."

"I don't know what you're talking about. All I know is you could be killed."

"Shhh," he said again and she laid her head on his shoulder.

"I will miss you. Will you write to me?" Nelly asked.

"Of course I will. And who knows, I might be such a terrible solider that they will send me back." Alex smiled, but he knew that he'd better be a good shot. He would need to be sharp, alert, and have plenty of *mazel* if he were going to survive.

After Nelly settled down, Alex went back to his barracks. He would never have told her, except that she would have found out after he had gone, and it would have been worse for her if he'd left without saying goodbye. He wondered if he should tell Anna....

Chapter 90

June 5, 1944

An American ship docked on an inlet
on the South Coast of Britain

Alex reflected on his life as he gazed up at the full moon. If the seas had been calmer and the winds less wicked, they would have landed in Normandy tonight. But the weather had forced them to stop.

There was a good chance he would die in battle tomorrow and he was afraid, afraid of death. Would it be painful? What was waiting on the other side? Perhaps nothing. What if there was nothing after death, just silence, a ceasing of existence? The thought terrified him and he refused to believe it; he knew there was a God. Although Alex didn't always understand God's actions, and he'd even been angry with God and argued with him, he'd felt God's presence so many times in his life. He was sure that it was God who'd gotten him of Dachau, although he couldn't understand why he was chosen to live, and his loved ones to die. God's will sometimes made no sense to him. Then, once again, he felt God's hand again after the fire when he hadn't known where to go or what to do to care for Anna. God had guided him, and he'd found his way. Alex began to pray, not prayers from a book, but his own words, words from his heart. Never had he felt closer to God then he did lying outside looking up at the moon and knowing that tomorrow he would be face-to-face with death. Whether death would claim him or not remained to be seen. But he could feel God beside him, and he allowed himself to put his trust in God. And as he did he felt at peace. God would guide him, and if he died, God would take his hand and all would be well.

Dear God, please take care of Anna. If I should die, if you should choose to take me now, please help Anna to find someone who will love and take care of her. And wherever he might be, please watch over Manny. I owe him so much. He saved my life once, but more importantly, he saved my Anna.

Alex sighed, and he thought about writing to Anna, but there was a good chance the letter would never arrive. The decision not to tell her about his being sent to combat began to worry him. If he didn't make it, it would come as such a shock to her. But at the same time, why worry her unnecessarily? What Anna had never understood about him was that he went away from her when things became rough to protect her from the depth of his emotions. Never once had he planned to leave her, but he didn't want to burden her. Instead he would go off and work things out on his own, then try to return with a solution. And now, again, he'd chosen not to burden her, to let fate take its course. Why have her waiting for the outcome on pins and needles? If need be, there would be time enough for crying later.

The men awakened as the ship pulled out of the inlet in the wee hours of the morning. "I have a message for you from General Eisenhower," General Montgomery said. Then he told the infantry what Eisenhower had said.

"You are about to embark upon a great crusade…" Montgomery began, reading from the wire Eisenhower had sent.

Some of the men cheered, others just sat looking out at the water, quiet, introspective. They'd been told that they would be landing at a division of the Normandy beach that had been code named Omaha. From what Alex understood there were five sections of the beach, Omaha, Utah, Gold, Sword, and

Juno. It had been planned that they would arrive when the tide was low, enabling the soldiers to wade through the water onto the land without the threat of drowning. An aerial invasion would take place simultaneously.

The sun had not fully risen as the ship arrived at its destination. Alex felt a wave of nausea hit him. The waters were choppy; men were seasick and vomiting over the side of the ship. Those unable to get to the side in time threw up right on the deck. Alex gagged at the smell. Because of low tide, the ship could not come close enough to shore to let the men out. Instead, they were loaded onto ducks, which could take them further in toward the beach. The men lined up to board the ducks, which ran back and forth picking up soldiers and dropping them off. When the men got off the ducks they were open targets for the machine-gun fire. But there was no way to bring them closer in; they had to go the rest of the way on foot. The men behind him in line pushed Alex forward. He boarded the duck, which bounced and jolted toward the shore. Dead bodies of soldiers who'd just left the ship floated all around them in a sea red with blood. Some of the men began to cry as the steel door of the duck opened, releasing them. But the others forced them forward; there was no time to lose. Men began to pile out of the duck and try to run against the force of the water toward the safety of land. They held their guns over their heads to keep them from getting wet. Alex fought the desire to vomit. Instead he began fighting his way through the water. Gunfire rained like a storm of death from the ten-foot cliffs that surrounded the beach. The bloody water splashed up in Alex's face as men fell on all sides of him. He pushed the bodies of his fellow soldiers out of the way and pressed on. Then the open eyes of a dead solder caught his glance, and for a moment Alex forgot the chaos around him. It was a young boy, maybe nineteen. Alex could not take his eyes off the dead man. He stopped moving. It felt as if he were glued to the spot. Poor boy, Alex thought, never to return home, never to see his loved ones again. A small voice in his head said, "Alex, don't stop. Don't look around you, and for God's sake, don't think. Just stay focused. Go forward; move as fast as you can toward the land. Get yourself to the safety of the trees."

His heart pounded in his ears. The Canadian soldier whom he'd sat beside on the ship last night waded right next to him. Then Alex heard him scream as a bullet flew into his chest, ripping a hole the size of a baseball into his flesh. That could have been me, Alex thought. It was only a few feet away.

Alex knew he must keep going, keep moving forward, no matter what he saw or felt. He must not stop. When he gently slid a dead body out of his way, Alex saw that one side of the young soldiers' faces was nothing but a mass of bloody matter.

"Don't think... You must not think. Get to the shore...alive."

The deafening roar of gunfire hurt his ears. If only he could move faster, but the weight of the water slowed him down. He struggled against the elements until finally he began to feel the sand more solid beneath his feet. A soldier sat on the beach crying. One shot, and he fell. Alex knew that he must not stop; he must concentrate on his own survival right now. *Just a few more steps and I'll be on land.*

When he reached the shore Alex started to run. He ran faster than he'd ever thought possible. He ran as if the devil were at his heels, as a hailstorm of bullets raced one step behind.

Chapter 91

Anna lay in Benny's arms. Since she'd become pregnant, Anna had begun to prefer spending quiet weekends with Benny at her apartment. She found dancing and running all over the city too taxing. He smoothed her hair. Soon she would be showing, and forced to leave work. Then they agreed that she would move into Benny's apartment. He would pay all of the bills and she would stay at home and raise their child. Every penny that Alex had sent her, Anna had saved in an envelope in her drawer. She would continue to save it and then give it to him when he returned. She didn't deserve that money. She was his wife, but she had sinned; she had given herself, heart and body, to another man. Benny and Anna had decided that Anna would ask Alex for a divorce, but not by mail, not until he returned safely home.

Even with Benny's love and constant support, Anna had misgivings. She owed Alex. She'd married him, and she loved him.

But she loved Benny too, loved him in a way she'd never been able to love Alex. Benny made the decisions. He took charge. He took care of Anna's every need, anticipated it before she knew it herself. But the biggest difference was a private one, one that Anna could not ever tell Benny or anyone else. It was sexual. With Alex, making love had been tender, gentle, warm, and loving. But Benny was different; his passionate, driven personality flowed over into an overpowering sexual whirlwind. His desire for her swept her up until she lost all touch with conscious thought. He was demanding as a lover, insatiable, taking her body to heights she'd never even known she could experience, and for the first time, with Benny, Anna had an orgasm. It was like heroin; once she tasted the sweetness she couldn't help but yearn for more.

At night, every time Benny left and Anna was alone, the guilt always came seeping back. *Alex… God only knows where he is, if he is even alive. I am a horrible person. All I can think of is myself, while Alex is out there somewhere, perhaps suffering.* She cried herself to sleep, often wishing she'd never met Benny, and cherishing every minute she spent with him.

"You'll probably miss the company picnic this year," Benny said, breaking Anna out of her personal thoughts

"Yes, I know I'll be almost into my second trimester by then. And goodness knows I'll have trouble hiding my belly." She patted her stomach. "Just look at how big I am already. When I look in the mirror I feel sick. I am so fat! None of my clothes fit."

"You are and have always been beautiful. Pregnancy only makes you more beautiful to me."

"And fat."

"Nope, just beautiful. Glowing, happy, and beautiful."

Benny leaned down kissing the top of Anna's head. "Would you like me to pick some food up for dinner?" he asked. It was a Friday afternoon, and Anna had gotten off early from work.

"Sure, what would you like?"

"Oh I don't know, you're the one with cravings. Anything you want is fine by me."

"How about some potato *latkes* from the deli around the corner?"

"Your wish is my command, my princess." he said. "I'd better hurry though; they'll close by sundown for the Sabbath. I'll take a walk over there now and pick them up. Would you like some corned beef and a rye bread to go with it?"

"Hmm. maybe roast beef for me. Corned beef is too spicy. Spice bothers me since I've been expecting." She smiled and he kissed her. "Why don't you order a little of both, corned beef for you, roast beef for me?"

"Sounds good. I'll be right back." He stood up, then leaned over her and kissed her again.

"Mmmm, your kisses could keep me here."

"But then you would be too late to get anything from the deli."

"Yep, but we have all night…"

She smiled at him and shook her head. "Benjamin Berman, you are incorrigible."

"That's what they say…" He winked at her and smiled.

Damn, she thought. He looks so much like Clarke Gable.

All of the windows were open in the entire apartment, but there was hardly a breeze. Benny bought Anna a fan, and it helped a little, but she still felt sweaty. Her hair, normally like silk, was frizzing around her rounded face. She hated the way pregnancy made her look, but the reward at the end would make it all worthwhile. Anna would be a mother; she would have a child of her own, Benny's child. A sad smile came slowly over her face as she remembered her own mother. God how she missed her parents. It had been years since she'd heard from them. She prayed that they'd gone into hiding and would contact her after the war. The alternative was unbearable. How could she be so happy and so miserable at the same time? She wanted the baby, but she didn't. Alex

310

would be so hurt. She could see the look on his face, and it made her feel sick to her stomach.

The downstairs bell rang on the wall of her apartment. Who could that be? Maybe Benny had forgotten his key, and wanted her to buzz him in, or it could be that they had the wrong apartment number. That happened quite often. She went to the intercom and pressed the button that allowed her to speak and listen.

"Who is it?" Anna asked.

"Telegram for Mrs. Mittelman. Are you Mrs. Mittelman?"

"Yes…" Anna's heart thundered in her ears.

"May I come upstairs and give you the telegram?"

Chapter 92

The cobblestone streets were crowded with automobiles as Benny navigated through the groups of people congregating on the sidewalk. Of all the places he'd traveled, Benny loved New York the most, the familiar old ethnic neighborhoods, the exotic foods that the immigrants from everywhere brought to the New World, but most of all the people.

He rounded the corner and entered, Appleman's Deli. As always, a small crowd waited in line to place their orders, with only one man serving behind the counter. Benny went to the end of the line.

"Aren't you that fellow who's with the union?" the man who stood behind him asked. He was a heavyset man, with thick skin and jowls that looked like two weights on the sides of his face.

"Yep, that's me."

"You're one of them Jew troublemakers, right? I should have known I'd see one of you assholes if I came here to the Jewish deli. But my wife likes this food. I sure as hell don't know why. Oh boy, do I know all about you and your damn unions."

"It depends on what you mean by a troublemaker," Benny said. He wasn't in the mood for a union-buster today. It would be nice to just go back to the apartment and enjoy a quiet dinner with Anna.

"You know what I mean, stirring up them workers causing problems, getting folks fired."

"Well, you see there are a lot of labor laws that need to be changed. If we don't start to organize, and join together, the company owners take terrible advantage of the workers. They make plenty of money, but hardly pay their employees a living wage and people out there are working long hours for very little money. Many of them work ten to twelve hour days without even a break to eat. Do you think that's fair?" Benny felt himself becoming angry.

"I think that folks are lucky to have jobs. And you want to mess that up. Shit, do you have any idea what it's like to stand in a fucking bread line? My son listened to one of you SOBs and you know what happened? He was fired, and then his wife left him, so he jumped off the bridge, my one son, my only boy. He left me with three kids to support. "

"I'm sorry that happened. I can imagine how you feel, and my heart goes out to you. But, with all due respect, sir, I can't help but try to make the scales to be a little more balanced. If the labor force has no rights, then the owners can take advantage, especially in a depressed economy."

"My only son…"

"Next," the owner of the deli wearing a white apron called out.

"I'm next," Benny said.

"No, you ain't. I was here before you," The man Benny had been talking to was itching for a fight.

"Go ahead. I can wait a few minutes."

"I want a pound of pastrami and pumpernickel bread."

The deli man packed up the order. "Here you go, sir."

The man with the jowls nodded, taking the bag and handing the owner a few dollars. Then he turned back to Benny and said, "You better watch your back. My boy lost his job because of one of them damn unions some good-for-nothing talked him into joining. Coulda been you."

Benny didn't answer, although he wanted to. His blood boiled. He wanted to hit the old guy right in the face, but it wasn't worth the aggravation.

"Sir, can I help you?" The deli clerk addressed Benny.

"Yeah, thanks. I need a half pound of roast beef and a half pound of corned beef, four potato pancakes, and a rye bread."

"Right away, sir."

Benny watched the other man leave the deli in his dirty tee shirt, with his oversized belly hanging over the belt of his pants. Bastard, he thought.

After he paid, Benny took his package and left. Put that guy outta your mind, he's not worth getting upset over, Benny thought, but he was still shaking as he walked back toward the apartment.

Benny passed an alleyway between two tall buildings. Before he realized what was happening he felt a hand covering his mouth pulling him into the alleyway. Although Benny could take care of himself in a fight, this assault caught him off guard. He lost his footing and slipped as he felt the sting of the blade of a knife tear across his throat. Blood poured like a river from his neck. The bag the deli manager had carefully packed in white paper dropped from his hand. At first, he couldn't believe what happened. But he felt the gush of wind come into his body from the open wound as he fell to the ground, his blood a crimson blanket on the concrete. I'm dying, he thought. It had happened so suddenly. He'd just been on his way to Anna's for a night of cuddling. If he continued to bleed this heavily, he would be dead in a few minutes. *What about Anna? The baby? Our future? How did this happen?* Benny's eyes closed for the last time as the man who'd murdered him picked up Benny's bag of food from where it had fallen, wiped the blood on to his tee shirt and straightened the contents, then shoved it under his arm and left. His wife sure would be happy that he brought home all that Jew food.

Chapter 93

Anna almost forgot to tip the delivery boy. Her hands trembled, as she found a quarter and pushed it into his right hand, taking the envelope and closing the door. She wished Benny had returned already, and then he would be here with her when she opened the telegram. But he had not yet returned and she couldn't bear to wait.

She tore open the envelope. For several minutes, she could not understand the words. She read them repeatedly. Alex had gone into combat. He was missing in action somewhere in France. The army did not know if he was dead or alive. Anna's hand covered her mouth. Alex, my God... Alex, all alone somewhere in France. He could be in agony. The Nazis might have him. Oh dear God, he needs me, and I'm not with him. Her heart cried out as she said his name over and over again. "Alex...Alex..."

Anna had to find Benny; she couldn't cope with this alone. Benny was her oak tree. He would know what to do. He'd been gone a long time, far longer than it took to buy some food at the deli around the corner. Anna slipped on her shoes, and with the letter still in her hand, she ran down the stairs to the main floor of the building. *Maybe someone stopped him to talk about building a union, and he got sidetracked.* That happened to the two of them all the time, so Anna had come to expect it.

As soon as she got outside, Anna heard the blaring of ambulances and saw the flashing lights of police cars. Something had happened up the street. Perhaps Benny was in the crowd of people who'd gathered on the sidewalk.

"What happened?" Anna asked a woman with an infant in her arms as she approached the scene.

"That union fella got killed in the alley over there. A fella and his little boy found his body. Somebody slit his throat."

"What union fella?" Anna asked, but she already knew. Her face turned white, she began to hyperventilate. *How was this possible? Could it really be Benny?*

She ran up to the front, pushing her way through the crowd.

"Who is it?" She asked a police officer who was loading the covered body into the ambulance.

"That union fella, his identification said his name is Benjamin Berman. Do you know him? Can you come with us to identify the body?"

Anna didn't answer... She walked away, deaf to the roaring crowds and blazing horns of the ambulance.

"Benny is gone, gone forever. Oh God..." Her voice came as a whisper.

Anna broke the heel of her shoe as she ran back to her apartment. Once she got inside she slammed the door, breathing heavily from the shock and exertion. She heard Wera next door, but she needed to be alone. Anna remembered that Alex had left a bottle of whiskey under the sink. She could count number of the times she'd had alcohol on one hand. She poured herself a shot. As always, the taste assaulted her senses; then it burned as it slid down her throat. But she didn't stop; she poured another and drank it quickly, then another. The bitter taste of whiskey lingered on her lips. In the past, when she'd taken a shot, she felt numb, easy, tired. But this time she felt as if she'd been struck with madness. Suddenly Anna was filled with anger, anger at Alex, at Benny, anger at her life and her wasted youth, rage at

Hitler, but most of all anger toward herself. She wanted to die. Alex was missing, and Benny was dead. Her mind was crazed. She could not believe all that had happened in just a few hours. She could see no point in trying to go on, no point in bringing a child into a world as cruel as this one. It would be better if she had never been born. Anna's hand trembled as she took the knitting needle out of her bag of yarn. Then she ripped off her underpants and lay down on her bed. "God forgive me, I can't take anymore. I can't bring this child into this hell, and care for it by myself. I can't do it. I give up. I'm tired, and I'm finished," she whispered, tears running down her cheeks. Anna shoved the needle inside of her. A pain the likes of which she had never felt before shot through her like a lightning bolt. She would abort this child, it would never have to endure the hell she had lived through, and hopefully she would die in the process. Sharp pains shot through her belly, familiar pains, but stronger than she'd ever felt them. Anna held her abdomen as an ocean of blood poured out of her. She rolled onto her side in a fetal position.

Then, because of the intense pain and the extreme loss of blood, Anna lost consciousness.

Anna awoke to bright overhead lights that stung her eyes. Her head felt as if a band of drummers pounded inside of her brain. Could she be dreaming? It looked like the hospital but her mind was fuzzy. What had happened? How had she come to be here? A nurse gently held her hand as she told Anna that she'd lost a lot of blood, and that she had miscarried. Anna turned away, her saliva tasted bitter in her mouth as her memory returned.

"And Benny? The union man who was attacked in the alley? Did, you hear about it? Was he brought here? Did he make it?" She hoped against all odds that somehow some way…

"I'm sorry. He didn't. Did you know him?"

Anna nodded and turned her face to the wall. *The baby…gone… Well, she'd caused that…killed it in a fit of madness... Benny…her rock, her oak tree…her friend and her lover…gone... Alex…dear sweet Alex, where was he? He might be dead; could he be swept from her life too?* An ocean of tears would not be enough to express the sadness and grief she felt. But she could not cry; her heart ached too much to weep. Now Anna was truly alone, and even if she wanted to, she could not return to Germany to her family. She didn't want to speculate what the Nazis might have done to her parents. It had been a long time since she'd heard from them. Anna had seen too much pain in her young life, and now everything had fallen apart, everything had failed. Maybe God was angry with her for betraying Alex, and so he'd punished her by taking Benny. And maybe her suicide attempt had failed because God wanted her to live so that she would suffer for what she had done. Well I deserve to suffer. I had an affair while my husband fought and perhaps died on foreign soil, and I killed my unborn child. I don't deserve any sympathy. I deserve to spend the rest of my life in agony.

"Anna…" Wera stood in the hallway and peeked her head around the corner into the room. "Are you all right? My God you gave me a scare. I went over to your apartment to borrow some milk and it's a damn good thing I did. I found you. What were you thinking Anna?"

"You found me? You're the one who called the hospital."

"Yes, I thought that you and Benny had gone out somewhere, so when I knocked and you didn't answer, I used my key."

"Oh, Wera, Benny is dead, and Alex is missing in action."

"Anna!" Wera took Anna's hand and sat down on the edge of the bed." I'm here Anna."

"I think I've lost my mind. When I heard about Alex and then Benny... Oh God, Wera, Benny! I wanted to die. I wanted to kill my baby. What was I thinking? Now the baby's dead. I've murdered my child...and I'm so weak from the loss of blood." Anna was as pale as the white hospital walls; her body shook violently.

"Are you cold? You look like you have the chills."

"Yes, very cold," Anna answered, her teeth chattering.

"I'm going to get you another blanket. I'll be right back."

Wera went to the nurse's station and got another blanket, which she spread over Anna.

"It's going to be all right, Anna. "Wera squeezed her hand. "We will get through this together. I'll help you."

"Wera, I'm so glad you came. I need you so much right now. I committed the most unspeakable crime against my own helpless baby."

"I think maybe you were in shock... and that's why you did this."

"What am I going to do, Wera? How am I ever going to go on living? I ran away from Germany, from Hitler, from the Nazis. I left my parents, and God only knows where they are now. But you know what? Hitler is here. He is still with me. The hatred he brought out in people has stayed with me, and with Alex, and with every Jew who tried to escape him. Because, you see, no matter what we do, our lives will never be the same. It will never be for us the way it would have been if we hadn't been forced out of our homes. The guilt I feel for my parents? Alex has the same guilt. And now, I'm so guilty about the baby. I wish I had died."

"You shouldn't say that. God's greatest gift is life."

"God is punishing me for my affair with Benny. That's why Benny is dead. Or maybe God has an anti-Semitic streak too. Why did he let this happen with the Nazis? Why, Wera, why are so many Jews forced to suffer? Tell me, Wera, tell me. I want to know…" She shook even more violently than before. The veins on her neck stood out like purple ropes.

"I don't know, Anna. I wish I had all the answers but I don't. But I refuse to believe that God is mean or vengeful. I think that God allows us to do what we want to do. Then, sometimes, bad things happen. But I know, no matter what, I know God loves you. We have never talked about Jesus, because you are Jewish, but Jesus loves you, Anna. No matter what you did, he loves you. And he forgives you."

"I killed the baby. How can I ever forgive myself for that? I couldn't bear to bring a child into this horrible world without a father. I was afraid, afraid of so many things, that I wouldn't be able to support the baby on my own."

"Well, you're right; it would not have been easy, and you probably would have lost your job when they found out that you had a child out of wedlock."

"But most of all, Wera, I couldn't have Benny's baby because I didn't know how I would face Alex with a child by another man. I am weak and I am selfish. "

"What's done is done. You acted in a state of madness."

"I am so alone. And I deserve to be alone. I deserve to suffer. Why didn't I just die? It would have been easier."

"You know what I think? I think you should move in with me, at least until we know more about Alex."

"Do you think he is dead?" Anna asked, and bit her lower lip hard, until she tasted blood.

"I don't know, but we will be together and wait for news. For now you must not lose hope."

Suddenly Anna's shoulders dropped and her body stopped trembling. Her head hung and she seemed to collapse. Then she began to weep. She wept in long, heart-wrenching sobs. It helped to cry, to let the pain out instead of burying it so deep that it ate her from the inside out, like a cancer.

Wera put her arm around Anna and held her. Anna buried her head in the comfort of Wera's ample breast.

"Do you still love Alex?" Wera asked, her voice soft.

"I've always loved Alex. I am not sure how it is possible, but I loved Benny too. I just can't believe he is dead. And I will never forgive myself for the baby. Look what I've done."

"I know... I know. Shhh... It will be all right." Wera patted Anna's back and held her like a child.

Chapter 94

Anna missed Benny's funeral because the doctor refused to release her from the hospital. But as soon as she was released, she went back to work. She preferred to be busy rather than sitting at home with her memories. However, everything around her reminded her of Benny: the counter at Gimbels where he would drop by to say hello, or have flowers delivered, the break room where he came meet with employees after the union had been established. Bette took great care not to mention Benny, knowing how much it would hurt Anna. Alice and Anna had not spoken since the Christmas party, but when Anna saw Alice one day in the break room, Alice looked as heartbroken as Anna felt.

Wera convinced Anna to move in with her.

"It's better you shouldn't live all alone. We'll wait together for mail from our husbands. And why should we pay rent for two places when we can pay for just one?"

Anna nodded. "Yes, all right." It would be better not to spend the evenings sitting on the same sofa she'd sat on with Benny, or sleeping in the same bed where they had once made love.

Together, Wera and Anna moved Anna's personal items into Wera's apartment. Anna did not have a private room, although Wera offered her the bedroom. Anna insisted on sleeping on the sofa in the living room. Still, Wera made an effort to give Anna plenty of privacy. And the two women got along well. For Anna, it came as a relief not to open the door after work to a dark and empty apartment.

Still, a day never passed that Anna didn't cry when something brought back a memory of Benny. And a day never went by that she didn't think of Alex, worry about him, and wonder if he was safe, alive. She fought thoughts of the baby that crept into her mind, but they returned at night in dreams. Silver-gray hair began to take over Anna's luxurious dark color, and although she still dressed well, and had an innate sense of style, she began to look weathered, tired, and worn.

Before Anna had left the hospital, the doctor had come into her room, and as gently as he could he told her that she would never have a child. In fact, after what happened, he said that she was lucky to be alive. She felt that she got what she deserved. After what she did, she didn't deserve to be a mother. Often, when she was alone, those words came back to her, and a bitter frown came over her face. "Lucky? The last thing I am is lucky," she thought.

Wera tried to ease Anna's guilt and pain, but Anna seemed to be adamant on self-punishment. Her self-hatred continued to grow and Wera worried about her constantly. After what Anna had done, Wera did not trust her not to take her own life.

As she rode home on the subway one Monday afternoon, Anna made a decision. It had become too difficult to continue working at Gimbels. The time had come to leave and find another position. She watched the buildings fly by outside the window as she considered applying for a job in the diamond district. She spoke fluent Yiddish, so she could get along well there. But, Anna had changed; her inner strength and excitement for life had left her. Most of the time she came home from work just longing to be left alone, to go to sleep. But Wera forced her to eat. She'd push the food around to please her friend, then lie down and close her eyes and try to fight off all of the terrible thoughts that eventually came anyway.

The tenement where Anna and Wera lived stood over two small retail stores. On one side a shoemaker, and the other a used-clothing store. Because of the rationing of shoes, the shoemaker had gotten very busy. Anna thought he might need help. It would be a lot easier to walk downstairs and go to work instead of taking the subway all the way into town. Where she had once thrived on the excitement of the big department stores, she now found them overwhelming.

Anna smoothed her hair down with her hands and walked inside.

"May I help you?" The shoemaker sat on a bench covered with old leather shoes, both men's and women's, and an array of tools, his two sons working beside him.

"I was wondering if you needed any help."

"No, I'm sorry, miss. I have my two boys to help me here. Try next door. The woman next door is all alone; maybe she'll need help."

"Thank you," Anna said.

Anna went into the clothing store. It had a musty smell, like an old closet. A woman with short, curly red hair and a thick waist came up to the front.

"Hello, miss. Please have a look around."

"I was wondering if you need any help," Anna asked. She glanced around quickly; the shop was a mess, clothing on chairs, tossed about on the counters. Nothing looked clean.

"You mean like a worker to help me here in the store?"

"Yes, I need a job. "Anna said.

The woman looked Anna up and down.

"Hmm… You sure do look nice. You make a nice impression. I can't pay much, but if you want a job. I can hire you."

"Yes, I want a job very badly."

"You can start tomorrow?"

"Yes…"

Chapter 95

Alex crouched under a bridge, listening to the heavy footsteps as a troop of enemy soldiers marched over his head. He had no idea how he'd gotten separated from his platoon. When they'd landed on Omaha Beach, he'd started running, and he hadn't stopped until the gunfire was far in the distance. In fact, he'd run until he got a stitch in his side so painful that it forced him to stop. Now he wandered somewhere in France, alone, searching for any Allies. For years Alex had battled depression, and considered suicide, but when death looked him in the eyes, his survival instinct had kicked in and he found that he had a stronger will to live than he'd ever imagined.

Before the ship had landed at Normandy, he'd heard a rumor that a shipment of nurses would follow. He wondered if Nelly had been among them. The thought of her coming through Omaha Beach sent shivers up his spine. It had been by far the most terrifying experience of his life, and he would never forget it.

He tried to find a good hiding place where he could sleep during the day, then wait and begin moving again after sundown, when he was sure that the Germans had passed. He lay on a rock under the bridge and closed his eyes, but he couldn't sleep. So he got up and began to move again.

Anna… If only he could get a letter to Anna to let her know he was alive and unharmed. If he ever found his way to safety, he would send her a letter as soon as he could. Alex looked up at the sky and wondered if Anna were looking at the stars too. If the army had told her that he'd gone missing she would be worried sick, and there was nothing he could do to protect her. All he could do was go forward and hope that somehow he would someday find his way home.

Chapter 96

Gnawing hunger and terrible thirst drove Alex to enter a small village in the darkest hour of the night, where he took the risk of being captured. He needed food and water to survive. Hiding in the shadows, he navigated the narrow cobblestone streets. Nazi flags hung from the buildings, moving softly in the breeze alongside pictures of Hitler. From where he stood, he could see a general store with a plate glass window and cans of food on the shelves. The streets were deserted. Alex picked up a rock and threw it at the window, but the window only cracked. He tried again, but still could not shatter the glass. He walked away, dejected.

Alex left the village and began walking through the countryside. When he grew too tired to continue, he hid in the safety of a forest, leaned against a tree, and fell asleep.

When he awakened, Alex started walking. He assumed he was headed inland, but had no idea what direction. Alex heard the rumble of a vehicle and hid behind a thick patch of bushes, his heart racing as a jeep filled with *Wehrmacht* soldiers rumbled by him. From where he crouched, he could hear them singing old German folk songs, songs he remembered from his childhood. How was it that Germany had turned on the Jews the way that they had? Growing up, Alex had always considered himself a German first, then a Jew. But he'd learned that no matter what country he lived in, he was a Jew first. That was the way the world saw him, and so it was the way he must see himself.

A half-mile up the road Alex came upon a barn. Looking in every direction to see if anyone was around, Alex pushed on the heavy wooden door and found it unlocked. He entered. A cow stood, its big soft brown eyes staring at him. He'd never milked a cow, but he must try. He pulled at the teats, but nothing happened. The cow let out a bellow that broke the silence, startling him. But he had to try again, still nothing. Alex searched the barn for food, a carrot, or potato, anything. But not even a morsel of food was in the barn. A fat-bodied insect walked across the hay. Alex caught it and forced himself to eat it, almost vomiting as he felt the wings crunch under his teeth. Then he sat down, leaning against the side of the barn, his head in his hands.

"Who are you?" A young girl, her dark hair in a braided bun, had entered so quietly that Alex had not heard her. She spoke in French.

Alex knew a little French. He'd studied it years ago when he was in school. "I am an American soldier," he said, unsure of how this information would be received. There was no way to know if this family were Nazi sympathizers.

"Why are you here?" she asked, putting her hands on her hips.

"I was separated from my troop."

Cocking her head to a side, she studied him for a moment.

"Come into the house, hurry. The Germans come around here all the time. If they find you they'll shoot you," she said.

Alex followed the girl. She led him up to a wooden farmhouse, badly in need of care. The paint had chipped and Alex could see the structure had once been white, but now had turned grey with age.

"Come on," she said as she opened a panel in the back of the house, revealing a hidden door.

He stood there for a moment, wondering if he should follow or run. This could be a trap.

"Don't just stand there. Come on…"

Alex needed food, water...

She pulled at his shirtsleeve, and he followed her inside.

Chapter 97

"Chantel, who is this?" A man in his early twenties stood in the kitchen when they entered.

"An American. I found him in the barn."

"You're an American?"

Alex nodded.

"Welcome. You look hungry. Chantel, give him some food."

"I am Marc, and this is my sister, Chantel." Another man a few years younger with a handsome face, a cleft chin and a crooked nose entered. "This is our brother, Luc."

"It's a pleasure to meet all of you, I'm Alex."

Luc pushed Alex against the wall. "Why do you speak French with a German accent? Are you a Nazi spy?"

"A spy?" Marc said and he came forward. Both men surrounded Alex.

"I am an American. I swear it."

"With a German accent?" Marc said. Then, turning to Luc, "I don't trust him."

Chapter 98

It was easier to walk down the stairs and go to work right outside of her apartment than to take the subway downtown. Anna had once loved to work downtown, with the tall buildings that were being erected, the well-dressed business people, and the sophisticated women shoppers. But now, everything in the city brought back memories of Benny. For that reason she'd not even considered applying to Macy's. Sarah's Second-Hand Store proved to be a godsend. Sarah appreciated Anna's ability to sell, and she also enjoyed the lunches Wera brought down to the store for them a few days a week. In turn, Sarah was kind to Anna, paying her well, and allowing her to sit down between customers. Gimbels had never allowed that. Sarah also offered sewing jobs to Wera when better-made clothing came in to the shop in need of repair.

"It will sell better if you fix the tear on the seam," Sarah said. She paid Wera a fair wage, and Wera was happy to stay busy.

Anna quickly developed a clientele, a following of sorts who enjoyed her excellent taste and her expert help in their fashion choices. Working at Gimbels had taught Anna to apply cosmetics properly. She wore mascara, lipstick, rouge, and powder, all perfectly applied. The women customers often asked her to help them with makeup, which gave Sarah an idea.

"What if we offered make up for sale, with lessons on how to use it? You could teach the women. Maybe we could buy the stuff at the five-and-dime, then after that we'd add a percentage, which we could split half-and-half. What do you think, Anna?"

"Sure, I think it's a wonderful idea."

"You'll have to go downtown and get the makeup because I don't know what to buy."

"How much makeup do you think we should get?"

"*Oy*, I have no idea. I wouldn't want to get stuck for all that money."

"No, I can understand."

"Should we take a poll and ask the customers how many of them would be interested?"

"Yes, that's a good idea."

Over the next several weeks, the women asked every customer if they would be interested in purchasing and learning to apply cosmetics. Almost all of them said yes! Anna and Sarah were ecstatic. For Anna the new business venture was a perfect distraction from her misery. She would go into town and buy products she felt would sell, and then Sarah would book appointments for her to teach women, sometimes in groups, other times individually. With the men overseas, many women had entered the workforce. They wanted to look nice, polished and professional.

Wera offered to come down and help to straighten up the store so that they could set up displays and make the cosmetics attractive. Sarah loved the idea and the three women redesigned the old second hand store into a resale boutique.

The new venture began slowly, with only one appointment the first week, and another the second. Sarah began to worry that their investment in the cosmetics had been a mistake, but by the end of the month Anna had between three and four appointments a day. They sold out of their stock in a week and Anna needed to buy more.

"I wonder how expensive it would be for us to develop our own line," Anna asked.

"We should look into it," Sarah agreed. "This could be even more profitable than the clothes."

However, the clothing sold in conjunction with the cosmetics. Sarah's little store had gone from a lower-income shop to a specialized boutique carrying better resalable items for the fashion-conscious woman. They even changed the name to "Sarah's Gently-Used Fashions."

Anna bought candles to cover the musty smell. And the business began to thrive.

Chapter 99

Wera received a telegram saying that her husband had been wounded and would be returning home in a month. Then Wera received a letter from her husband reassuring her that he was only slightly disabled. Wera prepared for his return, relieved and excited, but sorry to see Anna move out. Anna's old apartment next door had already been rented, so she would have to find a new place to live. The whole purpose of working at the secondhand store had been to avoid commuting, so she did not want to move too far away. Anna searched the neighborhood, looking for an available flat. She found a room in the back of a house where another family lived, but it had a private entrance and a location right across the street from Wera's apartment and the shop. She rented it.

Chapter 100

"I am not a spy. I promise you that," Alex said, his voice cracking with desperation. "Look, look at my dog tags."

"You could have stolen those off of a dead soldier," Luc said.

"Put him in the cellar. When it gets dark I'll take him over to the Americans; let them decide what to do with him," Marc said, holding Alex's gun.

Chantel led Alex downstairs. "Here," she handed him the heel of stale bread. "I'll get you some water, but don't tell my brothers."

He nodded. "Thank you. I won't."

They were going to take him to the Americans. As soon as they saw his dog tags they'd know he was one of them and he would be all right. Alex breathed a sigh of relief and waited for the nightfall.

For the first time in Alex's life, it had been an advantage to be born a Jew. When Marc and Luc delivered him to a troop of American soldiers that night, the Americans were suspicious of his accent. However, four of the soldiers were Jewish and they'd heard about the Nazi persecution of Jews in Germany. Alex told them how he'd come to America and how he'd earned his citizenship, and how he'd joined the army and landed at Omaha Beach. Then he proved his Jewish heritage the only way he could think of to prove it... by showing them his circumcision.

"We are headed toward Germany. You will come with us."

"Yes," Alex agreed. He had just joined with the U.S. Army's 45th Infantry Division.

Chapter 101

Over the next year Alex saw combat, even had the opportunity to shoot at some Nazis. However, he could never determine if his bullet was the one that caused death. Still, at night he sometimes thought about all of the men who died: the Americans and the Germans. Once they'd been children, had friends, maybe they'd even been friends with each other; then they had gone to school. Later perhaps they'd danced with a girl, kissed her, or even gotten married. Some of them probably left children behind. And…any one of them could have been him.

Never again did Alex experience anything as brutal as the landing at Normandy. It added another vision to his nightmares.

As soon as Alex was able, he posted a letter to Anna, telling her that he loved her and letting her know he was alive and unharmed. Her answer came within a week. As he read her letter he cried, and he could feel her relief.

In every town that Alex entered, he searched for Manny, asking strangers if they'd ever heard of him, But always, he got the same answer…no one had.

On the last Sunday in April, Alex and the rest of his platoon, walked through the gates of Dachau. Memories flashed in Alex's mind.

Dachau.

His parents had died here.

His sister, too.

And he had suffered…and still suffered…

The U.S. Army's 45th Infantry Division had arrived; they had come to liberate the prisoners.

The smell of death, of urine and of feces slapped them in the face as they marched into Hitler's death camp. The soldiers found themselves surrounded by dead bodies, and bodies so close to death from torture and starvation that it was hard to tell the living from the dead.

All of the soldiers looked at each other in shock. "How could anyone do this? This is atrocious," Alex heard them say, their faces horrified. And Alex knew that their sympathies were real. But for him it was different. Alex felt it firsthand.

He walked into the barracks where he'd once slept on the dirty straw. Bending down he touched the pile of hay filled with mold and lice. Tears streamed down his face, and he began to cry out… "Manny… Manny… Are you here?"

Alex ran from bunk to bunk, then through all of the barracks and to the ovens, screaming "Manny! Manny!" This was where they'd burned his mother, his father, his baby sister.

"God…where were you? Answer me… Answer me…"

He tripped on a rock and fell forward, tearing the knee out of his pants leg and breaking the skin. But Alex could not feel the pain. He got up and started running again through the barracks, crying out, "Manny! Are you here?"

"Alex… Come on… Grab hold of yourself." His sergeant tried to hold his arm, but Alex shook himself away.

"MANNY! MANNY!"

Finally, exhausted, Alex fell to the ground, his face in the dirt. He wept and wept until the other soldiers carried him away.

Although Alex knew that the war had ended, and that Germany had lost, and Hitler was dead, he could not remember much. There had been a plane ride back to the states and admittance to the psychiatric ward at the V.A. hospital, but all of that was a blur. The first clear memory he had was of Anna.

He'd been awakened by the screaming of the man in the bed next to him, who was tied down to keep him from harming himself or anyone else. Alex turned his head to see the man, red-faced, veins standing straight out of his neck as he tried to hurl himself off the bed, fighting against the restraints.

How long had he been lying in this bed? Was he still in Germany? France?

And then he saw her…"Anna, my Anna." His throat parched. He could barely speak above a whisper. Could it be a dream?

"Anna? Is it really you?" It took all the strength he had to reach his hand out to her. He wanted to feel her touch, to know that she stood there, before him, real, flesh and blood.

She bent beside him and he saw that she was crying. "Alex…" Taking his hand, she brought it to her lips. "Alex."

"I love you," he said. "I love you with all my heart."

"I know. I love you too," she said. "Do you want some water?"

He nodded. She held the glass to his lips. He sipped slowly.

"Anna…" he said, "Something happened while I was in England." Alex said. "There was a girl, a nurse…"

Anna looked at him, shaken.

"One night we walked to her room. She invited me in…"

Anna began to feel sick. She knew she shouldn't; after all, hadn't she done the same thing? This knowledge should free her from guilt, but it didn't. It hurt.

"Alex," she said. "Oh Alex, please don't be hard on yourself. I did something terrible too. I need to tell you. I must tell you." She took a deep breath. "Maybe if we both confess, we can start all over again." She couldn't look directly at him, but she knew she must continue; he must know the truth. "When you were gone... I had a lover... I got pregnant. And I aborted the baby purposely."

"Anna?" His face turned white. The grip he had on her hand loosened.

"Yes, I am sorry. I was so lonely... I never meant to hurt you."

"I wanted to go with Nelly, Anna... I wanted to be with someone to feel warm and safe. But I couldn't. I didn't because I love you. I love you too much to ever take another woman as a lover. That's what I wanted to tell you. How could you do this to me?"

She started to cry. "Oh, Alex, I am so sorry. Please forgive me."

He took his hand out of hers. His face felt hot; then the heat spread over his entire body. "Go home, Anna. I need to be alone. I need time to think."

"Please, Alex... Please don't do this... I never stopped loving you...not even..."

"Anna...go. Please, just go."

She stood up and walked out the door of his room, out of the hospital, and took the subway home.

That night Wera came by her apartment.

"You want to come for dinner?"

"No thanks, Wera. I'm tired, worn out."

"You look terrible. How is Alex?" Wera asked. She knew that he was in the hospital. Anna had been waiting for several days for him to regain consciousness.

"I told him about Benny."

"Oh my God, Anna, why did you tell him, especially now when he is so weak?"

Anna just shrugged her shoulders and shook her head. "I don't know. I shouldn't have told him, but I was afraid that a lie like that would keep us from ever being close again."

Wera touched Anna's cheek.

"Do you think he will divorce me?"

"I don't know, but if he does you are a strong woman, Anna. You will survive."

Chapter 102

Anna called the hospital every day to check on Alex's condition, but he refused to speak to her and eventually placed her on a no-call, no-visitor list. Whatever they'd shared was over. Anna would have to go on without him. She had no choice. She continued to work at the thrift store and tried to find out information about her parents, sending letters to the Red Cross in search of their names on the survivor lists.

Three months passed before she received an answer. Both her parents had been killed by the Nazis. Even though Anna, had assumed they were gone, when she received the official papers she wept. Now she need not search anymore. They were not in hiding; they would never contact her. Her mama, and papa, who had loved and nurtured her, saving her life by sending her away on the *St. Louis*, never even thinking of their own lives, had been brutally murdered and their bodies burned in an oven. Anna folded the letter and put it into the desk. She wished she could talk to Alex; he would understand her pain. But Alex, too, was gone.

Sarah kept Anna busy. Even though the men had returned from the war and most women had left their jobs, the little boutique continued to thrive.

At night Anna returned to a dark apartment. She no longer ran to the mailbox. She knew that nothing would arrive, nothing of importance, only bills and sales notices.

When Anna had moved into this small room she'd had a phone installed. It almost never rang, but it gave Sarah and Wera the opportunity to call her if they needed her. That night she picked up the phone and called Wera to let her know that she'd gotten a good price on a dozen apples and Wera was welcome to come over and take some. "I can't come tonight. Would tomorrow be all right for you?"

"Yes, but I have a late appointment tomorrow, a woman coming in for a cosmetic lesson, so it would have to be around eight."

"I'll bring you something for dinner. I have to cook anyway, so I'll bring something by," Wera said. "Then maybe I'll make a pie with some of the apples and bring you half. Sounds good?"

"You don't have to. I'm fine."

"Of course you are. I know that but I like to bring food… It makes me feel good. So you'll do it for me."

"Well, thank you. See you tomorrow."

"Goodbye."

Anna hung up the phone. She missed living with Wera, missed the camaraderie of having a friend always there to talk with. And she missed Benny and his sweet smile. But most of all, she missed Alex.

As she ate a cheese sandwich after work on that Wednesday night Anna thought about moving out of the city. It would be nice to get away from everything. But her job was there. So maybe she would get a puppy or a kitten. Yes, that might be a good idea. Cats were a little easier to care for. They didn't require that you be at home all the time. Yes, perhaps she would get a little kitten, a companion.

She placed the plate with the half-eaten sandwich on the table beside the bed and picked up the newspaper looking for animals for sale.

The telephone rang.

Anna picked it up on the first ring. Wera's probably calling to change the time tomorrow, she thought.

"Hello."

"Anna… It's Alex."

"Alex…" She could barely speak. His voice touched a place deep inside of her. "How are you?"

"I'm feeling better, thank you." He sighed, "Listen," he said, hesitating for a moment. "I have been talking to someone here in the hospital, a doctor. He made a suggestion to me. He thinks that if I write a book about everything that happened in Dachau and on the *MS St. Louis*, it might help me to come to terms with all of the thoughts and feelings that constantly haunt me. I have decided that I am going to write it and dedicate it to Manny."

"I think that is a wonderful idea."

"But Anna…I can't do it without you."

She could hear in his voice that he was crying. She was crying too.

"Please, Alex, come home. I miss you. I need you. I know I was wrong, but please, Alex, forgive me. We'll write it together. Only we know the story the way it really happened."

"Yes, that's very true. Only we know what really happened." She heard him sigh, and then there were several minutes of silence. "Anna…I will come home."

"I love you so much, Alex. I am so sorry for everything."

"Anna, my Anna... We will write it together."

Chapter 103

The roar of the crowd finally died down as Anna Mittelman walked slowly up the stairs to the stage. Even though she was well past her prime, true to her nature, she still looked elegant.

"Thank you, ladies and gentlemen," Anna said. "It is truly an honor for me to be here, and I know if Alex were still alive he would feel the same way. I lost my dear husband a little over two years ago to cancer. Our lives were not always easy, but they were always filled with love. Alex was not only my husband, but also my best friend. He survived Dachau, D-day and combat, but I lost him to a small tumor that formed on his pancreas. A day does not go by that I do not think of him and as those of you who have lost a spouse will understand, I find myself talking to him as I go about my daily routine. As most of you know, my husband and I co-authored the book, "A Life with Purpose," a memoir of our voyage on the ill-fated *MS St. Louis*. We dedicated this book to Manny. If you have read it you will understand. Without Manny's sacrifice, there is a very good chance that neither Alex nor I would have survived. Until his death, my husband and I searched for Manny, but we never found him, nor were we able to find any information about what happened to him. However, for reasons of his own Alex kept procrastinating on publishing this book. It was on his deathbed that he finally said to me, "When I am gone, Anna, take the book to a publisher and release it to the world." I can remember sitting at his bedside and crying because I knew that soon he would be leaving me, and the next time we would meet, it would be on the other side. On the day that I was notified that the book had become available at bookstores I remembered the last day of Alex's life. He refused to die in a hospital room, so I brought him home. It was early on a winter morning and a cold front had just come through. Alex lay in bed. I lay beside him and we were watching the sunrise. "Are you cold? Should I get some more blankets or turn the heat higher?" I asked him. He shook his head, smiled, and squeezed my hand; then he said, "Well... I think it's time for me to go." I sat up and looked at him and he winked at me. "I'll see you on other side. Don't forget. Publish the book, for me, for yourself...and for Manny." I was stunned. Even though I knew he was dying for a long time, when the time finally arrived it felt like a knife in my heart. "Alex..." was all I could say. Then he smiled at me and said, "Don't be afraid, Anna. This book is our reason for living. It was our purpose for being on earth. We must be sure to let the world know what happened so that it never happens to our people again. Publish it." He kissed my hand. "Anna, my Anna..." he said, and then he was gone.

With all of the Holocaust survivors growing older, I feel that it is very important that we educate the young people, both Jewish and Gentile, about the Holocaust. We must tell them what happened. We must tell them over and over to be sure that they never forget.

As a special gift to each of you, I will be offering signed copies at no charge to survivors. Alex would have wanted each of you..."

The light at the front of the room began to blink, interrupting Anna's speech. A man at one of the tables with a big sign that said "Germany" stood up.

"Anna Mittelman?" he called out.

"Do I know you?" she asked, squinting to see him in the semi-darkness. From where she stood, he didn't look old enough to be a survivor unless he was a baby during the war.

"My name is Sepp Hahn. We have never met. I have come a long way to be here today, to see you, Anna, and to speak before this audience. I wish Alex were here as well, because I believe he would want to hear what I am about to say."

Anna cocked her head. What was this all about? Was this someone who knew Alex?

"So if you would like some answers to your questions in "A Life with Purpose," if you want to know what happened to the people left on the ship that could not get into Cuba, I can tell you what happened I know the answers. I also know became of Elke and Manny after you and Alex left the ship."

Anna studied him. He looked familiar, but she was sure she had never met anyone by the name of Sepp Hahn. Who was he and what did he know of Elke and Manny? Was he just a fan, a reader who had become obsessed with the characters in "A Life with Purpose?" Or was he somehow connected to all of this? It would probably be best to meet with him in private. After all, he could be anyone, even the son of a former Nazi. That would be upsetting to the audience of survivors. However, it was hard to say whether Mr. Hahn would be willing to meet later, and she and Alex had spent years trying to find their friends, coming up empty handed every time. This man who stood before her claimed that he knew the answers. She could not let him leave without hearing him out; she must allow him to speak. "Yes, please, tell me," she said. "I would very much like to know…everything."

Chapter 104

The MS St. Louis, May 30, 1939

Elke kissed Anna and Alex goodbye. Manny waited in his stateroom, he'd asked Elke to come for him after they'd left the ship. She knocked on his door softly. "They just got off…" she said.

Manny did not answer right away. "Thank you for letting me know," he said.

"Would you like to have a drink perhaps?"

"Sure, why not?"

As Elke and Manny sat on the deck, glasses in hand, Anna and Alex had just been cleared to go into the country. From their spot on deck where they sat they could see Alex carrying Anna's suitcase as the young couple left the *MS St. Louis* behind them on their way to freedom, a freedom Elke and Manny believed that they would never know.

Manny smiled a cynical smile and patted Elke's hand.

"Well, kid, we had fun anyway, didn't we? All the plans we made about this dream of freedom in America," he said with a wry smile.

"Always the optimist," she said, smiling.

"Yes, I suppose I am. What good does it do to cry?"

"You really loved her?"

"I did and I do," he said.

"Enough to sacrifice your own life for her happiness…"

"What is life without love?" he said.

For a few minutes they sat in silence, staring out over the water.

"What do you think will become of us? Do you think we will go back to Germany?" Elke asked.

"Who knows? Maybe the negotiations will turn in our favor and we will be allowed off the ship. It's possible, right?'

"Of course it is. Of course," she said, wringing her hands together. "Manny, I am glad that we had that afternoon together. You know, when we... It was very special for me."

"I am glad too. You are a wonderful, beautiful woman, Elke. And I will probably someday regret not having run away with you when we had the chance."

"Yes. Thank you for the kind words, Manny. But, I'm tired. I am going to lie down for a while."

"Good idea. " He smiled.

"I'll see you later tonight at dinner."

Manny entered the room he'd shared with Alex. He looked at the blanket on Alex's bed. Walking over he ran his hand along the coarse wool. *I am a fool, an idealistic fool. Ah, well, so what? He loved her, and she loved him. What of it? I did the only thing that I could do. I gave them freedom to live and to love.*

Sitting down on his bed, Manny considered the future. Alone, he was not nearly as optimistic as he appeared to others. He was smart enough to know what was in store, and he knew he could not bear it. But Manny's optimism came from a lifetime of living with wealthy parents who bailed him out of every mess he ever got into. And secretly he believed that somehow his family money and influence would save him again. He didn't believe that he would ever see the camps because if things really got out of hand he would be forced to write to his father and beg for money and forgiveness for squandering the funds he'd already received. Manny hated to do that. He knew that his father thought of him as a burden. He called Manny his son without ambition or responsibility, a reckless ne'er-do-well, who would never succeed at anything. So before he would contact his father, Manny decided to try another means. He began to write a wire to his cousin in France.

Joseph,

I have run out of money. It's a long story, I'll explain the next time I see you. But this is a desperate situation here on the St. Louis *and I need you to send me cash as quickly as possible so that I can pay my way out of Germany. We passengers on the* MS St. Louis *have been denied entrance into Cuba and from the way things appear, we will be sent back to Germany. I cannot write to my father; he would complain. You know how he can rant and rave. He'd say that I should have used the money he gave me to buy my freedom. But you see, something happened to the money while I was on board. It's far too complicated to explain in a letter. However, if you wire me the cash I will repay you as soon as I arrive in the States. Once I see my father in person, I will explain everything and he will repay pay my debt. Please help me, Joseph. I am depending on you.*

Manny

Manny left the note on the table beside the bed. He'd take it upstairs and send it in the morning. A flask of whiskey lay hidden in the bottom of his suitcase; Manny brought it out and took a swig, and then another. The more he drank the more he regretted his decision. What was he thinking? Of course, he wanted to be noble, to do the right thing, to behave like one of the heroes he admired in books and films. But deep inside Manny knew he was no hero, in fact he was a coward. He had proved that to himself once long ago. An incident that made him ashamed… An event that he'd buried but could never forget. And, now…now it could be possible that he might pay for his rash behavior with his life. Why did he always act first and then think things through afterwards? This was not the first time he'd made an error that had cost him. He'd lost count of how many times. However, if his family did not come through, this one might cost him more dearly than he'd realized when he had made the gesture. Could that happen? Was it possible? Could Manny get caught up in a web with no way out? He took another swig of whiskey and glanced over at Alex's bed. Manny liked Alex, but it was more that he wanted to show Anna how decent a man he was. It felt crucial to his self-worth that she see him as a hero. But now that she had left the ship, her importance in his mind had diminished. Anna was just a woman, and there were millions of women. If he'd gotten off the ship in Cuba, he'd have forgotten her in time and even eventually erased the connection she sparked to that terrible secret memory of what he had done. But when he went to the captain and paid for the freedom of the two lovers, he'd seen himself like the hero in "A Tale Of Two Cities." It had all been so romantic, so dramatic. For a moment Manny was not the weak, spoiled rich boy who ran from danger; he was the knight who rode in on a white steed to save the damsel in distress. It had felt so good to see himself that way. However, now, with the glory and romance gone, he wasn't sure he had ever loved Anna. He loved the idea of being desperately, hopelessly in love, and of courting the woman he loved in a way that Alex could not. But most of all, she reminded him of Lieb, the girl who haunted him. The girl whose shame he hid deep inside of his heart. Manny had never actually admitted it to himself before, but he always knew it: Anna and Lieb could have been sisters. Their eyes, their smiles, the bone structure of their faces… That face, that face… Those eyes, Lieb's eyes… He saw those eyes in his mind…pleading with him. Raising the flask, he toasted aloud, "To Lieb… To Anna… To guilt… And to the man I am not and never will be because of my own fucking weakness." Then he gulped down another swig of whisky and got dressed for dinner. Manny hated himself, but he wasn't ready to die, not now, not yet. Well, if his cousin didn't come through, his father would. In the end they would bail him out; they always did.

No music played in the dining room that night. Where the band had once been an empty space now stood. Manny drank incessantly, until he lost comprehension; then he began to tell Elke how he felt.

"I think I made a mistake, giving them all my money. I could have been off this godforsaken ship. Ah, shit... Well, anyway, it doesn't matter. My family will get me out of this mess. They'd better get me out," he said, smiling as he took another gulp of straight whiskey.

"Maybe you have had enough to drink, Manny," Elke said. "Let's go up on the deck and get some air."

"Yes, if you would like…"

They walked on the deck. A warm tropical breeze danced through Elke's golden hair.

"You know, you're much prettier than Anna. But there was just something about her."

Elke didn't answer. Manny was stumbling on the deck.

"Let's sit down," Elke said, taking his arm and leading him to a chair.

Out of nowhere Manny began laughing, laughing so hard that tears fell on his cheeks, and then suddenly he was weeping, choking with out-of-control sobbing.

Elke reached up and touched his head.

"Manny? Manny?" She didn't know what to say, so she tried to hold him close to her to ease the pain inside of him.

Manny pushed away. "I don't deserve to be comforted. Do you want to know a secret, something I have never told anyone before? I'll bet when I am finished you won't think I am so wonderful anymore." His head was bobbing up and down like a marionette.

"You don't have to tell me. Perhaps you should go to bed. You're tired and you've had a lot to drink."

"No, I want to tell you. I want to finally tell someone what I did. The world should know that Manny is not the man he pretends to be."

She looked away from him. His nose was running, tears stained his face, and he looked as if he'd been struck with insanity. Elke glanced out over the ocean, the water black under the night sky, the land barely visible.

Then Manny began to speak, slowly at first...

"On the night of *Kristallnacht*, I was out painting the town. Oh, yes, I did that quite often. You see nobody knew what was coming. I had this girl with me; her name was Lieb. We grew up together, but she was always the reserved one. That night I wanted to show her some action, so I took her out of the Jewish section to a nightclub in downtown Berlin. A wild place, filled with decadence and excitement. I liked it. I went there pretty often. I talked her into having a few drinks, and we danced. I'd been trying to convince her to spend the night with me for years. But on this night, although it took a lot of convincing and quite a bit of liquor, she finally agreed. As we were walking back toward my apartment we saw a terrible sight in the distance. Flames filled the sky, coming from the Jewish Temple... I could hear the noise and chaos: people shouting, glass breaking, but I thought it was all due to the blaze. I looked over at Lieb. 'The synagogue is on fire. Hurry, maybe we can help.' I said. And so we both ran headlong right into the claws of the Nazi persecutors. Once we saw what was happening, it was too late; we were too close.

Angry German boys ran down the streets smashing windows with clubs. I saw people being torn out of their homes and thrust onto the street, then kicked and beaten, and sometimes killed. It was a bloodbath."

"Come on, run...' I said to Lieb. 'We've to get out of here fast. But she couldn't run, you see. She was wearing high heels. I grabbed her arm and tried to pull her along, but Lieb kept tripping on her shoes. 'Take them off," I said. Hurry, get rid of those damned shoes now.' She had to stop to undo the buckles in order to get them off. 'The streets are filled with broken glass. I'll cut my feet to shreds.' She hesitated, looking at the glass. 'I don't know what to do,' she said. The angry mob surrounded us on all sides, closing in quickly, like predators coming in for the kill. I wanted to stop, to help her, to wait for her, I really did, but my feet wouldn't let me. My feet wanted to fly, to escape. I ran, like the coward that I am. I ran as fast as I could and I left Lieb behind. I heard her scream. I turned around and I saw two hefty boys grab her and throw her on the ground. She was screaming for me, 'Manny! Manny, help me!' But you know what I did? I kept running, Elke. I kept on running." Manny was choking on his words. "Only once more did I stop for a brief second to look back. She saw me stop, and I still remember the hope and desperation in her eyes, those eyes that still haunt me... She thought I was going to come back and help her. She called out my name. It was all a matter of seconds. Then I saw the boy raise a club, and Lieb let out a blood-curdling scream. The club came down, and her screaming stopped, but I still heard it in my mind. 'Manny, help me! Manny!" I gagged and vomit spilled out of my mouth as I ran past a pool of blood filled with blood-drenched human tissue. Then, as I raced by, I caught the stinking odor of the spoiled garbage of the fishmonger. I slipped into the alleyway behind Abram's fish store. Everyone in the neighborhood knew that the smell of the rotting fish was unbearable. It wafted out on to the street just enough to discourage anyone from venturing too close to the discarded refuse. I hid under the back stairs right by the garbage can. Heads of fish with black and accusing eyes glared at me under the streetlight. I hoped the attackers would avoid searching this area because the odor was so foul. And I was right; it was the stench of that garbage that saved my life. They ran past the storefront cursing the odor. I heard the glass window next door shatter, and the animal cries of the mob. My heart pounded. I thought of Lieb, but I didn't' have the guts to go back and help her, not even to see if she was alive. I am a coward, Elke. I am nothing but a coward. All I could think of was my own safety, my own life. The following morning, I found out that Lieb had died, all alone on the street that night. It was my fault, all my fault…"

An old man with hair as silver as the moon and skin that matched his hair walked slowly by them. He turned to Elke and Manny, his eyes rheumy and yellowed; he spoke like the voice of doom.

"We'll never leave this ship safely. We are all going back to Germany, to Hitler, to die…just the way Hitler always wanted it to be… He tricked us; he gave us hope."

"Shut up, you old bastard," Manny said.

"Manny, he's just an old man," Elke said.

"You mark my words; you'll both see what happens. You'll see that I am right." The old man pointed his index finger at Manny.

Manny's face turned red with anger. He got up and punched the old man, who staggered across the deck with a look of shock on his face. Manny punched him again. "Damn you!" he yelled, staggering and grabbing the old man by the shirt. A younger man came from behind and punched Manny. Elke began to scream.

Manny fell, but he was trying to get up.

"Stop… Stop fighting. Please stop. Someone is going to get hurt," Elke said.

Viktor came rushing up from the lower deck; he'd heard Elke's voice.

"What's going on here?"

Both Manny and the old man were bleeding from different parts of their faces.

Manny turned and punched the old man's son in the stomach; he doubled over trying to catch his breath.

As soon as he could stand upright, the son went after Manny again.

Viktor held him off. Then, as Manny tried to hit the man again, Viktor called for help and another crewmember came to hold Manny off.

In his drunken state, Manny had gotten a burst of strength, but as soon as the stronger man detained him, his body went limp.

The old man's son shook himself off.

"I'm sorry," he said to Viktor. "That drunk just hit my father."

Viktor nodded. "Just go on your way, please," he said. The man nodded, took his father's arm and led him away.

Then Viktor turned to Manny who was still in the other sailor's strong grasp. "I think you'd better go to bed for the night. You've had far too much to drink and I think you'd best sleep it off."

Manny nodded, tired and spent from the fight and his confession.

Viktor escorted Manny to his stateroom. Elke followed. Once Manny went into the room and closed the door, she turned to Viktor.

"Thank you."

"Of course," he said. "Would it be too bold for me to ask you to take a walk on the deck with me?" Viktor asked.

"I'd like that." Elke smiled.

Chapter 105

Manny finished the whiskey in the flask in his room; then he lay down on the bed, fully dressed, and tried to sleep. He fell asleep for an hour, then awakened, unable to fall back asleep. He reached for the flask only to find it empty. Damn, he thought, if I go back upstairs and try to get another drink that big Nazi sailor will stop me. Then he remembered... Of course he couldn't rest; he'd forgotten to take his sleeping pills. During the day, he could fake an air of ease, but at night things always crept back to bother him, so his family doctor had prescribed sleeping pills. And tonight, after telling Elke his secret, he felt even worse than usual. Instead of unburdening him, it had brought it all back as vividly as if it had happened yesterday. Well, no matter, he would take a couple of the pills and they would help him sleep, dull his overactive mind.

A few hours later Manny awoke again, dazed and restless, his head aching. Perhaps he needed another sleeping pill. Talking with Elke had brought on a dream of Lieb. In his dream he saw Lieb's face; she was calling to him, begging for his help, but he was glued to the sidewalk. Then Lieb's face changed just a little, into Anna's. "I helped you Anna... I helped you," Manny said in the dream. "Doesn't that count? Can I be released from my guilt and shame now? "

"But you let them murder me. How could you do that, Manny, how? Are you less than a man? Don't you know that if you escort a woman it's your responsibility to protect and take care of her? Unless of course you aren't a real man..." It was Lieb again.

The dream had terrified Manny, lying awake, breathing hard, bathed in sweat with his heart racing. So it turned out that he'd been right all along, Anna was his *bashert*, but not in the way, he'd originally thought. The meaning of the word *bashert* is destiny, what is meant to be. Meeting her should have changed his life, should have eased his mind, his guilt, his pain, because in paying for her freedom he'd tried to pay off the debt he owed to Lieb. In Manny's mind it all became clear as glass, what he'd done, what it meant, and why. It should have worked. Why didn't it work? He took three more pills. He had to stop his thoughts from racing or he would never rest. There was no water by the bed, so he swallowed the pills dry and grimaced at the bitter taste. There, that should help to calm him and get him through the night. In the morning he'd send off the letter, and then forget he'd ever met Anna, forget he'd ever boarded this miserable ship.

Chapter 106

When Manny did not come to breakfast the following morning Elke just assumed he was sleeping off his hangover. But when he did not arrive for dinner that night, Elke knew something happened. She went to a crewmember and asked him to unlock the door to Manny's stateroom. The man refused, saying that perhaps her friend just needed privacy, just needed some time alone to digest all that had happened.

Elke nodded, but she knew that something wasn't right.

Then when Manny did not come to breakfast the following morning, Elke began to panic. She could not eat. She got up and went over to the table where Viktor sat with a group of crewmembers.

"May I speak with you please?" she said, tapping Viktor on the shoulder.

"Of course," he said, rising immediately. "Excuse me, gentlemen." Then turning to Elke, he said, "Follow me, we can speak more privately on the deck."

They climbed the stairs and walked up onto the deck.

"Sit, please…" Viktor said, looking concerned.

"I think something has happened to Manny. He didn't' show up to dinner last night or to breakfast this morning. Can you do something for me?"

"Anything, if it is in my power…"

"Can you get the key and take me into his room?"

"Yes, sure," he said. "Wait right here. I will be right back."

Chapter 107

As they opened the door, a foul odor wafted from the room. Elke walked ahead.

Viktor knew that smell, He'd smelled it aboard the ship before. He raced after Elke; she would need comfort very soon.

Elke moved too fast for him even to offer his arm for support. Within seconds she had entered the stateroom. Manny lay on the bed on his side, a small pool of vomit running out of his mouth. A scream escaped from her lips, and then she fell to her knees crying, "Oh, Manny...Manny..."

She saw the letter addressed to his cousin Joseph on the table beside him.

For a few minutes, Viktor just stood there feeling inept, not knowing what to do, his hands limp at his sides. Then he knelt beside Elke and put his arm around her shoulder.

"It's all right," he whispered. "Come away from here." He helped her to her feet and led her out of the stateroom. She leaned against him for support as they made their way upstairs onto the deck. She was gasping for breath. He held her.

"Manny, poor Manny," Elke said, thinking about what Manny had told her the night before.

Viktor listened as she tried to make sense of what had taken place. She mumbled to herself. He could not understand what she was saying so he rubbed her back trying to calm her nerves.

"Let me get you some water."

"Yes, that would be good. Thank you, Viktor. You have been so kind."

He nodded and went to the bar where he filled a glass with water. He brought it back to her.

She sipped slowly and began to calm down.

When she'd regained control she sat up straight, releasing herself from his arms.

"I'm all right now," she said.

"Sit here for a moment. I am going to let the captain know what has happened and I will be right back."

She nodded.

Viktor returned quickly. He sat back down beside Elke.

"How are you?" he asked not knowing what else to say.

"How should I be? Two of my friends just left the ship; I will probably never see them again. Manny is dead, and things don't look good for us in Cuba."

"Have faith in the captain. He is a good man, a truly good man. Somehow he will find a solution. He has already told the crew that he refuses to take the passengers back to Germany. He declared that all of you are passengers on his vessel, and as the captain, your safety is his responsibility. He will do all he can to protect you. I know it."

She looked across the water at Cuba. Had she ever really believed that she would be allowed to go there, to live in peace, and leave the past behind her? Elke shook her head involuntarily.

Viktor reached for her hand and gave it a gentle squeeze.

"I'm sorry about the way that I treated you," Elke said. "I just didn't want to get involved with a German man when I

366

thought I was going to America. I just wanted to leave everything German behind me."

"That's understandable," he said, glad that she'd allowed him back into her life.

Viktor spent the day at Elke's side. She sat staring out into space for most of the afternoon. When lunchtime arrived, she refused to eat. Viktor knew that if Cuba continued to refuse entrance to the passengers the ship would soon be faced with another problem, a food shortage. Well, no matter, somehow he would find food for Elke. She would not go hungry. As much as Viktor wanted to see the passengers disembark safely in Cuba, in a way their being detained gave him a chance to get to know Elke. What a double-edged sword, he thought. If the passengers did not get into Cuba, they would most likely be returned to Germany. This would put Elke in terrible danger. However, if she got off the ship in Cuba and left for America, he would most probably never see her again. The longer they remained at sea, the longer Viktor had to spend with Elke. His selfish thoughts disgusted him. He wanted what was best for her, but he dreaded saying goodbye.

Over the next several days Viktor only left Elke's side to do his work, returning as often as possible to check on her. The atmosphere on the ship had changed from one of optimism to one of gloom. There were no more parties and little-by-little, the passengers became aware that the food supply was running out. Very few people went to the pool anymore. Most just sat waiting for the captain to announce any developments. After six days docked just outside of Cuba, word finally arrived. The passengers waited anxiously for the captain to come up on the deck and tell them the news.

Elke sat beside Viktor, holding his hand as the captain walked onto the deck. He wore a grim expression and Elke felt her heart sink as she looked at him.

"Ladies and gentlemen," he said. "It is with great regret that I must inform you that the *MS St. Louis* has been ordered by President Bru of Cuba to exit Cuban waters. Initially they gave us three hours to depart; however after explaining our need for additional time they extended their deadline until Friday, June second. On that date, we must sail out of Cuban waters. "

"Captain, where will we go? Are you going to take the ship back to Germany?" A man shouted from the back of the crowd.

"I have no intention of returning this ship to Germany. We will sail along the coast of Florida while I send a wire to President Roosevelt of the United States of America requesting permission for all of you to enter the country. I am sorry for this terrible mishap; however, I will do everything in my power to see you to a safe destination. I remain Gustav Schroder, captain of the *MS St. Louis*."

Then Captain Schroder, tall, blond and handsome, walked back to his office.

After the captain left the deck there was a hum of conversation. Elke heard several of the passengers who had come from influential backgrounds say that they planned to send personal wires to President Roosevelt.

"Do you think America will let us in?" Elke asked Viktor.

"I don't know. I hope so." He shrugged.

Elke and Viktor walked along the deck. The hours seemed to stretch forever as the uncertainty drove Elke crazy. Viktor, anxious too, decided to devise a plan. He refused to let this beautiful woman slip out of his life. And even more, he would not see her taken to one of those concentration camps. He'd heard rumors about those places. Although he doubted they could possibly be as atrocious as people proclaimed, he knew that Elke would never see the inside of one, not as long as he lived.

On Friday, the *MS St. Louis* began her voyage out of Cuban waters. Relatives of some of the passengers had rented small boats on which they sailed out to meet the *MS St. Louis*. The passengers stood on the deck waving goodbye, their faces frozen in horror. Many of the women cried; some of the men did too.

No one came out on a small boat to bid Elke farewell, and no one waited for her in Cuba. When she'd left Germany, her mother, the only person she had in the world, had hardly taken the time to say goodbye. Elke stood on the deck watching relatives both on the ship and on the small rafts crying and reaching for each other, longing to be together. She decided that there was a benefit to never having loved or been loved by anyone. Elke felt no pain or loss, only fear of what was in store. She and Viktor left the deck and went down to the lounge, which they shared with two other couples. Most of the passengers had gone off to their cabins or stood on the deck, watching their hopes and dreams disappear on the horizon.

"Elke," Viktor said. "Do you like me?"

"What?" She was startled by the strangeness of his question. "That's a silly question. Of course I like you."

"No, I mean, do you really like me? I guess I am trying to ask you if you could see yourself learning to love me."

"Oh, Viktor, I don't know. With everything that is happening here on the ship I haven't even thought about anything like that."

"Well, would you? I mean would you think about it?"

She wanted to laugh. It all seemed so childish to her. But he looked so vulnerable, like a little boy. And she did like him, but love him? She did not love him, and right now she was glad that she didn't love anyone. Loving could only end in pain and loss; look at Manny. And with all of the uncertainty surrounding the Jewish passengers, it was best not to have any ties to anyone or anything. Viktor didn't seem to understand what it meant to be a Jew. He wanted a silly whirlwind romance, and nonsense like that could not be good for either of them. He had no money to buy her freedom. He had no influence. He had nothing to offer her, and besides all of that, he was going back to Germany, and God only knew where she was headed.

"I suppose I will think about it if you would like me to." She would say she loved him if it made him feel better. Why not? What was there to lose?

"I would very much…"

Poor man.

Perhaps he wanted to sleep with her and he felt that she had to be in love to be bedded. How she wished that were true. Elke looked into Viktor's eyes; he gazed at her with such sincerity that she felt sorry for him. *I am so cynical. Still, if Viktor knew my past, he would surely find me repulsive. He has no idea who I am or what I have done. Viktor is just a man. Like all the other men, he looks only at my blonde hair and my fine figure, and so he thinks he is in love. Perhaps it is a blessing, for now; after all, he is very kind to me. He will make sure that I have plenty to eat. And soon I am afraid that food will be hard to come by, but because he is a crewmember, he will have access to supplies that the rest of us will not. Also I must consider that since Manny's suicide, Viktor has been here for me. He is a comfort, always willing to listen, and I've never met a man like that. But most of all, he has been a good friend.*

"Would you like to come to my cabin?" Elke asked. She would do this for him. For all that, he had done for her.

"You are asking *me*?"

"I don't see anyone else here." She smiled.

He was stunned. Could she be serious? He'd hardly expected this.

"Yes, yes I would…," he said.

They spent the afternoon making love. For her, it was an escape from the grim reality of her future. For him, it was a culmination of every dream he'd ever had of finding the perfect woman. Viktor knew in that afternoon, in that brief time span of joy that he would do whatever he must, even if his own life were in jeopardy; he would protect this woman. Viktor had fallen hopelessly in love.

Chapter 108

Viktor shared a small cabin in the crew's section of the ship with another crewmember, where he returned to freshen up after spending time with Elke before beginning his shift. After he took a bath and dressed in a clean uniform he sat down on his bed for a moment to think things over. He knew that the captain would always act in the best interest of the passengers, but so far there had been no answer from the President of the United States. If America refused these poor souls entrance what would become of them? More importantly, what would become of Elke?

Viktor lit a cigarette just as the door to his cabin opened and his roommate, Olof, entered.

"Hahn, I haven't seen much of you this voyage. Work keeping you busy?"

"Not really."

"So what is it? You look so forlorn. Is this problem with the docking in Cuba bothering you? Or is it that our food supply is diminishing so fast? You eat like a horse; I don't know how you keep in such good shape."

"Neither. Olof, can you keep a secret?"

"We've been best friends for over ten years. If I couldn't keep a secret, you would know it already. With all of the things you have told me…"

"Yes, well, sit down. I have something to tell you. Maybe you'll have a suggestion."

Olof sat on the edge of his own cot and studied his friend. "Go ahead; you have my full attention."

"There is a girl on board… a special girl."

"You mean the blonde whom you brought to dinner at the captain's table the other night?"

"Yes, she is the one. Her name is Elke."

"Pretty name. She is a Jew, no?"

"Yes, she is. And, I'm in love with her. Olof, you have many friends back in Germany, and many of them quite influential. Do you think that you can help me to buy papers for her?"

"You mean forged papers?"

"Yes. Can you do anything?"

"I don't know," Olof said, stroking his chin. "Viktor, you are entering dangerous territory. You know that this is against the law. "

"I am only thinking that I might need to have papers made for her if the ship should return to Germany."

"What would you do with her in the meantime? Where would you hide her? I have heard that if we are forced back to the Fatherland that all of the passengers who are aboard this ship will be taken right from the dock to camps."

"*Oh my God!*" Viktor stood up and began to pace, puffing continuously on his cigarette.

"Viktor, you shouldn't' get so involved with these people. I feel bad for them too, but Jews are not like us. I know she is beautiful and looks pure Aryan, but there are things you don't know about her. Once you get to know her you will find out that Jews think differently; they act differently. It would be best for you to stay away from her."

"I can't. I am in love with her. I will give my own life for her if it comes to that." Viktor put the cigarette into an ashtray and sat down beside Olof. "Please," he said

"This is pure folly. You must be mad. Viktor get hold of yourself. You must stop this. The *Gestapo* won't play games with you. If you are caught, you will be killed, or at best sent to a camp. Do you understand the seriousness of this?"

"What can I do? Olof, you are my best friend. You must help me. I have nowhere else to turn." Viktor grabbed Olof's sleeve.

Olof looked away and took a deep breath. Then he turned back to see his friend's eyes pleading with him.

"I don't know why I am agreeing to this. I must be crazy. But you are like a brother to me, so if there is any way that I can help you, I will.

"I am thinking that if we are forced to go home to Germany I will hide her in the engine room until everyone has left the ship. Then during the night I will sneak her out and keep her hidden in my flat until we can have papers drawn up. Do you know someone who can falsify papers for me?" Viktor asked.

"Perhaps. I know of someone who has forged some documents and sold them. He's an old friend I knew from gymnasium. I will look into it, if we return to Germany."

"I will owe you my life if you can do this."

"You will owe me only your friendship. However, it will cost money. I am sure I will be required to pay him. I don't know how much, but it won't be cheap. He, too, will be putting himself at risk."

"I have a little saved. I hope it's enough."

"We will have to wait and see what happens. I am not sure that he will even agree to do this. Anything having to do with

Jews makes the crime more illicit, and consequently the severity of the punishment if one is caught it is far worse. So, again, don't get your hopes up. We will have to see what my friend can do, and what he is willing to do."

Chapter 109

The following morning the passengers found that they were able to see the coast of Miami from the ship's deck.

At breakfast Elke heard several people talking. Another passenger had attempted suicide during the night. He had jumped overboard and had to be rescued. It had posed danger not only to the passenger but to the crew member. Elke searched for Viktor; her concern for his well-being surprised her. When she did not see him at his usual table, she got up and began walking toward his room.

"Good morning," Viktor said as he walked out of the radio room. "Have you eaten yet?"

Elke sighed with relief; the crewmember involved in the rescue was not Viktor.

"No."

"Well, come, let's have breakfast together."

She nodded,

After that a committee was formed to prevent passengers from jumping overboard and trying to swim to shore. And a suicide watch was put into effect.

Every day the passengers grew more edgy as their lives and futures hung in the balance.

And still no word came from President Roosevelt.

The captain received information that the world press had begun covering the story of the MS *St. Louis,* and he hoped that somehow this might help his passengers to find a friendly country that would accept them. Or even better, it might stir Roosevelt to answer with a letter of permission.

People began to talk, their uncertain futures made them panicky and nervous. A distrust of the captain infiltrated the ship like a deadly disease. Rumors began to fly that the entire voyage had been nothing but a Nazi hoax from the beginning, in which the captain had played a part. The crew began to fear an uprising.

Viktor worked in the radio room as the alarm bell sounded, indicating trouble on deck. He raced up the stairs and outside to find that several of the young male passengers had staged a mutiny. The men stood upon the bridge of the ship shouting down to the other passengers who stood dumbfounded, but listening.

"Our captain pretends to be our friend. But he is nothing but a pawn for Hitler. You can be sure that he was in on this all along. These Nazis wanted us to believe that they would give us our freedom while they plotted to destroy us. We must take control of the ship if we are to live, or you can be assured you are going back to Germany." Several of the other passengers shook their fists, yelling out in agreement.

It began to look as if more passengers would join the mutiny, and if enough of them banded together they could be successful. The sounds of chaos filled the ship and more people came up on deck to see what the ruckus was about. As the crowd grew larger, the young men who stood in charge demanded to know what the captain planned to do to ensure everyone's safety.

Viktor wished he had an answer. He wished it for them, but more than that, he wished it for Elke.

Viktor and the rest of the crew climbed the bridge. They must subdue the rabble-rousers before all of the passengers got out of control. Panic spread through the crowd. Several woman and children cried; others screamed and shouted. Men stared at the crewmembers with makeshift weapons in their hands, their eyes filled with rage.

When Viktor and his fellow workers reached them, the angry men who were trying to overthrow the ship fought the seamen with fists and bottles that they'd found on the ship. Viktor, a good fighter, could hold his own with almost any man. Fists flew, blood splattered, and the mutiny was underway. Elke heard the racket from her cabin, and she came on deck to see what was happening. When she saw Viktor fighting she screamed as he took a hit in the face. Blood spurted from his split lip. Elke stood still as the angry mob ran around her in every direction. Her hand covered her mouth in shock and horror. It took the better part of a half an hour, but finally the mutiny was overthrown.

Viktor wiped the blood from his face with a handkerchief he kept in his pants pocket; then he walked down the bridge to where Elke stood staring at him, her eyes wide with terror.

"Are you all right?" she asked.

"Yes, I am fine. I've been hurt worse in a football game." He smiled.

"You're bleeding…"

"Yes, I suppose I am." He wiped the cut again.

"Here, let me." She took the handkerchief from him and touched it to his lip gently.

"I'd gladly get a split lip or a broken nose every day if it meant that you would take care of me." He smiled at her.

"Oh Viktor, you talk such nonsense," Elke said.

His heart ached with longing and love as he saw the worry in her eyes.

The commotion began to die down and the passengers left the area. Only a group of young children playing with marbles remained on the deck. They sat on the floor at the corner of the ship and pitched the marbles against the wall.

Elke watched the children play, so innocent and unaware. She wondered about their future. Would they have a future? They were so busy being children that they didn't even realize the danger. Well, wasn't that better? A little girl with curly black hair giggled as she picked up one of the larger marbles. The swirls of blue and red shone gaily in the sunshine.

"I win," she said, holding the marble up in her small dimpled hand so everyone could see her treasure," and it almost made Elke want to cry.

"I have to go back to work," Viktor said as he reached over to squeeze Elke's hand. "I will come to your cabin as soon as my shift is finished. Would that be all right?"

"Yes, of course."

"I will come and get you and we will have dinner together?"

"Yes." She smiled.

"It looks like I'll have to go back to my cabin and change clothes." He shrugged, looking at the blood all over the front of his shirt. But he hesitated, not wanting to leave her.

"That would be a good idea. You'd best hurry," she said with a wry smile.

Once again quiet came over the passengers…the stillness of a bomb about to explode.

And still no word from America.

Chapter 110

"Viktor," Olof said as he came into the radio room.

"Yes."

"Come with me. You should really see this. It's sort of horrifying."

Viktor gave Olof a confused look. "Why would I want to see something horrifying?"

"Because it shocked me terribly. Come with me?"

Viktor put his work aside and followed Olof onto the deck.

A large group of passengers had gathered together in what appeared to be a meeting.

"There must be at least three hundred families here," Viktor said.

"Yes, I am afraid they are planning another attempt at a mutiny."

"Friends, fellow Jews," a dark, burly man who stood at the front of the ship said, and the other passengers grew silent to listen to him. "We know that with all that has taken place there is a very good chance that we will be forced to sail back to Germany. What awaits us there is beyond comprehension. I believe we will face a terrible death through torture at the hands of the Nazis. That is why I have arranged this meeting. I have a proposal for all of you. Together we must make an impression on the world. The press is following our situation and that is good. It gives us an opportunity, one we must take... *We* must show all of the countries of the world the horror of Hitler and his Third Reich. Then perhaps they will be forced to pay attention. Now, I realize that what I am suggesting is very drastic. And feel free to leave if you are not with me in this. But I am proposing that once it is decided that for certain we are going to be sent back to Germany, we must agree to commit mass suicide. Only something so shocking and terrible will shake all of these leaders into opening their eyes. It will ring like a warning bell, one they can no longer ignore. And I am aware that we will be sacrificed, and it will not help us, but maybe it will help our fellow Jews who are still in Germany. And for us, well, it is far better to jump into the water and die by our own hands then to be tortured by the Nazis.

Viktor looked at Olof. "They are not planning a mutiny, they are planning mass suicide."

"My God," Olof gasped.

"Who is with me?" the burly man asked.

Slowly everyone in the crowd raised their hands.

"Then it is decided. Once we are sure that we have no chance and that our fate is sealed, we will meet here on the deck and do what we must do."

Women were gripping their children to their breasts. Men held their head in their hands or embraced their wives. As Viktor glanced at the crowd he felt an overwhelming sadness and shame at being German, followed by a pang of terror that shot through him like a hot blade. He must find a way to save Elke from harm, he must.

Chapter 111

Captain Schroder was beside himself. He walked along the deck watching the passengers on his ship. He'd taken an oath as captain of this vessel to protect them. They trusted him, depended upon him, and even if it cost him his life, he must do everything in his power to ensure their safety. He stopped to watch a group of children jumping rope and singing songs. Schroder could not imagine anyone forcing these children to suffer and be tortured. It was horrific, inhumane. He refused to send these children back to Germany. He would sink the ship first… But before he took such drastic measures he would try everything he could think of. There must be something he could do.

Captain Schroder climbed down the stairs and entered the radio room.

"Gentlemen," the captain said to the radio operators. "Send another telegram to America; this time addresses it to Mrs. Eleanor Roosevelt. Plead with her to allow the children from our ship to enter the United States. Be sure to explain that these little ones will face terrible consequences if they go back to Germany, perhaps death. She is a woman; with God's help she will find it in her heart to take them. I am praying that she will be willing to do that much at the very least."

The telegram was sent…marked urgent from the *MS St. Louis*.

Chapter 112

THE OFFICE OF THE PRESIDENT
OF THE UNITED STATES OF AMERICA
WASHINGTON D.C.

"Give me your tired, your poor,
Your huddled masses yearning to breathe free,
The wretched refuse of your teeming shore.
Send these, the homeless, tempest-tossed, to me:
I lift my lamp beside the golden door. "

From the Statue of Liberty

Franklin Delano Roosevelt sat quietly in his wheelchair facing the window, sipping a cup of coffee in the small sitting room where he often went to take time to reflect. Today he awaited the arrival of his wife Eleanor. Although her looks disappointed him and he attributed his lifetime of indiscretions to that, she'd been his best friend, his wisest consultant and most importantly, he trusted her. President Roosevelt had already discussed the matter of the *St. Louis* with both Hull and Kennedy, and he'd listened to what they had to say, had even taken it into consideration. But in the end, Eleanor's opinion ranked the highest. He knew that she always had his best interests at heart no matter what happened between them personally. For the fifth time this morning, he picked up the telegram that had arrived the previous week from the *MS St. Louis* and reread it, a messy business for sure. Soon he would face reelection, and he knew that permitting a ship filled with immigrants in need of food, money and jobs into the already financially depressed Unites

States would cause lots of dissention amongst his supporters. And to make things worse, they were Jews. Contrary to popular belief, Roosevelt didn't have anti-Semitic leanings. In fact, in the prior election he'd enjoyed tremendous Jewish support. However, there was a great show of anti-Semitism in the country and he was afraid that opening the door to a ship full of Jewish refugees would only stir the pot and hurt his chances of being reelected.

The great mahogany door opened and Eleanor entered. Her hair caught up neatly in a twist at the nape of her neck, she wore a tailored cotton navy blue dress and matching low-heeled shoes. Eleanor gave him the regular half-smile she'd given him every morning since they'd been married; then she walked over and poured herself a cup of steaming coffee. Pulling out the chair, Eleanor sat across the desk from her husband and studied him.

"Have you eaten breakfast?" she asked.

"No, I can't eat."

"I am assuming that you want to discuss the *St. Louis*." She looked into his eyes.

"Yes, how did you know?"

"Because I know you. I am sure it is weighing heavily on your mind."

"It is. There are helpless people on board that ship. And isn't America the world power that's always ready to help the needy? That's what makes this country great."

"I received a wire myself this morning. It's from the captain of the *St. Louis*; he's requested that I take the children, just the children. He says that if they are returned to Germany there is a good chance they will die. But if we take them in, then they will become wards of the state. America will be responsible for supporting them. Right now, in the state we are in, we can't afford to do that."

"I know. I've been working day and night trying to find every avenue I possibly can to create work for Americans. Our own people are standing in bread lines. If we open our doors, refugees from all over the world will come pouring in and our economy would never recover," he said.

"And if you refuse, you will look insensitive and anti-Semitic. It's a dilemma. But still, you must never forget that you were elected by the American people. You promised them that you would rebuild the United States, that you would make America rich and strong again. You, Mr. President, are in the employ of the people of this great country and they have trusted you to put their needs first. That was your promise when you took the oath. You owe it to the people."

"If this ship full of Jews is returned to Germany, Hitler, that sadistic bastard, will torture them. Possibly even kill them."

"Yes, I am aware, and you must know that I wish we could do something. But there is another thing we must consider. If we antagonize Hitler it could plunge America into a war. Now you have been more than generous with supplies and money to England and the Americans have accepted that, but there is a strong consensus amongst our citizens against entering this war. And don't get me wrong, Franklin, I wish we could do even more. But I am afraid of the consequences of all of this."

He nodded. "It's hard to look the other way when a ship of helpless people is begging for your mercy and you feel as if their fate lies in your hands."

"Yes, it is. Harder than the world will ever know. And I doubt they will ever understand. But you will do what you must to rebuild America, and someday you will be known as the best president who ever lived," she said.

"God willing. I hope so, Eleanor. And God forgive us."

Chapter 113

Elke stayed on deck breathing the fresh air. Only a young couple and a group of children remained on deck. Thoughts of Manny trickled into her mind. How well he'd hidden his pain. She had never suspected that he of all people, carefree Manny, would end his life. The doctors could not determine if he'd committed suicide or accidently taken too many pills in combination with alcohol. She chose to believe his death was accidental. Poor Manny, even after all that he told her about *Kristallnacht* and what had happened with the girl Lieb, she knew him to be a good soul. Elke had grown up with a selfish, self-serving mother who'd forced her into terrible acts with egotistical men. Knowing Manny had affected her in so many ways. It made her realize that perhaps there were people who actually cared about others. He cared enough about that girl, Lieb, to carry the guilt in his heart, and he'd cared enough about Alex and Anna to give them the gift of a future. He thought of himself as a heartless self-indulgent playboy. Everyone made mistakes.

For years Elke had avoided questioning the identity of her birth father. She'd forced herself not to wonder where she came from. She'd closed that chapter when as she just a child. She'd asked her mother about her father, and her mother had responded by slapping her.

"Don't ever ask about that bastard. He left us to fend for ourselves. Let me tell you he was a good-for-nothing man. To think I once believed I actually loved him."

Seeing the fury in her mother's eyes, Elke never dared to ask again. The only information she had about her father was information that her mother had volunteered willingly, and that had only happened when her mother drank too much.

Life had forced her mother into becoming a strong and demanding woman whom Elke had feared. She had raised Elke alone, without love or tenderness. Because she'd been saddled with a child, as she called it, at a young age, she'd had no time to acquire any education or skills. Her mother had told Elke that with a baby hanging on her neck she would never find a husband either. So, her mother had taken care of her child the only way she knew how, by selling her body and then secretly cursing the men who bought her wares, and beating her daughter while blaming Elke for forcing her into a life of poverty and prostitution. Often she'd told Elke, "If it's good enough for me, it's good enough for you," and as soon as her clients began to find Elke desirable, her mother made her earn her keep.

But now, sitting here on this doomed ship, uncertain of her future or the future of Jews in general, Elke allowed herself to wonder about her father. From her blonde hair and light eyes, she'd always assumed that her father had been Gentile. But actually, there were blond Jews, she'd seen them here on this ship, and she'd met them even before she'd left Germany. So her coloring did not give her any definite indication as to who or what nationality her father might be. It was hard to accept, but she thought that he was probably a customer of her mother's, although her mother claimed she'd only begun prostitution after her father left them. In fact, once her mother had even claimed to have been married to her father. However, Elke knew that her mother could stretch or change the truth to suit her needs; she'd seen her do it often. So there could be no telling fact from fiction. Once Elke had had a dream that she'd finally met her father. In the dream, she was a little girl again. Her father had turned out to be, of all people, Adolf Hitler. He'd come to see her mother to pay for her services like all the other men who came to trade money for sex. Elke had been cowering in the corner hoping that this customer would not set his sights on her and force her into the terrible, painful acts that the others did. Hitler had looked in the corner and smiled. Then he told her in a calm and inviting voice that he was her father, luring her out of her hiding place. She'd come out slowly, trusting him. "Come sit by me," he'd said, pulling a bunch of hard candies out of his suit-jacket pocket. Then as the dream had continued, she'd come to trust him, and as they talked she told him that she was a Jew and her mother was too. Then she'd begged him to stop his persecution of the Jews. She'd told him how afraid she was every day of her life, and although the fear of the Nazis had only come upon her over the last few years, in the dream the fears had come to her as a child, even before she understood what the Nazis stood for. But dreams can be like that, where the time sequences made no sense at all. He'd immediately changed from the smiling father image to a monster with horns growing out of his head; his face had been covered in red, bulging veins and he'd growled with anger and disgust. Then he'd roared for his *Gestapo* agents and they'd come rushing in. They too had been monsters rather than men. She and her mother had been handcuffed, beaten to near death and then sent to a concentration camp. Elke had had this dream more than once and each time it occurred, she'd awaken shaken and afraid to go back to sleep. I am so troubled, she thought. My mind is not stable. I should consider myself fortunate to have someone like Viktor who cares about me in my life. He always shows me kindness and he is very gentle and generous. Not like the others, the ones my mother allowed to force themselves on me before I even knew what it was that happened between a man and a woman. She envisioned Viktor's face in her mind. *He could never do such a thing; he would never force himself upon a child, or anyone else for that matter. His heart is good.*

It was at that moment as she sat on the deck of the *MS St. Louis* gazing out at the coast of Miami, the smell of seaweed in the air and a light dusting of salt from the ocean spray upon her lips, that Elke Berman, the girl who was never going to fall in love, allowed herself to fall in love with Viktor Hahn.

Chapter 114

Elke waited in the dining room for Viktor. He was late, but she wasn't concerned; she knew he would come. The waiters brought a large tureen and served each passenger a bowl of soup. There was bread on the table, enough for one slice per person. These meals were nothing like the opulent meals they'd served on the way to Cuba. They must preserve the food supply that was still available. The others at the table cursed the captain and his crew.

"I think this was a trick from the beginning. This ship flies the Nazi flag. When we first got on, there was a picture of Hitler right here in the dining room," a middle-aged man with graying hair and a tailored suit said.

"I am afraid you could be right," said one of the other men at the table.

"I don't believe that," Elke said. "I know for a fact that the captain is doing all he can for us."

"Well, he's sent a wire to the President of America. At least he claims he did."

"I know he did. He is waiting, as we all are."

"Perhaps, but his life is not at stake. Ours are. If we are returned to Germany there is no telling what will become of us," the middle-aged man's wife said.

"But that is not his fault. He is trying," Elke said.

"You say that because you are dating one of them, a Nazi," the woman spoke again and shook her head, looking like she would like to spit.

"He is a German, but he is not a Nazi. I know you can't believe this, but not all Germans are Nazis. Before I got on this ship, I didn't believe it either. But now I know it for a fact," Elke said.

"You know only what they tell you. But what you don't know or don't understand is how badly they lie. The Nazis wanted our money, the money we had hidden outside of Germany, the money they would never have found, never have gotten their filthy hands on, so they arranged this voyage to force us to pay them for our lives. And we did. Once they had our money, we were worthless to them, and all of the passports they sold us with all of the promises they made fell through. The visas that we paid for with our life savings weren't worth the paper they were written on. And now I am afraid our lives are worth even less," the man with graying hair said as he lit a cigar.

"I hope you are wrong…" a young woman holding a child, who'd been silent thus far said. "If you are right, we are finished."

Just then, Viktor came dashing into the dining room. His smile reached across his face and his eyes twinkled as he walked up to Elke.

"Come with me, onto the deck. I have something to tell you," Viktor said, grabbing Elke's hand.

"Wouldn't you like to have something to eat first?" she asked.

"I am too excited to eat."

Elke took the napkin off her lap and got up from the table. "Please excuse me," she said to the other diners who frowned at her and Viktor.

He pulled her up the stairs so fast that she felt as if she might fall. Laughing, she said, "Viktor. Slow down! I am wearing high heels."

"I'm sorry. I am just so excited. I have news. It won't be announced to the rest of the ship until later tonight. But I will tell you now."

They were on the deck, standing next to the railing.

"Go on…" she said turning to look in his eyes.

"The captain has made contact with the Dominican Republic and also a small island off the coast of Cuba called Isla de la Juventud. The Dominican Republic hasn't answered. But the island is willing to take the passengers."

"All of us?"

"Yes, all of you."

"Oh, Viktor, that is such good news."

"It is, isn't it?"

"But…" She looked away from him as emptiness filled her heart. How could she be so silly at such a crucial moment? This was a matter of life and death. Why did she care about leaving him behind? Somehow losing him seemed almost as important as losing her life. "I guess this is goodbye for us… I mean, I will get off the ship and you…you will return to Germany."

"I thought about that. I thought about that long and hard. Elke," he got down on one knee. "I am afraid I was unable to buy a ring. There is no jewelry shop onboard."

"You are so silly, even now…"

"I am not being silly. I love you. Will you marry me? If you say yes, I will finish this voyage; then I will come to the Isla de la Juventud and we will live out our lives together. I have a little money saved. We can start over."

She swallowed hard to hold back the tears, but they came anyway.

"Yes, Viktor, I will marry you. I will be your wife."

He stood up and lifted her in the air, swirling her in a circle of joy. She giggled. He put her down carefully and pressed his lips against hers.

"I will get you a ring."

"It's not necessary. Keep the money; we may need it for more important things."

"Whatever you want," he said. "Tonight you have made me the happiest man in the world."

"Let's go to my room," she said. Why was it so hard for her to say "I love you," even when it was true?

He nodded. "Yes, let's go to your room. But first let me get us a couple of hard rolls. I was so excited about the news that I forgot to eat. I haven't eaten since this morning."

She smiled. "It is exciting. Go to the kitchen and get something for yourself. I am fine. I've eaten plenty today."

"Are you sure?"

"I'm sure." She smiled, touching his hair. "Then meet me at my room?"

"I'll be there soon...very soon."

Later that night the announcement about the Isla de la Juventud was sounded over the loud speaker.

"Ladies and gentlemen, this is your captain speaking. I sent out wires to Canada, The Dominican Republic, and to a small island off the coast of Cuba called Isla de la Juventud asking them for permission to dock at their ports. Unfortunately, the answers from Canada and the Dominican Republic were not favorable. However, I received a wire from the Isla de la Juventud. They have agreed to accept the passengers of the *MS St. Louis* onto their shores. This is wonderful news for all of us. Tomorrow morning I will be turning the ship around and heading back toward Cuban waters. As always, I remain your faithful servant, Captain Gustav Schroder."

Cries of jubilation could be heard all over the ship. A few minutes later the band began to play and the passengers got up to dance.

But still they had not heard even a word from America...

Chapter 115

Elke lay in Viktor's arms. He caressed her shoulder, marveling at the softness of her skin.

"Why me?" she asked.

"I'm sorry? I don't understand."

"Why did you choose me to love?"

"You don't choose who you will love. Love just happens. I don't know why."

"I don't agree. I think that you chose to allow yourself to love or not to love," she said.

"I will say this: the first time I saw you I thought you were the most beautiful girl I'd ever seen. But it's far more than that. There is something in you that touches something deep within me. It makes me want to protect and care for you."

"But I was so rude to you …in the beginning."

"That's because you liked Manny," he said

"You knew that?"

"I knew. I knew what attracted you to him, too. He was suave, and rich. And I suppose I hated him. He was so carefree. At least that was what I thought."

"Yes, that was what we both thought."

"I am sorry he died, but I am glad you are mine."

"He never wanted me anyway. He was in love with Anna."

"What a triangle."

"Yes, I suppose it was. But you know, this is interesting to me anyway. I had gone through life, I mean before I got on this ship, certain that I would never allow myself to care for anyone or anything. I'd suffered far too much. Everything I'd ever cared for or wanted was taken away from me, so I learned early not to become attached to anything."

"I can understand."

She began toying with a loose string on the blanket that covered them. "When I was a little girl, I brought a dog home. I'd found it on the street and it had licked my hand. I fell instantly in love with the pup. I can still remember her she was a little brown-and-white dog with a tail that never stopped wagging. I named her Brownie. My mother said I could keep her. I was so excited. But two days later after one of her drinking sprees, she got rid of the dog while I was at school. I came home and Brownie was gone. Oh, how I cried. And when I cried my mother slapped my face and said that we barely had money to feed ourselves. How were we going to feed a dog?"

"That must have hurt you very badly."

"Oh yes, it did. But there is even more. Something I must tell you before you become involved with me."

"I think it might be too late for that," he said.

"Hear me out. You might decide I am not the angel you thought I was."

"Go ahead. I am listening."

"This is hard for me. But I must tell you. My mother, she was a prostitute. I don't know who my father was. But, Viktor, the part that is even worse, is that she forced me to be a prostitute too. She sold me to older men who had deviant attractions to children. I am dirty. They did strange and awful things to me. But if it weren't for a group of Nazis who were my customers, I would never have gotten passage on this ship. They took pity on me. And although they hurt me in many ways, they also saved my life. I am ashamed of my past. And I know that you deserve better. So there it is..."

He was silent for a moment. She was suddenly afraid that he would get up, get dressed, and walk out of this room, and once again she would be alone. Her heartbeat quickened. She wanted to speak, but she couldn't think of anything more to say... Elke had told him what he must know before she could become his wife. Finally he turned and took her into his arms. Then she felt his face against hers. He was crying.

"Oh, Elke, that is so terrible. My darling, I wish I could have been there to help you."

"You are not going to leave me?"

"I am never going to leave you."

"You forgive me?" she asked.

"Forgive you? You were just a child. You had no choice in the matter. It was what your mother demanded of you, and so you did what you were told. There is nothing to forgive. This does not change my feelings for you. In fact, if anything they are even stronger."

"That is why I thought I wanted Manny. I was looking for a comfortable life where I would never have to earn money that way again, and I could escape from my terrible beginnings."

"And you saw Manny as the one to do that for you? I can't say I blame you after what you'd been through."

"Yes, I did think he was the one. I liked him, but I never loved him."

"Dare I ask?"

"Ask what?"

"Do you love me?" Viktor asked.

"It comes as a surprise even to me, me who thought I was incapable of love…but yes, Viktor, I love you."

"Say it again…"

She laughed. "I love you."

"And I love you too, with all my heart. Elke, we are going to have a wonderful life together, I promise. And if I have to work around the clock, you will never have to sell yourself again."

"And we will live in an island paradise."

"Yes on the Isla de la Juventud. Before today, I'd never even heard of this place, this small island that has brought me immeasurable joy when just this morning I was almost at the depths of despair. Elke, I was so worried. But now I know that you will be safe. That is such a relief to my mind and to my heart. I know that as long as we are together, this little island we will call home will be heaven on earth," Viktor said and he kissed her.

`

Chapter 116

The passengers stood on deck watching, and they cheered as the ship turned around heading back toward Cuba. A handsome young man with dark curling hair and sparkling green eyes was playing the piano while a group of passengers surrounded him singing songs in Yiddish. Viktor had gone to work with a promise of returning to Elke as soon as his shift ended. Elke sat on the deck. She'd taken a book from the library to entertain her until Viktor was done with his shift. As she began reading, a little girl of no more than ten years old came over and sat beside her.

"Hello," the child said. "My name is Judith. What are you reading?"

"It's a book about the different regions in Germany. There wasn't much to choose from, I'm afraid. And this one is awfully boring."

"It sounds boring," Judith said. "My mother says that Hitler burned all the books that were written by people he didn't like. And we are not allowed to read anything unless he says it's all right with him."

"That's true. He's banned many books in Germany. And this is a German ship, so I guess they have to abide by his rules," Elke said, laying the book down on the chair beside her.

"What does that mean, to abide by his rules?"

"It means that the ship must do what Hitler tells them to do."

"What if he says that we have to go back to Germany? I heard my parents talking when they thought I was asleep. They said that the Nazis would kill us. Could that be true? Would they really kill us? That makes me so scared. I wish that Hitler would just leave us alone."

"Don't be afraid. We are on our way right now to a nice little island right by Cuba. I would bet that they even have conga dancing there." Elke looked at the child. It saddened her to think that a little girl had to worry about dying. Her own childhood had been filled with fear, so she felt for this little one very deeply.

"I saw some of the passenger's conga dancing when we first got on the ship. It looked like fun," Judith said, breaking Elke's train of thought.

"You will probably learn how to do that dance and maybe some others as well once we are on the island."

"I would really like that," Judith said, smiling.

The bell sounded and the captain came over the loud speaker.

"Ladies and gentlemen…" He cleared his throat. "It is with deepest regret that I must inform you that the Isla de la Juventud has withdrawn their offer. We are no longer welcome on their shores. I immediately wired the JDC to inform them of the news. I am turning the ship back again toward the United States. Please do not lose hope. A few minutes ago I received word that the JDC, the committee for the assistance of Jewish refugees is working diligently to help you find a safe harbor. They promise that they will not stop trying until we are able to land. We must hold fast to the belief that they will be successful. It breaks my heart to bring you this news. But as always, I remain your captain, here to serve you, Captain Gustav Schroder, of the *MS St. Louis*."

Judith lost her color. Her eyes filled with panic as she looked at Elke. "What does that mean? Does that mean that the island doesn't want us? Why not? What did we do wrong? Can't we tell them we're sorry and we won't do it again? They have to take us, or Hitler will kill us. Can't we tell them that?"

"Judith," Elke said, reaching over and putting her arm around the little girls shoulder. "We did nothing wrong. Don't worry. We will find a place to land."

"I don't think anyone wants us. I don't know why. I don't understand why they all hate us. But I am really scared that we are going back to Germany, and then I think we will die. My mother says so, and I'm afraid to die. I think it will hurt a lot."

"Don't say such things. Don't even think them…" Elke said just as Viktor came bounding up the stairs on to the deck. He ran over to Elke.

"When I heard the news I went to your cabin. You weren't there, so I thought you might be up here."

She nodded. "I was getting a little fresh air."

"We are going back to Germany," Judith said. She had begun to cry. "I know it."

"I don't believe that. We have a very good captain. He will find a way for you; you'll see…"

"I don't believe you. I don't believe any Germans who aren't Jewish anymore… They hate us. They want to hurt us…" Judith got up and ran to the stairs that lead back to the staterooms.

"Terrible news," Elke said.

"Yes, it is, but I have an alternate plan. I want to talk to you about it."

"All right," she said.

"Not here, not out in the open. Let's go to your room."

"Of course." Elke stood up and followed him.

He looked at the book she carried. "Such nonsense," he said, shaking his head in disgust. "You can't even read what you want to read. The only books available to us are books that proclaim Germany as the greatest place on earth and Hitler the supreme leader. These books are so far from the truth that it's disgusting."

They walked back to Elke's stateroom. After they closed the door and Elke locked it, Viktor sat down on the bed. He patted the area next to him for Elke to sit.

"I don't have much time. I have to get back to work. However, I didn't want you to despair over the news. I wanted to ensure you that I already have a plan."

"Can you tell me?"

"Of course. I will tell you quickly. If we are forced to go back to Germany, I am planning to hide you in the engine room once we dock. Then I will wait until dark, when I will come back and sneak you off the ship. I have an apartment where I will hide you while a very good friend of mine has papers forged by a professional forger, papers that declare you a Gentile. At that time, we will leave Germany and go to Switzerland and get married. What do you think?"

"I am afraid that I will be missed. They took a head count when we got on board. Won't the authorities know that I've disappeared?"

"Yes, that's a valid point, but you could have fallen from the ship during the night while we were at sea and gone unnoticed. It isn't likely, but it's not impossible either. It is our only option. I think it's worth the risk."

"If you think so, then this is what we will do."

"And no matter what, I will be beside you. If you go to a camp, I will tell them that they might as well arrest me and send me too."

Chapter 117

On June 6, 1939, the *MS St. Louis* had run out of options. They were almost out of fuel and food, so the captain was forced to turn the ship around and head back to Europe.

The passengers gave up hope of ever finding a safe harbor. The mood on the ship was one of impending doom. The time had come to face the fact that soon they would be back in Germany, under the rule of the Third Reich, and at the mercy of a heartless madman who hated them.

The band played; the captain insisted that the music go on in an effort to keep up morale, but no one danced. At mealtime the dining room was half full, and now very few people went up on deck to take walks or sit and enjoy the sunshine. Instead, they stayed alone in their staterooms, contemplating the future.

Viktor began making plans. His mind raced with constant plotting, assessing the danger of different strategies. He'd already arranged for Olof to go forward with plans of securing papers for Elke as soon as the ship landed, if he could only be sure that nobody would check the engine room too closely when the ship docked. He'd thought of all of the possible hiding places on board and decided that the engine room was the safest. But even so, there were no guarantees.

Viktor could not eat or sleep. The plan was far from foolproof, and anything could happen, anything could go wrong. And if it did, Elke would be in even greater danger than she would if she cooperated with the authorities, In fact, she might be shot on the spot. He'd gladly take the risk himself, but he couldn't bear to think of what might happen to Elke if all this failed. He found it difficult to concentrate on his work that morning in the radio room. He felt as if he might jump out of his skin with anxiety when a message came in on the wireless. He had to read it twice to believe the words that stood in black ink upon the white page.

It was from the American Joint Jewish Distribution Committee.

It is with delight that we send you the following information. After an exhaustive search, we have found homes for the passengers of the MS *St. Louis*. Please follow these instructions: the St. Louis is expected to dock in Antwerp, Belgium, where the passengers will be divided as follows: Belgium has agreed to take 214, The Netherlands 181, France 224, and Great Britain 287.

Although he wanted to dash up to Elke's room and tell her right away, Viktor knew that he must first deliver the news to the captain, who he knew would be relieved beyond measure.

Viktor found Captain Schroder in his office, head in hand. The captain had refused food for the last two days and the crew had begun to worry about him. Schroder looked up, his brow wrinkled and his eyes lined with red veins, as Viktor entered the room, forgetting to knock.

"Yes, what did you want Mr. Hahn?"

"I 'm sorry, sir, I should have knocked before entering your office; however I have an important message for you." Viktor handed the captain the paper and waited.

A light seemed to shine from Captain Schroder's face as he read the words. By the time he'd finished he looked as if he'd grown younger by twenty years. Tears fell from his eyes.

"Praise God," Captain Schroder said, gripping the note in his hand. "Praise God…"

Chapter 118

Viktor took the stairs two at a time up to Elke's cabin. He knocked and she opened the door.

"You've finished work so early?"

"Can you speak French?" he asked, breathless with excitement.

"What? Why?"

"Can you?"

"Well, maybe a little. Not much… Why?"

"Perhaps it is best if you go to Belgium, to Luxembourg, where they speak fluent German. That way you won't have a language problem. Yes, I think so. You will go to Luxembourg. I will arrange it, and then you will wait for me there…"

"What? What are you talking about? Slow down, Viktor. I don't understand."

"Yes, yes. Let me explain…"

He told her about the message from the Joint Commission. Then he explained his plan. Elke would leave the ship in Antwerp and take the train to Luxembourg. He would try to stay with her for a few days if possible, and then give her all the money he could. As a crewmember, he must complete the voyage and sail with the *St. Louis* back to Germany. There he would wait while Olof drew up the papers that would give Elke her new identity as a Gentile. As soon as he had the papers, he would return to Belgium where they would marry and then either go back to Germany or live in Belgium as an Aryan couple.

"But if we are living in Luxembourg I won't need a new identity. I don't think that the anti-Semitism is a strong there as it is in Germany."

"This may very well be true. But, if we don't have papers made up for you, it will not be safe for us to return to Germany to see my family. If I am unable to have the papers made up, I will be forced to lose contact with my family forever. I want to be able to go home. I want you to know my mother, father and brother. I love them. They are good people, Elke, and they will love you as much as I do."

"You're right. It would be best this way, if it all works out. Where are we going to land, and how soon do you think we will be there?"

"It will all work out. I have faith. The plan is to land in Antwerp. The captain will try to get there quickly because we are almost out of food."

Viktor took Elke into his arms. She felt his heart pounding though his shirt against her chest. She knew he was afraid. She was afraid too, but she was also grateful for the love of this man she hardly believed she deserved.

Chapter 119

On the seventeenth of June the *MS St. Louis* docked in the port of Antwerp, Belgium. The passengers, sea weary but grateful to be alive, disembarked from the ship. They walked in lines onto the dock, their eyes wide with anticipation and disbelief.

Upon Viktor's request, the captain granted his leave of absence for three days while the ship restocked before sailing for Germany. On that same sun-kissed afternoon, Viktor and Elke took the train to Luxembourg. Outside the window, the scenery exploded into summer colors, wildflowers and quaint little cottages slipped by as they held hands like an ordinary couple on an afternoon excursion. Viktor sat beside Elke with his golden hair, tanned skin, and white uniform. She could not help but swell with pride as she saw the other girls on board give Viktor appraising glances. Viktor saw Elke peek at a group of young women who'd been smiling across the aisle at him. He didn't return the smile; he wanted to assure Elke that he had no interest in other women, so he squeezed her hand and whispered in her ear.

"I'm all yours, only yours, until the day I die."

What had she done to deserve such happiness? When she had boarded the *MS St. Louis*, so many weeks ago, she'd never in her wildest dreams imagined that she might find such joy. Elke turned to Viktor and touched his cheek gently with her fingers.

"I love you too," she said.

Chapter 120

It was almost dinnertime when they arrived in Luxembourg. It had been a long day and neither had eaten since breakfast. They stopped at a café for a bowl of soup and thick slices of grainy bread. Sitting outside at a table under an umbrella, Elke and Viktor ate quickly; they wanted to find a flat before sunset. Most of the places that they looked at were either too expensive or too rundown. By nightfall it became apparent they would be forced to use some of the money that they'd saved to stay in a hotel. Viktor entered a bakery shop that was closing and asked the owner where he might find a hotel. The owner, a thick man with hanging jowls covered in perspiration, gave them directions.

"Go out the door and turn left. Then you will walk for about five blocks," the baker said.

Viktor bought a loaf of bread and they left.

When they arrived, a young girl with light blonde hair and golden eyes sat at the reception desk sorting papers. When she heard the customers enter she looked up and smiled at them.

"Can I help you?"

"My wife and I need a room for the night."

"Very good. Let me see what I have available."

"By the way, by any chance, do you happen to know of any nice, reasonably-priced apartments for rent near here?" Viktor asked. The girl looked close in age to Elke and seemed as if she might understand. "You see, I need a safe place for my wife to stay. I am going to be shipping out to sea in a few days and it might be a while before I return."

"Well, I don't know of any apartments, but we are looking for a housekeeper for the hotel and the job comes with a free room. I don't know if your wife would be interested."

"My wife will not be a maid." Viktor was appalled.

"I don't mind. I would be very interested. In fact, it would give me something to do," Elke said, turning to look at Viktor.

"I don't know…" he said shaking his head and looking around at the modest but tastefully decorated hotel lobby.

"Why don't we get a room and talk about it?" Elke said.

"All right." Viktor sounded skeptical

"Can we let you know in the morning?" Elke asked.

"Of course," the girl said. "By the way, I'm Lara."

"I'm Elke."

Viktor hated the idea of Elke cleaning rooms, scrubbing toilets, and making beds where other couples had made love, but he did like the idea that at least she might have a friend in this girl, someone to talk with or share a meal. It might help to alleviate the loneliness until he returned.

Lara handed the room key to Viktor, and he and Elke went to their room.

It was a simple room, not fancy, but clean, with a well-maintained bathroom right down the hall where they both took turns cleaning up.

When Elke returned to the room, Viktor sat in a wooden chair at a small desk in front of the window eating a slice of the bread he'd bought.

"Want some?"

"No, thank you." She smiled.

Viktor dropped the bread on the desk and stood up. He kissed Elke and lifted her face so that their eyes met.

"Talk to me. Tell me what you want. Do you want to work here until I get back?"

"I think that it would be a good idea. I know you have some savings and so do I, but this will help us to save what money we have in case we need it later. It will also be good for me to be around other people instead of staying alone day after day in a flat somewhere."

He nodded. It wasn't what he wanted for her, not by far, but he did agree that the waiting would be less nerve-racking if she were to have something to fill her time and people to talk with.

"I will agree to this. I don't like it, but I don't know what else to do right now. Now Elke, listen to me, this is very important," he said, sitting down and taking her hand until she sat beside him.

"Go on. I'm listening."

"You must remember that no one is to know your true identity. You cannot tell anyone our plans. We still don't know whom we can trust. You must say that you are a German woman, visiting Luxembourg for a while until your husband returns from a voyage. You cannot ever let them know that you are Jewish."

"Yes, but there is no problem for Jews here in Luxembourg. The problem is in Germany."

"Sweetheart, there are spies everywhere. I am buying illegal papers. This is a dangerous operation. I can't take any risks, even here.. Do you understand? If anyone finds out what we are doing we could find ourselves in more trouble than I care to think about."

Elke nodded. She would do as he asked. But she wanted to live in Belgium, never to return to Germany at least not to live. Because she loved him, Elke would agree to visit his family, but only for short periods of time. Germany had too many ugly memories and too many dangers for her as a Jew. She wanted to leave everything that had to do with that country of her birth in her past.

Viktor agreed.

That night they lay in each other's arms, spent from the day followed by a brief but tender hour of lovemaking.

"Viktor?"

"Yes, my love…"

"Are you sure that this is what you want? You are getting involved in something that you don't need to be drawn into. All you have to do is go back home and your worries are gone."

"What do you mean?"

"I mean, leave me here in Luxembourg. I will find a way to get by. If you go back to Germany and to your family, you will be safe. I feel very guilty about you getting mixed up in all of this, with the illegal papers and me being Jewish… It's just dangerous for you."

He got up on one elbow and looked into her eyes.

"I couldn't leave you now even if I wanted to, and I don't. You are my love, the other half of me. Before we met, I never knew what it meant to truly love another person. I will not leave you here in Luxembourg. Whatever the danger, for me, it's worth the risk to be your husband."

She put her arms around him and held him tight, her mind spinning. She'd recently made a discovery, but she could not bear to tell him, not here, not now. Not when everything felt so beautiful, so perfect.

Chapter 121

The next three days were like a honeymoon. Viktor insisted on showing Elke around Luxembourg, a city filled with old world charm. They walked through the ruins of a twelfth-century castle. Holding hands, they explored an old fort. Every night they made love, holding tight to each other until morning. Both of them knew that soon they would be separated, and neither could speculate for how long. In the mornings they took long walks, stopping for breakfast at small cafes. They tried to keep their meals fairly inexpensive, but still they dined on smoked pork shoulder with fried potato patties, or pan-fried trout with dishes of steaming *sauerkraut*. On the last night before he sailed out, Viktor insisted that they splurge and enjoy a French-inspired dinner of veal with cream and mushrooms topped off with a delicious Riesling wine. They sat in a dimly-lit restaurant with white tablecloths and white-gloved waiters as a harpist played softly in the background.

"I'll always remember this night," Viktor said.

"Why this night?"

"Because everything is so perfect."

She smiled at him. The flame from the candle on the table illuminated his eyes; they looked so sincere, so filled with love. And that reminded her that keeping things from him made her untrustworthy. If only she could tell him, come clean. He took her hand and brought it to his lips. Not yet, it would spoil the evening. And besides, the words would not come. When the time was right...then... Perhaps after he returned safely and everything fell into place. Yes, there would be time to tell him then.

When dawn broke, Viktor knew he must return to the ship. Elke sat up in bed watching him dress. He glanced over at her. She'd forgotten to pull the sheets over herself and her naked breasts were exposed, her golden hair falling in curls over her shoulders.

"Have I told you how beautiful you are?" he said.

She smiled.

"Right now, as I am looking at you, I am amazed that any person can be so stunning. Please forgive me if I stare, but I am taking a picture in my mind. I'll carry this picture of you, just the way you are right now with me all the way to Germany, and then until you are safely back in my arms."

"I look a mess," she turned away from him, blushing

He just shook his head. "I love you. God, how I love you."

She stood up and walked over to him, kissing him and then holding him tightly, inhaling the clean fragrance of his newly-shampooed hair. Outside a light rain fell from an overcast gray sky. Elke quickly slipped on a dress and shoes; then she walked Viktor down the stairs and to the train station. A flock of pigeons flapped their wings as they flew overhead.

"I am so afraid for you," she said, a lump forming in her throat. Elke suddenly felt desperate, terrified. "Why can't you just stay here with me and forget all about the papers? We don't need them." She pulled on the collar of his uniform.

"Then we can never go to Germany. I will never see my brother or my parents again."

"They could visit us here. This is so terribly risky, Viktor. What if you are caught? You will be punished... My God,

Viktor...punished by the Nazis..." She felt a shiver run like a sharp fingernail down her spine.

"My parents are too old to travel. I will be all right. I will be back soon. You must trust me. Don't forget everything I told you to do."

"Viktor..." Elke squeezed the sleeve of his raincoat, "I love you."

"I know, and I love you. And with God's help we will be together again soon."

The train rolled into the station with a horn blaring to announce its arrival.

Viktor turned to Elke and she grabbed him hard and fast, holding him close, "Be safe..." she said.

He kissed her, then turned and boarded the train. Elke watched and waved until Viktor was completely out of sight. Then she returned to the loneliness of her hotel room and sat looking out the window at the street. She was glad to be starting work the following day. It would take her mind off the waiting and wondering. She took off her shoes and went to the bed. Laying her head on the pillow he'd slept on, she turned and clutched it to her face inhaling deeply, then began to cry. Had it been better when she'd had no feelings at all? Hard to say when but with Viktor beside her the world seemed to glow in a golden light only she could see. And somehow that light made any sacrifice she might be forced to make worthwhile. Elke tried to nap; she drifted in and out of sleep. Because she'd been on the *St. Louis* and knew her way around it so well, she could picture Viktor on the deck or in the radio room. She longed to be there with him, but she knew she was lucky, lucky to have found a country willing to open its doors to Jews.

By five o'clock that night Elke needed to find something to eat. They'd finished the bread Viktor bought the previous night. As she forced herself to get up and go down the hall to wash the tears off her face. Then she went to see if Lara would like to join her for a light dinner somewhere.

Lara sat at the front desk. She greeted Elke as soon as she saw her.

"My husband left today," Elke said. "I thought maybe you would like to join me for a quick meal?"

"I would love to, but I can't; I have a date tonight. Perhaps later in the week?"

"Yes, anytime. I am by myself, just waiting for my husband's return, and I would love to have the company."

"Of course. Then let's plan to have dinner later this week."

"I look forward to it."

Viktor had given Elke as much money as he could afford, still keeping enough to pay for the papers, and she had a little cash of her own that she'd brought with her to begin her life in Cuba. How different things had turned out than she's thought they would when she boarded the *St. Louis*. Then she'd been looking for money and security; love had never even entered her mind. Strange, love… If anyone had asked her, she'd have told them that love was nothing but a prison for fools. Well, she couldn't say that she regretted the way that things had turned out. As long as Viktor returned safely, everything would be fine. And she was glad that she had not told him her secret. The shocking news might well have made him nervous and careless, two things he could not afford to be right now.

Chapter 122

Elke started working that Monday morning. Going from room to room, changing beds, sweeping floors, dusting wood furniture until it shined, and cleaning the bathrooms at the end of the halls… The work exhausted her, especially since she'd spent an entire month on the ship, not doing anything at all.

During the day she moved at such a fast pace that she hardly had a moment to think, but at night when she lay in the bed she'd shared with Viktor, her mind would not allow her to rest. She still had not changed the sheets, because she didn't want to lose touch with him. The fresh scent of his hair on the pillow, the fragrance of his cologne on the sheets, was all she had left of him now.

It was over two weeks before Lara had time to share a meal with Elke. They met at a bakery that served food just a few blocks from the hotel. Elke was so glad to have someone to talk to. Lara went on and on about the men she was seeing, about her new hairstyle, and a dress she was saving money to buy. She talked so much that Elke hardly said a word. Elke didn't mind listening. Although the girls were very close in age, Elke felt many years older, and for her Lara's untroubled life served as a much-needed distraction from her own worries.

When they parted, Elke and Lara decided they would try to meet once a week for dinner. That meeting became the highlight of Elke's otherwise lonely and worried days.

Chapter 123

It had been almost a month since Elke had last seen Viktor. Every possible scenario raced through her mind. It became difficult to sleep. She would drift off for an hour only to awaken with terrible images of Viktor being caught by the Nazis and arrested. For the rest of the night she would lay in bed watching the clock on the wall, unable to rest. And then, exhausted, she would drag herself out of bed in the morning and go to work.

Every week she would open her pay envelope and hide the contents in the drawer beneath her bras and panties.

Elke decided to save money and stop eating out, with the exception of the evenings that she met Lara. At the bakery she purchased a loaf of bread and from a vendor she bought some apples, she would live on these for now.

Lara reminded Elke of a brightly-colored butterfly; she flitted from subject to subject, and from boyfriend to boyfriend. Her frivolity amused Elke, who even during her very young years had not enjoyed a life of lighthearted pleasures. Elke longed to open up to Lara. It would help to have someone to share her fears about Viktor's return, her concerns about her pregnancy, and even her thoughts about her mother back in Germany. Often Lara and Elke would sit across the table eating a light meal of salads and fried potatoes, Lara giggling about a new dress, while Elke bit her lip as a reminder that she must not share her personal information with anyone. She'd promised Viktor.

One night after Elke finished dinner with Lara, on her way home she saw a card shop. A single bulb flickered in the window where she saw lovely cards and stationery, but what drew her attention was a thick leather-bound book. On the cover in gold letters it said, "Journal." She went inside and picked up the book. It was encased in rich burgundy leather. She ran her hand over the cover. *This would be good for me; I could release my feelings by writing about them. It would do me good to rehash it all: my childhood, my mother, Viktor, and everything that has happened since I left Germany on the* St. Louis.

She splurged and bought the book, and a lovely fountain pen and ink as well. It was exciting to have a project, something to do, to keep her busy on the long, lonely nights ahead.

As another week passed, Elke began to believe that Viktor had returned home and decided to stay in Germany. After all, his family and all of his friends lived there. If he came to live in Luxembourg, she would be all he had. She couldn't blame him if he had decided after being away from her that what they had was just not enough in exchange for what he would be sacrificing.

When Elke had left for Cuba, she thought that starting a new life on her own would be easy. And perhaps it would have been, then. But that was before she fell in love. Now, life without Viktor seemed impossible. Except for Lara, she had no friends or family in Luxembourg. And with each day that passed that Viktor did not return, instead of things becoming easier, she missed him even more.

Chapter 124

Elke's secret began to stir and grow inside of her. She was pregnant. But that wasn't the entire problem. Elke tried several times to accurately calculate the dates in order to make a solid determination; however, she was not sure if the baby belonged to Viktor or Manny. And this was why she had not told Viktor before he left. She agonized over this. How could she expect Viktor to raise a child that might have been fathered by another man? But then again, the baby could very well belong to Viktor. She had no idea what to do.

Chapter 125

Elke awoke early one morning feeling slight cramps. When she went to the bathroom she saw a spot of blood on her underwear. She needed a doctor or a midwife to help her or she would surely lose the baby. Over the past several weeks, she had become attached to the tiny soul that grew inside her womb. Being alone much of the time, once the infant had begun to move, it became very real to her. She talked to the baby and found that although she could not hold it or see it, she no longer felt lonely. The longer her pregnancy went on, the more she convinced herself that Viktor had fathered the child, and she wanted that child, wanted it with all her heart.

Elke pulled a small pile of money out of her drawer. Working and not spending, she had acquired a small savings, certainly enough to pay for medical help. But how would she ever find a doctor? She didn't know anyone except Lara in Belgium, and Lara did not know about her condition. Well, perhaps she would ask her anyway, but not mention the pregnancy. She wanted to wait for Viktor, wanted him to be the first to know.

Elke went downstairs to find Lara at the front desk; she told Lara that she'd been feeling very tired lately and need to see a doctor. Lara recommended her family physician. Although she seemed concerned, Lara didn't press her for details. Work took a toll on her that day; she completed her tasks, but the quality suffered. As soon as she finished her shift, she walked four blocks and turned the corner as Lara had instructed to find the office of Dr. Moens. His receptionist, a young girl with wavy auburn hair and warm honey-colored eyes said he was busy, but if she had an emergency, Elke could wait and she would get her into the office as soon as possible. Elke waited for over an hour until the doctor had an opening in his schedule. He examined her and recommended bed rest, insisting that she must quit her job immediately.

"The work that you do is too strenuous for you right now, in your condition. If you want this baby, you cannot continue this way."

Elke nodded. What would she do for money?

"Now if the bleeding gets worse you must call me right away. Do you understand?" he said, his face kind but stern.

"Yes, I understand."

Then he also told her that she must make plans with either him or a midwife to assist with the birth. Again she nodded.

The appointment cost her more money than she expected. If her bleeding increased, forcing her to see the doctor again, and then had to pay for delivering the baby too, it would wipe out everything she had.

What if Viktor never returned? What then? She must not deplete her savings.

She left the building and began walking.

Vomit rose in her throat and she turned into an alleyway just in time to spew the contents of her stomach on the pavement. Elke leaned her head against the side of a building. The bricks felt cool on her cheek. She was even more lightheaded and nauseated than she'd been before she'd seen the doctor. As she caressed her cramping belly, blood trickled down her leg. She forced herself to begin walking again. Only four more blocks and she would be back at the hotel, then she could lie down. Perhaps the pain would subside.

Chapter 126

As the *St. Louis* sailed out of the port at Antwerp, Viktor had heavy heart. He'd been forced to leave Elke alone in a strange city, knowing no one. If anything happened to her, he would never forgive himself. And besides all of that, he missed her terribly.

The crew on the ship seemed relieved to have found suitable destinations for the Jewish travelers, but none more than Captain Schroder. As captain of his ship, he'd fulfilled his responsibility and the voyage had been a success. Over the month that he'd spent with his Jewish charges, Captain Schroder had grown to care deeply for them, not just as a captain but also as a friend. It did his heart good to know they were safe. As the *St. Louis* sailed back toward Hamburg the captain and crew had found peace at last, all except for Viktor.

Viktor and Olof made plans to meet on the first Saturday following the ship's landing. During the week Olof would go to see his friend and request that the papers be drawn up. Then once he had more information, Olof would meet Viktor at the neighborhood pub, a place they regularly frequented when they came into town. There Olof would tell Viktor exactly what must be done to go forward with the forgeries and how much it would cost.

When he got off the ship in Hamburg, Viktor noticed the Nazi flags and pictures of Adolf Hitler on all of the buildings. Oh, he had seen them before, but he'd never paid attention until now. As he walked through the familiar streets, Viktor realized that he'd boarded the *St. Louis* as a boy in search of adventure, and left it as a man in love with a woman in grave danger. Still, he would not trade even a second of the time he'd spent with Elke. The love he felt for her trumped any fear he had for The Third Reich.

Viktor arrived at the small cottage in Dinkelsbuhl, where he'd grown up, only to find his father ill with a bad case of influenza and his brother Axel gone. While Viktor had been sailing with the *St. Louis*, Axel had enlisted in the Germany army, leaving his parents anxiously awaiting a letter, which they had not yet received.

Viktor had gone with Olof to Austria on his last leave, and so he had not been home for several months. As he watched his parents, he saw how much they had aged. His mother's hip bothered her and she'd developed a slight limp when she walked. His father's illness sent him into fits of coughing that left him gasping for breath. With Axel gone, Viktor became the one light in their lives, and they watched him with joy, their eyes hopeful that Viktor would stay with them for a long time before he went back out to sea.

"You should not be going back on the ship for at least a month, yes?" Viktor's mother asked.

"I don't know. I may have to leave sooner." Viktor felt guilty. They needed him. The house had begun to fall apart. Still young and strong, Viktor could take care of things for his parents that they could no longer do themselves. But Elke needed him too.

"Well, stay as long as you can, please, Viktor. Your Papa is sick and it's hard for me to take care of him."

His father, a barber by trade, had never earned enough money for the family to be able to save. Before Hitler, the country suffered a great depression and except for the very rich, most wives cut their husbands' hair and mothers their sons.' So the family lived hand to mouth. But once Viktor began working, he helped them by giving them cash each time he returned from a voyage with a pay envelope. This time he could not give them anything; he must hold on to every penny in order to pay for the forged papers. In fact, he hoped he would have enough.

Viktor went to his father's bedside.

"Hello, Papa. I just got back."

"It's good to have you home." He coughed. "Hand me my cigarettes; your mother has taken them away again."

"You shouldn't smoke when you're so sick."

"Yes, I know, but if I am going to die, I'd like to at least die happy. Now, hand them to me."

Viktor did as his father asked. He watched his father light a cigarette with trembling fingers and then lean back against the pillows to inhale deeply.

"That's good…"

"You are not going to die, Papa. Not for a while anyway," Viktor said. "So you should at least make some effort to take care of yourself."

"Yes, yes, I know. Axel has made us very proud. He's enlisted."

"Mother told me."

"You don't approve?" his father asked.

"It's not that. It's just that I'm not sure Hitler is as good for Germany as all of you might think he is."

"He is good for Germany. Since he's come in to power things are much better for us, much better. When I am not sick, and I can work, I actually have some customers. People have a little bit of money to spend now."

"Perhaps, but still he is a cruel madman. Do you realize what he is doing to the Jews? To the Gypsies, to the Jehovah's Witnesses? To anyone he doesn't approve of?"

"What do I care about this? I have enough trouble taking care of my family. Now I should worry about Jews and Gypsies? Don't be an idealist, Viktor. Join the navy and make a career for yourself. Help to rebuild the Fatherland. God knows, Germany needs this."

His father began coughing again. Viktor patted his back. He knew that his mother would be in agreement with his father, so Viktor decided that it would be best if neither of his parents ever knew that Elke was Jewish.

That Saturday as planned Viktor walked the three blocks to the pub to meet Olof. They usually met around noon, had lunch followed by a few beers. Viktor waited all day. Olof never came.

Over the next several weeks, Viktor did what he could to help his parents while he waited to hear from Olof. He needed those papers, but he'd also begun to worry about Olof. He'd put Olof in danger asking him to see a forger. Had Olof been arrested? Viktor agonized over all the what-ifs, but he dared not mention anything about it to anyone, not even to his mother…

Remarkably, at his age, and despite the haphazard way he took care of himself, his father's health began to improve. He regained his color and his strength, and within a couple of weeks he was able to return to work.

Viktor called Olof, leaving several messages with his family, but received no reply. He had no idea where to begin to look for other avenues to purchase forged papers, and he dared not trust anyone. Time was passing and Viktor had to take some kind of action, so he finally decided that he would return to Luxembourg without the papers, marry Elke and stay in Luxembourg where she would be safe. It would be hard to leave his parents, especially with his brother gone, but he could not find another solution. When he could he would visit, but he knew that if Elke did not have papers, he would be forced to come alone. His family would probably never know his wife.

Viktor packed everything he thought he might need. He spent hours sitting on the floor of his room and going through his old box of memories. His diploma when he graduated from gymnasium. A photo of his brother and him in front of a Christmas tree in the town square when his brother was only ten and he was only eight. The edges of the paper had turned yellow, but Viktor could still see his brother's eyes, and if he thought hard enough he could still feel Axel's arm around his shoulder. Oh, Axel, don't die in the army. Please come back safe…

There were ribbons he'd won in competitions when he'd been in the Hitler Youth. How little he really knew about the Nazi Party then. He'd spouted the propaganda like all of the other boys, but he'd not realized what it meant. Now he did. And now he knew that he could never truly be a Nazi. He squeezed one of the red ribbons in his hand, and then opened his palm to look at it. In the center of the award was a swastika. Viktor wanted to burn the ribbon, to see it go up in flames before his eyes. But his mother would surely smell the smoke and come into his room to investigate, and he didn't' feel like explaining. Once he was fully packed and ready he decided to give Olof one more week before he departed from Germany, leaving behind everyone and everything he had known all of his life.

Almost a month had passed and Viktor had still received no word from Olof. He began to worry about Elke. He'd left her alone, and they had not had any communication since he'd left Belgium. He prayed that she was safe and hoped that she still wanted him. But things could happen; another man could have come into her life. He wanted to call and tell her that he planned to return without the papers and live with her permanently in Belgium. If he reassured her, then perhaps she would continue to wait, that is if he were not already too late.

He dialed the number of the hotel where he had left her. He expected the girl Lara to answer, but instead a man answered and claimed he did not know anyone by the name of Elke Berman. Now Viktor was even more distressed. Either she was using an alias, or she had gone off with another man, or God forbid, she could be in trouble. Perhaps, she'd been forced to leave the hotel. Where would she go and how would he find her? He went to the telegraph station and sent a wire, being careful not to reveal anything illegal. When she did not answer the wire, he knew he must make his way back to Belgium immediately. He would not wait another minute.

Chapter 127

Walking back to the hotel, Elke caressed her belly. If she had to rely on her savings it would diminish fast, but she couldn't help the situation. If she wanted this child, she must quit her job. When she'd told Dr. Moens what she did for a living he'd said that the work was far too heavy for a woman in her condition.

Elke arrived back at her room, out of breath and still bleeding badly. She lay down upon her bed and stared at the ceiling. Where was Viktor? Would he ever return?

In the morning, her face pale as an Easter lily, she went downstairs and quit her job, and then she paid for the room for the next month. As she peeled the bills off, her small pile of money looked much smaller.

The entire day she stayed in bed. The cramps increased and grew more painful.

Chapter 128

The morning Viktor planned to leave, Olof knocked on the door of his parents' home.

"Olof, where have you been? I've been waiting and trying to reach you."

"I was trying to get the papers for you, but my friend was arrested. The *Gestapo* caught him working with some underground agency. I don't know where they've sent him."

"So you should have come by and told me."

"I should have. But I was afraid, considering I'd just met with my friend the night before he was caught. I thought they might be watching me and since you are trying to get papers, I decided it would be best you have as little association with me as possible until all of it settled down."

"So I am assuming that you cannot help me find anyone else to draw up papers?"

"The strange thing is I can. One of the men who work with the organization that my friend was affiliated with has contacted me. He said my friend had asked him forge these papers for you before he was arrested. He is willing to it, but he wants a great deal of money. Viktor, are you sure this is what you want? You are home now. You will find another girl, and you will fall in love again. This one is too much trouble. You could end up in a work camp. And certainly you will end up broke buying these papers. He wants 200 Reich*smarks*. That's a lot of money, and we didn't earn anywhere close to that amount working on the last two voyages."

"I'm sure. I want the papers. I will get the money one way or another."

"Viktor?" Olof looked at him. Their eyes connected and then Olof shook his head, grabbing Viktor's shoulder. "If this is what you want… You're 100 percent sure?"

"It is. I am sure of it. How soon can it be done?"

Viktor borrowed money from his parents, from every friend he had, including Olof, and even from the priest he'd known all of his life, to whom he confessed the entire operation. The priest was kind and understanding, willing to help, but very concerned about Viktor's safety. They prayed together. Then Viktor took all the money he'd put together and went to see Olof.

"I have the money."

Olof took the envelope. "I'll bring this to him tonight. Then I'll come by your house tomorrow."

The following day Olof arrived early in the morning. Viktor's parents were still asleep when the knock on the door awakened Viktor.

Olof came in.

"Her name will be Edda Beckenbauer. She will be a Catholic."

Viktor nodded.

"I will have the papers tonight. It might be late, but as soon as I get them, I will bring them to your home. I'll come to your window and knock, so that I don't wake your parents. The way we used to do it when we wanted to escape and go fishing when we were kids."

"I remember, and I will be waiting."

True to his word, Olof arrived at a little past eleven the following evening, papers in hand. "God be with you, my friend. Please be careful," Olof said. Viktor reached through the window and took the papers; then he tucked them inside of his socks, burying them deep within his suitcase.

"I will, and Olof, I don't know how I can ever thank you. But as soon as I find work, I will pay back every penny you gave me."

"I'm not worried about the money. I don't care about it. Just be careful, and for God sake don't get caught."

"Olof, the first train ticket I was able to get was for the day after tomorrow, would you come with me to the pub tomorrow night? I'd like to buy you a few beers."

"How could I turn down a drink?" Olof smiled. "Although I'm surprised you still have any money left at all."

"I hardly have any. But I still want to say goodbye and thank you."

"Well, maybe you'll let me buy the beer." Olof said.

"We'll see. I will miss you, my friend. I will miss our days at sea together." Viktor said.

"As will I."

Chapter 129

The night before Viktor was to leave for Belgium, Viktor and Olof went to the same pub they had been going to all of their lives. For Viktor, not only was he saying farewell to his friend, but also goodbye to his bachelorhood. They sat at a table with red and white checked tablecloths and drank mugs of thick dark beer. They'd grown up on this brew, so the bitter taste brought back memories for both of them.

"So, you're sure you are never going back out to sea?" Olof asked.

"I don't think so. I will be a married man now."

"She's a beautiful girl, but Viktor, you've been a sailor your entire life. You know how much we have enjoyed our travels together. How can you throw it all away now? My God, you are giving up so much, and for a woman?"

"Because I am in love."

Olof laughed. "Love's like a disease, my friend. And you have been struck with it. In fact I think you might have the worst case I've ever seen."

"It's wonderful. I hope it happens to you someday," Viktor said.

"Please spare me. I'm not looking for anything like this. I would rather have several different girls than one permanent one. Too much work." Olof laughed again. "But I must admit you do look very happy and for that I am truly glad."

"I will think of you often, Olof. I'll remember all the fun we had together"

"Yes, we certainly had some good times and got into plenty of trouble, too. Remember that girl in France, the one with the red hair? And the night when we all got drunk in her apartment and she did that crazy little dance?"

"I'm trying not to remember. I've gone respectable," Viktor laughed.

Olof laughed too. "It was fun anyway."

"I don't know how to thank you for what you have done, getting these papers for Elke," Viktor said.

"No need to thank me. I only did what anyone would do for a best friend. If the shoe was on the other foot you would have done the same for me."

"You're right. I would have. No doubt about it."

Olof took a sip of beer. "How truly strange life is. When were chosen as the crew for that ship of Jews I would never have dreamt that you would fall in love with one of them."

"If you only knew her better, you would understand."

"I saw her. She is stunning, but this is your entire life. Sleeping with a pretty girl is one thing, but marriage? I'm sorry, but I have to ask you just one more time. Are you sure about all of this, Viktor?"

"More sure about marrying her than anything I have ever done before in my entire life."

"So," Olof said, "if you are not going back out to sea what will you do?"

"Find a job, I suppose. Neither of us has much money, so I am going to have to think of something."

"And we always swore that we could never give up the sea…" Olof said.

"Yes, the sea is like a woman. You fall in love with her depth and beauty. But the only thing that can make you forget one woman is another. And I have found a woman I love far more than the ocean, a woman who makes my heart beat faster, stirs my blood, and fills me with a sense of purpose."

"Have you become a poet too?" Olof laughed. "So where is my friend Viktor? Has he been possessed by Shakespeare?"

"No, Olof, just by love."

"Well, who am I to say. Perhaps I will fall in love one day." Olof shrugged. "Let's hope not." Then he took a gulp of beer and smiled at Viktor. "Would you mind if I saw you off tomorrow morning at the train station? I have a little something for you, a gift. I forgot to bring it with me tonight."

"Of course not. I would welcome seeing you."

"What time does your train leave?"

"Eight o'clock in the morning. Are you sure you want to come after a full night of drinking?"

"I'll be there."

Chapter 130

Viktor stood on the platform waiting to board the train. A cool breeze filtered through the station, as the sun had just risen and had yet to warm the earth. He'd arrived at seven in case Olof came early, but there was no sign of his friend. Viktor decided that Olof had probably changed his mind about getting out of bed after the late night they'd had. The large round clock on the wall said five minutes to eight. Viktor assumed his friend wouldn't make it before he left.

"All aboard!" the conductor cried out. "Have your papers ready for inspection."

Viktor had his papers in his front pocket. He knew there would be no problem. He was pure German, Aryan as they had come to call it.

"Next!" the man at the boarding desk called.

Viktor presented him the papers. He nodded his okay, and Viktor lifted his suitcase and stepped up the stairs on to the train. He slid into a window seat and gazed out at the train station. The next time he came to Germany he would be a married man. Strange how life could be… As he drifted off, daydreaming of Elke, the train let out a whistle and then rumbled to life. He prayed that he had not left Germany too late, and that he had not lost Elke by leaving her alone for so long. Soon he would be in Belgium, and if she still loved him, and he hoped with all of his heart that she did, he would take Elke into his arms and make love to her until they both were so worn out that they had to get some sleep. He missed her terribly.

Outside, Olof came running across the platform. Viktor saw him through the window, and leaned forward as if he could reach out and touch him, but the train was already beginning to move, so he waved. Olof did not see Viktor. Instead, Olof was looking around frantically as is something had gone wrong. Then two *Gestapo* agents came running onto the platform. They grabbed Olof's arms. Viktor could not hear the conversation, but he saw the panic on his friends face and jumped up to get off the train. However, the train had begun to pick up speed. Viktor watched in horror as the *Gestapo* took Olof away, and the train pulled out of the station.

Viktor sunk back into his seat. His heart was racing so fast he felt dizzy. *What had happened? Had Olof been caught? How? Why? What had gone wrong? Now what would happen to Olof? Would he be questioned? Sent to a work camp? Killed? And all of this for me? What if the Gestapo tortured Olof and forced him to tell them about Elke and the papers? Would they come as far as Belgium to find both of them, and did Hitler have any power there?* He had no answers, only terrifying questions. Perhaps he should never go back to her, never bring her the papers. Maybe the Nazis were following him, too, to see where he went and who he met. That would be just like them. Sweat began to trickle down his brow. Worse yet, maybe they already knew everything and had arrested Elke. Maybe that was why the hotel clerk did not find her name registered. Could the Nazis arrest Elke if she were in Belgium? He had no idea. He didn't think that they could, but what if they did or if they just took her? Elke. He couldn't leave her there in Belgium all alone. He would go to her, and no matter what happened they would face it together.

Chapter 131

Every time the train stopped at a station on its way to Antwerp, the guards checked Viktor's papers. Although he tried to remain calm, he found his hands trembling as he handed the documents over to be scrutinized. Viktor watched the guards' faces and wondered if they were searching for him, if the guards at the stops had been alerted. A thin line of sweat ran down the side of Viktor's face. He wanted to grab the papers, jump off the train, and run as fast as he could. The pounding in his ears made him feel as if he might vomit.

But then the guard just handed Viktor his papers, nodded, and went on to the next rider.

"Papers..." the guard said. The man in the seat behind Viktor handed the guard his documents.

The guard nodded, and then went on to the next person.

Viktor sighed, his body relaxing for the moment with relief.

Finally the train arrived in Belgium. The ride from Antwerp to Luxembourg was far less nerve-racking; after all, he was no longer under Nazi rule. He could loosen up a little. However, his nagging worries would not allow him to sleep.

It was close to midnight when Viktor arrived at the hotel where he'd last seen Elke. He climbed the stairs to the little room that they shared and knocked on the door painted red. She answered almost instantly, as if she had not been asleep at all.

"Who's there?" she asked.

"It's me, Viktor."

The door flung open and Elke began to cry, and then to laugh, and then cry again as she threw herself into his arms. Viktor found he was crying too. They kissed, and continually touched each other to be sure that the dream was real.

"You're here…" she said.

"I'm here," he whispered in her ear.

"Viktor, I missed you so much."

"An hour never went by that I didn't think of you. I am so glad to be here with you again…" he said, slamming the door and locking it. Then he lifted Elke into his arms; she was light as a child, and laid her on the bed.

"I have something I must tell you." she said looking up into his eyes.

"Yes, go on…" he was suddenly afraid. Maybe she had found someone else, or changed her mind?

"I'm pregnant."

He bent down and kissed her. "Oh, Elke," he said, his voice husky with emotion. Never did he consider that the child might not be his.

She reached up and wiped a tear from his cheek. He was here. Viktor was here.

"We are going to have a wonderful life. Your new name is Edda Beckenbauer."

"You got the papers?" she asked. At that moment, Elke decided that Viktor must never know that the child she carried might not be his. Why tell him? Why hurt him? What happened with Manny no longer meant anything to her. Together she and Viktor would raise this baby, and she would do everything she could to ensure the lifelong happiness of her husband and their child.

"Yes, I have them in my suitcase. You can feel free to travel with me back to Germany and meet my family," he said, but he wanted to wait for a long time to let this thing with Olof settle before he ever set foot in Nazi-occupied territory.

Chapter 132

On a sunny Sunday morning in early September, in the year of 1939, Edda Beckenbauer married Viktor Hahn in St. Mary's Catholic Church. They moved to Antwerp, where no one knew Elke by her real name. She would officially be Edda Hahn.

The couple found a small two-bedroom apartment above a bakery shop. They bought enough secondhand furniture to be comfortable, including a wooden crib, which Viktor sanded down and painted white. They made friends with a couple who lived upstairs with their three young children. The wife taught Edda to knit booties and blankets while she grew big waiting for the baby's birth. Every Sunday, Viktor and Edda went to church with their upstairs neighbors and another couple who lived just a block away. Often the three couples shared dinners at each other's homes and stayed to play games of cards, or just sip strong coffee and talk.

They began to feel safe, and as time passed Viktor let go of his fears. Edda could not work, and money was tight, but Viktor found a job working on repairing fishing boats. He missed going out to sea, but would not have traded his life with Edda to sail again.

That February, on a cold, snowy afternoon, in a small local hospital, Sepp Hahn came quietly into the world. A sweet infant who almost never cried, Sepp grew into a self-reliant one-year-old, capable of playing alone on his blanket on the floor while Edda cleaned the small apartment where they lived. When Edda looked at her son, as much as she wanted to she could not deny that he belonged to Manny. He was born with a full head of dark curls, and his eyes danced the same way Manny's had. Both Edda and Viktor were blondes, but Viktor never seemed to notice; maybe he just assumed that the dark hair was a trait in Edda's family tree. He bonded with the little boy and the two were as close as a father and son could be. When Viktor arrived at home after a day of working, Sepp immediately raised his arms to request that his father pick him up and hold him. Viktor laughed and lifted the boy high in the air, making him laugh aloud. All during dinner, Viktor held his son on his lap, never tiring of the child or needing time to himself.

Enough time had passed for Viktor to feel comfortable returning to Germany. Although it was difficult, he forced thoughts of Olof from his mind. He wanted his family to know his wife and their son. So they planned a trip to coincide with his brother's leave from the army, a reunion.

Viktor's family took to Edda right away, and they adored little Sepp, who amused everyone with his childish antics. Nobody suspected Edda was really Elke, born a Jew. Although it was difficult for both Edda and Viktor when his brother Axel appeared wearing the uniform of the German army, neither said anything to the family. However, at night, alone in their room, they discussed their feelings. "My family loves you."

"I am glad. I love them too. However, it is hard for me to live this lie with them. I feel dishonest."

"I know, but it is best that they never know. Can you forgive me for asking you to pose as something you are not? It is not only for my family, but we are in Germany. If you were discovered…"

"I can forgive you and I do. You are doing what is best for me, what is best for little Sepp, and us too. I have learned to live as a Gentile so that nobody ever suspects. It is good to know that we can travel back and forth to Germany without

445

worry. We have wonderful Gentile friends and the priest at the church is a kind man. I like him very much. But seeing your brother wearing his uniform sends chills up my spine. I can't help it. It is a constant reminder of everything."

"Yes, I know. I feel the same way, but he's my brother. What can I do? I don't want to risk your safety telling them the truth. I know they are my family, but it is just better this way."

She nodded. "I know you're right."

The following day, Edda went out for a walk. She needed the fresh air and time alone. Axel and his father had spent the better part of the morning discussing Hitler's virtues, and how he'd saved Germany from ruin. It took everything she had for Edda to keep quiet. Viktor offered to accompany her but she refused. Her golden hair tossed in the wind as she tucked her hands into her pockets. It was a beautiful crisp day, and she had a lot to be grateful for. She may have given up her identity, but she was alive. And even more, she had a wonderful husband and a healthy son. What more was there to life?

Chapter 133

Viktor sat in the living room staring blankly out of the large picture window, watching the children across the street play tag. His mother was baking and the fragrance filled the air. He couldn't hear what they were saying, but his brother and his father were laughing about something. It felt good to be home, even if the conversations between his father and Axel were sometimes difficult to endure. He was glad that they loved his wife, his precious Edda, and he could see how much his son fulfilled a need for his aging parents. Sometimes, as hard as he tried not to, he still thought of her as his Elke.

"Come and taste this sauce. Tell me if it needs some more salt," Viktor's mother called to him.

He got up, and as he did he heard the most unnerving sound. It was the blaring horn of the *Gestapo*. It rang like a death bell and pierced his heart like a dagger. And for some reason it was getting louder, coming closer, then closer. Suddenly he wanted to break out, to run, but he felt as if he were locked in a cage.

"Come on, Viktor. Taste this for me, please."

Had Olof told them something? Had they been waiting for him to come back to Germany? His heart pounded so hard he was afraid it might explode.

My God, where was Elke? He prayed that she would stay away. If she weren't there, maybe they would take only him. But what if they told his family that she was a Jew? Axel could very well turn on her and report her as soon as she returned.

"Viktor…I keep calling you to come in the kitchen and taste this for me." His mother peeked her head around the corner and looked into the living room.

He couldn't move. The sound moved closer, louder. Closing in on him and then…it was deafening. So loud, it threatened to break his eardrums. His hands covered his ears as he looked out the window dreading what he knew he would see. The black *Gestapo* automobile had stopped right in front of his house. Two agents got out of the car wearing trench coats. One lit a cigarette.

Chapter 134

Elke couldn't wait to return home to Belgium. Viktor had enjoyed the visit so much and she was glad that she'd come, for his sake. It had been a good visit. Everyone had welcomed her with warmth and affection, but in truth, sitting across from Viktor's brother in his SS uniform disturbed her greatly. It brought back the horrific memories of the men who'd come to the apartment she'd shared with her mother. Not only did she have unpleasant thoughts of the past, but she also felt the pain of her fellow Jews. And because she knew how much they suffered, she was overcome with guilt because it seemed to her that by living this lie she had betrayed her people. But the worst part of it all was that she wondered if Viktor's family would be so accepting of her if they knew the truth.

As she walked along the brown and red cobblestone sidewalk, she thought about what a pretty country Germany was, especially here where Viktor had grown up, the streets so clean, the children so blond and well mannered. But even here, one could not miss the Nazi flags that hung from the windows or the pictures of Adolf Hitler over the storefronts. She found it hard to believe that a country that had been so filled with culture and knowledge could have turned into a land that forced ignorance upon its people, burning books, committing mass murders and falling under the demonic spell of a madman.

Chapter 135

Viktor's mother walked over to him and shook him.

"Are you feeling all right?" She asked.

He could not speak. All he could do was nod his head.

"Why can't you answer me? Viktor what is wrong with you?"

Then she looked out the window.

"That's the *Gestapo*; they come to the neighborhood often just to investigate this or that. Did the siren upset you? It does sound like an ambulance. But no need to worry…"

Viktor nodded again, but could not turn his face away from the two men standing outside.

After crushing his cigarette, the *Gestapo* agent and his partner began to walk up the walkway to Viktor's home. The clicking heels of their shoes could be heard through the window. Viktor felt sure he would soon pass out because he couldn't catch his breath.

Then he saw one of the men look over at the address that was written on the side of the building.

"This is the wrong address, Rudolf. It's next door," the *Gestapo* agent said to his partner who nodded and squinted to read the numbers.

"Yes, you're right." Rudolf said. "It is next door."

They walked across the lawn to the little cottage next door. For a few minutes no sound came from the house, only dead quiet. Then Viktor heard screaming, a commotion. His mother looked at him questioning.

The screams grew louder.

Now his mother bent down to look out the window just as the *Gestapo* agents dragged the woman who lived next door by her arm that looked dislocated. She fell and grabbed onto the *Gestapo* agent's pants leg, crying and pleading. One of the agents took a pistol out of his pocket and hit her across the face. Then she was silent, lying on the grass as a pool of blood began to form around her head. But even more shocking, the other agent led three people away at gunpoint.

Viktor heard him say something but he couldn't make out what he said. The only word that was clear to him was "*Juden* (Jew)."

"Oh my God," Viktor's mother said. "They were hiding Jews right next door, right under our noses."

Viktor thought of Elke. He was hiding her right under their noses, wasn't he? Suddenly Viktor said a silent prayer of thanks that they he and Edda, he must remember to call her Edda, were leaving for Belgium in the morning.

It had been a wonderful visit, but the time had come to say goodbye.

Chapter 136

Two weeks after Viktor and Edda returned to Belgium, a letter arrived addressed to Viktor, with no return address, only a postmark from Germany. Viktor had gone off to work when it arrived, so Edda opened it. It read:

My Brother,

I send this message to you at great risk to myself and to our parents. However, because you are my brother, because we shared the same womb and the blood that runs through our veins is the same, I am forced to take this risk. Listen to me and please heed my warning. You must never, under any circumstances return to Germany. Your friend Olof was arrested and tortured until he confessed his crime and named everyone involved, you and your wife included. Because of my position in the SS, I was notified, reprimanded also. However, I was fortunate; things could have gone far worse. Apparently, Olof was selling falsified papers. From what I gather, he had several other clients. When you came I already knew all of this, but I did not say anything. I felt that if you were aware that the authorities were looking for you, you might have become nervous and suspicious. If I had known you were coming I would have told you not to come. While you were here, I was on edge every minute, because if you had been caught, mother and father would have been arrested, and I might have been as well. You are probably wondering if I knew that your wife was a Jew when the two of you were here, and the answer is yes. But again, I did my best to cover for you. That was why I discouraged you from going to the pub that night that you wanted me to accompany you. I told you that I was ill because I knew that you would not go without me. Viktor, your wife is a lovely woman, but you have made a grave mistake and I am afraid it will cost you dearly. You should never have married a Jew. This will cause you a life of misery. Now you cannot come home, and I cannot associate with you. It is far too dangerous. I am sorry, my brother. Be well, be safe, and Goodbye.

Axel.

Edda read the letter over twice. Then she sunk down into a chair. Axel had never let on that he knew. She remembered that night that she and Viktor had wanted to go into town with his brother to have a few beers. Axel had discouraged it. It shocked her that he knew and yet had remained so cool and calm. Her hand went to her throat. She felt terribly guilty for all that she had taken away from Viktor: his family, his home. And now they would never be at peace. Every day for the rest of their lives they would have to be watching and looking behind them. The Nazis, just as the wolf in the story of the three little pigs, would always be just a few steps away from their door, waiting, knocking...

That night when Viktor returned from work, he read the letter. When he finished he laid it on the table. Then he ran his hand through his hair and looked at Edda who sat beside him.

"We must destroy this letter," he said.

"I know," Edda answered.

"And to ward off suspicion we must become a very active couple in the Christian community. Even more active than we are right now."

"Yes," she said.

Viktor nodded.

There was silence for several minutes. Viktor took her hand and rubbed it with his thumb. Then Viktor got up and took the letter. He lit it on fire and placed it in a metal soup pot.

Then the couple watched as it burned. Neither spoke until the flames had consumed the paper, turning it to black ash.

Then in a very soft voice, barely a whisper, Edda asked, "Viktor…"

"Yes?"

"Are you sorry? Do you regret marrying me?" She wasn't sure she wanted to hear the answer, but she had to know.

He looked into her eyes. She saw the sadness in his face and guilt came over her.

"I've ruined your life," she said.

He shrugged.

"I'm sorry."

"I'm not," he said taking her hand. "I love you. You are my wife, you are the mother of my son, and I don't regret what I have done."

She fell into his arms and wept.

Chapter 137

At the beginning of January, Edda found herself pregnant once again and expecting her second child in mid-September.

On the seventeenth of September, Irmgard Hahn was born. She would grow up to have her parents' blonde hair and light eyes, and would be affectionately known to family and friends as Irma.

In early October of 1940, just a month after the birth of their daughter, Edda and Viktor watched in horror as Hitler's army invaded Belgium and broke right through the bubble of false security that they had built.

Viktor thanked God repeatedly that Edda had papers proclaiming her a Gentile, that they had been living as Gentiles, and that no one in Belgium but he and his wife knew the truth. However that haunting memory of Olof and what had happened in Germany never left the back of his mind, and Viktor prayed every day that the Nazis would be too busy conquering the world to worry about looking for the two of them. They both agreed that children must never hear them discuss their mother's Jewish ancestry or her real name. They were only babies, and at any time they could repeat something, unaware of the danger it might cause. Best for the children to believe that both of their parents were born Catholics and they, too, were Catholics.

When the Jews in Belgium were rounded up in the streets, Edda watched from the window. She held her back stiff and straight, but her hands gripped the windowsill with white knuckles. Viktor stood beside her. Both he and Edda looked far older than their years. Occasionally they glanced at each other; they said nothing, but their eyes said everything. A Nazi guard beat a man and his wife with his rifle. They lay in a pool of blood on the street. The Hahns didn't know them, but Edda thought that they looked familiar and that she might have remembered them from the *St. Louis*. Another guard walked by and kicked the woman in the back of the head. She let out a cry, her legs trembled violently, and then she lay silent. Edda ran to the bathroom and vomited.

The commands of the Nazi invaders filled the streets as they roared over their loudspeakers, and although it was a lovely fall day, Edda closed the window in an effort to drown them out. Still, even through the bolted windows she could hear them, harsh angry voices, mingled with the cries of victims. She put her hands to her ears, feeling as if she would go mad.

The baby started crying in her crib. Little Sepp came over and tugged at his mother's skirt. "Mama, the baby…" he said.

Her son's face looked worried. "Mama," he said again, pulling harder. She had to get herself together for her children.

"Yes, Sepp. I'm sorry, sweetheart," she said, running her hand over his light brown hair. "Mama is coming."

As she followed Sepp over to the crib, Viktor still stood at the window, spellbound. Even through the closed window, they heard a man begging for the life of his child. "Please, I beg you, leave my son. Take me…not my son."

Then she heard a shot, and the man let out such a cry of anguish that it reached inside of her and grabbed her very soul. She stopped frozen.

"Mama?" Sepp said again, his voice louder. The baby continued to wail.

Edda looked outside. The man lay on top of the body of a little boy. He was covered in blood, and weeping. The Nazi officer walked over and kicked the man.

"Get up, you lazy Jew. Get up."

But the man didn't move. Edda held her breath.

"Mama…" Sepp called to Edda. "Mama, please, come on…"

She turned her head to look at her son. A shot rang out. Edda turned back to the window to see that the father now lay dead, his body covering his son.

"Mama…" Sepp said even louder and more insistent than before.

Edda forced herself away from the window. She went over to Sepp and picked him up into her arms. Then she buried her face in his neck and took in the innocent, childlike smell of him. She felt tears threaten to fall. The baby was screaming. She carried Sepp and went to the crib. After all she'd done to escape the Nazis, they had followed her here to Belgium. Thank God Viktor had gotten those papers. They had not known it at the time, but if by the grace of God the Nazis had forgotten the business with Olof and what had happened, those documents would save her life.

Chapter 138

Within a few days, the entire city of Antwerp was covered with pictures of Adolf Hitler. Nazi flags flew from the tops of buildings, and what once was a peaceful seaside town was now a community of quiet and fearful residents.

When Edda had visited Viktor's parents, his mother had given her a gift of a gold cross. It had been Viktor's grandmothers and she'd wanted to give it to his wife as a family heirloom. Edda thought the gesture kind, but she had not been able to wear it. Somehow, it felt like a betrayal to her Jewish background, and to all the Jews still suffering. On the day the Nazis entered Antwerp, Edda took the necklace out of her drawer. Then Viktor, with a solemn expression on his face, helped her to put it on.

"I will wear this from now on, until our daughter is old enough and then it will be hers," Edda said.

Viktor nodded. "We are the lucky ones, Edda. We are both safe and alive…"

"And guilty," she said looking down at the worn carpet.

"Yes, and guilty."

Chapter 139

Edda sighed with relief, after an hour of coaxing both children had finally gone down for a nap. They usually slept for at least two hours, which meant that if everything worked out as planned she and Viktor might have a precious half hour to spend making love when he came home from work for lunch. Since the children's births, their time alone together took scheduling. Most nights Viktor returned late from work, and by the time the children were asleep, he was too. However, because their time was limited, it became even more special for both of them.

Viktor would be hungry when he got home, so Edda went into the kitchen to prepare something that he might eat quickly. She took out a hunk of dark yellow cheese and thick black bread. There was a knock at the door. Probably Christina from upstairs, she thought. Often Christina would come over and the two would share a cup of coffee. Christina and her family were their good friends. They attended church together and the women belonged to the women's club at the church as well. Christina's youngest child just started school, so she had plenty of time to visit. Well, Edda would just explain that Viktor would be home soon and she could not sit and talk. She wiped her hands on her apron and opened the door.

"Telegram for Viktor Hahn." A boy in short black pants wearing a band with a swastika around his arm stood holding the wire.

She took the envelope and put it on the counter. "Wait just a moment," she said. Then went to her handbag and got a coin out of her change purse, which she handed him.

"Thank you, Frau Hahn," he said.

She nodded.

After she closed and locked the door, she sat down on the sofa and opened the letter. It read:

Viktor,

I am writing because I believe that you have a right to know. They were your parents too. Mother and father have both passed away. Father came down with tuberculosis last year and mother took care of him until the end. She never contacted me. I never knew. I wish she had. I would have wanted to see father one last time. I suppose she didn't want to burden me. However, I missed his funeral, and I feel I should have been there. After father's death, she finally sent me a letter to inform me of what happened. I wanted to come home and spend some time with her, but she refused. Then last month, I suppose she was weak from all she had gone through, she got very sick. It was a bad year for influenza this year and she caught a terribly strong strain of it. Mr. and Mrs. Krautz from across the street were bringing her food. Finally, they sent me a cable informing me of her condition and I came home immediately. I wanted her to go into a hospital but she refused.

Mother's funeral took place two days ago. As I stood there under the gray sky watching them lower her casket into the ground, I thought of you. I wished that you could be here with me. We are orphans now, Viktor. And you are my only brother. However, because of circumstances, we both must go on as if we are all alone in the world. In a few days, I will be leaving for the Ukraine. Perhaps I will die there, who knows? Mr. Krautz says that he will keep an eye on the house until I return. When I am able, I will sell it and send you some of the money. I suppose losing our parents has made me soppy and sentimental, but I cannot help but think of us as children and I must admit, I miss you. Well, enough of all of that. Once again, I must remind you, do not return to Germany under any circumstances. It is unsafe for you. I wish you well.

Axel

Edda dreaded giving this letter to Viktor. It would devastate him. She thought of Axel; he'd gone a different route, certainly, but she could see that he still cared for his brother. *What have I done to the man I love?*

The door opened and Viktor came in. He walked over and kissed her.

"What's wrong?" he said looking at her.

She handed him the telegram. He read it, then sat down on the sofa.

"My parents, Elke." His face bloodless, he called her by her real name. "They are both dead."

She nodded. "I know. I am so sorry."

"I wasn't there for them. They died old, sick, and alone. My God, Elke."

"I'm sorry."

He shook his head. He would not look into her eyes. "I am going back to work." He dropped the paper on the worn coffee table.

"Viktor."

He stood up to leave.

"Stop, please."

He turned to look at her. "What is it?"

"I must know…You resent me for this…"

"No," he said, turning away.

"Don't lie to me, just tell me. Say it, Viktor. You do. I can see it in your eyes."

"Elke, stop."

"Say it."

"No, I won't."

"Say it," she said. Her voice rose.

"Goddamn it… Okay, I'll say it. I resent you."

She started to cry.

He walked out of the house and slammed the door. The baby woke up and started wailing. Tears in her eyes, Elke went to the crib and began rocking it. Irma settled down and fell back asleep.

I should leave him. I should take the children and go. But, how can I take the only family he has left away from him? I should never have married him. I knew it when we were on the ship. I knew that he would come to hate me for everything that he lost because of me. She was sobbing when the door opened.

Viktor walked in.

"This is what you wanted. You wanted me to say that I resent you. Well all right, I said it, but not for the reasons that you might think. I resent you for being everything any man could ever want in a wife. I resent you for making me love you. But I wouldn't change it for anything," he said, his face red with anger, his body shaking.

"I'm sorry for what I have done to you. You could have been at home with your family, with your friends. If only you had married a non-Jew. God, Viktor, I feel so guilty. I knew this would happen one day…"

"Yes, it was inevitable. We knew they were old and that soon they would pass on. And I feel guilty too. But it isn't your fault and it isn't mine either. You want to know whose fault it is... It's Hitler's, and Himmler's, and Goebbels,' and Goering's, and Eichmann's, and all of those sons of bitches who did this to us. Every single person we know has suffered because of them. Each one of us has lost something. Think about it, Elke... Anna and Alex lost their homes and families. My parents, my brother, Olof... Dear God, poor Olof... And Manny? What about him? The Nazis took a piece of each of us, and left us guilty and broken. But you and I, Elke, this is the good part of life. What we have together is a gift from God himself. We have love, we have each other, and we have two wonderful children. If we let ourselves become resentful of one another for any reason, we will have given the Nazis our lives. Haven't they taken enough?"

She nodded, wiping the tears from her cheeks with the back of her hand. "I'm sorry, Viktor. I'm sorry."

"Shhh, it's all right," he whispered. "Hold fast to our love, Elke. It's true we don't have much material wealth, but make no mistake, we share a beautiful gift that even Hitler could not take away from us."

He walked over to her and took her into his arms. "I love you."

"I love you, too..."

"Come lie with me. Let me hold you. Let me know the wonderful gift that God has given me," he said.

And she saw a single tear fall down his cheek.

Viktor never saw or spoke to Axel again.

The war ended with the Nazis' defeat. The concentration camps were liberated, and displaced persons camps were formed. The Jewish refugees began searching for their lost loved ones. For a single moment, Edda longed to reveal her identity, but then she thought about her friends, and her children. Her friends would be angry that she had lied to them. The children would be ostracized, no longer a part of the good Catholic community where they had grown up and were comfortable. No, Edda thought, there was no reason to tell anyone anything. She'd lived as a Gentile for so long, and she would go to her grave with her secret.

When Irma turned seventeen, she married the son of the neighborhood shoemaker, a boy she'd known all of her life. Edda and Viktor hosted a wedding for the couple, inviting all of their friends at St. Mary's Catholic Church. It was a lovely occasion, and the bride and groom were sent off in a hail of good wishes. It was a good thing for her children to be a part of a community, Edda thought.

Sepp shipped off to college on a scholarship to study philosophy.

"Ehh, a waste of education… What kind of job are you going to get with a degree that means nothing?" Viktor asked his son. "Get some kind of training so that you can make a decent living."

"Perhaps I will go into law…" Sepp said.

Edda turned her head sharply to look at him. Manny had studied the law. Sepp looked just like Manny. She took a deep breath and sighed. There was no reason to bring this up with Viktor now, after all of these years. Sepp might be Manny's son by blood, but he was Viktor's son in every other way. When at age three he'd had the measles, Viktor had stayed up all night and walked the floors carrying him, rocking him, comforting him. At seven years old, Viktor taught him to throw a ball and to fish. Sepp belonged to Viktor; he was his father's heart, and his pride and joy. For the sake of both father and son, Edda would never reveal what she knew to be the truth.

Chapter 140

On a cold winter morning in the year of 2008, Viktor passed away, at 92 years old. Edda never left his side; she held his hand and longed to go with him. His two children both came home to stay with their parents through the night.

Only four months later, Edda followed her husband to heaven. The children were with her.

"I am glad to go," she said. "I miss your father every day. Now we will be together."

Irma broke into tears. Her husband hugged her close to him. Sepp held his mother's hand.

After the funeral, brother and sister returned together to the small apartment where they'd grown up. The time had come to clean out the remains of their parents' lives.

Irma couldn't stop crying; her eyes were bloodshot. Sepp put his arm around his younger sister.

"Mom couldn't go on once dad died. They were too close to be separated," Irma said.

"It's true. Everyone said it. They were so in love, inseparable, even when they were old. If I ever meet someone and get married, I hope it's like that," Sepp said.

"Come on Sepp, you're an incurable playboy. You'll never settle down. It's not in your nature."

"You don't know that for sure…"

"Come on Sepp. My children are getting married and their uncle is still single. If you were going to get married you would already have done so."

"Yeah, I guess you're right. Well, when your kids have kids, can I share the grandchildren?"

"Of course," she said and squeezed his arm.

The apartment was filled with memories. Edda had never removed a single piece of Viktor's clothing. It was as if she were waiting for his return. All of the tiny knick-knacks brought back memories, as well as the boxed-up Christmas tree ornaments. Even Sepp felt the tears threaten.

"We had good parents, Sepp."

"Yeah, they really tried to do the best they could for us," Sepp said.

"Hey, look at this." Irma pulled a book bound in burgundy leather out of her mother's drawer. On the cover it said *Journal*. "Did you know Mama kept a journal?"

"Hell no. Let me see it." Sepp reached out and Irma handed him the book. As his hands touched the pages he felt a tingling in his fingers. "Do you mind if I take this back to the hotel tonight and read it?"

"No, go ahead. Let me know what it says," Irma said.

Chapter 141

Ft. Lauderdale, Florida
Café Europa

The room was silent except for the clanking of the ceiling fan.

"Sepp Hahn," Anna said, her voice cracking with the recollection of her friends and the time they spent together…so long ago. When they were all still so young… "You are Elke and Viktor's son."

Sepp nodded. "My mother believed that Manny was my birth father. It was all in her journal, everything. After I learned about my Jewish heritage I knew that I had to see you."

"Oh my God, Manny had a son." Anna's hand went to her throat. "Your father did a great deal for my husband and me. I owe him my life, and now that I know that he is no longer alive, I owe everything to you, his last legacy, his only remaining heir."

"You owe me nothing. I didn't come here today expecting anything. I came because, until you knew everything that happened, the story was not over. Now you know that you no longer need to search for Elke or Manny."

"It's none of my business, but Sepp…did you have a good life?" Anna asked, the words catching in her throat. She was rich now since she'd published the book. If only she could have helped Elke and Viktor.

"I had the best parents a child could have. I never knew Manny. To me, Viktor Hahn was, and always will be my father."

"Please, join me up here on the podium. This book, this story, is as much yours as it is mine…" Anna said.

Sepp walked up to the podium. Anna hugged him.

"I am glad I came. I am glad that I met you, and that after all of these years there is no shame in telling the world that my mother was Jewish. I am proud of everything she was. And the fact that she survived with my father's love and assistance against incredible odds only increases my admiration for both of them."

The room was silent. Many of the survivors had tears running down their faces. Then, quietly at first, one person began it, but then the chant caught on, "Never again! This must never happen again! We must never forget!" It rose in volume until the room shook with the noise of those who had seen hell and lived through it.

"Never forget. Keep the story alive, tell your children's children. It is only through education that we can prevent a horror like this from ever happening again!" Anna shouted through the microphone over the raised voices of the survivors.

Epilogue

Although Alex, Anna, Manny, Elke, Viktor, Benny, Sepp, Irma, and Rebecca Morgenstern are fictional characters, the doomed voyage of the *MS St. Louis* actually took place. I've taken some liberties with the timing of events on board as well as the purchase of the visas because this is a work of fiction. However, Captain Schroeder was a very real person. He was the captain of the ship, and after the war ended, he was named Righteous Among Nations at the *Yad Vashem* Holocaust Memorial in Israel, and also awarded the Order of Merit by the Federal Republic of Germany. Captain Schroder, an anti-Nazi, was honored for having made every effort to treat his passengers as he would any passengers on his ship. He did everything in his power to maintain their dignity. Never once did the captain exhibit or allow his crew to exhibit any form of anti-Semitism. When the ship was not permitted to land in Cuba, Captain Schroder refused to sail back to Germany. As captain of the *MS St. Louis*, he never neglected the responsibility of the safety of his passengers and crew. In fact, he refused to dock until he received notification that the passengers would be safe, and would be divided between Belgium, the Netherlands, Great Britain, and France. He, of course, had no idea that soon Hitler's tentacles of hatred and horror would stretch out and seize all of these countries except for Great Britain, and his efforts to protect those on board would be in vain, for the passengers would face Nazi persecution anyway. Years later, after the war, Captain Schroder fell upon hard financial times. He was so beloved that when the survivors of the St. Louis discovered the captain's predicament, they joined together to send him gifts of money. As I mentioned in the beginning of the book, I had the honor of meeting with Herbert Karliner, the man responsible for having Captain Schroder listed in the Avenue of the Righteous Among Nations. Mr. Karliner is a remarkable man and I feel very privileged to have met him. I also saw a play that I would highly recommend to anyone interested in this subject. The play was written by Robert M. Krakow, and was called "The Trial of Franklin D. Roosevelt." It was a mock trial concerning the actions of the president in the case of the *MS St. Louis*. It was well written, and although I did not agree with every part of it, it was filled with terrifying, but thought provoking messages.

I was also informed by a very reputable source that many Jews became Catholics through forged papers during the Holocaust. They became rooted in the Catholic communities and many of their families remain Catholics today.

The thirties were a booming time for the building of unions in America, and the union strike at Gimbels in New York actually did take place in the summer of 1941.

Every year, and sometimes, more often than once a year, the holocaust survivors have a meeting. It is usually a luncheon in a hotel, and it is called "Café *Europa*." It is there that these extraordinary people sometimes reconnect with friends and relatives with whom they had lost contact during the war. I had the opportunity of volunteering at one of these events. It was an experience like no other. I have done my best to describe the scene with as much accuracy as possible in this novel. The centerpieces on the tables with the names of various occupied countries were as I describe them. The large boards flashing names of those searching for others who might be in attendance is factual. During the entire luncheon the board continues to flash, one name after another of survivors, in the hope someone will recognize the names and come forward to greet them, even after all these years. When people reconnect, and believe it or not, they still do, even if they were once only neighbors, it is an amazing moment. One might think that this luncheon would be a grim occasion; however, it is anything but. It is actually a celebration of life. As the survivors grow older and leave us, it becomes more crucial that we keep their memory alive in order to assure that a tragedy such as the Holocaust never happens again.

Please visit www.RobertaKagan.com for news and upcoming releases by Roberta Kagan. Join the email list!

Authors Note

First and foremost, I want to thank you for reading my novel and for your continued interest in my work. From time to time, I receive emails from my readers that contest the accuracy of my events. When you pick up a novel, you are entering the author's world where we sometimes take artistic license and ask you to suspend your disbelief. I always try to keep as true to history as possible; however, sometimes there are discrepancies within my novels. This happens sometimes to keep the drama of the story. Thank you for indulging me.

I always enjoy hearing from my readers. Your feelings about my work are very important to me. If you enjoyed it, please consider telling your friends or posting a short review on Amazon. Word of mouth is an author's best friend.

If you enjoyed this book, please sign up for my mailing list, and you will receive Free short stories including an USA Today award-winning novella as my gift to you!!!!! To sign up, just go to...

www.RobertaKagan.com

Many blessings to you,

Roberta

Email: roberta@robertakagan.com

Come and like my Facebook page!

https://www.facebook.com/roberta.kagan.9

Join my book club

https://www.facebook.com/groups/1494285400798292/?ref=br _rs

Follow me on BookBub to receive automatic emails whenever I am offering a special price, a freebie, a giveaway, or a new release. Just click the link below, then click follow button to the right of my name. Thank you so much for your interest in my work.

https://www.bookbub.com/authors/roberta-kagan.

Continue on to the next page to discover more work by Roberta Kagan.

MORE BOOKS BY THE AUTHOR
AVAILABLE ON AMAZON

Not In America

Book One in A Jewish Family Saga

"Jews drink the blood of Christian babies. They use it for their rituals. They are evil and they consort with the devil."

These words rang out in 1928 in a small town in upstate New York when little four-year-old Evelyn Wilson went missing. A horrible witch hunt ensued that was based on a terrible folk tale known as the blood libel.

Follow the Schatzman's as their son is accused of the most horrific crime imaginable. This accusation destroys their family and sends their mother and sister on a journey home to Berlin just as the Nazi's are about to come to power.

Not in America is based on true events. However, the author has taken license in her work, creating a what if tale that could easily have been true.

They Never Saw It Coming

Book Two in A Jewish Family Saga

Goldie Schatzman is nearing forty, but she is behaving like a reckless teenager, and every day she is descending deeper into a dark web. Since her return home to Berlin, she has reconnected with her childhood friend, Leni, a free spirit who has swept Goldie into the Weimar lifestyle that is overflowing with artists and writers, but also with debauchery. Goldie had spent the last nineteen years living a dull life with a spiritless husband. And now she has been set free, completely abandoning any sense of morals she once had.

As Goldie's daughter, Alma, is coming of marriageable age, her grandparents are determined to find her a suitable match. But will Goldie's life of depravity hurt Alma's chances to find a Jewish husband from a good family?

And all the while the SA, a prelude to the Nazi SS, is gaining strength. Germany is a hotbed of political unrest. Leaving a nightclub one night, Goldie finds herself caught in the middle of a demonstration that has turned violent. She is rescued by Felix, a member of the SA, who is immediately charmed by her blonde hair and Aryan appearance. Goldie is living a lie, and her secrets are bound to catch up with her. A girl, who she'd scorned in the past, is now a proud member of the Nazi Party and still carries a deep-seated vendetta against Goldie.

On the other side of the Atlantic, Sam, Goldie's son, is thriving with the Jewish mob in Manhattan; however, he has made a terrible mistake. He has destroyed the trust of the woman he believes is his bashert. He knows he cannot live without her, and he is desperately trying to find a way to win her heart.

And Izzy, the man who Sam once called his best friend, is now his worst enemy. They are both in love with the same woman, and the competition between them could easily result in death.

Then Sam receives word that something has happened in Germany, and he must accompany his father on a journey across the ocean. He is afraid that if he leaves before his beloved accepts his proposal, he might lose her forever.

When The Dust Settled

Book Three in A Jewish Family Saga

Coming December 2020

As the world races like a runaway train toward World War 11, the Schatzman family remains divided.

In New York, prohibition has ended, and Sam's world is turned upside down. He has been earning a good living transporting illegal liquor for the Jewish mob. Now that alcohol is legal, America is celebrating. But as the liquor flows freely, the mob boss realizes he must expand his illegal interests if he is going to continue to live the lavish lifestyle he's come to know. Some of the jobs Sam is offered go against his moral character. Transporting alcohol was one thing, but threatening lives is another.

Meanwhile, across the ocean in Italy, Mussolini, a heartless dictator, runs the country with an iron fist. Those who speak out against him disappear and are never seen again. For the first time since that horrible incident in Medina, Alma is finally happy and has fallen in love with a kind and generous Italian doctor who already has a job awaiting him in Rome; however, he is not Jewish. Alma must decide whether to marry him and risk disappointing her bubbie or let him go to find a suitable Jewish match.

In Berlin, the Nazis are quickly rising to power. Flags with swastikas are appearing everywhere. And Dr. Goebbels, the minister of propaganda is openly spewing hideous lies designed to turn the German people against the Jews. Adolf Hitler had disposed of his enemies, and the SA has been replaced by the even more terrifying SS. After the horrors they witnessed during Kristallnacht, Goldie's mother, Esther, is ready to abandon all she knows to escape the country. She begs her husband to leave Germany. But Ted refuses to leave everything that he spent his entire life working for. At what point is it too late to leave? And besides, where would they go? What would they do?

The Nazis have taken the country by the throat, and the electrifying atmosphere of the Weimar a distant memory. The period of artistic tolerance and debauchery has been replaced by a strict and cruel regime that seeks to destroy all who do not fit its ideal. Goldie's path of depravity is catching up with her, and her secrets are threatened. Will her Nazi enemies finally strike?

Book Four in A Jewish Family Saga

Coming Early 2021....

The Smallest Crack

Book One in a Holocaust Story series.

1933 Berlin, Germany

The son of a rebbe, Eli Kaetzel, and his beautiful but timid wife, Rebecca, find themselves in danger as Hitler rises to power. Eli knows that their only chance for survival may lie in the hands of Gretchen, a spirited Aryan girl. However, the forbidden and dangerous friendship between Eli and Gretchen has been a secret until now. Because, for Eli, if it is discovered that he has been keeping company with a woman other than his wife it will bring shame to him and his family. For Gretchen her friendship with a Jew is forbidden by law and could cost her, her life.

The Darkest Canyon

Book Two in a Holocaust Story series.

Nazi Germany.

Gretchen Schmidt has a secret life. She is in love with a married Jewish man. She is hiding him while his wife is posing as an Aryan woman.

Her best friend, Hilde, who unbeknownst to Gretchen is a sociopath, is working as a guard at Ravensbruck concentration camp.

If Hilde discovers Gretchen's secret, will their friendship be strong enough to keep Gretchen safe? Or will Hilde fall under the spell of the Nazis and turn her best friend over to the Gestapo?

The *Darkest Canyon* is a terrifying ride along the edge of a canyon in the dark of night.

Millions Of Pebbles

Book Three in a Holocaust Story series.

Benjamin Rabinowitz's life is shattered as he watches his wife, Lila, and his son, Moishe, leave to escape the Lodz ghetto. He is conflicted because he knows this is their best chance of survival, but he asks himself, will he ever see them again?

Ilsa Guhr has a troubled childhood, but as she comes of age, she learns that her beauty and sexuality give her the power to get what she wants. But she craves an even greater power. As the Nazis take control of Germany, she sees an opportunity to gain everything she's ever desired.

Fate will weave a web that will bring these two unlikely people into each other's lives.

Sarah and Solomon

Book Four in a Holocaust Story series

"Give me your children" -Chaim Mordechaj Rumkowski. September 1942 The Lodz Ghetto.

When Hitler's Third Reich reined with an iron fist, the head Judenrat of the Lodz ghetto decides to comply with the Nazis. He agrees to send the Jewish children off on a transport to face death.

In order to save her two young children a mother must take the ultimate risk. The night before the children are to rounded up and sent to their deaths, she helps her nine year old son and her five year old daughter escape into a war torn Europe. However, she cannot fit through the barbed wire, and so the children must go alone.

Follow Sarah and Solomon as they navigate their way through a world filled with hatred, and treachery. However, even in the darkest hour there is always a flicker of light. And these two young innocent souls will be aided by people who's lights will always shine in our memories.

All My Love, Detrick

Book One in the All My Love, Detrick series.

Book One in the All My Love, Detrick Series

Can Forbidden Love Survive in Nazi Germany?

After Germany's defeat in the First World War, she lays in ruins, falling beneath the wheel of depression and famine. And so, with a promise of restoring Germany to her rightful place as a world power, Adolf Hitler begins to rise.

Detrick, a handsome seventeen-year-old Aryan boy is reluctant to join the Nazi party because of his friendship with Jacob, who is Jewish and has been like a father figure to him. However, he learns that in order to protect the woman he loves, Jacob's daughter, he must abandon all his principles and join the Nazis. He knows the only way to survive is to live a double life. Detrick is confronted with fear every day; if he is discovered, he and those he loves will come face to face with the ultimate cruelty of the Third Reich.

Follow two families, one Jewish and one German, as they are thrust into a world of danger on the eve of the Nazis rise to power.

You Are My Sunshine

Book Two in the All My Love, Detrick series.

A child's innocence is the purest of all.

In Nazi Germany, Helga Haswell is at a crossroads. She's pregnant by a married SS officer who has since abandoned her. Left alone with the thought of raising a fatherless child, she has nowhere to turn -- until the Lebensborn steps in. They will take Helga's child when it's born and raise it as their own. Helga will now be free to live her life.

But when Helga has second thoughts, it's already too late. The papers are signed, and her claim to her child has been revoked. Her daughter belongs to Hitler now. And when Hitler's delusions of grandeur rapidly accelerate, Germany becomes involved in a two-front war against the heroic West and the fearless Russians.

Helga's child seems doomed to a life raised by the cruelest humans on Earth. But God's plan for her sends the young girl to the most unexpected people. In their warm embrace, she's given the chance for love in a world full of hate.

You Are My Sunshine is the heartfelt story of second chances. Helga Haswell may be tied to an unthinkable past, but her young daughter has the chance of a brighter future.

The Promised Land:

From Nazi Germany to Israel

Book Three in the All My Love, Detrick series.

Zofia Weiss, a Jewish woman with a painful past, stands at the dock, holding the hand of a little girl. She is about to board The SS Exodus, bound for Palestine with only her life, a dream, and a terrifying secret. As her eyes scan the crowds of people, she sees a familiar face. Her heart pounds and beads of sweat form on her forehead…

The Nazis have surrendered. Zofia survived the Holocaust, but she lives in constant fear. The one person who knows her dark secret is a sadistic SS officer with the power to destroy the life she's working so hard to rebuild. Will he ever find her and the innocent child she has sworn to protect?

To Be An Israeli

Book Four in the All My Love, Detrick series.

Elan understands what it means to be an Israeli. He's sacrificed the woman he loved, his marriage, and his life for Israel. When Israel went to war and Elan was summoned in the middle of the night, he did not hesitate to defend his country, even though he knew he might pay a terrible price. Elan is not a perfect man by any means. He can be cruel. He can be stubborn and self-righteous. But he is brave, and he loves more deeply than he will ever admit.

This is his story.

However, it is not only his story; it is also the story of the lives of the women who loved him: Katja, the girl whom he cherished but could never marry, who would haunt him forever. Janice, the spoiled American he wed to fill a void, who would keep a secret from him that would one day shatter his world. And...Nina, the beautiful Mossad agent whom Elan longed to protect but knew he never could.

To Be an Israeli spans from the beginning of the Six-Day War in 1967 through 1986 when a group of American tourists are on their way to visit their Jewish homeland.

Forever My Homeland

The Fifth and final book in the All My Love, Detrick series.

Bari Lynn has a secret. So she, a young Jewish-American girl, decides to tour Israel with her best friend and the members of their synagogue in search of answers.

Meanwhile, beneath the surface in Israel, trouble is stirring with a group of radical Islamists.

The case falls into the hands of Elan, a powerful passionate Mossad agent, trying to pick up the pieces of his shattered life. He believes nothing can break him, but in order to achieve their goals, the terrorists will go to any means to bring Elan to his knees.

Forever, My Homeland is the story of a country built on blood and determination. It is the tale of a strong and courageous people who don't have the luxury of backing down from any fight, because they live with the constant memory of the Holocaust. In the back of their minds, there is always a soft voice that whispers "Never again."

Michal's Destiny

Book One in the Michal's Destiny series.

It is 1919 in Siberia. Michal—a young, sheltered girl—has eyes for a man other than her betrothed. For a young girl growing up in a traditional Jewish settlement, an arranged marriage is a fact of life. However, destiny, it seems, has other plans for Michal. When a Cossack pogrom invades her small village, the protected life Michal has grown accustomed to and loves will crumble before her eyes. Everything she knows is gone and she is forced to leave her home and embark on a journey to Berlin with the man she thought she wanted. Michal faces love, loss, and heartache because she is harboring a secret that threatens to destroy her every attempt at happiness. But over the next fourteen tumultuous years, during the peak of the Weimar Republic, she learns she is willing to do anything to have the love she longs for and to protect her family.

However, it is now 1933. Life in Berlin is changing, especially for the Jews. Dark storm clouds are looming on the horizon. Adolf Hitler is about to become the chancellor of Germany, and that will change everything for Michal forever.

<u>A Family Shattered</u>

Book Two in the Michal's Destiny series.

In book two of the Michal's Destiny series, Tavvi and Michal have problems in the beginning of their relationship, but they build a life together. Each stone is laid carefully with love and mutual understanding. They now have a family with two beautiful daughters and a home full of happiness.

It is now 1938—Kristallnacht. Blood runs like a river on the streets, shattered glass covers the walkways of Jewish shop owners, and gangs of Nazi thugs charge though Berlin in a murderous rage. When Tavvi, the strong-willed Jewish carpenter, races outside, without thinking of his own welfare, to save his daughters fiancée, little does his wife Michal know that she might never hold him in her arms again. In an instant, all the stones they laid together come crashing down leaving them with nothing but the hope of finding each other again.

Watch Over My Child

Book Three in the Michal's Destiny series.

In book three of the Michal's Destiny series, after her parents are arrested by the Nazis on Kristallnacht, twelve-year-old Gilde Margolis is sent away from her home, her sister, and everyone she knows and loves.

Alone and afraid, Gilde boards a train through the Kinder-transport bound for London, where she will stay with strangers. Over the next seven years as Gilde is coming of age, she learns about love, friendship, heartache, and the pain of betrayal. As the Nazis grow in power, London is thrust into a brutal war against Hitler. Severe rationing is imposed upon the British, while air raids instill terror, and bombs all but destroy the city. Against all odds, and with no knowledge of what has happened to her family in Germany, Gilde keeps a tiny flicker of hope buried deep in her heart: someday, she will be reunited with her loved ones.

Another Breath, Another Sunrise

Book Four, the final book in the Michal's Destiny series.

Now that the Reich has fallen, in this—the final book of the Michal's Destiny series—the reader follows the survivors as they find themselves searching to reconnect with those they love. However, they are no longer the people they were before the war.

While the Russian soldiers, who are angry with the German people and ready to pillage, beat, and rape, begin to invade what's left of Berlin, Lotti is alone and fears for her life.

Though Alina Margolis has broken every tradition to become a successful business woman in America, she fears what has happened to her family and loved ones across the Atlantic Ocean.

As the curtain pulls back on Gilde, a now successful actress in London, she realizes that all that glitters is not gold, and she longs to find the lost family the Nazi's had stolen from her many years ago.

This is a story of ordinary people whose lives were shattered by the terrifying ambitions of Adolf Hitler—a true madman.

And . . . Who Is The Real Mother?

Book One in the Eidel's Story series.

In the Bible, there is a story about King Solomon, who was said to be the wisest man of all time. The story goes like this:

Two women came to the king for advice. Both of them were claiming to be the mother of a child. The king took the child in his arms and said, "I see that both of you care for this child very much. So, rather than decide which of you is the real mother, I will cut the child in half and give each of you a half."

One of the women agreed to the king's decision, but the other cried out, "NO, give the child to that other woman. Don't hurt my baby."

"Ahh," said the king to the second woman who refused to cut the baby. "I will give the child to you, because the real mother would sacrifice anything for her child. She would even give her baby away to another woman if it meant sparing the baby from pain."

And so, King Solomon gave the child to his rightful mother.

The year is 1941. The place is the Warsaw Ghetto in Poland.

The ghetto is riddled with disease and starvation. Children are dying every day.

Zofia Weiss, a young mother, must find a way to save, Eidel her only child. She negotiates a deal with a man on the black market to smuggle Eidel out in the middle of the night and deliver her to Helen, a Polish woman who is a good friend of Zofia's. It is the ultimate sacrifice because there is a good chance that Zofia will die without ever seeing her precious child again.

Helen has a life of her own, a husband and a son. She takes Eidel to live with her family even though she and those she loves will face terrible danger every day. Helen will be forced to do unimaginable things to protect all that she holds dear. And as Eidel grows up in Helen's warm maternal embrace, Helen finds that she has come to love the little girl with all her heart.

So, when Zofia returns to claim her child, and King Solomon is not available to be consulted, it is the reader who must decide…

Who is the real mother?

Secrets Revealed

Book Two in the Eidel's Story series.

Hitler has surrendered. The Nazi flags, which once hung throughout the city striking terror in the hearts of Polish citizens, have been torn down. It seems that Warsaw should be rejoicing in its newly found freedom, but Warsaw is not free. Instead, it is occupied by the Soviet Union, held tight in Stalin's iron grip. Communist soldiers, in uniform, now control the city. Where once people feared the dreaded swastika, now they tremble at the sight of the hammer and sickle. It is a treacherous time. And in the midst of all this danger, Ela Dobinski, a girl with a secret that could change her life, is coming of age.

New Life, New Land

Book Three in the Eidel's Story series.

When Jewish Holocaust survivors Eidel and Dovid Levi arrive in the United States, they believe that their struggles are finally over. Both have suffered greatly under the Nazi reign and are ready to leave the past behind. They arrive in this new and different land filled with optimism for their future. However, acclimating into a new way of life can be challenging for immigrants. And, not only are they immigrants but they are Jewish. Although Jews are not being murdered in the United States, as they were under Hitler in Europe, the Levi's will learn that America is not without anti-Semitism. Still, they go forth, with unfathomable courage. In New Life, New Land, this young couple will face the trials and tribulations of becoming Americans and building a home for themselves and their children that will follow them.

Another Generation

Book Four in the Eidel's Story series.

In the final book in the Eidel's Story series the children of Holocaust survivors Eidel and Dovid Levi have grown to adulthood. They each face hard trials and tribulations of their own, many of which stem from growing up as children of Holocaust survivors. Haley is a peacemaker who yearns to please even at the expense of her own happiness. Abby is an angry rebel on the road to self-destruction. And, Mark, Dovid's only son, carries a heavy burden of guilt and secrets. He wants to please his father, but he cannot. Each of the Levi children must find a way to navigate their world while accepting that the lessons they have learned from the parents, both good and bad, have shaped them into the people they are destined to become.

The Wrath Of Eden

The Wrath of Eden Book One.

Deep in them Appalachian hills, far from the main roads where the citified people come and go, lies a harsh world where a man's character is all he can rightly claim as his own. This here is a land of deep, dark coal mines, where a miner ain't certain when he ventures into the belly of the mountain whether he will ever see daylight again. To this very day, they still tell tales of the Robin Hood-like outlaw Pretty Boy Floyd, even though there ain't no such thing as a thousand dollar bill no more From this beautiful yet dangerous country where folks is folks comes a story as old as time itself; a tale of good and evil, of right and wrong, and of a troubled man who walked a perilous path on his journey back to God.

The Wrath of Eden begins in 1917, in the fictitious town of Mudwater Creek, West Virginia. Mudwater lies deep in mining country in the Appalachian Mountains. Here, the eldest son of a snake-handling preacher, Cyrus Hunt, is emotionally broken by what he believes is his father's favoritism toward his brother, Aiden. Cyrus is so hurt by what he believes is his father's lack of love for him that he runs away from home to seek his fortune. Not only will he fight in the Great War, but he will return to America and then ramble around the United States for several years, right through the great depression. While on his journey, Cyrus will encounter a multitude of colorful characters and from each he will learn more about himself. This is a tale of good and evil, of brother against brother, of the intricate web of family, and of love lost and found again.

The Angels Song

The Wrath of Eden Book Two.

Cyrus Hunt returns home to the Appalachian Mountains after years of traveling. He has learned a great deal about himself from his journey, and he realizes that the time has come to make peace with his brother and his past. When he arrives in the small town where he grew up, he finds that he has a granddaughter that he never knew existed, and she is almost the same age as his daughter. The two girls grow up as close as sisters. But one is more beautiful than a star-filled night sky, while the other has a physical condition that keeps her from spreading her wings and discovering her own self-worth. As the girls grow into women, the love they have for each other is constantly tested by sibling rivalry, codependency, and betrayals. Are these two descendents of Cyrus Hunt destined to repeat their father's mistakes? Or will they rise above their human weakness and inadequacies and honor the bonds of blood and family that unite them?

One Last Hope

A Voyage to Escape Nazi Germany

Formerly *The Voyage*

Inspired by True Events

On May 13, 1939, five strangers boarded the MS St. Louis. Promised a future of safety away from Nazi Germany and Hitler's Third Reich, unbeknownst to them they were about to embark upon a voyage built on secrets, lies, and treachery.

Sacrifice, love, life, and death hung in the balance as each fought against fate, but the voyage was just the beginning.

A Flicker Of Light

Hitler's Master Plan.

The year is 1943

The forests of Munich are crawling with danger during the rule of the Third Reich, but in order to save the life of her unborn child, Petra Jorgenson must escape from the Lebensborn Institute. She is alone, seven months pregnant, and penniless. Avoiding the watchful eyes of the armed guards in the overhead tower, she waits until the dead of night and then climbs under the flesh-shredding barbed wire surrounding the Institute. At the risk of being captured and murdered, she runs headlong into the terrifying, desolate woods. Even during one of the darkest periods in the history of mankind, when horrific acts of cruelty become commonplace and Germany seemed to have gone crazy under the direction of a madman, unexpected heroes come to light. And although there are those who would try to destroy true love, it will prevail. Here in this lost land ruled by human monsters, Petra will learn that even when one faces what appears to be the end of the world, if one looks hard enough, one will find that there is always A Flicker of Light.

The Heart Of A Gypsy

If you liked Inglorious Basterds, Pulp Fiction, and Django Unchained, you'll love The Heart of a Gypsy!

During the Nazi occupation, bands of freedom fighters roamed the forests of Eastern Europe. They hid while waging their own private war against Hitler's tyrannical and murderous reign. Among these Resistance fighters were several groups of Romany people (Gypsies).

The Heart of a Gypsy is a spellbinding love story. It is a tale of a man with remarkable courage and the woman who loved him more than life itself. This historical novel is filled with romance and spiced with the beauty of the Gypsy culture.

Within these pages lies a tale of a people who would rather die than surrender their freedom. Come, enter into a little-known world where only a few have traveled before . . . the world of the Romany.

If you enjoy romance, secret magical traditions, and riveting action you will love The Heart of a Gypsy.

Please be forewarned that this book contains explicit scenes of a sexual nature.

Printed in Great Britain
by Amazon

53847428R00279